GHOSTS OF THE
SHADOW MARKET

Also by Cassandra Clare

THE MORTAL INSTRUMENTS

City of Bones
City of Ashes
City of Glass
City of Fallen Angels
City of Lost Souls
City of Heavenly Fire

THE INFERNAL DEVICES

Clockwork Angel
Clockwork Prince
Clockwork Princess

THE DARK ARTIFICES

Lady Midnight
Lord of Shadows
Queen of Air and Darkness

THE ELDEST CURSES
With Wesley Chu

The Red Scrolls of Magic

The Shadowhunter's Codex
With Joshua Lewis

The Bane Chronicles
With Sarah Rees Brennan and Maureen Johnson

Tales from the Shadowhunter Academy
With Sarah Rees Brennan, Maureen Johnson,
and Robin Wasserman

Ghosts of the Shadow Market

CASSANDRA CLARE

SARAH REES BRENNAN

MAUREEN JOHNSON

KELLY LINK

ROBIN WASSERMAN

This is a work of fiction. Names, characters, places and incidents are either the product of the author's imagination or, if real, used fictitiously. All statements, activities, stunts, descriptions, information and material of any other kind contained herein are included for entertainment purposes only and should not be relied on for accuracy or replicated as they may result in injury.

First published 2019 by Walker Books Ltd
87 Vauxhall Walk, London SE11 5HJ

2 4 6 8 10 9 7 5 3 1

This book has been typeset in Dolly

Printed and bound by CPI Group (UK) Ltd, Croydon CR0 4YY

British Library Cataloguing in Publication Data:
a catalogue record for this book is available from the British Library

Export/airside edition ISBN 978-1-4063-8537-3
Hardback edition ISBN 978-1-4063-8536-6

www.walker.co.uk

For our wonderful readers

Whatever you are physically, male or female, strong or weak, ill or healthy—all those things matter less than what your heart contains. If you have the soul of a warrior, you are a warrior. Whatever the color, the shape, the design of the shade that conceals it, the flame inside the lamp remains the same. *You* are that flame.

GHOSTS OF THE
SHADOW MARKET

CONTENTS

CONTENTS

Cast Long Shadows

By Cassandra Clare and Sarah Rees Brennan

Old sins cast long shadows.
—English proverb

The Shadow Market, London, 1901

The railway viaduct passed only a hairsbreadth away from St. Saviour's Church. There had been discussion among the mundanes about the possibility of demolishing the church to make way for the railroad, but it had met with unexpectedly fierce opposition. Instead the railway took a slightly more circuitous route, and the spire of the church still remained, a silver dagger against the night sky.

Beneath the arches, crosses, and rattling rails, a mundane market was held by day, the largest association of grocers in the city. By night, the market belonged to Downworld.

Vampires and werewolves, warlocks and fey, met under the stars and under glamour that human eyes could not pierce. They had their magic stalls set up in the same pattern as the humans' stalls, under the bridges and through tiny streets, but the Shadow Market stalls did not hold apples or turnips. Under the dark arches the stalls shone, laden with bells and ribbons, gaudy with color: snake green, fever red, and the startling orange of flames. Brother Zachariah smelled incense burning and heard the songs of werewolves for the distant beauty of the moon, and faeries calling for children to *come away, come away*.

It was the first Shadow Market of the New Year by English standards, though it was still the old year in China. Brother Zachariah had left Shanghai when he was a child, and London when he was seventeen, to go to the Silent City, where there was no acknowledgment of time passing save that the ashes of more warriors were laid down. Still he remembered the celebrations of the New Year in his human life, from eggnog and fortune-telling in London to the setting off of fireworks and nibbling of moon dumplings in Shanghai.

Now snow was falling on London. The air was crisp and cold as a fresh apple, and felt good against his face. The voices of his Brothers were a low hum in his head, affording Brother Zachariah a little distance.

Zachariah was here on a mission, but he took a brief time to be glad he was in London, in the Shadow Market, to breathe air clear of the dust of the departed. It felt something like freedom, like being young again.

He rejoiced, but that did not mean the people of the Shadow Market rejoiced with him. He observed many Downworlders, and even mundanes with the Sight, casting him looks that were the opposite of welcoming. As he moved, a dark murmur threaded through the hum of conversation all around him.

The denizens of Downworld considered this Market time as space snatched away from angels. They clearly did not relish his presence among them. Brother Zachariah was one of the Silent Brothers, a voiceless fraternity that lived long amid old bones, sworn to seclusion with hearts dedicated to the dust of their City and their dead. Nobody could be expected to embrace a Silent Brother, and these people would not be likely to take pleasure in the appearance of any Shadowhunter at all.

Even as he doubted, he saw a stranger sight than any he had expected in the Market.

There was a Shadowhunter boy dancing a cancan with three faeries. He was Charlotte and Henry Fairchild's younger son, Matthew Fairchild. His head was thrown back, his fair hair bright by firelight, and he was laughing.

Brother Zachariah had an instant to wonder if Matthew was spellbound before Matthew caught sight of him and sprang forward, leaving the faeries behind him looking discomfited. The Fair Folk were not accustomed to having mortals skip out on their dances.

Matthew did not appear to notice. He ran up to Brother Zachariah, threw an exuberant arm about his neck, and ducked his head under the hood of the Silent Brother to give him a kiss on the cheek.

"Uncle Jem!" Matthew exclaimed joyfully. "What are you doing here?"

Shadowhunter Academy, Idris, 1899

Matthew Fairchild hardly ever lost his temper. When he did, he tried to make the occasion memorable.

The last time had been two years ago, during Matthew's short-lived stint at Shadowhunter Academy, a school intended to mass-produce perfect demon-fighting bores. It began with half the school crowded on a tower top, watching the parents arrive after an incident in the woods with a demon.

Matthew's usual good humor had already been sorely tried. His best friend, James, was being blamed for the incident, simply because James happened to have a tiny, insignificant amount of demon blood and the—Matthew thought prodigiously lucky—ability to transform into a shadow. James was being expelled. The actual people to blame, unmitigated wart Alastair Carstairs and his rotten friends, were not being expelled. Life in general, and the Academy in particular, was a positive parade of injustice.

Matthew had not even had the chance to ask James if he wanted to be *parabatai* yet. He had been planning to ask him to be sworn warrior partners in a very elaborate and stylish fashion so Jamie would be too impressed to decline.

Mr. Herondale, James's father, was among the first of the parents to arrive. They saw him stride in the doors with his black hair turbulent from wind and rage. Mr. Herondale undeniably had an air.

The few girls permitted to come to the Academy were casting James speculative glances. James shuffled about the place with his head in a book and had an unfortunate haircut and an unassuming demeanor, but he bore a very marked resemblance to his father.

James, Angel bless his oblivious soul, failed to notice anyone's attention. He slunk away to be expelled, sunk in despair.

"Gosh," said Eustace Larkspear. "It would be *something* to have a father like that."

"I heard he was mad," said Alastair, and let out a bark of laughter. "You'd have to be mad, to marry a creature with infernal blood and have children who were—"

"Don't," said little Thomas quietly. To everyone's surprise, Alastair rolled his eyes and desisted.

Matthew wanted to be the one who had made Alastair stop,

but Thomas had already done it and Matthew could not think of any way to stop Alastair permanently short of challenging him to a duel. He was not even sure that would work. Alastair was not a coward, and would probably accept the challenge and then talk twice as much. Besides which, getting into fights was not precisely Matthew's style. He could fight, but he did not think violence solved many problems.

Aside from the problem of demons laying waste to the world, that was.

Matthew left the tower top abruptly and wandered the halls of the Academy in a foul mood. Despite his commitment to dark brooding, he knew he was duty bound not to lose track of Christopher and Thomas Lightwood for long.

When he was six, Matthew's older brother, Charles Buford, and their mama had left the house for a meeting at the London Institute. Charlotte Fairchild was the Consul, the most important person of all the Shadowhunters, and Charles had always been interested in her work instead of resenting the bothersome Nephilim for taking up her time. As they prepared to go, Matthew had stood in the hall crying and refusing to let go of his mother's dress.

Mama had knelt down and asked that Matthew please take care of Papa for her while she and Charles were gone.

Matthew took this responsibility seriously. Papa was a genius and what most people considered an invalid, because he could not walk. Unless he was carefully watched, he would forget to eat in the excitement of invention. Papa could not get on without Matthew, which was why it was absurd that Matthew had been sent to the Academy in the first place.

Matthew liked to take care of people, and he was good at it.

When they were eight, Christopher Lightwood had been discovered in Papa's laboratory performing what Papa described as a very intriguing experiment. Matthew had noticed that there was now a wall missing in the laboratory, and he took Christopher under his wing.

Christopher and Thomas were real cousins, their fathers brothers. Matthew was not a real cousin: he only called Christopher's and Thomas's parents Aunt Cecily and Uncle Gabriel, and Aunt Sophie and Uncle Gideon, respectively, out of courtesy. Their parents were only friends. Mama had no close family and Papa's family did not approve of Mama being Consul.

James was Christopher's blood cousin. Aunt Cecily was Mr. Herondale's sister. Mr. Herondale ran the London Institute, and the Herondales tended to keep to themselves. Unkind people said it was because they were snobbish or thought themselves superior, but Charlotte said those people were ignorant. She told Matthew the Herondales tended to keep to themselves as they had experienced unkindness due to Mrs. Herondale being a warlock.

Still, when you ran an Institute, you couldn't be completely invisible. Matthew had seen James at various parties before and tried to acquire him as a friend, only Matthew was impeded because he felt he should contribute to parties being a success and James tended to be in a corner, reading.

It was usually a simple matter for Matthew to make friends, but he did not see the point unless it was a challenge. Friends who were easy to get might be easy to lose, and Matthew wanted to keep people.

It had been rather shattering when James seemed to actively

dislike Matthew, but Matthew had won him over. He still was not entirely sure how, which made him uneasy, but James had recently referred to himself, Matthew, Christopher, and Thomas as the three Musketeers and D'Artagnan, from a book he liked. Everything had been going splendidly aside from missing Papa, but now James was expelled and everything was ruined. Still, Matthew could not forget his responsibilities.

Christopher had a tempestuous relationship with science, and Professor Fell had commanded Matthew not to let Christopher come into contact with any flammable materials after the last time. Thomas was so quiet and small they were always losing him, rather like a human marble, and if left to his own devices he would inevitably roll toward Alastair Carstairs.

This was a hideous situation with only one bright side. It was a simple matter to locate Thomas when he was lost. Matthew only had to follow the sound of Alastair's irritating voice.

Unfortunately, this meant being forced to behold Alastair's irritating face.

He found Alastair soon enough, gazing out a window, with Thomas shyly standing at his elbow.

Thomas's hero worship was inexplicable. The only things Matthew could find to like about Alastair were his extraordinarily expressive eyebrows, and eyebrows did not make the man.

"Are you very sad, Alastair?" Matthew heard Thomas ask as he approached, bent on retrieval.

"Stop bothering me, pip-squeak," said Alastair, though his voice was tolerant. Even he could not strongly object to being adored.

"You heard the low, snaky serpent," said Matthew. "Come away, Tom."

"Ah, Mother Hen Fairchild," sneered Alastair. "What a lovely wife you will make for somebody one of these fine days."

Matthew was outraged to see Thomas's tiny smile, though Thomas quickly concealed it out of respect for Matthew's feelings. Thomas was meek and much afflicted by sisters. He seemed to think Alastair being rude to everyone was daring.

"I wish I could say the same for you," said Matthew. "Has no kind soul thought to inform you that your hairstyle is, to use the gentlest words available to me, ill-advised? A friend? Your papa? Does nobody care enough to prevent you from making a spectacle of yourself? Or are you simply too busy perpetrating acts of evil upon the innocent to bother about your unfortunate appearance?"

"Matthew!" said Thomas. "His friend *died*."

Matthew strongly desired to point out that Alastair and his friends had been the ones to unleash a demon upon James, and their nasty prank going wrong was no more than their just deserts. He could see, however, that would distress Thomas extremely.

"Oh, very well. Let us go," he said. "Though I cannot help but wonder whose idea their nasty little trick was."

"Wait a moment, Fairchild," snapped Alastair. "You can go ahead, Lightwood."

Thomas looked deeply worried as he went, but Matthew could see he was loath to disobey his idol. When Thomas's worried hazel eyes flicked to Matthew, Matthew nodded, and Thomas reluctantly departed.

When he was gone, Matthew and Alastair squared off. Matthew understood that Alastair had sent Thomas away for a purpose. He bit his lip, resigned to a scuffle.

Instead Alastair said, "Who are *you* to play the moralist, talking about tricks and papas, considering the circumstances of your birth?"

Matthew frowned. "What on earth are you driveling about, Carstairs?"

"Everyone talks about your mama and her unwomanly pursuits," said awful, unthinkable worm Alastair Carstairs. Matthew scoffed but Alastair raised his voice, persisting. "A woman cannot be a good Consul. Nevertheless your mother can continue her career, of course, since she has such strong support from the powerful Lightwoods."

"Certainly our families are friends," said Matthew. "Are you unfamiliar with the concept of friendship, Carstairs? How tragic for you, though understandable on the part of everyone else in the universe."

Alastair raised his eyebrows. "Oh, great friends, no doubt. Your mama must require friends, since your papa is unable to play a man's part."

"I beg your pardon?" said Matthew.

"Odd that you were born so long after your papa's terrible accident," Alastair said, all but twirling an imaginary mustache. "Strange that your papa's family will have nothing to do with you, to the extent of demanding that your mother renounce her married name. Remarkable that you bear no resemblance to your papa, and your coloring is so like Gideon Lightwood's."

Gideon Lightwood was Thomas's papa. No wonder Alastair had sent Thomas away before making a ridiculous accusation like that.

It was absurd. Perhaps it was true that Matthew had fair hair, while his mama's was brown and his father's and Charles

Buford's was red. Matthew's mama was tiny, but Cook said she thought Matthew would be taller than Charles Buford. Uncle Gideon was often with Mama. Matthew knew he had spoken for her when she was at odds with the Clave. Mama had once called him her good and faithful friend. Matthew had never thought much about it before.

His mama said his papa had such a dear, friendly, freckled face. Matthew had always wished he looked like him.

But he didn't.

Matthew said, his voice strange in his own ears, "I do not understand what you mean."

"Henry Fairchild is not your father," spat Alastair. "You are Gideon Lightwood's bastard. Everybody knows it but you."

In a white and blinding rage, Matthew struck him in the face. Then he went to find Christopher, cleared the area, and gave him matches.

A short but eventful time passed before Matthew left school, never to return. In that interval, a wing of the Academy blew up.

Matthew realized it had been rather a shocking thing to do, but while he was deranged, he also demanded James be his *parabatai*, and by some miracle James agreed. Matthew and his papa arranged to spend more time at the Fairchilds' London home so that Matthew could be with both his papa and his *parabatai*. It had all, Matthew considered, worked out rather well.

If only he could forget.

The Shadow Market, London, 1901

Jem halted in the midst of the dancing flames and black iron arches of the London Market, startled by the appearance of a familiar face in an unexpected context, and even more so by the warmth of Matthew's greeting.

He knew Charlotte's son, of course. Her other boy, Charles, was always very cool and distant when he encountered Brother Zachariah on official business. Brother Zachariah knew that the Silent Brothers were meant to be detached from the world. His uncle Elias's son, Alastair, had made that very clear when Brother Zachariah reached out to him.

This is how it should be, said his Brothers in his mind. He could not always tell one of their voices from the others. They were a quiet chorus, a silent, ever-present song.

Jem would not have held it against Matthew if he felt the same way as many others, but he didn't seem to. His bright, delicate face showed dismay all too clearly. "Am I being too familiar?" he asked anxiously. "I only supposed since I was James's *parabatai* and that is what he calls you, I might do so as well."

Of course you may, said Brother Zachariah.

James did, and James's sister, Lucie, and Alastair's sister, Cordelia, had taken to doing so as well. Zachariah considered that they were the three sweetest children in the world. He knew he might be a little partial, but faith created truth.

Matthew glowed. Zachariah was reminded of Matthew's mother, and the kindness that had taken in three orphans when she was hardly more than a child herself.

"They all talk about you all the time in the London Institute," Matthew confided. "James and Lucie and Uncle Will and Aunt Tessa too. I feel as if I know you a great deal better than I actually do, so I beg pardon if I trespass on your kindness."

There can be no trespass when you are always welcome, said Jem.

Matthew's smile spread. It was an extraordinarily engaging expression. His warmth was closer to the surface than Charlotte's, Jem thought. He had never been taught to close himself off, to do anything but delight and trust in the world.

"I would like to hear all about your and Uncle Will's and Aunt Tessa's adventures from your point of view," Matthew proposed. "You must have had a very exciting time! Nothing exciting ever happens to us. The way everyone talks about it, one might think you had a dramatic star-crossed passion with Aunt Tessa before you became a Silent Brother." Matthew stopped himself. "Sorry! My tongue ran away with me. I am heedless and excited to talk to you properly. I'm sure it is strange to think of your past life. I hope I did not upset or offend you. I cry peace."

Peace, echoed Brother Zachariah, amused.

"I am certain you could have had a torrid affair with any person you wanted, of course," said Matthew. "Anyone can see that. Oh Lord, that was a heedless thing to say too, wasn't it?"

It is very kind of you to say so, said Brother Zachariah. *Is it not a fine night?*

"I can see you are a very tactful fellow," said Matthew, and clapped Brother Zachariah on the back.

They wandered through the stalls of the Shadow Market. Brother Zachariah was searching for one warlock in particular, who had agreed to help him.

"Does Uncle Will know you are in London?" asked Matthew. "Are you going to see him? If Uncle Will finds out you were in London and did *not* come to call, and I knew about it, that will be curtains for me! Young life cut off in its prime. A bright flower of manhood withered untimely. You might think of me and my doom, Uncle Jem, you really might."

Might I? asked Brother Zachariah.

It was fairly obvious what Matthew was angling to know.

"It would also be very kind of you if you refrained from mentioning that you saw me at the Shadow Market," Matthew wheedled, with his engaging smile and a distinct air of apprehension.

Silent Brothers are terrible gossips as a rule, said Brother Zachariah. *For you, though, Matthew, I will make an exception.*

"Thanks, Uncle Jem!" Matthew linked his arm with Jem's. "I can see we are going to be great friends."

It must be a horrible contrast for the Market to behold, Jem thought, seeing this bright child hanging so carelessly off the arm of a Silent Brother, hooded and cloaked and shrouded in darkness. Matthew seemed blissfully unaware of the incongruity.

I believe we will be, said Jem.

"My cousin Anna says the Shadow Market is tremendous fun," said Matthew happily. "Of course, you know Anna. She's always tremendous fun herself and has the best taste in waist-coats in London. I met some very agreeable faeries who invited me, and I thought I would come see."

The faeries Matthew had been dancing with previously whisked past, streaks of light in flower crowns. One faerie boy, lips stained with the juice of strange fruit, paused and winked at Matthew. He appeared not to resent being deserted in their dance, though appearances were seldom reliable with faeries. Matthew hesitated, casting a wary eye upon Brother Zachariah, then winked back.

Brother Zachariah felt he had to warn: *Your friends may mean mischief. Faeries often do.*

Matthew smiled, the lovely expression turning wicked. "I mean mischief frequently myself."

That is not exactly what I mean. Nor do I intend to insult any Downworlders. There are as many trustworthy Downworlders as there are Shadowhunters, which means the opposite is also true. It might be wise to remember that not all those at the Shadow Market look with favor on the Nephilim.

"Who can blame them?" said Matthew airily. "Stuffy lot. Present company excepted, Uncle Jem! My papa has a warlock friend he talks of frequently. They invented Portals together, did you know? I would like to have an intimate Downworlder friend too."

Magnus Bane would be a good friend for anyone to have, Brother Zachariah agreed.

It would have seemed disrespectful to Magnus, who had been such a good friend to Jem's *parabatai,* to press the issue with Matthew any further. Perhaps he was being too cautious. Many of the Downworlders were sure to be taken with Matthew's ready charm.

Will had made it clear his Institute was there to help Downworlders who sought aid, as surely as it was for mundanes and Shadowhunters. Maybe this new generation could grow up in more charity with Downworlders than any before them.

"Anna is not here tonight," Matthew added. "But you are, so all's well. What are we going to do together? Are you looking for something special? I rather thought I might buy Jamie and Luce a book. Any book would do. They love 'em all."

It made Jem warm to him even more to hear him speak of James and Lucie with such obvious affection.

If we see a suitable book, he said, *let us buy it for them. I would rather not buy them a tome of dangerous enchantment.*

"By the Angel, no," said Matthew. "Luce would read it for sure. Bit of a daredevil in a quiet way, Lu."

As for me, said Jem, I have a commission from someone else whom I hold in high regard. Out of respect for them, I can say nothing more.

"I completely understand," said Matthew, looking pleased to be this far in Jem's confidence. "I won't ask, but is there anything I can do to help? You could rely on me, if you would. We love all the same people, don't we?"

Thank you most sincerely for the offer.

There was no way for this child to help him, not in this current search, but his presence made Zachariah feel as if he could borrow some of Matthew's delighted wonder as he looked around the Market, and they strolled around taking in its sounds and sights together.

There was a stall selling faerie fruit, though there was also a werewolf outside the stall making dark remarks about being cheated and not making deals with goblin men. There were stalls with red-and-white-striped awnings selling cinder toffee, though Brother Zachariah had doubts about its provenance. Matthew stopped and laughed for sheer joy at a warlock woman with blue skin who was juggling toy unicorns, mermaids' shells, and small wheels on fire, and he flirted until she told him her name was Catarina. She added that he certainly might not call on her, but when he smiled, she smiled back. Brother Zachariah imagined people usually did.

The Shadow Market as a whole seemed rather bemused by Matthew. They were accustomed to Shadowhunters arriving on the hunt for witnesses or culprits, not demonstrating huge enthusiasm.

Matthew applauded when another stall sidled up to him, walking on chicken feet. A faerie woman with dandelion-fluff hair peered out among vials of many-colored lights and liquids.

"Hello, pretty," she said, her voice rasping like bark.

"Which one of us are you talking to?" asked Matthew, laughing and leaning his elbow against Brother Zachariah's shoulder.

The faerie woman regarded Zachariah with suspicion. "Oooh, a Silent Brother at our humble market. The Nephilim would consider that we were being honored."

Do you feel honored? asked Zachariah, shifting his stance slightly to stand protectively in front of Matthew.

Oblivious, Matthew sauntered past Zachariah to examine the vials laid out before him.

"Jolly nice potions," he said, flashing his smile on the woman. "Did you make them yourself? Good show. That makes you something of an inventor, does it not? My papa is an inventor."

"I am happy to have anyone at the Market who has an interest in my wares," said the woman. "I see you have a honey tongue to match your hair. How old are you?"

"Fifteen," Matthew replied promptly.

He began to sort among the vials, his rings clinking against the glass and their wood-and-gold or wood-and-silver stoppers, chattering about his father and faerie potions he had read about.

"Ah, fifteen summers, and by the look of you it has been all summer. Some would say only a shallow river could flash so bright," said the faerie woman, and Matthew looked up at her, an unguarded child surprised by any hurt dealt him. His smile flickered for an instant.

Before Jem could intervene, the smile resumed.

"Ah well. 'He has nothing, but he looks everything. What more can one desire?'" Matthew quoted. "Oscar Wilde. Do you know his work? I heard faeries like to steal poets. You should definitely have tried to steal him."

The woman laughed. "Perchance we did. Do you wish to be stolen, honey-sweet boy?"

"I do not think my mama the Consul would like that at all, no."

Matthew continued to beam radiantly on her. The faerie looked discomfited for a moment, then smiled back. Faeries could prick like thorns because it was their very nature, not because they meant harm.

"This is a love charm," said the faerie woman, nodding to a vial filled with a delicately sparkling pink substance. "No use to you, fairest child of the Nephilim. Now this would blind your opponents in a battle."

I imagine it would, said Brother Zachariah, studying the vial full of charcoal-colored sand.

Matthew was transparently pleased to hear about the potions. Zachariah was sure Henry's boy had been regaled with tales of the elements over dinner time and time again.

"What's this one?" Matthew asked, pointing to a purple vial.

"Oh, another one that would be of no interest to the Nephilim," said the woman dismissively. "What need would you have of a potion that would make the one who took it tell you all the truth? You Shadowhunters have no secrets among each other, I hear. Besides which, you have that Mortal Sword to prove one of you is telling the truth. Though I call that a brutal business."

"It *is* brutal," Matthew agreed vehemently.

The faerie woman looked almost sad. "You come of a brutal people, sweet child."

"Not me," said Matthew. "I believe in art and beauty."

"You might be pitiless one day, for all that."

"No, never," Matthew insisted. "I don't care for Shadowhunter customs at all. I like Downworlder ways much more."

"Ah, you flatter an old woman," said the faerie, waving a hand, but her face wrinkled up like a pleased apple as she smiled once more. "Now come, since you are a darling boy, let me show you something very special. What would you say to a vial of distilled stars, guaranteeing the one who carried it long life?"

Enough, said the voices in Zachariah's head.

Shadowhunters do not make bargains for their own lives, said Brother Zachariah, and towed Matthew away by his sleeve.

Matthew flailed and squawked a protest.

The woman's potions were in all likelihood colored water and sand, said Zachariah. *Do not waste your money or make any bargains with the fey. You must be careful at the Market. They sell heartbreak as well as dreams.*

"Oh, very well," said Matthew. "Look, Uncle Jem! That werewolf is running a book stall. Werewolves are surprisingly ardent readers, you know."

He dashed over and began to ask artless questions of a lady werewolf in a prim dress, who was soon patting her hair and laughing at his nonsense. Brother Zachariah's attention was suddenly arrested by the warlock he had been searching for.

Wait for me here, he told Matthew, and went to meet Ragnor Fell by the side of a fire built under one of the railway arches.

As the fire leaped, it birthed green sparks that matched the clever face of the warlock and lit his snowy white hair, curling around the sterner curl of his horns.

"Brother Zachariah," he said, nodding. "A pleasure, but I wish I had better news for you. Ah well. Bad news comes like rain and good news like lightning, barely seen before a crash."

A cheerful thought, said Brother Zachariah, his heart sinking.

"I went to several sources about the information you asked for," said Ragnor. "I have a lead, but I have to tell you—I was warned that this quest might prove fatal: that it has already proved fatal to more than one person. Do you truly want me to follow up on the lead?"

I do, said Brother Zachariah.

He had hoped for more. When he had met Tessa on the bridge that year, she had seemed concerned as she talked to him. It had been a gray day. The wind had blown her brown hair back from the face that trouble could touch as time could not. Sometimes it seemed like her face was all the heart he had left. He could not do much for her, but he had once promised to spend his life guarding her from the very wind from heaven.

He intended to keep his word in that at least.

Ragnor Fell nodded. "I will keep searching."

So will I, said Brother Zachariah.

Ragnor's face changed to a look of deep alarm. Brother Zachariah turned and beheld Matthew, who had wandered back to the faerie woman's stall of potions.

Matthew! Brother Zachariah called. *Come here.*

Matthew nodded and came reluctantly forward, smoothing his waistcoat.

The look of alarm on Ragnor's face deepened. "Why is he coming over? Why would you do this to me? I had always considered you one of the more sensible Shadowhunters, not that this is saying much!"

Brother Zachariah studied Ragnor. It was unusual to see the warlock rattled, and he was usually very discreet and professional.

I thought you had a long and cherished history of mutual esteem with the Fairchilds, said Brother Zachariah.

"Oh, certainly," said Ragnor. "And I have a long and cherished history of not getting blown up."

What? asked Zachariah.

The mystery was explained when Matthew caught sight of Ragnor and beamed.

"Oh, hello, Professor Fell." He glanced in Jem's direction. "Professor Fell taught me at the Academy before I was expelled. Very expelled."

Jem had been aware that James had been expelled, but he had not known Matthew was too. He had thought Matthew had simply chosen to follow his *parabatai*, as anyone would if they could.

"Is your friend with you?" asked Ragnor Fell, and twitched. "Is Christopher Lightwood on the premises? Is our Market shortly to be engulfed in flames?"

"No," Matthew said, sounding amused. "Christopher is at home."

"At home in Idris?"

"In the Lightwoods' London home, but it is far away."

"Not far enough!" decided Ragnor Fell. "I shall decamp to Paris forthwith."

He nodded at Brother Zachariah, visibly shuddered at Matthew, and turned away. Matthew waved forlornly after him.

"Good-bye, Professor Fell!" he called. He looked up at Brother Zachariah. "Christopher did not *mean* to cause any of the accidents, and the large explosion was entirely my fault."

I see, said Brother Zachariah.

Brother Zachariah was not sure he did see.

"You must know Gideon quite well," Matthew remarked, his quicksilver mind flashing onto another topic.

I do, said Brother Zachariah. *He is the best of good fellows.*

Matthew shrugged. "If you say so. I like my uncle Gabriel better. Not as much as Uncle Will, of course."

Will has always been my favorite too, Jem agreed solemnly.

Matthew chewed on his lower lip, clearly considering something. "Would you care to accept a wager, Uncle Jem, that I can clear that fire with a foot to spare?"

I would not, said Brother Zachariah with conviction. *Matthew, wait—*

Matthew charged at the flames sparkling with jade light, and leaped. He twisted in midair, slim black-clad body like a dagger thrown by an expert hand, and landed on his feet in the shadow of the church spire. After a moment, several members of the Shadow Market began to clap. Matthew mimed taking off an imaginary hat and bowed with a flourish.

His hair was gold even by strange flames, his face bright even in shadow. Brother Zachariah watched him laugh, and foreboding crept into his heart. He experienced sudden fear for Matthew, for all the shining, beloved children belonging to his dear friends. By the time he was Matthew's age, he and Will had been through fire and burning silver. His generation had suffered so they could bring the next one forth into a better world, but now it occurred to Jem that those children, taught to expect love and walk fearless through shadows, would be shocked and betrayed by disaster. Some of them might be broken.

Pray disaster never came.

Fairchild Residence, London, 1901

Matthew was still thinking about his visit to the Shadow Market the next day. In some ways it had been rotten luck, coming upon Uncle Jem like that, though he had been glad for the chance to become better acquainted. Perhaps Uncle Jem would think Jamie had not made a bad choice in his *parabatai*.

He rose early to help Cook with the baking. Cook had arthritis, and Matthew's mama had asked if she was not getting along in years and wishing to retire, but Cook did not wish to retire and nobody had to know if Matthew lent a hand in the early morning. Besides, Matthew liked to see his papa and mama and even Charles eating breakfast he had prepared. His mother always worked too hard, lines of worry etched between her brows and around her mouth that never disappeared even if Matthew managed to make her laugh. She liked scones with cranberries baked in, so he tried to make them for her whenever he might. Matthew could not do anything else for her. He was not a strong support for her like Charles.

"Charles Buford is so serious-minded and reliable," one of his mother's friends had said when they were taking tea together in Idris. She had bit into one of Mother's special scones. "And Matthew, well, he is . . . charming."

That morning at breakfast Charles Buford reached for the plate of Mama's scones. Matthew gave him a smile and a very decided shake of his head, moving the plate to his mother's elbow. Charles Buford grimaced in Matthew's direction.

Charlotte gave him a distracted smile, then returned to contemplating the tablecloth. She was in a brown study. Matthew wished he could say that was an unusual occurrence these days, but it was not. For months there had been something wrong in the atmosphere of home, with not only his mother but his father and even Charles Buford looking abstracted and occasionally snapping at Matthew. Sometimes Matthew dreaded the thought of what he might be told: that it was time he knew the truth, that his mother was going away forever. Sometimes Matthew thought if he only knew, he could bear it.

"My dear," said Papa. "Are you feeling well?"

"Perfectly, Henry," said Mama.

Matthew loved his father beyond reason, but he knew him. He was well aware that there were times when the entire family could have had their heads replaced with parakeet heads and Papa would simply tell the parakeet heads all about his latest experiment.

Now his father was watching his mother with worried eyes. Matthew could picture him saying, *Please, Charlotte. Do not leave me.*

His heart lurched in his chest. Matthew folded his napkin three times over in his hands and said: "Could somebody tell me—"

Then the door opened, and Gideon Lightwood came in. Mr. Lightwood. Matthew refused to think or speak of him as Uncle Gideon any longer.

"What are you doing here?" said Matthew.

"Sir!" Mama said sharply. "Really, Matthew, call him sir."

"What are you doing here?" said Matthew. "Sir."

Mr. Gideon Lightwood had the cheek to give Matthew a brief smile before he walked over and put his hand on Mama's shoulder. In front of Matthew's papa.

"Always a pleasure to see you, sir," said Charles Buford, that wretch. "May I serve you some kippers?"

"No, no, not at all, I already ate breakfast," said Mr. Lightwood. "I merely thought to accompany Charlotte through the Portal to Idris."

Mama smiled properly for Mr. Lightwood, as she had not for Matthew. "That's very kind, Gideon, though not necessary."

"It is most necessary," said Mr. Lightwood. "A lady should always have the escort of a gentleman."

His voice was teasing. Matthew usually waited until after breakfast to take his father down in his chair to his laboratory, but he could not bear this.

"I must see James at once upon urgent business!" he declared, bolting upright.

He slammed the door of the breakfast parlor shut behind him, but not before he heard Mama apologize for him, and Mr. Lightwood say: "Oh, that is all right. The age he is at is a difficult one. Believe me, I remember it well."

Before Matthew left, he ran up to his bedroom mirror to adjust his hair and cuffs and smooth his new green waistcoat. He stared at his face in the glass, framed in gold. A pretty face, but not a clever one like everyone else's in his family. He remembered the faerie woman saying, *Some would say only a shallow river could flash so bright.*

He tilted his head as he looked into the glass. Many people thought his eyes were dark like his mama's, but they were not. They were such a dark green that they fooled people, except when light struck the dark a certain way and the depths flashed emerald. Like the rest of him, his eyes were a trick.

He drew the vial of truth potion from his sleeve. Uncle Jem had not seen him buy it. Even if he suspected Matthew had it, Uncle Jem would not peach on him. When Uncle Jem said something, you believed it: he was that kind of person.

Matthew had refrained from ever mentioning his thoughts about Gideon to James, because Matthew was the soul of discretion and Jamie had an awful temper on him sometimes. Last summer a perfectly amiable Shadowhunter named Augustus Pounceby had come to the London Institute on his tour abroad, and Matthew had left Pounceby in James's sole company for less than half an hour. When Matthew returned, he found Jamie had thrown Pounceby into the Thames. All James would say was that Pounceby had insulted him. It was quite a feat, since Pounceby was a Shadowhunter fully grown and Jamie was fourteen at the time. Still, however impressive, it could not be considered good manners.

Neither James nor Uncle Jem would buy potions like a sneak, or consider administering them. Only, what harm would it do to finally learn the truth? Matthew had considered adding a drop from the vial to breakfast this morning; then Father and Mother would *have* to tell them all what was happening. Now that Mr. Gideon Lightwood had started popping in of a morning, he wished he had.

Matthew shook his head at his reflection and determined to banish melancholy and dull care.

"Do I look dapper?" he asked Mr. Oscar Wilde. "Do I look dashing and debonair?"

Mr. Oscar Wilde gave him a lick on the nose, because Mr.

Oscar Wilde was a puppy Jamie had given Matthew on his birthday. Matthew took this as approval.

He pointed to his reflection.

"You may be a waste of space in a waistcoat," he told Matthew Fairchild, "but at least your waistcoat is fantastic."

He checked his pocket watch, then tucked the pocket watch and vial into his waistcoat. Matthew could not linger. He had an important appointment at a most exclusive club.

First Matthew had to breeze into the London Institute to collect a parcel known as James Herondale. He had a shrewd idea of where James was likely to be, so he told Oscar to stay and guard a lamppost. Oscar obeyed: he was very well behaved for a puppy, and people said Matthew must have trained him well, but Matthew only loved him. Matthew threw a grappling hook up to the library window, climbed up while being careful of his trousers, and tapped on the glass.

James was in the window seat, his black head bent over— what a surprise!—a book. He looked up at the tap and smiled.

James had never really needed Matthew. James had been so shy, and Matthew had wanted to take care of him, but now that James was growing into his angular features and accustomed to having the certain company of three good friends, he was far more collected during social gatherings. Even when Jamie was shy, he never seemed to doubt or wish to alter himself. He never looked to Matthew for rescue. There was a quiet, deep certainty to James that Matthew wished he had himself. From the start, there was something between them that was more equal than between him and Thomas or him and Christopher. Something that made Matthew want to prove himself to James. He was not sure he ever truly had.

James never looked relieved to see Matthew, or expectant. He only looked pleased. He opened the window and Matthew crawled in, upsetting both James and the book from the window seat.

"Hello, Matthew," said James from the floor, in slightly sardonic tones.

"Hello, Matthew!" chimed Lucie from her writing desk.

She was a picture of dainty disarray, clearly in the throes of composition. Her light brown curls were half pulled out of a blue ribbon, one shoe dangling precariously from her stockinged toes. Uncle Will frequently gave dramatic readings from the book he was writing on the demon pox, which were very droll. Lucie did not show her writing around. Matthew had often considered asking her if she might read him a page, but he could think of no reason why Lucie would make a special exception for him.

"Bless you, my Herondales," said Matthew grandly, scrambling up from the floor and making Lucie his bow. "I come upon an urgent errand. Tell me—be honest!—what do you think of my waistcoat?"

Lucie dimpled. "Devastating."

"What Lucie said," James agreed peacefully.

"Not fantastic?" Matthew asked. "Not positively stunning?"

"I suppose I am stunned," said James. "But am I positively stunned?"

"Refrain from playing cruel word games with your one and only *parabatai*," Matthew requested. "Attend to your own attire, if you please. Heave that beastly book away. The Misters Lightwood await us. We must hook it."

"Can't I go as I am?" asked James.

He looked up at Matthew with wide gold eyes from his position on the floor. His pitch-black hair was askew, his linen shirt rumpled, and he was not even wearing a waistcoat. Matthew nobly repressed a convulsive shudder.

"Surely you jest," said Matthew. "I know you only say these things to hurt me. Off with you. Brush your hair!"

"The hairbrush mutiny is coming," warned James, making for the door.

"Come back victorious or on the hairbrushes of your soldiers!" Matthew called after him.

When Jamie had flown, Matthew turned to Lucie, who was scribbling intently but who looked up as if sensing his glance and smiled. Matthew wondered how it would be, to be self-sufficient and welcoming with it, like a house with sturdy walls and a beacon light always burning.

"Should I brush my hair?" Lucie teased.

"You are, as always, perfect," said Matthew.

He wished he could fix the ribbon in her hair, but that would be taking a liberty.

"Do you wish to attend our secret club meeting?" asked Matthew.

"I cannot, I am doing lessons with my mother. Mam and I are teaching ourselves Persian," said Lucie. "I should be able to speak the languages my *parabatai* speaks, shouldn't I?"

James had recently started calling his mother and father Mam and Da rather than Mama and Papa, since it sounded more grown-up. Lucie had instantly copied him in this matter. Matthew rather liked hearing the Welsh lilt in their voices when they called their parents, their voices soft as songs and always loving.

"Of a certainty," said Matthew, coughing and making a private resolution to return to his Welsh lessons.

There had been no question of Lucie attending Shadowhunter Academy. She had never demonstrated any abilities like James's, but the world was cruel enough to women who were even suspected of being the least bit different.

"Lucie Herondale is a sweet child, but with her disadvantages, who would marry her?" Lavinia Whitelaw had asked Matthew's mama once over tea.

"I would be happy if either of my sons wished to," said Charlotte, in her most Consul-like manner.

Matthew thought James was very lucky to have Lucie. He had always wanted a little sister.

Not that he wanted Lucie to be his sister.

"Are you writing your book, Luce?" Matthew asked tentatively.

"No, a letter to Cordelia," Lucie answered, shattering Matthew's fragile plot. "I hope Cordelia will come to visit, *very* soon," she added with earnest eagerness. "You will like her so much, Matthew. I know you will."

"Hmm," said Matthew.

Matthew had his doubts about Cordelia Carstairs. Lucie was going to be *parabatai* with Cordelia one day, when the Clave decided they were grown-up ladies who knew their own minds. Lucie and James were acquainted with Cordelia from childhood adventures that Matthew had not been part of, and which Matthew felt a bit jealous about. Cordelia must have some redeeming qualities, or Lucie would not want her for a *parabatai*, but she was Alastair Loathly Worm Carstairs's sister, so it would be strange if she was entirely amiable.

"She sent me a picture of herself in her latest. This is Cordelia," Lucie continued in tones of pride. "Is she not the prettiest girl you ever saw?"

"Oh, well," said Matthew. "Perhaps."

He was privately surprised by the picture. He would have thought Alastair's sister might share Alastair's unpleasant look, as if he were eating lemons he looked down on. She did not. Instead Matthew was reminded of a line in a poem James had read to him once, about an unrequited love. "That child of shower and gleam" described the vivid face laughing up at him from the frame exactly.

"All I know is," Matthew continued, "*you* have every other girl in London beat to flinders."

Lucie colored faint pink. "You are always teasing, Matthew."

"Did Cordelia ask you to be *parabatai*," Matthew said casually, "or did you ask her?"

Lucie and Cordelia had wanted to be made *parabatai* before they were parted, but they were warned that sometimes you regret a bond made young, and sometimes one partner or other would change their mind. Particularly, Laurence Ashdown had remarked, since ladies could be so flighty.

Lucie was not flighty. She and Cordelia wrote to each other faithfully, every day. Lucie had even once told Matthew she was writing a long story to keep Cordelia amused since Cordelia was always so far away. Matthew did not really wonder why someone like Lucie found it difficult to take someone like him seriously.

"I asked *her*, of course," Lucie said promptly. "I did not wish to miss my chance."

Matthew nodded, confirmed in his new belief that Cordelia Carstairs must be something special.

He was sure that if he had not asked James to be *parabatai*, James would never have thought of asking him.

James returned to the room. "Satisfied?" he asked.

"That is a strong word, Jamie," said Matthew. "Consider my waistcoat wrath somewhat appeased."

James still had his book tucked under his arm, but Matthew knew better than to fight doomed battles. James told him about the book as they walked the London streets. Matthew enjoyed the modern and humorous, such as the works of Oscar Wilde or the music of Gilbert and Sullivan, but Greek history was not so bad when it was Jamie telling him. Matthew had taken to reading more and more literature of old, stories of doomed love and noble battles. He could not find himself in them, but he saw James in them, and that was enough.

They walked unglamoured, as Matthew always insisted they do in his quest to make Jamie feel less self-conscious after the disasters of the Academy. A young lady, arrested by Jamie's bone structure, stopped in the path of an omnibus. Matthew seized her waist and whirled her to safety, giving her a tip of his hat and a smile.

Jamie seemed to miss the whole incident entirely, fiddling with something beneath his shirt cuff.

There were crowds protesting the mundane war outside the Houses of Parliament.

"The Bore War?" asked Matthew. "That cannot be right."

"The Boer War," said James. "*B-o-e-r*. Honestly, Matthew."

"That makes more sense," Matthew admitted.

A lady in a shapeless hat caught hold of Matthew's sleeve.

"May I be of any assistance, madam?" asked Matthew.

"They are committing unspeakable atrocities," said the lady.

"They have children penned up in camps. Think of the children."

James fastened his hand on Matthew's sleeve and towed him away, with an apologetic hat tip to the lady. Matthew looked over his shoulder.

"I do hope affairs go right for the children," he called.

James appeared pensive as they went. Matthew knew James wished Shadowhunters could solve problems like mundane war, though Matthew felt they were rather overstretched as it was with all the demons.

In order to cheer Jamie up, he stole his hat. Jamie burst into startled laughter and pursued Matthew, both of them racing and jumping high enough to amaze the mundanes, under the shadow of St. Stephen's Tower. Matthew's puppy lost his head, forgot his training, and dashed under their feet, yapping with the sheer joy of being alive. Their rushing footsteps outpaced the steady tick of the Great Clock, under which was written in James's beloved Latin, *O Lord, keep safe our Queen Victoria the First*, and their laughter mingled with the gleeful chime and roar of the bells.

Later Matthew would look back and remember it as his last happy day.

"Do I sleep, do I dream, or are these visions I see?" demanded Matthew. "Why are Aunt Sophie and *both of Thomas's sisters* taking tea in the same establishment as our private and exclusive club room?"

"They followed me," said Thomas in beleaguered tones. "Mama was understanding, or they would have followed us directly into the club room."

Aunt Sophie was a good sport, but that did not make

Matthew feel any less uneasy about the advent of Thomas's sisters. They were not kindred spirits, and they were liable to consider all the doings of their little brother both their business and very silly.

Matthew loved their club room and would brook no interference. He had chosen the materials for the curtains himself, made certain that James put the works of Oscar Wilde in their extensive book collection, and reinforced the corner that was Christopher's laboratory with steel sheets on the walls.

Which led Matthew to another grievance. He regarded Christopher with a steely gaze.

"Did you sleep in those clothes, Christopher? I know Aunt Cecily, Uncle Gabriel, and Cousin Anna would never let you inflict these horrors on the populace. What are those peculiar lavender stains upon your shirtfront? Did you set your sleeves on fire?"

Christopher regarded his sleeves as if he had never beheld them before. "A bit," he said guiltily.

"Ah well," said Matthew. "At least the purple stains match your eyes."

Christopher blinked said eyes, the improbable shade of violets in summer, and smiled his slow-blossoming smile. He clearly did not understand Matthew's objections, but was vaguely pleased they had been overcome.

It was not like with James, who actually presented a very fine appearance to the world. Christopher was incorrigible. He could rumple leather boots.

He could certainly set fire to anything. Matthew had not meant for Christopher to be asked to leave Shadowhunter Academy, but as it emerged, they did not let you remain in school if you blew up any portion of it. Besides which, Professor Fell had threatened to leave the Academy forever if Christopher remained.

Thomas had stayed out the full year, but found no reason to return with his friends gone and Alastair God-Help-Us Carstairs graduated.

So by luck, the closeness between their families, and an irresponsible attitude to flammable materials, more often than not all Matthew's bosom friends could live near each other in London. They trained together at the London Institute and took lessons together in various schoolrooms, and Lavinia Whitelaw had referred to them as "that notorious bunch of hooligan boys." Matthew and James had called themselves Shadowhooligans for some time after that remark. They had decided it was long past time to have a room of their own, inviolate from parents—however well-meaning—and preserved from siblings; though Cousin Anna and Luce were always welcome, due to being kindred spirits. So they had rented a room from the proprietor of the Devil Tavern, who owed the Herondales some sort of favor. They paid a monthly fee and had it all to themselves.

Matthew regarded their room with deep satisfaction. It looked very well, he thought, and best with all four of them sitting in it. In honor of Ben Jonson's Apollo Club, which had once held its meetings in this very tavern, a bust of the god hung over the fireplace with words cut into the marble beneath the head and shoulders:

Welcome all, who lead or follow,
To the Oracle of Apollo

All his answers are divine,
Truth itself doth flow in wine.

There was, of course, a window seat for Jamie, and Jamie was already installed with his book upon his lap. Christopher sat in his laboratory, adding an alarming orange liquid to a bubbling purple liquid, his face a picture of contentment. Thomas was seated cross-legged upon the sofa and earnestly practicing his blade work. Thomas was very conscientious and worried about not being a good enough Shadowhunter due to being undersized.

Thomas's sisters were a good deal taller than he was. So was everybody. Aunt Sophie, Tom's mama, said that Thomas would shoot up someday. She said she believed one of her grandpapas had been a blacksmith and a giant of a man, small as a pea until he was seventeen.

Aunt Sophie was a kind lady, very beautiful and most interesting with her tales of mundanes. Matthew did not know how Mr. Gideon Lightwood could live with himself.

He turned over the vial of truth potion in his waistcoat.

"Friends, now we are all gathered together, shall we share secrets?"

Jamie fiddled with his shirt cuff again, which he always did upon certain occasions, and pretended not to hear. Matthew suspected he had a secret love. He sometimes wondered whether James would have confided in him if he had been a different sort of person, more serious-minded and dependable.

Matthew laughed. "Come now. Any deadly hatreds you harbor in your bosom? Any ladies of your heart?"

Thomas flushed a deep red and dropped his knife. "No."

Oscar bounded over to fetch the knife for Thomas, and Thomas stroked his floppy ears.

Matthew sauntered closer to the laboratory corner, though he knew it was rash.

"Is there anyone who has caught your eye?" he asked Christopher.

Christopher eyed Matthew with alarm. Matthew sighed and prepared himself to explain further.

"Is there a lady you find yourself thinking of more often than other ladies?" he asked. "Or a fellow," he added tentatively.

Christopher's face cleared. "Oh! Oh yes, I see. Yes, there is a lady."

"Christopher!" Matthew exclaimed, delighted. "You sly dog! Do I know her?"

"No, I cannot think so," said Christopher. "She is a mundane."

"Christopher, you dark horse," said Matthew. "What is her name?"

"Mrs.—"

"A married lady!" Matthew said, overwhelmed. "No, no. I beg your pardon. Please go on."

"Mrs. Marie Curie," said Christopher. "I believe her to be one of the preeminent scientists of the age. If you read her papers, Matthew, I believe you would be most interest—"

"Have you ever met this lady?" said Matthew in dangerous tones.

"No?" said Christopher, heedless of danger as he often was around irate teachers and naked flames.

Christopher had the audacity to look surprised when Matthew began to belabor him mightily about the head and face.

"Watch the test tubes!" cried Thomas. "There is a hole in the floor at the Academy that Professor Fell calls the Christopher Lightwood Chasm."

"I suppose I hate some people," offered James. "Augustus Pounceby. Lavinia Whitelaw. Alastair Carstairs."

Matthew regarded his very own *parabatai* with deep approval.

"This is why we are chosen warrior partners, because we share such a perfect bond of sympathy. Come to me, Jamie, that we might share a manly embrace."

He made incursions upon Jamie's person. James thwacked him over the head with his book. It was a large book.

"Betrayed," said Matthew, writhing prone upon the floor. "Is that why you insist on carrying about enormous tomes everywhere you go, that you might visit violence upon innocent persons? Done to death by my best friend—my heart's brother—my own dear *parabatai*—"

He snagged James around the waist and brought him crashing to the floor for the second time that day. James hit Matthew with the book again, then subsided, leaning his shoulder against Matthew's. They were both thoroughly rumpled, but Matthew did not mind being rumpled for a good cause.

Matthew jostled James, very thankful that he had brought up Alastair and provided Matthew an opening to tell his secret.

"Alastair is not so bad," said Thomas unexpectedly from the sofa.

They all looked at him, and Tom curled up like an earwig under their scrutiny but persisted.

"I know what Alastair did to James was wrong," Thomas

said. "Alastair knows that very well too. That was why he was prickly whenever it was mentioned."

"How is that different from his usual ghastly demeanor?" Matthew demanded. "Besides him being particularly noxious the day everybody else's parents came to the Academy."

He paused to consider how to tell them, but that gave Thomas a chance to speak.

"Yes, exactly. Everybody's papa came but Alastair's," Thomas said quietly. "Alastair was jealous. Mr. Herondale came rushing to Jamie's defense, and nobody came for Alastair."

"Can one truly blame the man?" asked Matthew. "Had I such an insufferable toad of a son, and were he blessedly to be sent away to school, I am not sure I could bring myself to blast my sight with his visage until the accursed holidays carried him back to me again."

Thomas did not look convinced by Matthew's sound argument. Matthew took a deep breath.

"You do not know what he said to me the day we were expelled."

Tom shrugged. "Some nonsense, I expect. He always speaks the most shocking nonsense when he is overset. You shouldn't listen to him."

James's shoulder was tense against Matthew's. James had been the chief object of Alastair's malice. Thomas clearly intended to defend Alastair stoutly. This line of argument was bound to upset either James or Thomas. Matthew was not about to soothe his own feelings at the expense of Jamie's or Tom's.

Matthew gave up. "I cannot imagine why anyone would listen to him."

"Oh well," said Tom. "I like his nonsense." He looked wistful. "I think Alastair masks his pain with cleverly turned phrases."

"What absolute bosh," said Matthew.

Thomas was too nice, that was his problem. Really, people would let you get away with being the worst sort of scoundrel if you simply had a secret sorrow or did not rub along terribly well with your father.

It was definitely something to look into.

His papa was the best papa in the world, so Matthew had no opportunity to be cruelly oppressed or sadly neglected. Perhaps he should spend his time brooding over a forbidden passion like James was currently doing.

Matthew decided to give unrequited love a try. He stared out the window with all the pensive force he could muster. He was preparing to pass a hand across his fevered brow and murmur, "Alas, my lost love," or some other such rot when he was abruptly rapped upon the head with a book.

Honestly, Jamie was lethal with that thing.

"Are you quite well, Matthew?" Jamie inquired. "Your face suggests you are suffering from an ague."

Matthew nodded, but he ducked his head down against Jamie's coat and stayed there for a moment. It had never occurred to Matthew that Alastair might be jealous of James's father. He could not imagine being jealous of anybody's papa. Having the best papa in the world, Matthew would be perfectly satisfied with him.

If only he could be certain that Henry *was* his papa.

Early in the morning, Matthew unstoppered the faerie's vial and tipped a drop in among the cranberries for his mama's scones. The scones came out of the oven plump, golden, and smelling delicious.

"You are the best boy in London," said Cook, giving Matthew a kiss.

"I am entirely selfish," declared Matthew. "For I love you, Cook. When shall we be married?"

"Get along with you," said Cook, waving her wooden spoon in a menacing fashion.

When Jamie was a little boy, he had his own beloved special spoon. The family always reminisced about this. It embarrassed Jamie to death, especially when Uncle Gabriel presented him with a spoon at family gatherings. Uncles thought all sorts of sorry jests were a fine idea.

Jamie kept the spoons Uncle Gabriel gave him. When asked why, he said it was because he loved his uncle Gabriel. James was able to say such things with a sincerity that would shame anyone else.

After James said that, Uncle Will loudly asked what was the point in even having a son, but Uncle Gabriel looked touched. Uncle Gabriel loved Anna and Christopher, but Matthew was not sure he entirely understood his children. James greatly resembled his aunt Cecily, and tried very hard at being a Shadowhunter, while Christopher might not be aware any of them even *were* Shadowhunters. Uncle Gabriel was especially fond of James. Of course, who would not be?

Matthew stole Cook's spoon to give to James.

"I suppose that is for some absurd jest," said Charles Buford when he saw the spoon at breakfast. "I wish you would grow up, Matthew."

Matthew considered this, then stuck his tongue out at

Charles. His puppy was not allowed in the breakfast parlor, because Charles Buford said Oscar was not hygienic.

"If you would simply make an effort to be sensible," said Charles.

"I shan't," said Matthew. "I might sustain a strain from which I would never recover."

His mother did not smile at his theatrics. She was staring at her teacup, to all appearances lost in thought. His father was watching her.

"Is Mr. Gideon Lightwood coming to conduct you to Idris this morning?" Matthew asked, and pushed the plate of scones toward his mother.

Mama picked up a scone, buttered it liberally, and took a bite.

"Yes," she said. "I would thank you to be civil to him this time. You can have no idea, Matthew, how much I—"

Mama stopped speaking. Her small hand flew to her mouth. She sprang to her feet as if trying to take action in an emergency, in the manner she always did. Under Matthew's horrified gaze, tears shimmered in her eyes and abruptly spilled in two long, bright tracks down her face. In the morning light, Matthew discerned a faint tinge of violet in her tears.

Then she collapsed, her hair falling out of its tidy coil, her gray skirts a sudden riot on the floor.

"Charlotte!" cried Father.

Henry Fairchild used all kinds of ingenious contraptions to get about, but at family breakfasts he had only an ordinary chair. Not that it mattered. He simply launched himself from the chair in his haste to get to Charlotte, and fell heavily on the ground. He hardly seemed to notice he had fallen. Instead he crawled on his elbows toward the inert heap that was Mama, dragging his body painfully across the carpet as Matthew watched, frozen in horror.

He reached Mama and clasped her in his arms. She was always so small, but now she looked small as a child. Her face was still and white as the face of the marble busts in mundane tombs.

"Charlotte," murmured Papa, as if he was praying. "Dearest. Please."

"Mama," Matthew whispered. "Papa. Charlie!"

He turned to his brother the way he had when he was small, when he had followed Charlie around everywhere and believed his brother could do anything in the world.

Charles had bolted out of his chair and was shouting for help. He turned back in the doorway, staring at his parents with a wretched expression that was very unlike him. "I knew how it would be, Portaling back and forth from London to Idris so that Matthew could be near his precious *parabatai*—"

"What?" asked Matthew. "I didn't know. I swear I didn't know. . . ."

Cook had appeared in the doorway in response to Charles's shouts. She gasped. "Mrs. Fairchild!"

Matthew's voice shook. "We need Brother Zachariah—"

Brother Zachariah would know what he had given Mama and what to do. Matthew began to explain the evil thing he had done, but then there was a noise from Charlotte, and the room went still.

"Oh yes," faltered Mama, her voice terrifyingly weak. "Oh, please. Fetch Jem."

Charles and Cook raced from the room. Matthew did not

dare approach his mother and father. Finally, after some long and terrible time, Brother Zachariah came, parchment-colored cloak swirling about him like the robes of a fell presence come to deliver judgment and punishment.

Matthew knew Brother Zachariah's always closed eyes still saw. He could see Matthew, through to his sinful heart.

Brother Zachariah bent and scooped Matthew's mother up in his arms. He carried her away.

All day Matthew heard the sounds of comings and goings. He saw the carriage from the London Institute rattle up to the door and Aunt Tessa emerge with a basket of medicine. She had been learning some warlock magic.

Matthew understood that they needed a Silent Brother *and* a warlock, and they still might not save his mother.

Charles did not return. Matthew had helped his father back to his chair. They sat together in the breakfast parlor as the light turned from the glow of morning to the blaze of day, then faded into the shadows of evening.

Papa's face looked carved out of old stone. When he spoke at last, he sounded as if he were dying inside. "You should know, Matthew," he said. "Your mama and I, we were . . ."

Separating. Ending our marriage. She loved another. Matthew braced himself for the horror, but when it came, it was greater than anything he could have imagined.

"We were in anticipation of—of a happy event," said Papa, his voice catching in his throat.

Matthew stared at him with blank incomprehension. He simply could not understand. It would hurt too much.

"Your mama and I had to wait some time for Charles Buford, and for you, and we thought you were both worth the wait," said Father, and even in the midst of that awful moment he tried to smile for Matthew. "This time Charlotte was hoping for—for a daughter."

Matthew choked on his horror. He thought he might never speak another word or eat another bite. He would be choking on horror for years.

We thought. We were in anticipation. It was entirely clear that Father was certain, and had reason to believe, his children were his.

"We were concerned since you and Charles are both now quite grown up," said Henry. "Gideon, good fellow, has been dancing attendance on Charlotte during Clave meetings. He has always stood as your mother's friend, lending her the Lightwood name and consequence whenever she needed support, and advising her when she wished for good counsel. I am afraid I have never truly understood the workings of an Institute, let alone the Clave. Your mama is a wonder."

Gideon had been helping his mother. Matthew was the one who had attacked her.

"I had thought we might name her Matilda," Father said in a slow, sad voice. "I had a Great-Aunt Matilda. She was very old when I was still a young rip, and the other boys used to tease me. She would give me books and tell me that I was smarter than any of them. She had splendid buttery-white wavy hair, but it was gold when she was a girl. When you were born, you already had the dearest fair lovelocks. I called her Aunt Matty. I never told you, because I thought you might not like to be named for a lady. You already have a great deal to endure with your foolish father, and those who cavil at your mother and your *parabatai*. You bear it all so gracefully."

Matthew's father touched his hair with a gentle, loving hand. Matthew wished he would pick up a blade and cut Matthew's throat.

"I wish you could have known your great-great-aunt. She was very like you. She was the sweetest woman God ever made," said Father. "Save your mother."

Brother Zachariah glided in then, a shadow amid all the other shadows crowding that room, to summon Matthew's father to his mother's bedside.

Matthew was left alone.

He stared in the gathering darkness at his mother's overturned chair, the dropped scone and its trail of crumbs going nowhere, the greasy remnants of breakfast over the disarranged table. He, Matthew, was always dragging his friends and family to art galleries, always anxious to dance through life, always prattling of truth and beauty like a fool. He had run headlong into a Shadow Market and blithely trusted a Downworlder, because Downworlders seemed exciting, because she had called Shadowhunters brutal and Matthew had agreed, believing he knew better than they. It was not the faerie woman's fault, or Alastair's, or the fault of any other soul. He was the one who had chosen to distrust his mother. He had fed his mother poison with his own hands. He was not a fool. He was a villain.

Matthew bowed the fair head that had been passed to him through his father, from his father's best-loved relative. He sat in that dark room and wept.

Brother Zachariah descended the stairs after a long battle with death, to tell Matthew Fairchild that his mother would live.

James and Lucie had come with Tessa and waited in the

hall all this long day. Lucie's hands were chilled when she clung to Jem.

She asked, "Aunt Charlotte, is she safe?"

Yes, my darlings, said Jem. *Yes.*

"Thank the Angel," breathed James. "Matthew's heart would break. All our hearts would."

Brother Zachariah was not so sure of Matthew's heart, after the mischief Matthew had wrought, but he wanted to offer James and Lucie what comfort he could.

Go to the library. There is a fire lit. I will send Matthew to you.

When he went into the breakfast room, he found Matthew, who had been all gold and laughter, cowering in his chair as if he could not bear what was to come.

"My mother," he whispered at once, his voice brittle and dry as old bones.

She will live, said Jem, and softened seeing the boy's pain.

James had known his *parabatai*'s heart better than Jem. There had been a time when Will was a boy everybody assumed the worst of, with good reason. Everybody except for Jem. He did not want to learn harsh judgment from the Silent Brothers, or a less forgiving heart.

Matthew lifted his head to face Brother Zachariah. His eyes told of agony, but he held his voice steady.

"And the child?"

Brother Zachariah said, *The child did not live.*

Matthew's hands closed on the edge of his chair. His knuckles were white. He looked older than he had a mere two nights ago.

Matthew, said Brother Zachariah, and walled off his Brothers in his head as well as he might.

"Yes?"

Rely upon a Silent Brother for silence, said Jem. *I will not tell anybody about the Shadow Market or any bargains you may have made there.*

Matthew swallowed. Jem thought he might be about to be thanked, but Jem had not done this for thanks.

I will not tell anybody, he said, *but you should. A secret too long kept can kill a soul by inches. I watched a secret almost destroy a man once, the finest man ever made. Such a secret is like keeping treasure in a tomb. Little by little, poison eats away at the gold. By the time the door is opened, there may be nothing left but dust.*

Brother Zachariah stared into the young face that had been so bright. He waited and hoped to see that face lit again.

"All this about the Shadow Market," Matthew faltered.

Yes? said Jem.

The boy flung back his golden head.

"I'm sorry," said Matthew coldly. "I do not know what you are talking about."

Zachariah's heart fell.

So be it, he said. *James and Lucie are waiting for you in the library. Let them give you whatever comfort they can.*

Matthew stood from his chair, moving as if he had grown suddenly old over the course of a day. Sometimes the distance Silent Brothers possessed moved them to dispassionate observation and too far from pity.

It would be a long time, Brother Zachariah knew, before there could be any comfort for Matthew Fairchild.

The library in Matthew's house was a far smaller and less loved and lived-in room than the library in the London Institute, but tonight there was a fire burning and Herondales waiting within. Matthew stumbled into the room as if he were walking in from midwinter cold, his limbs too chilled to move.

As one, as if they had only been waiting for his coming, James and Lucie looked up at him. They were pressed together on a sofa at the hearth. By firelight, Lucie's eyes were as eerie as James's, a paler and more fiercely burning blue than her father's. It was as though James's gold were the corona of a flame and Lucie's blue its burning heart.

They were a strange pair, these two Herondales, thorned mysterious plants in the hothouse of the Nephilim. Matthew could not have loved either of them more dearly.

Lucie leaped to her feet and ran to him with her hands out-stretched. Matthew shuddered away. He realized, with dull pain, that he did not feel worthy of being touched by her.

Lucie glanced at him sharply, then nodded. She always saw a lot, their Luce.

"I will leave you two together," she said decisively. "Take as long as ever you may."

She reached out her hand to touch his, and Matthew shrank away from her again. This time he saw that it hurt, but Lucie only murmured his name and withdrew.

He could not tell Lucie this, and see her disgust of him, but he and James were bound. Perhaps James would try to understand.

Matthew advanced, every step a terrible effort, toward the fire. Once he was near enough, James reached out and clasped Matthew's wrist, drawing him close to the sofa. He laid Matthew's hand over James's heart, and covered it with his own. Matthew looked down into James's fire-gold eyes.

"*Mathew*," said Jamie, pronouncing his name in the Welsh way and with the Welsh lilt that let Matthew know he meant it as an endearment. "I am so sorry. What can I do?"

He felt he could not live on with this massive stone of a secret crushing his chest. If he was ever going to tell anyone, he should tell his *parabatai*.

"Listen to me," he said. "I was talking about Alastair Carstairs yesterday. What I meant to tell you was that he insulted my mother. He said—"

"I understand," said James. "You do not have to tell me."

Matthew drew in a small shaky breath. He wondered if James really could understand.

"I know the kind of thing they say about Aunt Charlotte," said James with quiet fierceness. "They say similar things about my mother. You remember that man Augustus Pounceby, last year? He waited until we were alone to cast slurs upon my mother's good name." A small grim smile curved James's mouth. "So I threw him in the river."

Aunt Tessa had been so glad to have a Shadowhunter visitor, Matthew remembered numbly. She displayed Shadowhunter family coats of arms on her walls to welcome any traveler to the London Institute.

"You never told me," said Matthew.

Jamie was telling him now. Tom had told him that whatever Alastair said was nonsense. If Matthew had asked his father about what Alastair had said, his father could have told him about Great-Aunt Matty, and they might even have laughed about how absurd it was to think some stupid malicious boy could ever make them doubt their family.

Jamie's mouth crooked down a little. "Oh well. I know you

have to hear a lot about me and my unfortunate antecedents already. I do not want you to think I am an unbearable nuisance and you got a bad bargain with your *parabatai*."

"Jamie," Matthew said on a wounded breath, as if he had been hit.

"I know it must feel wretched to remember anything hurtful that worm Carstairs said about your mother," James plunged on. "Especially when she is—she is unwell. The very next time we see him, we will punch him in the head. What do you say to that, Mathew? Let's do it together."

Matthew's father and his mother and his brother and his *parabatai* had all been trying not to burden him, while Matthew pranced on thinking he was no end of a fine fellow and dealing remarkably by himself. James would not have done what Matthew had. Nor would Christopher or Thomas. They were loyal. They were honorable. When someone had insulted Jamie's mother, Jamie had thrown him in the river.

Matthew pressed his palm against James's linen shirt, over the steady beat of his loyal heart. Then Matthew clenched his hand into a fist.

He could not tell him. He could never do it.

"All right, old chap," said Matthew. "We will do it together. Do you think I could have a moment alone, though?"

James hesitated, then drew back.

"Is that what you want?"

"It is," said Matthew, who had never wanted to be alone in his life, and never wanted to be alone less than in this moment.

James hesitated again, but he respected Matthew's wishes. He bowed his head and went out, Matthew assumed to rejoin his sister. They were both good and pure. They should be together and comfort each other. They deserved comfort as he did not.

After James was gone, Matthew could not keep standing. He fell to his hands and knees in front of the fire.

There was a statue above the fire showing Jonathan Shadowhunter, the first Shadowhunter, praying for the world to be washed clean of evil. Behind him was the Angel Raziel flying to gift him with strength to defeat the forces of darkness. The first Shadowhunter could not see him yet, but he was standing firm, because he had faith.

Matthew turned his face away from the light. He crawled, as his father had crawled across another floor at the beginning of this endless day, until he was in the darkest and farthest corner of the room. He had not believed. He laid his cheek against the cold floor and refused to let himself weep again. He knew he could not be forgiven.

It was long past time for Brother Zachariah to return to the City of Bones. Tessa stood with him in the hall and touched his hand before he went.

The sweetest woman God ever made, he had heard Henry say earlier. Jem loved Charlotte, but he had his own image of the sweetest this world could offer.

She was always his anchor in cold seas, her warm hand, her steadfast eyes, and it was as if a flame leaped between them and a mad hope. For a moment Jem was as he had been. It seemed possible to be together in sorrow, united as family and friends were, to sleep under the Institute roof and go down in the morning to breakfast, sad but safe in the warmth of a shared hearth and human hearts.

He thought, *Yes, ask me to stay.*

He could not. They both knew he could not.

Good-bye, Tessa, he said.

She swallowed, her long lashes screening the shine of her eyes. Tessa was always brave. She would not let him take a memory of her tears back to the Silent City, but she called him by the name she was always careful not to call him when anybody but they could hear. "Good-bye, Jem."

Brother Zachariah bowed his head, his hood falling about his face, and went out into the winter cold of London.

Finally you leave, said Brother Enoch in his mind.

All the Silent Brothers hushed when Brother Zachariah was with Tessa, like small animals in the trees hearing the approach of that which they did not understand. In a way, they were all in love with her, and some resented her for that. Brother Enoch had made it clear he was tired of two names ceaselessly echoing in their minds.

Brother Zachariah was halfway down the street where the Fairchilds lived when a tall shadow struck his across the pale streets.

He looked up from the shadows and saw Will Herondale, head of the London Institute. He carried a walking stick that had once been Zachariah's, before Zachariah took a staff into his hands.

Charlotte will live, said Brother Zachariah. *The child never had a chance to.*

"I know," said Will. "I already knew. I did not come to you for those tidings."

Brother Zachariah should really have learned better by now. Of course Tessa would have sent word to Will, and while Will often traded upon Brother Zachariah's position as a Silent

Brother to command his services and thus his presence, he very seldom spoke to Zachariah of his duties as a Silent Brother, as if he could make Zachariah not what he was by dint of sheer determination.

If anyone could have done it, Will would have been that one.

Will threw him the walking stick, which he must have stolen from James's room, and confiscated Brother Zachariah's staff. Jem had asked them to give James his room at the Institute, fill it with their son's bright presence, and not keep it as some dreary shrine. He was not dead. He had felt when they made him a Silent Brother as if he had been cut open and all things inside him ripped out.

Only, there was that which they could not take away.

"Carry it awhile," said Will. "It lightens my heart to see you with it. We could all do with lighter hearts tonight."

He traced a carving upon the staff, the Herondale ring winking by moonlight.

Where shall I carry it?

"Wherever you please. I thought I would walk with you a little way, my *parabatai*."

How far? asked Jem.

Will smiled. "Need you ask? I will go with you as far as I possibly may."

Jem smiled back. Perhaps there was more hope and less sorrow in store for Matthew Fairchild than he feared. None knew better than Jem that someone could be not fully known yet still entirely loved. Forgiven all sins, and dearest in darkness. James would not let his *parabatai* travel any shadowy paths alone. No matter what catastrophe came, Jem believed the son had as great a heart as his father.

New streetlights showed Will's and Jem's silhouettes, walking together through their city, as they had of old. Even though both knew they must part.

Across London the bells rang all together in a sudden terrifying clamor. Frightened birds in mad wheeling flight cast deeper shadows across the city at night, and Jem knew the queen was dead.

A new age was beginning.

Every Exquisite Thing

By Cassandra Clare and Maureen Johnson

London, 1901

This one was stained with something purple.

This one had a hole in the sleeve.

This one was missing a . . . back. An entire *back*. It was just a front of a shirt and two sleeves clinging on for dear life.

"Christopher," Anna said, turning the garment over in her hands, "how do you do these things?"

Everyone had their small wonderland. For her brother Christopher and Uncle Henry, it was the laboratory. For Cousin James and Uncle Will, the library. For Lucie, her writing desk, where she wrote her long adventures for Cordelia Carstairs. For Matthew Fairchild, it was any troublesome corner of London.

For Anna Lightwood, it was her brother's wardrobe.

In many ways, it was very good to have a brother who was largely oblivious about his clothes. Anna could have taken Christopher's coat right off his back and he would hardly have noticed. The only downside was that Christopher's clothes had suffered fates no clothes should suffer. They were dipped in acids, brushed by fire, poked with sharp objects, left out in the rain. . . . His wardrobe was like a museum of experiment and disaster, tattered, stained, charred, and stinking of sulfur.

To Anna, though, the clothes were still precious.

Christopher was over visiting the Institute and Uncle Henry, so he would be gone for hours. Her mother and father were both out in the park with her baby brother, Alexander. This was her golden hour, and there was no time to waste. Christopher was taller than her now and growing all the time. This meant that his older trousers suited her frame. She chose a pair and found the least-damaged shirt and a satisfactory gray-striped waistcoat. She dug through the pile of ties, scarves, kerchiefs, cuffs, and collars that lay on the bottom of Christopher's wardrobe and selected the most passable items. On his dressing stand she found a hat that had a sandwich in it. It was ham, Anna noted, as she tipped it out and dusted away the crumbs. Once she had everything she needed, she bundled it all under her arm and slipped out into the hall, shutting his door quietly.

Anna's room was so different from her brother's. Her walls were papered in a dusty rose. There was a white lace coverlet, a pink vase with lilacs next to her bed. Her cousin Lucie thought her bedroom quite charming. Anna had different tastes. Given her choice, the paper would be a rich, deep green, her decor black and gold. She would have a deep chaise longue on which she could read and smoke.

Still, she had a long dressing mirror, and that was all that mattered right now. (Christopher's mirror had met its fate in an experiment in which he attempted to magnify the effect of glamours. It had not been replaced.) She drew the curtains against the warm summer sun and began to change. Anna had long forsworn wearing a corset—she had no interest in squeezing her internal organs into a lump or pushing her small bosom up. She slipped out of her tea gown, letting it drop to the floor. She kicked it away. Off went the stockings, down came the hair. The trousers were tucked in at the ankle to adjust for height. A few adjustments of the waistcoat hid the damage to the shirt. She put one of Christopher's black ascots around her slender neck and tied it expertly. Then she took the derby that had been hosting the ham sandwich and placed it on her head, tucking her black hair carefully up under it and arranging it until it appeared that her hair was shorn short.

Anna stood before the mirror, examining the effect. The waistcoat flattened her chest a bit. She tugged it up and adjusted it until the fit was right. She rolled the legs of the trousers and knocked the hat down over her eye.

There. Even in these clothes—stains and ham sandwiches and all—her confidence swelled. She was no longer a gangly girl who looked awkward in ribbons and flounces. Instead she looked elegant, her lean body complemented by more severe tailoring, the waistcoat nipping in her slim waist and flaring over her narrow hips.

Imagine what she could do with Matthew Fairchild's wardrobe! He was a real peacock, with his colorful waistcoats and ties, and the beautiful suits. She walked back and forth a bit, tipping her hat to imaginary ladies. She bowed, pretending to be taking the hand of a fair maiden, keeping her eyes turned up. Always keep the fair maiden's eye as you press your lips to her hand.

"Enchanted," she said to her imaginary lady. "Would you care for a dance?"

The lady would be delighted to dance.

Anna crooked her arm around the waist of her phantom beauty; she had danced with her many times. Though Anna could not see her face, she swore she could feel the fabric of her lover's dress, the soft swooshing noise it made as it brushed the floor. The lady's heart was fluttering as Anna pressed her hand. Her lady would wear a delicate scent. Orange blossom, perhaps. Anna would press her face closer to the lady's ear and whisper.

"You are quite the most beautiful girl here," Anna would say.

The lady would blush and press closer.

"How is it you look more lovely in every light?" Anna would go on. "The way the velvet of your dress crushes against your skin. The way your—"

"Anna!"

She dropped her airy companion to the floor in her surprise.

"Anna!" her mother called again. "Where are you?"

Anna hurried to her door and opened it just a crack.

"Here!" she said in a panic.

"Can you come down, please?"

"Of course," Anna replied, already pulling at the ascot around her neck. "Coming!"

Anna had to step right through her fallen dancing partner in her haste. Off with the waistcoat, the trousers. Everything off, off, off. She shoved the clothes into the bottom of her wardrobe. The discarded dress was hastily put back on, her fingers fumbling on the buttons. Everything about girls' clothing was fussy and complicated.

Several minutes later, she hurried downstairs, attempting to look composed. Her mother, Cecily Lightwood, was sifting through a stack of letters at her desk in the sitting room.

"We ran into Inquisitor Bridgestock while we were walking," she said. "The Bridgestocks have just arrived from Idris. They've asked us to dine with them this evening."

"Dinner with the Inquisitor," Anna said. "What a thrilling way to spend an evening."

"It is necessary," her mother said simply. "We must go. Can you keep an eye on Christopher while we are talking? Make sure he doesn't set anything on fire. Or anyone."

"Yes," Anna said automatically, "of course."

It would be a dreadful affair. Clave business accompanied by overcooked beef. There were so many other things she could be doing on a fine summer night in London. What if she could walk the streets, finely dressed, a beautiful girl on her arm?

Someday, the lady would not be imaginary. The clothes would not be borrowed and ill-fitting. Someday she would stride down the street and women would fall at her feet (not failing to notice her perfectly polished brogues) and men would tip their hats to a lady-killer more accomplished than they.

Just not tonight.

It was still sunny when the Lightwood family got into their carriage that evening. There were costermongers out and flower sellers and bootblacks . . . and so many lovely girls, walking in their light summer dresses. Did they know how lovely they were? Did they look at Anna and see the way she looked at them?

Her brother Christopher bumped gently against her as they rode.

"This seems like a long route to the Institute," he noted.

"We're not going to the Institute," Anna said.

"Aren't we?"

"We're having dinner with the Inquisitor," her father said.

"Oh," Christopher said. And with that, he was off in his own thoughts, as ever—inventing something in his mind, working out a calculation. In this, Anna felt close to her brother. They were both somewhere else in their minds at all times.

The Bridgestocks lived in Fitzrovia, just off Cavendish Square. Theirs was a fine three-across town house. The paint on the shiny black door looked like it could have still been wet, and there were electric lights outside. A servant showed them into a dark and close reception room where the Inquisitor and his wife greeted them. They took little notice of Anna except to say what a charming young lady she was. She and Christopher sat politely on stiff chairs and added a decorative element to a dreary occasion.

The dinner gong finally sounded, and everyone shuffled through to the dining room. Anna and Christopher were seated at the far end of the table, and there was an empty place set across from her. Anna ate her asparagus soup and stared at a painting of a ship on the wall. The ship was in the throes of a storm, the masts on fire, and on the verge of disintegrating into the sea.

"Did you hear they are building a Portal in the Gard?" the Inquisitor asked Anna's parents.

"Oh dear," Mrs. Bridgestock said, shaking her head, "is that a good idea? What if it were to let demons through?"

Anna envied the ship in the painting and all who sank in her.

"Of course," the Inquisitor droned on, "there's also the

matter of money. The Consul has rejected the proposal to create an official currency of Idris. A wise decision. Very wise. As I was saying earlier—"

"I'm so sorry for my lateness," said a voice.

In the doorway of the dining room stood a girl, probably Anna's age, in a midnight-blue dress. Her hair was jet-black, like Anna's, but fuller, more luxurious, deep as night sky against her soft brown skin. But what captured Anna were her eyes—eyes the color of topaz—large, the lashes thick.

"Ah," the Inquisitor said. "This is our daughter, Ariadne. These are the Lightwoods."

"I was meeting my tutor," Ariadne said as a servant pulled out her chair. "We were delayed. I do apologize. It sounds like I came in just as you were debating the new currency. Shadowhunters are an international group. We must blend seamlessly with many international economies. Having our own currency would be a disaster."

On that, she plucked up her napkin and turned to Anna and Christopher and smiled.

"We have not met," she said.

Anna had to force herself to swallow, then to breathe. Ariadne was something beyond the realm of humanity or Shadowhunter. The Angel himself must have made her.

"Anna Lightwood," Anna said.

Christopher was pushing peas onto the back of his fork, unaware that a goddess had seated herself across from him.

"And this is my brother Christopher. He can be a bit distracted."

She gave him a nudge.

"Oh," he said, noticing Ariadne. "I'm Christopher."

Even Christopher, now that he had seen Ariadne, could not help but be mesmerized by her. He blinked, taking in the sight.

"You're . . . you're not English, are you?"

Anna died several deaths inside, but Ariadne simply laughed.

"I was born in Bombay," she said. "My parents ran the Bombay Institute until they were killed. I was adopted by the Bridgestocks in Idris."

She spoke very plainly, in the tone of someone who has long accepted a set of facts.

"What killed your parents?" Christopher asked conversationally.

"A group of Vetis demons," Ariadne said.

"Oh! I knew someone at the Academy that was killed by a Vetis demon!"

"*Christopher*," Anna said.

"You go to the Academy?" Ariadne asked.

"Not anymore. I caused one of the wings to explode." Christopher took a bread roll from a plate and happily began buttering it.

Anna looked at the painting of the ship again, trying to will herself onto the deck and then into the black, pitiless waters. The most lovely girl in the world had just walked into her life and in thirty seconds her dear brother had managed to bring up the death of her family, a death at school, and the fact that he had blown up part of the Academy.

But Ariadne was not looking at Christopher, even as he inadvertently placed his elbow into the butter dish.

"Have *you* caused any explosions?" she asked Anna.

"Not yet," Anna replied. "But the evening is young."

Ariadne laughed, and Anna's soul sang. She reached over and lifted her brother's elbow from the butter, never taking her gaze from Ariadne. Did she know how beautiful she was? Did she know her eyes were the color of liquid gold, and that songs could be written about the way she turned out her wrist to reach for her glass?

Anna had seen beautiful girls before. She had even seen a few beautiful girls who looked at her the way she looked at them. But that was always in passing. They went by on the street, or their gaze lingered a bit long in a shop. Anna had practiced the art of the prolonged stare, the one that invited them: *Come. Tell me of yourself. You are lovely.*

There was something in the way Ariadne was looking at Anna that suggested . . .

No. Anna had to be imagining it. Ariadne was being polite and attentive. She was not eyeing Anna romantically over the dinner table, over the roasted potatoes and the duck. Ariadne's perfection had caused Anna to hallucinate.

Ariadne continued to contribute to the conversation at the other end of the table. Anna had never been so interested in the economic policies of Idris. She would study them night and day if she could join Ariadne in discussing them.

Every once in a while, Ariadne would turn back to Anna and look at her knowingly, her mouth twisting in a smile like a bow. And each time this happened, Anna would wonder again what was happening, and why that particular look made the room spin. Maybe she was ill. Maybe she had developed a fever from looking at Ariadne.

The pudding came and went, and Anna vaguely remembered eating it. As the dishes were cleared and the women stood to leave the table, Ariadne came and hooked her arm through Anna's.

"We have quite a good library," she said to Anna. "Perhaps I could show it to you?"

Anna, with a show of supreme self-control, did not immediately fall to the floor. She managed to say yes, the library, yes, she would love to see it, yes, library, yes, yes . . .

She told herself to stop saying she wanted to see the library and looked over at her mother. Cecily smiled. "Go on, Anna. Christopher, would you mind accompanying us to the greenhouse? Mrs. Bridgestock has a collection of poisonous plants that I think you will quite enjoy."

Anna cast Cecily a grateful look as Ariadne led her from the room. Her head was full of Ariadne's orange-blossom perfume and the way her tumble of dark hair was pinned up in a gold comb.

"It's this way," Ariadne said, leading Anna to a set of double doors toward the back of the house. The library was dark and had a chill. Ariadne released Anna's arm and illuminated one of the electric lights.

"You use electricity?" Anna said. She had to say something, and that was as good a thing as any.

"I convinced Father," Ariadne said. "I am modern and possessed of all sorts of advanced notions."

The room was full of crates, and only some of the books had been unpacked and shelved. The furniture, however, had been placed. There was an ample desk, and many comfortable reading chairs.

"We're still settling in here," Ariadne said, sitting herself prettily (she had no other way) on a deep red chair. Anna was too nervous to sit, and paced along the opposite side of the room. It was almost too much to look at Ariadne here in this dark, private place.

"I understand your family has a very interesting history," Ariadne said.

Anna had to speak. She had to figure out a way to *be* around Ariadne. In her mind she donned her real clothing—the trousers, the shirt (the mental one had no stains), the fitted waistcoat. She slipped her arms through the sleeves. Thus attired, she felt confident. She managed to sit opposite Ariadne and meet her gaze.

"My grandfather was a worm, if that's what you mean," Anna said.

Ariadne laughed aloud. "You didn't like him?"

"I didn't know him," Anna said. "He was, quite literally, a worm."

Clearly, Ariadne didn't know that much about the Lightwoods. Usually, when one's demon-loving relative develops a serious case of demon pox and turns into a giant worm with massive teeth, word gets around. People will talk.

"It's true," Anna said, now examining the gilded edge of a writing desk. "He ate one of my uncles."

"You *are* funny," Ariadne said to Anna.

"I'm glad you think so," Anna replied.

"Your brother's eyes are quite extraordinary," Ariadne noted.

Anna heard this a good deal. Christopher's eyes were lavender in color.

"Yes," Anna said. "He's the good-looking one in the family."

"I quite disagree!" Ariadne exclaimed, looking surprised.

"Gentlemen must compliment you all the time on the shade of your eyes."

Then Ariadne blushed and looked down, and Anna's heart skipped a beat. It wasn't possible, she told herself. There was simply no chance that the Inquisitor's beautiful daughter was . . . like her. That she would look at another girl's eyes and note their color as lovely instead of simply asking her what fabrics she wore to bring out their shade best.

"I'm afraid I am quite behind on my training," Ariadne said. "Perhaps we could . . . train together?"

"Yes," Anna said, maybe too quickly. "Yes . . . of course. If you . . ."

"You may find me clumsy." Ariadne twisted her hands together.

"I'm sure I won't," Anna said. "But that is the point of training, in any case. It is a delicate thing, training, despite the obvious violence, of course."

"You will have to be delicate with me, then," Ariadne said very softly.

Just as Anna thought she might faint, the doors opened and Inquisitor Bridgestock came in, with Cecily, Gabriel, and Christopher in tow. The Lightwoods looked vaguely exhausted. Anna was conscious of her mother's eyes on her—a sharp and thoughtful look.

". . . and we have our map collection . . . ah. Ariadne. Still in here, of course. Ariadne is a fiendish reader."

"Absolutely *fiendish*." Ariadne smiled. "Anna and I were just discussing my training. I thought it would be sensible to partner with another girl."

"Very sensible," Bridgestock said. "Yes. A very good idea.

You shall be partners. Anyway, Lightwood, we'll look at the maps at some point. Now, Ariadne, come into the parlor. I'd like you to play the piano for our guests."

Ariadne looked up at Anna.

"Partners," she said.

"Partners," Anna replied.

It was only on the way home that Anna realized that Ariadne had asked her to the library and not shown her a single book.

"Did you like young Ariadne Bridgestock?" said Cecily as the Lightwoods' carriage rumbled home through the dark streets of the city.

"I thought her very amiable," said Anna, looking out the window at London sparkling in the vast night. She longed to be out there among the earthbound stars, walking in the streets of Soho, living a life of music and adventure and dancing. "Very pretty, too."

Cecily tucked a stray lock of hair back behind her daughter's ear. In surprise, Anna looked at her mother for a moment—there was a little sadness in Cecily's eyes, though she couldn't have guessed why. Perhaps she was simply tired after being bored by the Inquisitor all night. Papa, for instance, was quite asleep in the other corner of the carriage, and Christopher was leaning against him, blinking drowsily. "She isn't nearly as pretty as you."

"*Mother,*" Anna said in exasperation, and turned back to the carriage window.

Under the arches of the railway viaduct, near the south end of London Bridge, a large gathering was taking place.

It was midsummer, so the sun set over London at nearly ten

o'clock. This meant the time to sell at the Shadow Market was reduced, and the whole place had a bit of a frenzied air. There was steam and smoke and flapping silks. Hands reached out, shoving wares under shoppers' noses—gems and trinkets, books, pendants, powders, oils, games and toys for Downworlder children, and items that could not be classified. There was a hum of smells. The tang of the river and the smoke from the trains overhead mixed with the remains of the day's produce from the mundane market—squashed produce, bits of meat, the odor wafting from oyster barrels. Vendors burned incense, which tangled with spices and perfumes. The miasma could be overpowering.

Brother Zachariah moved through the crush of stalls, immune to the smells and the crowding. Many Downworlders drew back at the approach of the Silent Brother. He had been coming here for weeks now to meet Ragnor Fell. Tonight, he also glanced around to see if he spotted the vendor he had seen on one of his previous visits. The stall he was looking for could move on its own; it had feet like a chicken. The woman behind it was an elderly faerie woman with a wild mass of hair. She sold colorful potions, and Matthew Fairchild had purchased one and given it to his mother. It had taken all of Jem's efforts to bring Charlotte back from death's door. She had not been the same since, nor had Matthew.

The stall was not present tonight; neither, it seemed, was Ragnor. He was about to take a final turn around the Market before departing when he saw someone he knew bent over a stall of books. The man had a shock of white hair and striking purple eyes. It was Malcolm Fade.

"Is that you, James Carstairs?" he said.

How are you, my friend?

Malcolm simply smiled. There was always something a little sad about Malcolm: Jem had heard gossip about a tragic love affair with a Shadowhunter who had chosen to be an Iron Sister rather than be with the one she loved. Jem knew that for some, the Law was more important than love. Even as he was now, he could not understand it. He would have given anything to be with the one he loved.

Anything except that which was more sacred than Jem's own life: Tessa's life, or Will's.

"How goes your quest?" said Malcolm. "Has Ragnor turned up any information for you about a certain demon you've been seeking?"

Jem gave Malcolm a quelling look; he preferred that not too many people knew of the quest he had undertaken.

"Malcolm! I have the book you wanted!" A warlock woman carrying a book bound in yellow velvet strode up to Malcolm.

"Thank you, Leopolda," said Malcolm.

The woman stared at Jem's face. Jem was used to this. Though he was a Silent Brother, his lips and eyes had not been sewn shut. He did not see or speak as humans did, but the fact that without runes he could have done so seemed to distress some people more than the sight of a Silent Brother who had bound himself less reluctantly to the quiet dark.

We have not met.

"No," the woman replied. "We have not. My name is Leopolda Stain. I make a visit here from Vienna."

She had a German accent and a soft, purring voice.

"This is Brother Zachariah," Malcolm said.

She nodded. There was no hand extended, but she continued to stare.

"You must forgive me," she said. "We do not often see Silent Brothers in our Market. London is a strange place to me. The Market in Vienna is not so bustling. It is in the Wienerwald, under the trees. Here, you are under this railway. It is quite a different experience."

"Zachariah is not quite like other Silent Brothers," said Malcolm.

Leopolda seemed to conclude the study she was making of Jem's face and smiled.

"I must bid you a good night," she said. "It is good to see you, Malcolm. It has been too long, *mein Liebling*. Too long. And it has been most interesting to meet you, James Carstairs. Auf Wiedersehen."

She slipped away through the crowd. Jem watched her go. She had decided to call him James Carstairs, not Brother Zachariah, and the choice seemed deliberate. There were certainly many denizens of Downworld who knew his Shadowhunter name—it was no secret—but suddenly Jem felt like a butterfly under a pin, caught in the gaze of the lepidopterist.

Can you tell me about her? he asked Malcolm, who had returned to examining the book in his hand.

"Leopolda is a bit of an odd one," Malcolm said. "I met her while I was traveling in Vienna. I don't think she leaves her city often. She seems to get around with some famous mundanes. She is . . ."

He hesitated.

Yes?

". . . more connected, I suppose, to her demon side than her human side than most of us are. More than me, certainly. She makes me feel uneasy. I'm glad that you came over. I was looking for a way to politely escape."

Jem looked in the direction that Leopolda had gone. Someone more connected to the demon side. . . .

That was someone he might need to speak with. Or watch.

Anna lay in her bed, eyes closed, trying to will herself to slumber. In her mind, she was dancing again. She wore her imaginary finest evening wear—a suit of deep gray, a waistcoat of sunny yellow with matching gloves. On her arm was Ariadne, as she had been tonight, in the blue dress.

Sleep was not coming. She pushed herself out of bed and went to the window. The night was warm and close. She had to do something with herself. Her brother's clothes were still in her wardrobe. She picked them out and smoothed them on the bed. She had planned on returning them, but . . .

Who would miss them? Not Christopher. Their laundress might, but no one would question that Christopher might simply *lose* his trousers, possibly in the middle of a crowded dance floor. And the older clothes—he wouldn't need them, not at the rate he was growing. The trousers were too long, but they could be hemmed. The shirt could be nipped in at the back. A few simple stitches were all it would take.

Anna was not a natural seamstress, but like all Shadowhunters, she possessed the basic skills to repair gear. She couldn't have made lace or done precise tailoring, but she could get this job done. She tacked his shirt and waistcoat in the back to make them fit and flatter her torso. The jacket was a bit more complex, requiring tucks on the back and the side. The shoulders were a bit wrong, and the effect a bit triangular, but all in all it was a passable effort. She practiced her walk in the fitted trousers, now that they no longer scraped the ground.

She had always loved gear as a child, its easy maneuverability, the way it allowed her to move unfettered. She had always been surprised that other girls, unlike her, didn't resent being pressed back into dresses and skirts when training was over. That they didn't resent the loss of freedom.

But it was more than the comfort of the clothes. In silks and ruffles Anna felt silly, as if she were pretending to be someone she was not. When she wore dresses out on the street, she was ignored as a gawky girl, or stared at by men in a way she did not like. She had been out in her brother's clothes only twice, both times late at night—but oh, women looked at her then, smiling women, conspiratorial women, women who knew that in donning the clothes of men, Anna walked in their power and their privilege. They looked at her soft lips, her long eyelashes, her blue eyes; they looked at her hips in tight trousers, the curve of her breasts under a man's cotton shirt, and their eyes spoke to her in the secret language of women: *You have taken their power for your own. You have stolen fire from the gods. Now come and make love to me, as Zeus made love to Danaë, in a shower of gold.*

In her mind's eye, Anna bent to take Ariadne's hand in hers, and the hand seemed real.

"You are so beautiful tonight," she said to Ariadne. "You are the most beautiful girl I have ever seen."

"And you," Ariadne answered in her mind, "are the most handsome person I have ever known."

The next day, Anna spent two hours writing a note to Ariadne that ended up reading:

Dear Ariadne,

It was very nice to meet you. I hope we can train together

sometime. Please do pay a call.
Regards,
Anna Lightwood

Two entire hours for that, and a pile of drafts. Time no longer had meaning, and might never have meaning again.

In the afternoon, she had plans to meet her cousins James, Lucie, and Thomas, along with Matthew Fairchild. James, Matthew, Thomas, and Christopher were inseparable, and always meeting at a house or a hideout. They were invading her aunt Sophie and uncle Gideon's home today. Anna attended their little gatherings only on occasion, as did Lucie—the girls had many occupations to amuse themselves with; today, she desperately needed something to do, something to moor her mind in place, to keep her from fighting and pacing her room.

She walked with Christopher, who was excitedly talking of some kind of device that would fly through the air by means of four rotating blades. It sounded like he was describing a mechanical insect. Anna made noises that indicated she was listening although she was most assuredly not.

It was not far to their cousins' house. Her cousins Barbara and Eugenia were in the morning room. Barbara was stretched out on a sofa, while Eugenia was furiously working at a bit of needlepoint as if she truly hated it and the only way she could express her hatred was by stabbing the stretched cloth with the needle as vigorously as she could.

Anna and Christopher went up to the rooms that had been set aside for the use of Sophie and Gideon's children. James was there, sitting on his window seat, reading. Lucie was sitting at the desk, scribbling away. Tom was throwing a knife at the opposite wall.

Christopher greeted everyone and immediately sat down in the corner with a book. Anna dropped down next to Lucie.

"How's Cordelia?" she asked.

"Oh, she's wonderful! I was just writing to her quickly before Thomas helps me go over my Persian lesson." Lucie was always writing to her future *parabatai*, Cordelia Carstairs. Lucie was always writing. Lucie could write in a room full of people talking, screaming, singing. Anna was sure that Lucie could probably write in the middle of battle. Anna approved of this highly—it was very good to see two girls so devoted to each other, even platonically. Women should value other women, even if society often did not.

Ariadne came into her mind again.

"What's wrong, Anna?" James said.

He was looking at her curiously. Anna loved all her cousins, but she had a very soft spot for James. He had been a somewhat awkward young boy, gentle and quiet and bookish. He had grown up into a young man Anna could see was extraordinarily handsome, like his father. He had a soft fall of the Herondale black hair; from his mother, he had inherited his demonic trait—his inhuman golden eyes. Anna had always thought they were rather pretty, though Christopher had told her that James had been teased relentlessly at the Academy because of them. It was the teasing that prompted Matthew to get the explosives and Christopher to arrange for a wing of the building to blow up.

It was honorable to defend your friends, your *parabatai*. Anna was proud of them for doing it. She would have done the same. James had been such a shy, delightful little boy—it made Anna furious to think that he had been mocked. He was older now, given a bit more to brooding and staring into the distance, but still kind under it all.

"Nothing," she said. "I just . . . need a new book to read."

"A most sensible request," James said, swinging his long legs off his reading perch. "What sort of book? Fortunately, Aunt Sophie and Uncle Gideon have a respectable collection. Adventure? History? Romance? Poetry?"

All the younger set were fearfully bookish. Anna put it down to Uncle Will and Aunt Tessa's influence. They seldom let one leave the Institute without a book they felt one simply must read.

Now that they were talking about this, perhaps this would be useful in talking to Ariadne. She was a fiendish reader, after all.

"I'm training with someone new," Anna said. "Her name is Ariadne. She does quite a lot of reading, so—"

"Ah! Ariadne. That's a name from mythology. We could start you on a course of that. Would you like to begin with *The Golden Bough*, by Frazer? There's a new edition of three volumes. Unless you want to start with the basics. There's always Lemprière's *Bibliotheca Classica*. . . ."

James flipped gracefully through the books on the wall. He was an accomplished fighter and excellent dancer. Perhaps it was these traits, combined with the fact that he was growing into his looks, that explained why he seemed to suddenly be so popular with girls. He couldn't walk through a room of them without them sighing and giggling. Anna supposed she was pleased for him, or would be if he ever noticed it was happening.

He had soon plucked a dozen books from the shelf, passing one to Christopher almost as an afterthought. A silver bracelet flashed upon his wrist as he held his arm out—a love gift? Anna wondered. Perhaps one of the sighing gigglers had attracted his interest after all. Anna supposed she ought to be more charitable toward them—she felt herself on the verge of sighing and giggling over Ariadne at any moment.

The door flew open, and Matthew Fairchild entered the room and draped himself dramatically over the back of a chair. "Good afternoon, you wonderful bunch of villains. James, why are you clearing the shelves?"

"Anna asked me for something to read," James said, surveying a table of contents with a furious eye. He set the book aside.

"Anna? Reading? What dark magic is this?"

"I am hardly an illiterate," Anna said, throwing an apple at him. He caught it easily and smiled. Matthew was normally very fastidious. He and Anna often spoke of gentlemen's fashion together, but today Anna noticed that his hair was a bit wild and one of the buttons on his waistcoat was undone. These were small things, to be sure, but on Matthew, they spoke of something larger.

"What is your interest?" Matthew asked.

"Is it a crime to want to become more literate?"

"Not at all," Matthew said. "I love literature. In fact, I've found a marvelous place. It's a salon, full of writers and poets. But it is a bit . . . disreputable."

Anna cocked her head in interest.

"Here we go," James said, bringing over a pile of a dozen or so books and setting it down with a heavy thump. "Do any of these appeal? Have a look and see. Of course, I can recommend others. Wait. No. Not these. Not these."

He scooped the books away and returned to the shelves. James was clearly absorbed in his task. Christopher was happily reading his book, which had a horribly scientific title. Lucie and Thomas were at the desk, Thomas helping Lucie go over some phrases: Lucie was learning for Cordelia, and Tom liked languages, since he spoke Spanish with Uncle Gideon and Welsh with his cousins. Angel bless their sweet studious souls, none of them seemed likely to hear Anna and Matthew hatching a dark plot. Nevertheless, Matthew pitched his voice very low.

"Why don't I come and get you at midnight," Matthew said. "We can go together. I could use a companion who knows how to have a bit of fun. You might need a disguise, though. No reputable young lady walks the streets of London at midnight."

"Oh," Anna said. "I think I can manage something."

Just before midnight, as promised, Anna heard a tapping at her bedroom window. Matthew Fairchild was there, dancing along the edge. Anna threw it open.

"My my!" he said approvingly. "Are those Christopher's?"

Anna had dressed herself in her brother's clothes. The sewing had helped a good deal.

"A disguise," she said simply.

He laughed, spinning carelessly on the sill. She could see he had been drinking—his reflexes were slow, and he only caught himself a half second before tumbling back out to the ground.

"They suit you better than they suit him, but still . . . we need to get you something nicer than that. Here."

He pulled the ascot from his neck and handed it to her.

"I insist," he said. "I could never let a lady go out in inferior menswear."

Anna felt herself exhaling slowly and smiling as she put on the tie. The two of them jumped from her window, landing noiselessly on the courtyard in front of the house.

"Where is this place?" Anna said.

"A nefarious corner of Soho," he said with a smile.

"Soho!" Anna was delighted. "How did you find out about it?"

"Oh, just through my wanderings."

"You do a lot of those."

"I have a periphrastic soul."

Matthew was more drunk than he had first appeared. He rolled back on his heels and spun around the occasional lamppost as they walked. He had been like this a lot in recent weeks—what was fun and light about Matthew had taken on an edge. On some level, she felt a bit of worry rising. But this was Matthew, and he did not do well under confinement. Perhaps the summer night had just gotten his spirits particularly high.

The house Matthew took Anna to was deep in the warren of Soho, off Brewer Street. It was painted black, with a green door.

"You'll like it here," Matthew said, smiling at Anna.

The door was opened by a tall, pale man in a maroon frock coat.

"Fairchild," he said, looking at Matthew. "And . . ."

"Fairchild's good friend," Matthew replied.

Anna could feel the intelligence of the vampire's gaze, as he took her in for a long time. He seemed intrigued, both by her and by Matthew, though his expression was unreadable.

At last he stepped aside and allowed them in.

"You see?" Matthew said. "No one can resist our company."

The hall was utterly dark—the fanlight had been covered in a velvet drape. The only light came from candles. The house was decorated in a style that Anna thoroughly approved of—heavy green paper run through with gold, velvet curtains and furniture. It smelled of cigars and strange, tiny, rose-colored cigarettes and gin. The room was crowded with a mix of Downworlders and mundanes, all elaborately dressed.

Anna noticed many people taking in the sight of her in her men's clothing and nodding appreciatively. The men seemed pleased or amused, the women either admiring or—interested. Quite a few raked Anna boldly with their eyes, their gazes clinging to the feminine body revealed by her fitted clothes. It was as if in casting off dresses she had cast off society's expectation of a woman's modesty and could allow herself to be admired, desired. Her soul soared with new confidence: she felt herself a gorgeous creature, neither a gentleman nor a lady. A gentlewoman, she thought, and winked at one of the only people she recognized: the werewolf Woolsey Scott, head of the Praetor Lupus. He wore a bottle-green smoking jacket and was puffing away on a hookah pipe while holding court for a cluster of fascinated mundanes.

"Of course," Anna heard him say, "they had a difficult time getting my bathtub into one of the tree houses, but I would hardly leave it behind. One must always bring one's own bathtub."

"That's Somebody Somebody Yeats over there," Matthew said, indicating a tall, bespectacled man. "He read a new work the last time I was here."

"And it was wonderful," said a voice. It came from a woman sitting near where Matthew and Anna stood. She was a stunning warlock with the scaled skin of a snake, colored silver, almost opalescent. Her long green hair tumbled over her shoulders and was strung through with a fine gold mesh. She wore a red gown that clung to her frame. She tipped her head up elegantly toward Matthew and Anna.

"Are all London Shadowhunters so handsome as you?" she asked. She had a German accent.

"No," Anna said simply.

"Definitely not," Matthew agreed.

The warlock smiled.

"Your London Shadowhunters are more interesting than ours," she said. "Ours are very tedious. Yours are beautiful and amusing."

Someone grumbled something at this, but the rest of the group laughed appreciatively.

"Do sit and join us," the woman said. "I am Leopolda Stain."

Most of the people around Leopolda seemed to be fawning mundanes, like the group around Woolsey Scott. One man wore a black robe covered in symbols Anna did not recognize. Matthew and Anna sat down on the rug, against a pile of tasseled pillows that served as a sofa. Next to them was a woman wearing a gold turban scarf pinned with a sapphire.

"Are you two of the Chosen?" she asked Matthew and Anna.

"Certainly," Matthew said.

"Ah. I could tell from the way Leopolda reacted to you. She is quite wonderful, is she not? She is from Vienna and knows simply *everyone*—Freud, Mahler, Klimt, Schiele. . . ."

"Marvelous," Matthew said. He probably did think it was marvelous—Matthew adored art and artists.

"She's going to help us," the woman said. "Obviously, we've had such troubles here. Why, Crowley wasn't even recognized here in London! He had to go to the Ahathoor Temple in Paris to be initiated to the grade of Adeptus Minor, which I'm sure you heard about."

"The moment it happened," Matthew lied.

Anna bit her lip and looked down to keep herself from laughing. It was always amusing to meet mundanes who had fantastical notions of how magic worked. Leopolda, she noticed, was smiling indulgently at the entire group, like they were adorable but somewhat dim-witted children.

"Well," the woman continued, "I was an Adept of the Isis-Urania temple, and I can assure you that I was adamant that—"

This was interrupted by a man standing in the middle of the room and raising a glass of something green.

"My friends!" he said. "I demand that we remember Oscar. You must raise your glasses!"

There was a general noise of agreement, and glasses were raised. The man began to recite Oscar Wilde's "The Ballad of Reading Gaol." Anna was struck by one of the stanzas:

> Some love too little, some too long,
> Some sell, and others buy;
> Some do the deed with many tears,
> And some without a sigh:
> For each man kills the thing he loves,
> Yet each man does not die.

She didn't quite know what it meant, but the spirit of it haunted her. It seemed to have an even more pointed effect on Matthew, who slumped down.

"It is a rotten world that would allow a man like Wilde to die," Matthew said. There was a hardness in his voice that was new and a bit alarming.

"You're sounding a bit dire," Anna said.

"It's true," he replied. "Our greatest poet, and he died in

poverty and obscurity, not so long ago. They threw him in jail because he loved another man. I do not think love can be wrong."

"No," Anna said. She had always known that she loved women the way she was expected to love men. That she found women beautiful and desirable, while men were good friends, brothers-in-arms, but nothing more. She had never pretended otherwise, and her close friends all seemed to accept this about her as a known fact.

But it was true that though Matthew and the others often joked with her about slaying the hearts of pretty girls, it was not something she and her mother had ever talked about. She recalled her mother touching her hair fondly in the carriage. What did Cecily truly think of her odd daughter?

Not now, she told herself. She turned to the woman in the turban, who had been trying to get her attention. "Yes?"

"My dear," the woman said. "You must be sure to be here in a week's time. The faithful will be rewarded, I promise you. The ancient ones, so long hidden from us, shall be revealed."

"Of course," Anna said, blinking. "Yes. Wouldn't miss it for the world."

While she was simply making conversation, Anna found that she would like to return to this place. She had come here dressed as she was, and she had received only approbation. In fact, she was sure that one of the vampire girls was examining her with a look that was not entirely wholesome. And Leopolda, the beautiful warlock, had not taken her eyes from Anna. Had Anna's mind and soul not been full of Ariadne . . .

Well, it could only be left to the imagination.

As Matthew and Anna left the house that night, they did not notice a figure across the street, standing in the shadows.

Jem recognized Matthew at once but was confused at first as to who was with him. The person resembled his *parabatai*, Will Herondale—not Will as he was now, but Will at seventeen, with his confident swagger and upturned chin. But that could not be. And the person was obviously not James, Will's son.

It took him several minutes to realize that the young man was not a young man at all. It was Anna Lightwood, Will's niece. She had inherited the dark hair and the profile from the Herondale side of her family, and clearly, she had inherited her uncle's swagger. For a moment Jem felt a pang in his heart. It was like seeing his friend as a young man again, as the two of them had been when they lived at the Institute together and fought side by side, as they had been when Tessa Gray first arrived at their door.

Was it really so long ago?

Jem shook the thought loose and focused on the present. Anna was in some sort of disguise, and she and Matthew had just been at a Downworlder gathering with a warlock he had come to observe. He had no idea what they were doing there.

A full week passed. A full week of Anna running for the post, looking from the window, walking partway to Cavendish Square before turning back. A lifetime. It was agony, and just as it was turning to acceptance, Anna was called downstairs early Friday morning to find Ariadne waiting for her in a yellow dress and a white hat.

"Good morning," Ariadne said. "Why aren't you ready?"

"Ready?" Anna said, her throat gone dry at the sudden appearance of Ariadne.

"To train!"

"I—"

"Good morning, Ariadne!" Cecily Lightwood said, coming in with Alexander.

"Oh!" Ariadne's eyes lit up when she saw the baby. "Oh, I must hold him—I simply adore babies."

The appearance of Alexander bought Anna enough time to scramble upstairs, catch her breath, splash water on her face, and collect her gear. Five minutes later, Anna was seated next to Ariadne in the Bridgestock carriage, rumbling toward the Institute. They were alone now, close to each other in the warm carriage. The smell of Ariadne's orange-blossom perfume wafted up and wrapped around Anna.

"Did I disturb you?" Ariadne said. "I had simply hoped . . . that you might be free to train with me. . . ." She looked worried. "I hope I did not presume. Are you angry?"

"No," Anna replied. "I could never be angry with you."

Anna tried to make it sound light, but a husky note of truth rang through.

"Good." Ariadne looked radiantly pleased at that and crossed her hands on her lap. "I would hate to displease you."

When they arrived at the Institute, Anna changed much more quickly than Ariadne. She waited in the training room, nervously pacing, taking knives from the walls and throwing them to steady her nerves.

Just training. Simple training.

"You have a good arm," Ariadne said.

Ariadne was stunning in her dresses; the gear revealed something else. She was still feminine, with her long hair and lush curves, but unencumbered by pounds of fabric, she moved with grace and speed.

"How would you like to begin?" Anna said. "Do you have a preferred weapon? Or should we do some climbing? Work on the beam?"

"Whatever you think is best," Ariadne replied.

"Shall we start with blades?" Anna said, taking one from the wall.

Whatever Ariadne had been doing in Idris, it did not involve much training. She had been accurate in that. When she threw, her arm was weak. Anna came up and guided her, forcing herself to maintain her composure as she took Ariadne's hand in hers and guided the toss. Ariadne was surprisingly good at climbing, but once on the ceiling beam, she took a bad tumble. Anna jumped underneath and caught her neatly.

"Oh, very impressive!" Ariadne said, smiling.

Anna stood there for a moment, Ariadne in her arms, unsure of what to do. There was something in Ariadne's gaze, in the way she was looking at Anna . . . as if mesmerized. . . .

How did she ask? How did this happen with someone like Ariadne?

It was too much.

"A very good attempt," Anna said, gently setting Ariadne on her feet. "Just . . . watch your footing."

"I think I've had enough of that for today," Ariadne said. "How does one have fun in London?"

Oh, so many ways.

"Well," Anna said. "There is the theater, and the zoo is—"

"No." Ariadne took hold of one of the pillars and gently spun around it. "*Fun.* Surely you know a place."

"Well," Anna said, searching her mind frantically, "I know

a place full of writers and poets. It is quite louche. It is in Soho and starts after midnight."

"Then I assume you will be taking me," Ariadne said, eyes sparkling. "I will wait for you by my window at midnight tonight."

The wait that evening was excruciating.

Anna picked at her dinner and watched the clock across the room. Christopher was forming his carrots into a pyramid and working something out in his head. Her mother was feeding Alexander. Anna was counting her heartbeats. She had to try not to appear conspicuous. She spent some time in the family room with her baby brother; she picked up a book and cast an eye blankly over the pages. By nine she was able to stretch and say she was going to have a bath and retire.

Back in her room, Anna waited until she heard the other members of the household go to bed before changing her clothes. She had taken the time to clean her outfit and mend it as best she could. When she dressed, she looked dapper and dangerous. She had decided now that this was how she would dress if she slipped out on adventures, even to meet Ariadne.

She climbed from her window at eleven, sliding down a rope, which she tossed back inside. She could have jumped, but it had taken her some time to arrange her hair under the hat correctly. She walked to Fitzrovia, and this time she did not bother to avoid the pools of streetlight. She wanted to be seen. She straightened her back and widened her step. The more she walked, the more she felt herself slipping into the gait, the attitude. She tipped her hat to a lady passing in a carriage; the lady smiled and looked away shyly.

Anna knew now that she was never going to go back to wearing dresses. She had always loved the theater, always loved the idea of a performance. The first time she had worn her brother's clothes it had been a performance, but with each time she did it again, it became more her reality. She was not a man and did not want to be—but why should men get to keep all the good pieces of masculinity for themselves because of an accident of birth? Why should she, Anna, not wear their clothes, and their power and confidence too?

You have stolen fire from the gods.

Anna's swagger faded a bit as she turned the corner onto Cavendish Square. Would Ariadne accept her like this? It had felt so right a moment before, but now . . .

She almost turned back, but then she forced herself on.

The Bridgestock house was dark. Anna looked up, fearing that Ariadne had been teasing. But then she saw a flick of a curtain, and the sash window opened. Ariadne looked down at her.

And she smiled.

A rope sailed out of the window, and Ariadne slid down it, more gracefully than she had in training. She wore a light blue dress, which fluttered as she dropped.

"Oh my," she said, walking up to Anna. "You look . . . quite devastating."

Anna would not have traded the way Ariadne looked at her in that moment for a thousand pounds.

They took a carriage to Soho. Though she and Ariadne were both glamoured to hide their Marks from mundanes, Anna enjoyed the look she got from the driver when he realized the handsome young gent in his cab was a handsome young lady. He doffed his cap as she and Ariadne alighted from the cab, muttering something about "young people these days."

They arrived at the house, but this time, when Anna knocked on the door, the person answering was less accommodating. He looked at Anna, then at Ariadne.

"No Shadowhunters," he said.

"That was not your previous policy," Anna said. She noticed that the windows were now covered by the heavy velvet curtains.

"Go home, Shadowhunters," he said. "I have made myself clear."

The door was slammed in their faces.

"Now I am curious," Ariadne said. "We must go in, don't you think?"

Ariadne certainly had a wicked streak in her that complemented her bubbly cheerfulness, a love of things that were just a bit . . . naughty. Anna felt she should encourage this impulse.

There was no clear point of access on the flat front of the house, so they moved down to the end of the street and found a narrow alley backing the houses. This was bricked up to the third floor. There was, however, a drainpipe. Anna got a hold on this and made the climb. She could not reach the third-story windows from there, but she could get onto the roof. She looked down to see Ariadne climbing up after her, again showing more skill than she had in the training room. They managed to pry open an attic window. From there they crept down the winding stairs, Anna first, with Ariadne behind. Ariadne kept a hand on Anna's waist, possibly for guidance as they walked, or . . .

Anna would not think about it.

They were burning a great deal of incense in the house tonight. It hummed through the hall and up the stairs, almost causing Anna to cough. It was not a pleasant smell—it was acrid and hard. She detected wormwood, mugwort, and something else—something with a metallic edge, like blood. The group was unusually quiet. There was only one voice, speaking low. A female voice with the Germanic accent. She heard the incantations.

Anna knew a summoning when she heard one. She turned to Ariadne, who had a look of concern on her face.

Anna reached for her seraph blade and murmured, "*Adriel*," indicating to Ariadne that she would go ahead and look. Ariadne nodded. Anna crept down the hall. She pushed back a bit of the velvet curtain that closed off the main sitting room. Everyone there was turned toward the center of the room, so mostly she saw backs and the faint flicker of candlelight.

Anna could make out the form of a circle drawn on the floor. The woman in the turban was just on the edge of it, her face tilted up in ecstasy. She wore a long black robe and held a book with a pentagram over her head. The book was bound in something odd. It looked like skin.

Towering above all was the warlock Leopolda, her eyes closed and her arms raised. She held a curved dagger in her hands. She was chanting in a demonic language. Then she looked to the woman in the turban and nodded. The woman took a long step into the circle. Green flame flashed all around, making the mundanes murmur and back away. There were not, Anna noticed, many Downworlders present.

"Come forth!" cried the woman. "Come forth, beautiful death. Come forth, creature, that we may worship you! Come forth!"

There was a terrible smell, and the room filled with darkness. Anna knew she could no longer stand still.

"Get out!" she yelled, pushing her way into the room. "All of you!"

The group had no time to be surprised. A massive Ravener demon burst forth out of the darkness. The woman in the turban went down on her knees before it.

"My lord," she said. "My dark—"

The Ravener whipped its tail around and easily severed the woman's turbaned head from her neck. The assembled let up a collective scream, and there was a rush for the door. Anna had to fight her way toward the demon. The Ravener was making short work of the woman's remains.

Leopolda Stain simply looked on the scene with gentle amusement.

It was hard to fight a demon in such close quarters without killing all the people as well. Anna shoved several mundanes aside and launched herself at the demon, her seraph blade raised. The demon made an angry screeching noise. This was because something had just struck out one of its eyes. Ariadne was next to her, holding an electrum whip and smiling.

"Very good aim," Anna said as the angry demon wheeled around. It made a leap and broke through one of the front windows. Anna and Ariadne went right after it, Anna making the jump easily in her new clothes. Ariadne went through the door, but she was fast on her feet, snapping her whip in the air. Between them, they quickly made short work of the beast.

There was a strange crackling noise. They turned to see that the demon had not come alone—a cluster of smaller Raveners poured through the broken window, their jaws dripping green liquid. Anna and Ariadne turned to face them, weapons drawn. A small Ravener jumped forward first. Ariadne sliced through it with her whip. Another sprang out, but as soon as it appeared, a staff swung through the air next to Anna, bashing its head in. She turned as it disappeared, to find herself looking at Brother Zachariah. She was well acquainted with her uncle's former *parabatai*, though she had no idea what he was doing here.

How many? he asked.

"I don't know," she said as another demon came forth from the house. "They're coming from a circle inside the house. There are people hurt."

He nodded and indicated that he would proceed inside, while Anna and Ariadne fought outside. One of the creatures was about to descend on one of the fleeing mundanes. Anna jumped on its back, dodging its angrily swinging tail, and plunged her seraph blade into the back of its neck. The stunned mundane crab-crawled backward as the Ravener fell dead to the ground. She turned to look for Ariadne, who was laying waste to one of the Raveners, slicing her electrum whip through the air and then right through the demon's legs. Anna was surprised—the only other electrum whip she had ever seen was owned by the Consul, Charlotte Fairchild.

Ariadne and Anna stood back-to-back, fighting like *parabatai* might, their movements in sync. Though they were certainly not *parabatai*. It would be very wrong to feel about a *parabatai* the way Anna felt about Ariadne. There was no mistaking it, Anna thought, though it was an awkward revelation to have in the middle of a demon fight.

She was definitely in love with Ariadne Bridgestock.

✳ ✻ ✳

Jem entered the house through the open door, his staff at the ready. The room was quiet. There was a tremendous amount of blood on the floor, and the torn remains of a human.

"Herein!" said a voice. "I was hoping you would come."

Jem turned. Leopolda Stain was sitting on a large brocade chair, holding the head of a woman in her lap. Jem raised his staff.

You have murdered innocent mundanes, Jem said.

"They slew themselves," Leopolda said. "They were playing with fire. They were burned. You know of such creatures. They believe they understand magic. They must come to understand its true nature. I do them a service. They will not call another demon. If I wanted to teach them a lesson, where's the harm? There is hellfire in me, but I do not think I am your chief concern."

Jem was torn. His instinct was to strike her down for what she had done, and yet . . .

"You hesitate, James Carstairs," she said with a smile.

My name is Brother Zachariah.

"You were James Carstairs, the Shadowhunter who was addicted to *yin fen*. You were acquainted with Axel Mortmain, the one they called the Magister, I think?"

At the sound of Mortmain's name, Jem lowered his staff.

"Ah," Leopolda said with a smile. "You remember dear Axel."

You knew him?

"Quite well," she said. "I know many things. I know a warlock helps run the Institute here, yes? Named Tessa Herondale. She is a Shadowhunter, and she can bear no Marks. She is married to your *parabatai*."

Why are you asking me about Tessa? Jem said. It was as if cold fingers were touching his spine. He did not like this warlock. He did not like her interest in Tessa and Will.

"Because you have been in the Shadow Market, asking many questions about her. About her father. Her *demonic* father."

She let the head roll from her lap.

"As I said, I knew Mortmain," she said. "Since you have been asking about him and how Tessa was created, news has trickled back to me—one of his only remaining friends. I believe you are curious about how Mortmain created Tessa. You seek the demon he summoned to be her father. If you put your weapon away, perhaps we can have a conversation."

Jem did not set down his staff.

"She might not have been too curious about her demon father before"—Leopolda played with the gold netting in her hair—"but now that she has *children* . . . and those children show signs of their demon heritage . . . I imagine things are very different?"

Jem stood coldly stricken. It was as if she had reached into his mind and touched his memory. Standing on Blackfriars Bridge with Tessa on a cold January day. The fear on her face. *I do not want to trouble Will . . . but I worry so over Jamie and Lucie. . . . James despairs of his eyes, calls them doorways into Hell, as if he hates his own face, his own bloodline. If I but knew who my demon father was, perhaps I could know, prepare them and myself . . . and Will.* Jem had feared even then that it was a dangerous errand, that knowledge would gift them only further worries and doubts. But it was something Tessa had wanted for Will and the children, and he loved them all too much to say no.

"Your friend Ragnor's queries have finally borne fruit," said

Leopolda. "I know who Tessa's father was." She narrowed her eyes. "In exchange I only need something small. Just the smallest amount of blood from a living Shadowhunter. You will not even feel it. I was going to get it from the girl, the one who dresses as a boy. I like her very much. I would like to collect her, if I could."

You will stay away from her.

"Of course I will," Leopolda said. "I will help you as well. Just the smallest amount of blood, and I can tell you of Tessa Herondale's true father."

"Brother Zachariah!" he heard Anna yell.

Jem turned for one moment, and Leopolda moved toward him. He flung up his staff, knocking her backward. She let out a hiss and darted away faster than seemed possible. She lifted her curved blade.

"Do not toy with me, James Carstairs. Do you not want to know of your Tessa?"

There was another cry from outside. Jem had no choice. He ran in the direction of Anna's voice.

Outside, Anna and the other girl were in a fierce fight with at least six Raveners. They were pressed to the wall, fighting back-to-back. Jem swung out with his staff and brought it down on the back of the closest one. He continued swinging until Anna and the girl were able to regain some ground. Jem took down another, while Anna destroyed two at once with a long swing of her blade. There was but one Ravener left. It extended its spiked tail and pointed it at the other girl's chest. In a second, Anna was diving through the air, knocking the other girl out of the way. They rolled together, Anna's arms around the girl, shielding her. Jem struck out at this last demon, landing a blow on its head.

The street fell quiet. Anna was in the girl's arms, very still.

Anna. Jem raced over. The Shadowhunter girl was already tearing away Anna's sleeve to get to the wound. Anna hissed as the poison stung the surface of her skin.

Behind them, Leopolda stepped out of the house and began to simply walk away.

"I'm fine," Anna said. "Go after her, Ariadne."

The other girl, Ariadne, exhaled and sat back. "The poison did not enter your system. But it did get on your skin. We must wash the site with herbs, immediately. And your wound is deep. You will need several *iratzes.*"

The girl looked up at Jem.

"I'll take care of her," she said. "I am well trained in healing. I was taught by Silent Brothers while I lived in Idris. Anna's right. Go after the warlock."

You are sure? Anna will need an amissio, *a blood-replacement rune—*

"Quite sure," the girl said, easing Anna to her feet. "Believe me when I say Anna would rather lose a bit of blood than have her parents find out what we did tonight."

"Hear, hear," agreed Anna.

Take care of her, said Jem.

"I will." Ariadne spoke with a firm confidence, and from the way she was handling the wound, her words appeared true.

"Come," Ariadne said to Anna. "My house is not far. Can you walk?"

"With you," Anna said, "I can go anywhere."

Thus assured, Jem turned in the direction of Leopolda Stain.

✳ ✳ ✳

They walked back to Ariadne's house, Anna occasionally lean-ing on her friend for support. The poison on her skin was start-ing to have an effect, which was a bit like having too much wine, too fast. She tried to keep herself steady. They were glam-oured now, walking unseen through the street.

When they arrived, Ariadne let them in quietly through the front door. They took the stairs gently, so as not to wake any-one. Luckily, Ariadne's room was on the opposite side of the house from her parents' room. Ariadne led Anna in and shut the door.

Ariadne's room was like the person who inhabited it— perfumed, perfect, delicate. There were lace curtains on the large windows. The walls were papered in silver and rose, and there were fresh-cut lilacs and roses in vases around the room.

"Come," Ariadne said, leading Anna to her bureau, where there was a water basin. She removed Anna's jacket and pushed up her sleeve. Having mixed a few herbs into the basin, she poured the mixture over the wound, which stung.

"It is a nasty injury," Ariadne said, "but I am a good nurse."

She moistened a cloth and gently cleaned the wound with soft strokes, careful to wipe away any poison that had splashed on Anna's skin. Then she got her stele and drew an *amissio* rune to speed blood replacement and an *iratze* to encourage healing. The wound began to close.

Throughout all of this, Anna was silent, breathless. She did not feel pain. She felt only Ariadne's careful hands on her.

"Thank you," she finally said.

Ariadne set her stele down. "It is nothing. You sustained this wound while saving me. You stepped in front of me. You protected me."

"I would protect you always," Anna said.

Ariadne looked at Anna for a long moment. The only light came in through the pattern in the lace.

"My dress," Ariadne said softly. "I think it is quite ruined. I look a fright."

"Nonsense," Anna replied. Then, after a beat, she added, "You have never looked more beautiful."

"It has blood on it, and ichor. Help me remove it, please."

With trembling fingers, Anna undid the many buttons on the front of the dress, and it slid to the ground in a pile. Ariadne turned so that Anna could undo the stays of her corset. Ariadne wore a cotton chemise underneath, trimmed in delicate lace. Her chemise and bloomers were stark white against her brown skin. Her eyes glowed.

"You must rest a bit, Anna," Ariadne said. "You cannot leave right now. Come."

She took Anna by the hand and led her to the bed. Anna realized as she sank into it how exhausted she was from the fight, and also that she had never been so awake and alive.

"Lean back," Ariadne said, stroking Anna's hair.

Anna put her head down on the pillow. Her boots were gone. Her hair had come down, and she pushed it back impatiently.

"I would like to kiss you," Ariadne said. Her voice shook with a fear Anna understood all too well. Ariadne was afraid Anna was going to push her away, reject her, run screaming. But how could Ariadne not know how she felt? "Please, Anna, may I kiss you?"

Unable to speak, Anna nodded.

Ariadne leaned forward and pressed her lips to Anna's.

Anna had lived this moment in her mind a hundred times

or more. She did not know her body would grow so warm, that Ariadne would taste so sweet. She returned the kiss, then kissed Ariadne along her cheek, her chin, down her neck. Ariadne made a low sound of delight. She brought her lips up to Anna's again, and they fell back against the pillows. They were tangled together, laughing and warm, intent on only each other. The pain was gone, replaced by rapture.

During the day, the streets and alleys of Soho could be hard to navigate. At night, they became a dangerous and confusing warren. Jem kept his staff aloft. At this late hour, the only people about were drunkards and ladies of the night. The alleys smelled of refuse, and there was broken glass and the assorted detritus of a London day.

Jem made his way to a storefront on Wardour Street. He knocked, and the door was opened by two young werewolves, neither of whom seemed surprised to see him.

Woolsey Scott is expecting me.

They nodded and guided him through a dark and empty shop that sold buttons and ribbons and through a door. On the other side was a dimly lit but tastefully furnished room. Woolsey Scott was stretched out on a low divan. Sitting opposite him was Leopolda Stain, surrounded by a half a dozen more werewolves. She seemed calm and composed, and was even sipping from a cup of tea.

"Ah, Carstairs," Scott said. "Finally. I thought we'd be here all night."

Thank you, said Jem, *for looking after her for me.*

"It was no trouble," said Scott. He tipped his chin at Leopolda. "As you know, this one arrived a few weeks ago. We've been keeping an eye on her ever since. I didn't think she would go as far as she did tonight. Can't have her egging on idiot mundanes to raise demons. It's the sort of thing that inspires anti-Downworlder sentiment."

Leopolda seemed to take no offense at the way he spoke.

Woolsey rose to his feet. "You had said you wanted to speak with her," he said. "Shall I leave the matter with you?"

Yes, Jem said.

"Good. I have an appointment with a rather staggering bottle of red. I'm sure she won't cause any further fuss, will you, Leopolda?"

"Of course not," Leopolda said.

Scott nodded, and the werewolves left the room as one. Leopolda looked up at Jem and smiled.

"It is good to see you again," she said. "We were so rudely interrupted earlier."

You will tell me what you know of Tessa.

Leopolda reached over to a teapot on a low table and refilled her cup.

"These terrible beasts," she said, nodding at the door. "They handled me quite roughly. I would like to leave this place now."

You will not be leaving until you tell me what I want to know.

"Oh, I will. Your Tessa . . . and she was yours, wasn't she? I may not be able to see your eyes, but I can see it in your face."

Jem stiffened. He was no longer that boy, the young man who had planned a wedding to Tessa, who had loved her as much as his heart could bear. He loved her still, but he survived it by having put that young man away, by putting away his human loves as he had put away the violin. Instruments for another time, another life.

Still, there was no joy in being so cruelly reminded.

"I imagine her powers are great," Leopolda said, stirring her tea. "I envy her. Axel was . . . so very proud."

There was nothing but the sound of the spoon hitting the sides of the china cup. In the depths of his mind, Jem heard the murmuring of the other Silent Brothers. He ignored it. This was his mission alone.

Tell me of Tessa's father.

"The blood," she said. "You will give me the blood first. It is a very small amount."

That will never happen.

"No?" she said. "You know, I am merely the humble daughter of a Vetis demon, but your Tessa . . ."

She waited to see the effect on Jem.

"Yes," she said. "I know all. You will put out your arm. I will take the blood, I will tell you what you so wish to know, and I will leave. We will both be satisfied. I assure you, what I give you is so much more than I ask. It is a bargain of the highest order."

You do not have the advantages you think you have, Leopolda Stain, he said. *I have known you were here since you set foot on these shores. I knew you were a friend of Mortmain's. I know you want this blood to continue his works, and I will never allow that.*

Her lip curled. "But you are kind," she said. "You are famous for it. You will not hurt me."

Jem took his staff, spinning it between his hands, and held it balanced lightly between himself and Leopolda. He knew a hundred different ways to kill her with it. He could break her neck.

That was my Shadowhunter self, he said. *I have killed with this staff, though I prefer not to. Either you tell me what I wish to know, or you die. It is your choice.*

He saw, from the look in her eyes, that she believed him.

Tell me what I want to know, and I will let you go with your life.

Leopolda swallowed. "First, swear upon your Angel that you will allow me to leave tonight."

I swear upon the Angel.

Leopolda smiled a long, vulpine smile.

"The ritual that created your Tessa was magnificent," she said. "Such glory. I never thought such a thing could be done, mating a Shadowhunter with a demon. . . ."

Do not delay. Tell me.

"Your Tessa's father is a prince, the greatest of Eidolon demons. The most beautiful creature in any hell, for he has a thousand shapes."

A Prince of Hell? Jem had feared it. No wonder James could turn himself to smoke and Tessa herself could take any form, even that of an angel. A line of Nephilim whose blood was mixed with demonic royalty? There was no history of such impossible beings. Even now, he could not think of Tessa and her children as new and strange creations with incredible powers. They were simply people he loved beyond measure. *You are saying Tessa's father is a Prince of Hell?*

The Clave could never know. He could not tell them. His heart lurched. Could he tell Tessa? Would it be better for her to know or not?

"Indeed a prince," Leopolda said, "brother to Asmodeus and Sammael. What an honor to be born of him. Sooner or later, Jem Carstairs, blood will out, and such a beautiful power will blaze through this city."

She rose to her feet.

The greatest of Eidolons? I need more than that. What is his name?

She shook her head. "The price for the name is blood, James Carstairs, and if you will not pay it, another will."

She brought her hand out from behind her back and flung a handful of powder at Jem. Had his eyes not been protected by magic, it would likely have blinded him. As it was, he staggered back long enough for her to run past him to the door. She reached it in seconds and threw it open.

On the other side of it were two huge werewolves, flanking Woolsey Scott.

"As expected," Woolsey said, looking at Leopolda with contempt. "Kill her, boys. Let her be an example to others who would freely spill blood in our city."

Leopolda screamed and whirled on Jem, wide-eyed. "You said you would let me leave! You swore!"

Jem felt very weary. *I am not the one who is stopping you.*

She cried out as the werewolves, already half-transformed, flung themselves on her. Jem turned away while the sounds of ripping flesh and shrieks tore through the room.

The summer dawn came early. Ariadne was sleeping gently, and Anna heard the maid stirring downstairs. She had not slept yet, even after Ariadne had dropped off. Anna did not want to move from this warm spot. She played with the lace edges of the pillow and watched Ariadne's eyelashes flicker as if she were in the depths of a dream.

But the sky was turning from black to the soft peach color of sunrise. Soon there would be a maid at the door with a tray. Soon, life would intrude.

It would only hurt Ariadne if she were found here. It was her duty to leave this place.

She kissed Ariadne softly, so as not to wake her. Then she dressed and slipped out the sash window. The dark did not quite obscure her now as she walked through the misty London morning in her men's clothes. A few people turned their heads to get a second look at her, and she was fairly sure that some of those looks were admiring, even if she was mostly missing one of her sleeves and had lost her hat. She decided to take a circuitous route home, along Regent's Park. The colors were soft in the sunrise, the waters of the boating lake still. She felt friendship toward the ducks and the pigeons. She smiled at strangers.

This was what love was. It was total. It brought her together with everything. Anna barely cared if she made it home before someone would notice her missing. She wanted to feel like this forever—exactly this, this soft and fragrant and friendly morning, with the feel of Ariadne still on her skin. Her future, so confused before, was clear. She would be with Ariadne forever. They would travel the world, fight side by side.

Eventually, she had to walk toward her home, where she climbed up to her window with ease. She removed her brother's clothing and slipped into bed. Within seconds, she dropped into the easy embrace of sleep and felt herself back in Ariadne's arms.

She woke just before noon. Someone had brought her a tea tray and left it next to her bed. She drank the now-cold tea. She took a cool bath and examined the wound on her arm. The healing runes Ariadne had drawn had done their work. The area was still red and angry, but she could cover it with a shawl. She dressed in her plainest, most severely cut gown—so funny now, to be dressed as a girl—and put a silk shawl over her shoulders, winding it carefully over the damaged arm. She went downstairs. Her mother sat in a sunny corner of the sitting room, little Alexander on her lap.

"There you are," her mother said. "Are you ill?"

"No," Anna said. "I was foolish. I stayed up quite late reading a book."

"Now I know you are ill," her mother said with a smile, which Anna returned.

"I need to take a walk in the sunshine. It is such a lovely day. I shall go see Lucie and James, I think, and discuss my book with them."

Her mother gave her a curious look, but agreed.

Anna did not walk to the Herondale house. She turned instead toward Fitzrovia, stopping to buy a bunch of violets from an old woman selling them in the street. Her steps were light. The world was perfectly arranged, and all things and beings in it were worthy of love. Anna could have done anything in that moment—fought off a hundred demons at once, lifted a carriage over her head, danced on a wire. She passed along the pavements she had been on only hours before, back to her love.

At the house off Cavendish Square, Anna knocked once, then stood nervously on the step, looking up. Was Ariadne in her room? Would she look down?

The door was opened by the Bridgestocks' unsmiling servant.

"The family is receiving guests at the moment, Miss Lightwood. Perhaps you would like to wait in the—"

At that moment, the reception-room door opened, and

the Inquisitor walked out with a young man who had familiar features and red hair—Charles Fairchild, Matthew's brother. Anna rarely saw Charles. He was always somewhere, usually Idris. He and the Inquisitor were mid-conversation.

"Oh," Inquisitor Bridgestock said, seeing Anna. "Miss Lightwood. How fortuitous. Do you know Charles Fairchild?"

"Anna!" Charles said with a warm smile. "Yes, of course."

"Charles will be the interim head of the Paris Institute," the Inquisitor said.

"Oh," Anna said. "Congratulations. Matthew didn't tell me."

Charles rolled his eyes. "I imagine he thinks of such things as political aspirations as crass and bourgeois. What are you doing here, anyway?"

"Anna and Ariadne have been training together," the Inquisitor explained.

"Ah," Charles said. "Excellent. You must visit us in Paris sometime, Anna."

"Oh," Anna said, not knowing what "us" Charles was talking about. "Yes. Thank you. I shall."

Ariadne stepped out of the morning room. She wore a dress of fresh peony pink, and her hair was coiled on her head. On seeing Anna, her cheeks flushed. Charles Fairchild stepped ahead with Inquisitor Bridgestock, and Ariadne stepped up to her.

"I did not expect to see you so soon," she said to Anna in a low voice.

"How could I keep away?" Anna replied. Ariadne was wearing her perfume again, and it wafted lightly through the air. Orange blossom was Anna's favorite scent now.

"Perhaps we can meet later," Ariadne said. "We are—"

"I will be back again in a year's time," Charles said, concluding whatever conversation he was having with Inquisitor Bridgestock. He returned to them, bowed, took Ariadne's hand, and kissed it formally.

"I hope to see more of you when I next return," he said. "It should not be more than a year."

"Yes," Ariadne replied. "I would like that very much."

"Anna!" Mrs. Bridgestock said. "We have a parrot. You must see it. Come."

Suddenly, Anna found that Mrs. Bridgestock had hooked her by the arm and was gently leading her into one of the other rooms, where there was a large multicolored parrot in a massive gold cage. The bird cawed loudly on their approach.

"It is a very nice bird," Anna said, confused, as Mrs. Bridgestock shut the door behind them.

"I do apologize, Anna," she said. "I just needed to give the two of them the chance to properly say their farewells. These things can be so delicate. I am sure you understand."

Anna did not understand, but there was a creeping numbness coming over her.

"It is our hope that they might wed in a few years' time," Mrs. Bridgestock went on. "Nothing has been settled, but it is such a good match."

The parrot screeched and Mrs. Bridgestock went on talking, but Anna heard only a ringing in her ears. She could still taste Ariadne's kiss on her lips; she saw Ariadne's dark hair spread out on the pillow. Those things had happened just hours before, and yet it was like a hundred years had passed and the world had grown cold and unfamiliar.

The door opened again, and a quiet Ariadne joined them.

"Has mother introduced you to Winston?" she said, looking at the parrot. "She dotes on him. Aren't you a nasty beast, Winston?"

She said it warmly, and Winston the parrot danced along his rail and extended a foot to Ariadne.

"Did you have a fruitful discussion?" her mother asked.

"Mother!" Ariadne protested. She was a little pale, but her mother seemed not to notice. "Please, may I speak to Anna?"

"Yes, of course," Mrs. Bridgestock said. "You girls have a good chat. I'll have the cook make up some nice strawberry lemonade and some biscuits."

When she left, Anna stared blankly at Ariadne.

"You are to be married?" she said, her voice gone dry. "You cannot *marry him.*"

"Charles is quite a good match," Ariadne said as if she were discussing the quality of a piece of cloth. "Nothing has been settled, but we should reach an agreement soon. But come, Anna, come. Sit."

Ariadne took Anna's hand and led her over to one of the sofas.

"That won't be for at least another year or more," Ariadne said. "You heard Charles. It's a year before I even see him again. All that time, I will spend with you."

She drew a small circle on the back of Anna's hand with her finger, a gentle motion that took Anna's breath away. Ariadne was so beautiful, so warm. Anna felt like she was being torn to pieces.

"Surely you cannot wish to marry Charles," said Anna. "There is nothing wrong with him, but he is . . . Do you *love* him?"

"No," Ariadne said, clutching Anna's hand tighter. "I do not love him that way, or any man that way. All my life, I have looked at women and known only they could pierce my heart. As you have pierced it, Anna."

"Then why?" Anna said. "Why marry him? Because of your parents?"

"Because that is the way the world *is*," Ariadne said, her voice shaking, the way it had when she had first asked Anna if she might kiss her. "If I were to tell my parents the truth about myself, if I were to reveal who I really am, they would despise me. I would be friendless, cast out, alone."

Anna shook her head.

"They would not," she said. "They would love you. You are their daughter."

Ariadne drew her hand back from Anna's. "I am adopted, Anna. My father is the Inquisitor. I do not have parents who are as understanding as yours must be."

"But love is what matters," said Anna. "I would have no one but you. You are all to me, Ariadne. I will not marry a man. I only want you."

"And I want children," Ariadne said, lowering her voice in case her mother was returning. "Anna, I have always wanted to be a mother, more than anything else in the world. If I had to bear Charles's touch, it would be worth it for that." She shuddered. "I shall never, never love him as I love you. I thought you understood—that this would be a bit of happiness we could snatch for ourselves before the world forced us apart. We can love each other for the next year, before Charles returns—we could have that time and always remember it, hold it close to ourselves—"

"But when Charles returned, it would be over," Anna said coldly. "He would claim you. That is what you are saying."

"I would not be unfaithful to him, no," Ariadne said quietly. "I am not a liar."

Anna stood up. "I think you are lying to yourself."

Ariadne raised her lovely face. Tears poured down her cheeks; she wiped them away with shaking hands. "Oh, Anna, won't you kiss me?" she said. "Oh, please, Anna. Do not leave me. Please kiss me."

She looked at Anna pleadingly. Anna's breaths were short, and her heart beat a wailing tattoo in her chest. The perfect world she had dreamed of was shattered into a million pieces, turned to dust, and blown away. What replaced it was something cruel and strange. There was not enough air to breathe. Hot tears stung her eyes.

"Good-bye, Ariadne," she managed, and staggered from the room.

Anna sat on the edge of her bed and cried for a very long time. She cried until no tears came and her body heaved reflexively.

There was a soft knock on her door, and her brother peeked his head in.

"Anna?" he said, blinking his lavender eyes. "Are you all right? I thought I heard something."

Oh, Christopher. Sweet Christopher. Anna roughly wiped her face.

"I'm fine, Christopher," she said, clearing her throat.

"Are you sure?" Christopher asked. "Is there nothing I can do to help you? I could perform a saving act of science."

"Christopher, get along with you." It was Anna's mother,

appearing silently as a cat in the corridor behind her son. "Go and do something else. Something without explosives," she added, shooing her second-born off down the hall.

Anna hastily scrubbed the last traces of tears from her eyes as her mother came into her room, carrying a long, beribboned box. She sat down on the bed and looked at her daughter placidly.

As always, Cecily was perfectly dressed and perfectly calm-looking, her dark hair in a smooth chignon at the back of her neck, her dress a becoming blue. Anna couldn't help but think how ghastly she must look in her nightshirt with her face blotchy and red.

"Do you know why I named you Anna?" Cecily said.

Anna shook her head, puzzled.

"I was awfully ill during my pregnancy," said Cecily. Anna blinked—she hadn't known that. "I was worried all the time that you wouldn't live to be born, or you would be sickly and ill. And then you were born, and you were the most beautiful, healthy, perfect child." She smiled. "Anna means 'favor,' as in 'God has favored me.' I thought the Angel had favored me with you, and I would make sure you were always happy, always content." She reached out to gently touch Anna's cheek. "She broke your heart, didn't she? Ariadne?"

Anna was speechless. So her mother did know. She had always thought her mother knew that she loved women, and that her father did as well . . . but they had never spoken of it until now.

"I am so sorry." Cecily kissed Anna's forehead. "My darling lovely one. I know it does not help to be told it, but someone else will come, and she will treat your heart as the precious gift it is."

"Mama," she said. "You do not mind—that I might not get married or have children?"

"There are many Shadowhunter children orphaned, as Ariadne was, seeking loving homes, and I see no reason why you might not provide one someday. As for marriage . . ." Cecily shrugged. "They said your uncle Will could not be with your aunt Tessa, that your aunt Sophie and uncle Gideon could not be together. And yet, I think you will find that they were wrong, and they would have been wrong even if marriage had been forbidden. Even where laws are unjust, hearts can find a way to be together. If you love someone, I have no doubt you will find a way to spend your life with them, Anna. You are the most determined child I know."

"I am not a child," Anna said, but she smiled, in some amazement. Ariadne might have disappointed her, but her mother was astonishing her in quite the opposite way.

"Still," her mother said. "You cannot keep wearing your brother's clothes."

Anna's heart fell. Here it was. Her mother's understanding could go only so far.

"I thought you didn't know," she said in a small voice.

"Of course I knew. I am your mother," Cecily said as if she were announcing that she were the queen of England. She tapped the long, ribboned box. "Here is a new outfit for you. Hopefully you will find it suitable for accompanying your family in the park today."

Before Anna could protest, a loud and demanding cry sounded through the house. Exclaiming, "Alexander!" Cecily swept out the door, instructing Anna to meet her downstairs in the sitting room when she was dressed.

Glumly, Anna untied the ribbons holding the box closed. She had received many clothes from her mother in the past. Another pastel silk? Another cunningly constructed dress, meant to make the most of her slight curves?

The ribbons and paper fell away, and Anna gasped.

Inside the box was the most gorgeous suit she had ever seen. Charcoal tweed with a thin blue stripe, the jacket was neatly tailored. A gorgeous silk waistcoat in radiant shades of blue complemented a crisp white shirt. Shoes, braces—nothing had been forgotten.

In a daze, Anna dressed herself and gazed into the mirror. The clothes fit perfectly—her mother must have given her measurements to the tailor. And yet there was still one thing not right.

She tightened her jaw, then crossed the room to get the pair of scissors. Standing before the mirror, she grabbed a thick fistful of hair.

She hesitated for only a moment, Ariadne's soft voice in her ears.

I thought you understood—that this would be a bit of happiness we could snatch for ourselves before the world forced us apart.

The hair made a satisfying sound as she cut through it. It rained down on the carpet. She took another fistful, then another, until her hair was to her chin. The cut brought her features into sharp relief. She trimmed more in the front, clipped away at the back, until there was just enough to sweep into a gentlemanly wave.

And now it was perfect. Her reflection gazed back at her, lips curved in an incredulous smile. The waistcoat brought out her eyes; the trousers, the slimness of her legs. She felt she could breathe, even with the ache of Ariadne's loss in her chest. She might have lost the girl, but she had gained herself. A new Anna, confident, dapper, powerful.

Hearts were broken across London every day. Perhaps Anna might break a heart or two herself. There would be others—lovely girls would come and go, and she would remain in control of her heart. She would never be torn like this again.

She was a Shadowhunter. She would take the blow. She would harden herself and laugh in the face of pain.

Anna descended the stairs soon after. It was late afternoon now, though the sun was still shining brightly through the windows. This day would last forever.

Her mother was in the sitting room with a tea tray, baby Alex in a basket by her side. Her father sat opposite, engaged in reading the newspaper.

Anna stepped into the room.

Both her parents looked up. She saw them take in her new clothes, as well as her short hair. She stood in the doorway, bracing herself for whatever response was coming.

A long moment passed.

"I told you the blue waistcoat was the one," Gabriel said to Cecily. "It brings out her eyes."

"I did not disagree," said Cecily, rocking the baby. "I just said she would also look very well in red."

Anna began to smile.

"Much better than your brother's clothes," Gabriel said. "He does dreadful things to them with sulfur and acids."

Cecily examined Anna's shorn locks.

"Very sensible," she said. "Hair can be cumbersome in battle. I like it very much." She rose to her feet. "Come sit," she added. "Stay with your brother and father a moment. There is something I meant to fetch for you."

As her mother left the room, Anna felt her limbs go tingly as she sat down on the settee. She reached down to Alex. He was looking all around the room, taking in all the wonders anew in the way that babies do whenever they awake and find that the world is still there, to be understood in all its myriad complexities.

"I understand how you feel," she said to her brother.

He smiled a toothless smile at her and reached up a chubby hand. She extended her own, and he grabbed her finger.

Her mother returned only a few minutes later with a small blue box.

"You know," Cecily said, sitting down and refilling her teacup, "my parents did not want me to be a Shadowhunter. They had fled the Clave. And your uncle Will . . ."

"I know," Anna said. Gabriel gazed fondly at his wife.

"But I was a Shadowhunter. I knew it then, when I was fifteen. I knew it was in my blood. Foolish people say so many things. But we know who we are, inside."

She set the blue box on the table and pushed it toward Anna.

"If you will accept it," her mother said.

Inside the box was a necklace with a glimmering red gem. Latin words were etched onto the back.

"For your protection," she said. "You know what it does."

"It senses demons," Anna said, astonished. Her mother wore it nearly every time she went out to fight, though that was rarer now that Alexander had come along.

"It cannot protect your heart, but it can protect the rest of you," Cecily said. "It is an heirloom. It should be yours."

Anna fought back the tears that sought to fill her eyes.

She took up the necklace and clasped it about her throat. She stood up and gazed at herself in the mirror over the fireplace. A handsome reflection gazed back at her. The necklace felt right, just as her short hair did. *I do not have to be only one thing,* Anna thought. *I can choose what suits me when it suits me. The trousers and jacket do not make me a man, and the necklace does not make me a woman. They are only what makes me feel beautiful and powerful in this moment. I am exactly as I choose to be. I am a Shadowhunter who wears gorgeous suits and a legendary pendant.*

She looked at her mother's reflection in the glass. "You were right," she said. "The red does suit me."

Gabriel chuckled softly, but Cecily only smiled.

"I have always known you, my love," Cecily said. "You are the gem of my heart. My firstborn. My Anna."

Anna thought of all the pain of the day again—the wound that had ripped her chest open and exposed her heart. But now it was as if her mother had drawn a rune over it and closed it. The scar was there, but she was whole.

It was like being Marked all over again, defining who she was. This was Anna Lightwood.

Learn About Loss

By Cassandra Clare and Kelly Link

Chattanooga, 1936

On the morning of October 23, the inhabitants of Chattanooga, Tennessee, woke up to discover posters tacked up on the sides of buildings on every street. FOR A LIMITED TIME ONLY, the posters declared, MAGIC & MUSIC & MOST MYSTERIOUS MERCHANTS' BAZAAR. PAY ONLY WHAT YOU CAN AFFORD & ENTER FAIRYLAND. SEE WHAT YOU MOST DESIRE. ALL WELCOME.

Some men and women passed these posters, shaking their heads. It was the height of the Great Depression, and even if the president, Franklin Delano Roosevelt, was promising more work on projects like the tunnel and trails and campgrounds underway in the Great Smoky Mountains National Park, jobs were scarce and times were hard and most people didn't have money to spare on fripperies or fun. And who wanted to travel all the way up Lookout Mountain only to be turned away because what you could afford was nothing? Besides, no one ever gave you something for nothing.

But plenty of other Chattanoogans saw the posters and thought that maybe better times really were just around the corner. There was a New Deal, and maybe there would be new fun, too. And there was not a single child who caught sight of the posters and didn't yearn with their entire heart for what the posters promised. The twenty-third of October was a Friday. On Saturday, at least half the city of Chattanooga lit out for the carnival. Some of them packed bedrolls or tarps to sleep under. If there was music and festivity, maybe they would stay longer than a day. The churches of Chattanooga were poorly attended on Sunday morning. But the carnival in the Fairyland neighborhood of Lookout Mountain was busier than a beehive.

Up on top of Lookout Mountain, a local boy named Garnet Carter had quite recently established the community of Fairyland, which included Tom Thumb Golf, the first miniature golf course in the United States. There was the eerie natural landscape of Rock City, where his wife, Frieda Carter, had laid out paths between towering, mossy rock formations, planting wildflowers and importing German statuary so that the trails were watched over by gnomes and characters from fairy-tale stories like "Little Red Riding Hood" and the "Three Little Pigs."

Rich people came on vacations and rode the funicular, which also happened to be the world's steepest passenger railway, the mile up from Chattanooga to the Lookout Mountain Hotel. The hotel was also known as the Castle In the Clouds, and if all the rooms were taken, well, there was also the Fairyland Inn. For the wealthy, there was golf and ballroom dancing and hunting. For the civic-minded, there was the site of the Battle Above the Clouds, where the Union Army had, in living memory, driven off at great cost the Confederates. You could still find minié bullets and other traces of the dead all down the slopes of the mountain, along with flint arrowheads used by the Cherokee. But the Cherokee had all been driven off, and the Civil War was over too. There had been a greater war in recent memory, and many a family in Chattanooga had lost sons or fathers to it. Human beings did terrible things to each other, and the traces of those terrible things were everywhere if you looked.

If your taste ran more to corn whiskey than history, well, there were plenty of moonshine stills up on Lookout Mountain too. And who knew what other illegal or immoral delights might be found at a Mysterious Merchants' Bazaar?

There were men and women of money and taste at the carnival on that first Saturday, rubbing alongside the thin-faced children and wives of farmers. The rides were free to all. There were games with prizes, and a petting zoo with a three-headed dog and a winged snake so large that it was able to swallow a full-grown steer each day at noon. There were strolling fiddle players who drew such melancholy and lovely songs out on their instruments that tears came to the eyes of all who heard them. There was a woman who said that she could speak with the dead, and asked no coin. There was a magician, too, Roland the Astonishing, who grew a dogwood tree from a seed on his stage and then caused it to flower, drop its leaves, and grow bare again as if all the seasons were passing in the blink of an eye. He was a handsome man in his sixties, with bright blue eyes, a luxuriant white mustache, and snowy white hair with a black streak running through it as if some devil had touched it with a sooty hand.

There were delicious things to eat at such a negligible cost, or freely given as samples, that every child ate himself or herself sick. As promised, the bazaar was full of remarkable objects on display, tended by even more remarkable people. Some of the customers, too, drew curious glances. Were there people in faraway lands who had curly tails or flames in their pupils? One of the most popular stalls had on offer a local product: a clear, potent liquor rumored to give dreams of a moonlit forest full of running wolves to those who drank it. The men at that booth were taciturn and did not smile often. But when they did, their teeth were unsettlingly white. They lived up in the mountains and mostly kept to themselves, but here at the bazaar they seemed quite at home.

One tent was staffed by nurses so very lovely it wasn't a chore at all to let them draw your blood. They took a cup or two, "for research purposes," they said. And to those who donated, they gave away tokens that could be used elsewhere in the bazaar, just like money.

Just beyond the tents of the bazaar was a sign that led to the Maze of Mirrors. It said SEE FOR YOURSELF. THE TRUE WORLD AND THE FALSE LIE NEXT DOOR TO ONE ANOTHER. Those who went through the Maze of Mirrors came out looking a little dazed. Some of them had found their way to the very center, in which they had been made an offer by an entity that each described differently. To some, the person in the room had appeared as a small child, or an old woman in an elegant gown, or even in the shape of a loved one long dead. The person in the room had a mask, and if you confessed a thing that you desired, the mask was put on you and, well, you should really go and see for yourself. If, that is, you could find your way through the maze and to the place where that person and the mask were waiting.

By the end of the first weekend, most of Chattanooga had come up to see for themselves the strange charms of the carnival. And many came back to the carnival in the following days, although by then rumors were beginning to spread of troubling behavior exhibited by some who had returned. A woman claimed that the man she was married to was an impostor who had killed her real husband: this claim would have been easier to dismiss if a body had not been discovered in the river, in all ways a double of the man she was married to. A young man stood up in church and said that he saw and knew the secrets of all the congregation by looking at them. When he began to say these secrets out loud, the pastor tried to shout him down until the man began to declaim the things he knew about the pastor. At this, the pastor fell silent, then left his church and went home and slit his throat.

Another man won again and again at a weekly game of poker, until, drunk, he confessed, sounding astonished, that he could see the cards every man there held as if they were his very own hand. He proved this by calling out each card in order, and after that was beaten soundly and left unconscious and bloody in the street by men who had been his friends since childhood.

A boy of seventeen, newly engaged to be married, came home from the carnival and that night woke up everyone in his household screaming. He had put out his own eyes with two hot coals, but refused to say why. In fact, he never spoke again, and his poor fiancée at last broke off the engagement and went to live with an aunt in Baltimore.

A beautiful girl turned up at the Fairyland Inn at dusk one evening, claiming that she was Mrs. Dalgrey, when the staff of the inn knew very well Mrs. Dalgrey was a bucket-faced dowager in her late seventies. She stayed at the inn every fall, and never tipped anyone no matter how good the service.

Other terrible incidents were reported in the neighborhoods of Chattanooga, and by the middle of the week after the carnival had put up its signs, word of these happenings had made its way to those whose business it was to prevent the human world from being troubled and tormented by the malicious whims of Downworlders and demons.

It is only to be expected that some amount of trouble will arrive with a carnival. Pleasure and trouble are brother and sister to each other. But there were indications that this particular carnival was more than it seemed. For one thing, the Bazaar of the Bizarre was not just trinkets and gaudy junk. The bazaar was a full-on Shadow Market where there had never been one before, and humans were strolling its aisles and freely handling its wares. And there were indications, too, that there was an artifact made out of *adamas* in the hands of one who should not have had it. For this reason, at sunset on Thursday, the twenty-ninth of October, a Portal opened at Lookout Point, and two individuals who had only just met stepped through it unnoticed by any of the human sightseers gathered there.

One was a young woman not yet fully invested as an Iron Sister, although already her hands showed the scars and calluses of one who worked *adamas*. Her name was Emilia, and this was the last task her Sisters had set her before she joined their company: to recover the *adamas* and bring it back to the Adamant Citadel. She had a smiling, watchful face, as if she liked the world but did not quite trust that it would be on its best behavior.

Her companion was a Silent Brother who bore the runic marks on his face, although neither his eyes nor his mouth had been sewn shut. Instead, they were merely closed, as if he had voluntarily chosen to withdraw inside the citadel of his own self. He was handsome enough that if any of the women at Lookout Point had seen his face, one or two might have thought of fairy tales where a kiss is sufficient to wake one who is under an enchantment. Sister Emilia, who could see Brother Zachariah quite plainly, thought he was one of the handsomest men she had ever seen. Certainly he was one of the first men she had seen in quite some time. And if their errands were successful and she returned to the Adamant Citadel with the *adamas* in her possession, well, it wouldn't be the worst thing if handsome Brother Zachariah was the last man she ever laid eyes on. There was no harm in appreciating beauty when you chanced upon it.

She said, "Nice view, isn't it?" Because from the place they stood you could see Georgia, Tennessee, Alabama, both North and South Carolina, and, on the horizon, Virginia and Kentucky too, all spread out and rumpled like a tapestry quilt haphazardly embroidered in green and blue, little pricks of red and gold and orange where, in places, the trees were already beginning to turn.

Inside her head, Brother Zachariah said, *It's extraordinary. Though, I confess, I had imagined America to look somewhat different. Someone I . . . knew . . . told me about New York City. That was where she grew up. We talked one day of going together to see the things and places that she loved. But we talked of many things that I knew, even then, would likely never happen. And this is a very large country.*

Sister Emilia was not at all sure that she liked having someone else talking inside her head. She had encountered Silent Brothers before, but this was the first time one had spoken directly into her mind. It was like having company show up when you hadn't had the inclination to do the dishes or straighten up your living quarters in a while. What if they could see all the untidy thoughts you sometimes just shoved under the carpet?

Her mentor, Sister Lora, had assured Emilia that although Silent Brothers could ordinarily read the minds of those around them, their Sisterhood was exempt. But on the other hand, what if this was part of the test she had been set? What if Brother Zachariah's task was also to look inside her brain, to be sure that she was a deserving candidate? She thought, as loudly as she could, *Excuse me! Can you hear me thinking?*

When Brother Zachariah didn't respond, she said, relieved, "Your first time in the States, then?"

Yes, Brother Zachariah said. Then, as if to be polite, he said, *And you?*

"Born and bred in California," Sister Emilia said. "I grew up in the San Francisco Conclave."

Is San Francisco very like this? Brother Zachariah said.

She almost choked. "Indeed," she said, "it is not. Not even the trees are the same. And the ground there is like as not to give you a little shake now and then. Sometimes just enough to move your bed a few inches while you're trying to sleep. Other times, it knocks buildings down without so much as a warning. Oh, but the fruits on the trees are the best thing you've ever tasted. And the sun shines every single day."

Her oldest brother had been an infant in their mother's

arms during the earthquake of 1906. Half the city had burned, and Emilia's father said that even demons had stayed away during the destruction. Their mother, who had been pregnant, had had a miscarriage. If that baby had lived, Emilia would have had seven siblings, all brothers. Her first night in the Adamant Citadel, she had woken up every hour because it was all so quiet and peaceful.

You sound as if you miss it, Brother Zachariah said.

Sister Emilia said, "I do miss it. But it was never home. Now, I believe the carnival is thataways, and here we stand jawing when we have work to do."

Although his eyes and ears and mouth had all been closed by the magic of the Silent City, Brother Zachariah could still smell and hear the carnival much better than any mortal—here was the scent of sugar and hot metal and, yes, blood as well, and the sounds of barkers and calliope music and excited shrieks. Soon enough he could see it too.

The carnival stood on mostly level ground where once there must have been quite a battle. Brother Zachariah could feel the presence of the human dead. Now their forgotten remains lay buried under a grassy field where a kind of stockade fence had been erected around all manner of brightly colored tents and fanciful structures. A Ferris wheel stood above these, carriages dangling from the central wheel, full of laughing people. Two great gates stood flung wide open, with a broad avenue between them welcoming all who approached.

Sweethearts in their Sunday clothes strolled through the gates, arms around each other's waists. Two boys pelted past, one with tousled black hair. They looked about the age that

Will and Jem had been, a very long time ago, when they'd first met. But Will's hair was white now, and Jem was no longer Jem. He was Brother Zachariah. A few nights ago, he had sat at Will Herondale's bedside and watched his old friend struggle to draw a breath. Jem's hand on the coverlet was the hand of a young man still, and Tessa, of course, would never grow old. How must it seem to Will, who loved them both, that he must go on so far ahead of them? But then, Jem had left Will first, and Will had had to let him go. It would only be fair when, soon, Jem would be the one left behind.

Inside his head, Brother Enoch said, *It will be hard. But you will be able to bear it. We will help you bear it.*

I will endure it because I must, Brother Zachariah said.

Sister Emilia had stopped, and he caught up with her. She was taking in the carnival, her hands on her hips. "What a thing!" she said. "Did you ever read *Pinocchio*?"

"I don't believe so," Brother Zachariah told her. Though he thought that once, when he'd been in the London Institute, he might have heard Tessa reading it to a young James.

"A wooden puppet yearns to be a real boy," Sister Emilia said. "And so a fairy gives him his wish, more or less, and he gets into all sorts of trouble at a place that I always thought would look rather like this."

Brother Zachariah said, almost against his will, *And does he?*

"Does he what?" Sister Emilia said.

Does he become real?

"Well, of course," Sister Emilia said. Then, saucily, "What kind of story would it be if he only ever got to be a puppet? His father loves him, and that's how he starts to become real, I guess. I always liked those stories the best, the ones where people could make things or carve things and make them come to life. Like Pygmalion."

In his head, Brother Enoch said, *She's quite lively, for an Iron Sister.* He didn't sound exactly disapproving, but neither was it a compliment.

"Of course," Sister Emilia said, "you're something of a story yourself, Brother Zachariah."

What do you know of me? Brother Zachariah said.

She said pertly, "That you fought Mortmain. That you once had a *parabatai* and he became the head of the London Institute. That his wife, the warlock Tessa Herondale, wears a pendant that you gave her. But I know something of you that perhaps you do not know yourself."

That seems unlikely, Brother Zachariah said. *But go on. Tell me what I do not know about myself.*

"Give me your staff," Sister Emilia said.

He gave it to her, and she examined it carefully. "Yes," she said. "I thought so. This was made by Sister Dayo, whose weapons were so exquisitely wrought that it was rumored an angel had touched her forge. Look. Her mark."

It has served me well enough, Brother Zachariah said. *Perhaps one day you too will find renown for the things that you make.*

"One day," said Sister Emilia. She handed him back the staff. "Perhaps." There was a formidable glint in her eyes. Brother Zachariah thought it made her look very young. The world was its own sort of crucible, and in it all dreams were tempered and tested. Many crumbled away entirely, and then you went on without them. In his head his Brothers murmured in agreement. After nearly sixty years, Brother Zachariah was almost used to this. Instead of music, he had this stern brotherly chorus. Once upon a time, he had imagined each of the Silent Brothers as a musical instrument. Brother Enoch, he'd thought, would be a bassoon heard through the high-up window of a desolate lighthouse, the waves crashing down at the base. *Yes, yes, Brother Enoch had said. Very poetic. And what are you, Brother Zachariah?*

Brother Zachariah had tried not to think of his violin. But you couldn't keep secrets from your Brothers. And that violin had lain silent and neglected for a very long time.

He said, attempting to think of other things as they walked, *Can you tell me if you know anything of an Annabel Blackthorn? An Iron Sister? She and a friend of mine, the warlock Malcom Fade, fell in love and made plans to run away together, but when her family discovered this, they forced her to join the Iron Sisterhood. It would ease his mind to know something of what her life had been in the Adamant Citadel.*

Sister Emilia said, "It's clear that you know very little about the Iron Sisters! No one is ever forced to join against their will. Indeed, it is a great honor, and many who attempt the path are turned away. If this Annabel became an Iron Sister, she chose that for herself. I know nothing of her, although it's true that most of us change our names when we are consecrated."

Brother Zachariah said, *If you come to know anything of her, my friend would be most grateful. He does not speak of her much, but I believe that she is always in his thoughts.*

When Brother Zachariah and Sister Emilia passed through the gates of the carnival, the first strange thing they saw was a werewolf eating cotton candy out of a paper cone. Sticky pink strands were caught in his beard.

"Full moon tonight," Sister Emilia said. "The Praetor Lupus

has sent down some of their people, but it's said the werewolves here are a law to themselves. They run moonshine and ride roughshod in the mountains. These boys should be steering clear of mundanes this time of the month, not eating cotton candy and peddling rotgut."

The werewolf stuck out its tongue at them and sauntered away. "Sauce!" Sister Emilia said, and would have pursued the werewolf.

Brother Zachariah said, *Hold. There are worse things here than Downworlders with terrible manners and a sweet tooth. Can you smell that?*

Sister Emilia wrinkled her nose. "Demon," she said.

They followed the smell through the winding alleys of the carnival, through the strangest iteration of the Shadow Market that Brother Zachariah had ever seen. The Market was, of course, much bigger than you would have expected a carnival, even one of this size, to encompass. Some of the vendors he recognized. Some watched warily as he and Sister Emilia passed. One or two, with looks of resignation, began to pack up their wares. The rules by which Shadow Markets existed were more the rules of long custom than those written down and codified, but everything about this Shadow Market felt wrong to Brother Zachariah, and the Silent Brothers in his head were all debating how it might have come to be. Even if a Shadow Market had been right and proper in this place, there should not have been mundanes browsing and exclaiming over the strange goods on offer. Here went a man, looking pale and dreamy-eyed, blood still trickling from two neat punctures in his neck.

"I've never actually been to a Shadow Market," Sister Emilia said, slowing down. "My mother always said it was no place for

Shadowhunters and insisted that my brothers and I stay away from it." She seemed particularly interested in a booth that sold knives and weapons.

Souvenirs later, Brother Zachariah said, pushing on. *Business first.*

They were suddenly out of the Shadow Market and in front of a stage where a magician was telling jokes as he turned a small shaggy dog into a green melon and then cut the melon in half with a playing card. Inside was a fiery sphere that rose up and hung in the air like a miniature sun. The magician (the sign above his head proclaimed him to be Roland the Astonishing) poured water out of his hat onto it, and the sphere became a mouse and ran off the stage into an audience that gasped and shrieked and then applauded.

Sister Emilia had stopped to watch, and Brother Zachariah stopped too.

She said, "Real magic?"

Real illusions at least, Brother Zachariah said. He gestured at the woman who stood at the side of the stage watching the magician perform his tricks.

The magician looked to be in his sixties, but his companion could have been any age at all. She was clearly of high fey lineage, and there was a baby in her arms. The way that she watched the magician on the stage made Brother Zachariah's chest grow tight. He had seen Tessa look at Will the same way, with that rapt attention and love mingled with the knowledge of future sorrow that must, one day, be endured.

Brother Enoch said, again, *When the day comes, we will bear it with you.*

A thought came to Brother Zachariah like an arrow, that

when that day came and Will left the world, he did not wish to share his grief with his Brothers. That others would be there with him when Will was not. And, too, there was Tessa. Who would stay to help her endure when Brother Zachariah took the body that Will had left behind back to the Silent City?

The faerie woman looked out over the crowd and then drew back suddenly behind a velvet curtain. When Brother Zachariah tried to see what she had seen, he saw a goblin perched on a flag above the top of a nearby tent. It appeared to be sniffing the wind as if it smelled something particularly delicious. Mostly what Brother Zachariah smelled now was demon.

Sister Emilia craned her neck to see where Brother Zachariah was looking and said, "Another faerie! It's nice to be out in the world again. I'll have such a lot to write about in my diary when I'm back in the Adamant Citadel."

Do Iron Sisters keep diaries? Brother Zachariah asked politely.

"That was a joke," Sister Emilia said. She actually looked disappointed in him. "Do Silent Brothers have any kind of a sense of humor, or do they stitch that up too?"

We collect knock-knock jokes, Brother Zachariah said.

She perked up. "Really? Do you have any favorites?"

No, Brother Zachariah said. *That was a joke.* He smiled. Sister Emilia was so very human that he found it was waking up some of the humanity he'd put aside so long ago. That too must have been why he was thinking of Will and Tessa and the person he'd been before. His heart would ache slightly less, he was sure, once he and Sister Emilia had completed their mission and been dispatched back to the places where they belonged. She had some of the same spark that Will had had, back when he and Jem had chosen to be *parabatai*. Jem had been drawn to that fire in Will, and Brother Zachariah thought that he and Sister Emilia could have been friends too, under other circumstances.

He was thinking this when a small boy tugged at his sleeve. "Are you part of the carnival?" the boy said. "Is that why you're dressed like that? Is that why your face looks like that?"

Brother Zachariah looked down at the boy and then at the runes on his arms to make sure they hadn't somehow rubbed off.

"You can see us?" Sister Emilia said to the boy.

"'Course I can," the boy said. "Nothing wrong with my eyes. Although I think there must have been something wrong with them before. Because now I see all sorts of things that I never used to see."

How? Brother Zachariah said, bending over to peer into the boy's eyes. *What's your name? When did you start seeing things that you never used to see?*

"My name's Bill," the boy said. "I'm eight. Why are your eyes closed like that? And how can you talk when your mouth isn't open?"

"He's a man of special talents," said Sister Emilia. "You should taste his chicken potpie. Where are your people, Bill?"

The boy said, "I live down in St. Elmo, and I came up here on the Incline Railway with my mother and today I ate a whole bag of saltwater taffy and didn't have to share a piece with anyone else."

"Maybe the taffy had magical properties," Sister Emilia said softly to Brother Zachariah.

"My mother said not to wander off," the boy said, "but I never pay any attention to her unless she's het up like a kettle. I went through the Maze of Mirrors all by myself, and I got all the way to the middle where the fancy lady is, and she said as a prize I could ask her for anything I wanted."

What did you ask her for? Brother Zachariah said.

"I thought about asking for a battle with real knights and real horses and real swords, like in King Arthur, but the lady said if what I wanted was real adventures, I should ask to see the world as it really was, and so I did. And after that she put a mask on me, and now everything's strange, and also she wasn't a lady at all. She was something that I didn't want to be around anymore, and so I ran away. I've seen all kinds of strange people, but I haven't seen my mother. Have you seen her? She's little but she's ferocious. She has red hair like me, and she's got an awful temper when she's worried."

"I know all about that kind of mother," Sister Emilia said. "She must be looking everywhere for you."

Bill said, "I am a constant trial to her. Or so she says."

Over there, Brother Zachariah said. *Is that her?*

A small woman standing by a tent advertising MYSTERIES OF THE WORM DEMONSTRATED THRICE DAILY was looking over in their direction. "Bill Doyle!" she said, advancing. "You are in a heap of trouble, my little man!"

She had a carrying voice.

"I see my fate is upon me," Bill said in grave tones. "You should flee before you become a casualty of battle."

"Don't worry for us, Bill," Sister Emilia said. "Your mother can't see us. And I wouldn't mention us to her either. She'll think you're making it all up."

"It appears I have gotten myself into a real predicament," Bill said. "Fortunately I am as good at getting out of tight spots as I am at getting into them. I've had lots of practice. A pleasure to have met both of you."

Then Mrs. Doyle was upon him. She seized her son's arm and began to pull him back toward the exit of the carnival, scolding him as they went.

Brother Zachariah and Sister Emilia turned to watch them go in silence.

Finally Sister Emilia said, "The Maze of Mirrors, then."

And even if they hadn't encountered young Bill Doyle, they would have known they'd found the place they were looking for when they came to the Maze of Mirrors at last. It was a pointy structure, painted all over in glossy forbidding black, fissures of red running through the black paint, the red paint looking so fresh and wet that the building appeared to be seeping blood. Through the entrance, mirrors and lights dazzled. THE TRUE WORLD AND THE FALSE, said the sign. YOU SHALL KNOW EVEN AS YOU ARE KNOWN. THOSE WHO SEEK ME WILL FIND THEMSELVES.

The reek of demon malignance here was so strong that even Brother Zachariah and Sister Emilia, wearing runes to keep from being overpowered by the stench, flinched.

Be careful, the voices in Brother Zachariah's head warned. *This is no ordinary Eidolon demon.*

Sister Emilia had drawn her sword.

Brother Zachariah said, *We should be careful. There may be dangers here that we are not prepared for.*

Sister Emilia said, "I think we can be at least as brave as little Bill Doyle was, facing danger."

He didn't know he was dealing with a demon, Brother Zachariah said.

"I meant his mother," Sister Emilia said. "Come on."

And so Brother Zachariah followed her into the Maze of Mirrors.

* ✳ *

They found themselves in a long, glittering corridor with many companions. Here was another Sister Emilia and another Brother Zachariah, stretched out monstrously thin and wavy. Here they were again, squashed and hideous. There they were, their reflections' backs turned to them. In one mirror, they lay on the shores of a shallow purple sea, dead and bloated and yet looking utterly content to be so, as if they had died of some great happiness. In another, they began to age rapidly and then to crumble away to bare bones, the bones to dust.

Sister Emilia had never been fond of mirrors. But she had a craftswoman's interest in these. When a mirror is made, it must be coated in some reflective metal. Silver could be used, though vampires were not fond of this kind. The mirrors in the Maze of Mirrors, she thought, must have been treated with some kind of demonic metal. You could smell it. Every breath she took in here coated her mouth, her tongue, her throat with a kind of greasy residue of despair and horror.

She walked forward slowly, her sword held in front of her, and stumbled into a mirror where she had thought there was an open space.

Careful, Brother Zachariah said.

"You don't come to the carnival to be careful," she said. This was bluster, and perhaps he knew it. But bluster is a kind of armor too, as much as taking care is. Sister Emilia had appreciation for both.

"If it's a maze, then how are we to know which way to go?" she said. "I could shatter the mirrors with my sword. If I broke them all, we would find the center."

Hold your sword, Brother Zachariah said.

He had paused in front of a mirror in which Sister Emilia was not present. Instead, there was a slender white-haired boy holding the hand of a tall girl with a solemn, beautiful face. They were on a city avenue.

"That's New York," Sister Emilia said. "I thought you hadn't been there!"

Brother Zachariah advanced through the mirror, which allowed passage as if it had never been there at all. The image was gone like a popped soap bubble. *Go toward the reflections that show you whatever thing you most long to see*, Brother Zachariah said. *But that you know to be impossible.*

"Oh," Sister Emilia said involuntarily. "Over there!"

Over there was a mirror where a Sister much like her, but with silvery hair, held a glowing blade between tongs. She plunged it into a bath of cold water, and steam shot up in the shape of a dragon, writhing and splendid. All her brothers were there too, watching in admiration.

They passed through that mirror too. They made their way through mirror after mirror, and Sister Emilia felt her chest grow tight with longing. Her cheeks burned red too, that Brother Zachariah could see the vainest and most frivolous longings of her heart. But she saw the things that he longed for too. A man and a woman she thought must have been his parents, listening to their son play his violin in a great concert hall. A black-haired man with blue eyes and laugh lines around his mouth, building up a fire in a drawing room while the solemn girl, smiling now, perched on the lap of Brother Zachariah, no longer a Brother but a husband and a *parabatai* in the company of the ones he loved most.

They came to a mirror where the black-haired man, now

old and frail, lay in a bed. The girl sat curled up beside him, stroking his forehead. Suddenly Brother Zachariah came into the room, but when he threw back his hood, he had open, clear eyes and a smiling mouth. At this sight, the old man in the bed sat up and grew younger and younger, as if joy had renewed his youth. He sprang out of bed and embraced his *parabatai*.

"It is horrible," Sister Emilia said. "We should not see inside each other's hearts like this!"

They passed through that mirror and now came face-to-face with one that showed Sister Emilia's mother, sitting before a window, holding a letter from her daughter. There was the most desolate look in her eyes, but then the mother in the reflection began, slowly, to compose a fire-message to her daughter. *I am so very proud of you, my darling. I am so happy you have found your life's work.*

I see nothing shameful in you, Brother Zachariah said in his tranquil voice. He held out his hand, and after a moment Sister Emilia looked away from the reflection of her mother writing all the things she had never said. She took the offered hand gratefully.

"It is shameful to be vulnerable," she admitted. "Or so I have always thought."

They passed through the mirror, and someone said, "And that is exactly what a weapon maker and armorer *would* think. Don't you agree?"

They had found their way to the heart of the maze, and a demon was there with them—a handsome man in a well-cut suit that was the worst thing that Sister Emilia had ever seen.

Belial, Brother Zachariah said.

"Old friend!" Belial said. "I was so hoping it would be you they sent sniffing after me."

This was Sister Emilia's first time encountering a Greater Demon. She held the sword she had forged herself in one hand, and Brother Zachariah's warm hand in the other. If it had not been for those two things, she knew she would have turned and fled.

"Is that human skin?" she asked, her voice wavering.

Whatever the suit was made of, it had the glazed, slightly cracked appearance of poorly tanned leather. It had a pink, blistered look to it. And yes, she could now see that what she had thought was an odd flower poking out of the boutonniere hole was actually a mouth pursed in agony, a cartilaginous lump of nose sagging over it.

Belial looked down at the stained cuff sticking out past the sleeve. He flicked a speck off. "You have an eye, my dear," he said.

"Whose skin is it?" Sister Emilia said. Her voice was steadier now, she found to her great relief. It was not so much that she wanted to know the answers, as that she had found quite early on in her training in the Adamant Citadel that asking questions was a way to discipline your fear. Taking in new information meant you had something to focus on besides how terrifying your teachers or your environment were.

"A tailor I employed," Belial said. "He was a very bad tailor, you see, but in the end he has made a very good suit after all." He gave her and Brother Zachariah the most charming smile. But in the mirrors all around them, his reflections gnashed their teeth and raged.

Brother Zachariah gave every appearance of calm, but

Sister Emilia could feel how tight his grip had grown. She said, "You're friends with him?"

We have met before, Brother Zachariah said. *Silent Brothers do not choose the company they keep. Though I will confess I find yours more to my taste than his.*

"Hurtful!" said Belial, leering. "And, I fear, honest. And I only enjoy one of those things."

What is your business here? Brother Zachariah said.

"No business at all," Belial said. "This is purely fun. You see, they turned up some *adamas* in the caverns underneath Ruby Falls. A small vein of it in the limestone. Do you know that people come from all over the country to gawk at Ruby Falls? A subterranean waterfall! I haven't seen it myself, but I hear it's spectacular. I did play a few rounds of Tom Thumb Golf, though. And then gorged myself sick on the famous salt-water taffy. Had to eat the taffy seller afterward to get the taste out of my mouth. I think there's still a little stuck in my teeth. Chattanooga, Tennessee! The slogan should be 'Come for the *Adamas*, Stay for the Saltwater Taffy!' They could paint it on barns.

"Did you know there's a whole city underneath the city of Chattanooga? They had such terrible floods over the last century that finally they built over the original buildings. The old buildings are still there, underground, hollowed out like rotten teeth. And sure, everything is on higher ground now, but the floods still come. They wash away all the limestone, and what happens eventually? The foundations will crumble, and everything will be washed away in a deluge. There's a metaphor there somewhere, little Shadowhunters. You build and you struggle and you fight, but the darkness and the abyss will come one day in a great tide and sweep away everything that you love."

We didn't have time to tour Chattanooga, Brother Zachariah said. *We're here for the* adamas.

"The *adamas!* Of course!" Belial said. "You people kept such a tight grasp on the stuff."

"You have it?" Sister Emilia said. "I thought it was death to demons, just the touch."

"Your ordinary sort will just explode, yes," Belial said. "But I am a Prince of Hell. Made of sterner stuff."

Greater Demons can handle adamas, Brother Zachariah said. *Though my understanding is that it is agonizing to them.*

"To-may-to of agony, to-mah-to of ah-gony," Belial said. His reflections in the various mirrors wept tears of blood. "Do you know what causes us pain? The one who made us has turned his face from us. We are not allowed before the throne. But *adamas,* that's angelic stuff. When we touch it, the pain of our absence from the divine is indescribable. And yet it's the closest we ever get to being in its presence. So we touch *adamas,* and we feel the absence of our creator, and in that absence we feel the smallest spark of what we once were. Oh, it's the most wonderful thing you can imagine, that pain."

Brother Zachariah said, *And God said, "I shall not retain Belial within my heart."*

A sly, wounded look came over Belial's face. "Of course you, too, my dear Brother Zachariah, have been cut off from the ones you love. We understand each other." And then he said something in a language that Sister Emilia did not recognize, almost spitting out the awful, hissing syllables.

"What is he saying?" she said. She thought that the room seemed to be growing hotter. The mirrors were blazing brighter.

He's speaking Abyssal, Brother Zachariah said calmly. *Nothing of any interest.*

"He's doing something," Sister Emilia hissed. "We have to stop him. Something is happening."

In all the mirrors, Belial was swelling up, the suit of skin bursting like the skin of a sausage. The mirror versions of Sister Emilia and Brother Zachariah were dwindling, shrinking and blackening as if scorched by the heat of Belial.

Knock, knock, Brother Zachariah said.

"What?" Sister Emilia said.

He said again, *Don't pay any attention to Belial. He thrives on it. It's not real. It's illusions. Nothing more. Demons won't kill those they owe a debt to. Knock, knock.*

"Who's there?" she said.

Spell.

Sister Emilia's throat was so dry she could barely speak at all. The pommel of her sword was blazingly hot, as if she had her hand in the heart of a forge. "Spell who?"

If you insist, Brother Zachariah said. *W-H-O.*

And when Sister Emilia understood the joke, it was so very ridiculous that she laughed in spite of herself. "That's terrible!" she said.

Brother Zachariah looked at her with his sealed-off face. He said, *You didn't ask me if Silent Brothers had a good sense of humor.*

Belial had stopped speaking Abyssal. He looked incredibly disappointed in them both. "This is no fun," he said.

What did you do with the adamas? Brother Zachariah said.

Belial reached down into the neck of his shirt and drew up a chain. Dangling on the end of it was an *adamas* half mask. Sister Emilia could see his skin go red and then grow raw and festering and yellow with pus where the mask touched him. And where he touched the mask, the metal flared up in coruscating ripples of turquoise, scarlet, viridian. But Belial's expression of proud indifference never changed. "I've been using it on behalf of your precious mundane folk," he said. "It strengthens my power as I strengthen its. Some of them want to be people other than themselves, and so I give them the illusion of that. Strong enough that they can fool others. Other people want to see something that they want, or that they've lost, or that they can't have, and I can do that, too. There was a young man the other day—a boy, really—he was to be married. But he was afraid. He wanted to know the worst things that might happen to him and the girl he loved, so that he could prepare for them and go on bravely. I hear he wasn't that brave after all."

"He put out his eyes," Sister Emilia said. "And what about Bill Doyle?"

"That one, I think, will have a remarkable life," Belial said. "Or else end up in a lunatic asylum. Care to wager which?"

There shouldn't be a Shadow Market here, Brother Zachariah said.

"There are many things that shouldn't be that are," Belial said. "And many things that aren't that might still be if you only want them enough. I'll admit, I hoped that the Shadow Market would provide better cover. Or at least a warning to me, when your kind showed up to spoil my fun. But you weren't distracted at all."

Sister Emilia will take the adamas, Brother Zachariah said. *And once you've given it to her, you will send the Market away because I ask it of you.*

"If I do so, will that cancel out the favor I owe you?" Belial said.

"He owes you a favor?" Sister Emilia said. She thought, *No wonder they stitch up the Silent Brothers' mouths. They have so many secrets.*

It will not, Brother Zachariah said to Belial. To Emilia, he said, *Yes, and that is why you need not be afraid of him. A demon cannot kill one it is indebted to.*

"I could kill her, though," Belial said. He took a step toward Sister Emilia, and she raised her sword, determined to make her death count.

But you won't, Brother Zachariah said calmly.

Belial raised an eyebrow. "I won't? Why not?"

Brother Zachariah said, *Because you find her interesting. I certainly find her so.*

Belial was silent. Then he nodded. "Here." He threw the mask at Sister Emilia, who let go of Brother Zachariah's hand to catch it. It was lighter than she would have expected. "I imagine they won't let you work it, though. Too worried I might have corrupted it in some way. And who is to say that I didn't?"

We're done, Brother Zachariah said. *Go from here and do not return.*

"Absolutely!" Belial said. "Only, about that favor. It pains me so to be in debt to you when I might be of some service. I wonder if there isn't a thing that I could offer you. For example, the *yin fen* in your blood. Do the Silent Brothers still not know what the cure might be?"

Brother Zachariah said nothing, but Sister Emilia could see how his knuckles grew white where his fist was clenched. At last he said, *Go on.*

"I might know a cure," Belial said. "Yes, I think I know a sure cure. You could be who you once were. You could be Jem again. Or."

Brother Zachariah said, *Or?*

Belial's long tongue flicked out, as if he was tasting the air and found it delicious. "Or I could tell you a thing you don't know. There are Herondales, not the ones you know, but of the same bloodline as your *parabatai*. They are in great danger, their lives hang by a thread, and they are closer to us as we stand here than you can imagine. I can tell you something of them and set you on the path to find them if that is what you choose. But you must choose. To aid them or else to be who you once were. To once more be the one who left behind those who loved him best. The one they still yearn for. You could be him again if that is what you choose. Choose, Brother Zachariah."

Brother Zachariah hesitated for a long moment.

In the mirrors around them, Emilia saw visions of what Belial was promising, of all that his cure would mean. The woman Brother Zachariah adored would not be alone. He would be with her, able to share her pain and to love her wholly once more. He could rush to the side of the friend he loved, see his friend's blue eyes shine like stars on a midsummer night as he beheld Brother Zachariah transformed. They could clasp hands with no shadow of grief or pain upon them, just once. They had been waiting all their lives for that moment, and feared it would never come.

In a hundred reflections, Brother Zachariah's eyes flew open, blind and silver with agony. His face twisted as if he were being forced to endure the most terrible pain or, worse, forced to turn from the most perfect bliss.

The real Brother Zachariah's eyes stayed closed. His face remained serene.

At last he said, *The Carstairs owe a life debt to the Herondales. That is my choice.*

Belial said, "Then here is what I will tell you about these lost Herondales. There is power in their blood, and there is great danger, too. They are in hiding from an enemy who is neither mortal nor demon. These pursuers are resourceful, and close on their heels, and they will kill them if they find them."

"But where are they?" Sister Emilia said.

Belial said, "The debt is not that great, my dear. And now it is paid."

Sister Emilia looked at Brother Zachariah, who shook his head. *Belial is what he is,* he said. *A fornicator, a miser, and a polluter of sanctuaries. A creator of illusions. If I had made the other choice, do you really think I would be better off?*

"How well we know each other!" Belial said. "We all play a role, and it would astonish you, I think, to know how helpful I am being. You think I have offered you only tricks and sleights, but truly I have extended the hand of friendship. Or do you think that I can simply draw these Herondales out of a hat like so many rabbits? As for you, Sister Emilia, I owe you no debt, but would do you a good turn. Unlike our acquaintance here, you have chosen the path that you are set on."

"I have," Sister Emilia said. All she had ever wanted was to make things. To shape seraph blades and be known as a master of the forge. Shadowhunters, it seemed to her, gloried in destruction. What she longed for was to be permitted to create.

"I could make it so that you were the greatest *adamas* worker the Adamant Citadel has ever seen. Your name would be spoken for generations."

In the mirrors, Sister Emilia saw the blades she could make. She saw how they were used in battle, how the ones who wielded them thanked the one who had made them. They blessed the name of Sister Emilia, and acolytes came to study with her, and they, too, blessed her name.

"No!" Sister Emilia said to her reflections. "I will be the greatest *adamas* worker the Adamant Citadel has ever seen, but it will not be because I accepted aid from you. It will be because of the work that I do with the aid of my sisters."

"Nuts!" Belial said. "I don't even know why I bother."

Brother Zachariah said, *Roland the Astonishing!*

And before Sister Emilia could ask him what he meant by that, he was running out of the maze. She could hear him knocking over mirror after mirror with his staff, in too much of a hurry to find his way out as they had found their way in. Or maybe he knew that all the magic was bound up to make the center hard to find, and that smashing things on the way out would work just fine.

"A little slow on the draw, that one," Belial said to Sister Emilia. "Anyhow, I ought to make tracks. See you around, girlie."

"Wait!" Sister Emilia said. "I have an offer to make you."

Because she could not stop thinking of what she had seen in Brother Zachariah's mirrors. How much he longed to be with his *parabatai* and with the girl who must have been the warlock Tessa Herondale.

"Go on," Belial said. "I'm listening."

"I know that the things you offer us aren't real," Sister Emilia said. "But perhaps the illusion of a thing that we can't have is better than nothing at all. I want you to give Brother Zachariah a vision. A few hours with the one he misses most."

"He loves the warlock girl," Belial said. "I could give her to him."

"No!" Sister Emilia said. "Warlocks endure. I believe one day he will have his hours with Tessa Herondale even if he does not dare to hope for it. But his *parabatai*, Will Herondale, is old and frail and drawing near the end of his life. I want you to give them both a span of time. Both of them in a time and place where they can be young and happy and together."

"And what will you give me in return?" Belial said.

"If I had agreed to your previous offer," Sister Emilia said, "I think that my name would have lived on in infamy. And even if I was one day celebrated for my work, still every blade that I made would have been tainted by the idea that you had had some part in my successes. Every victory would have been poisoned."

"You're not as stupid as most Shadowhunters," Belial said.

"Oh, stop trying to flatter me!" Sister Emilia said. "You're wearing a suit made of human skin. No one of any sense should care what you have to say. But you should care very much about what I say to you. And that is this. I promise you if you do not give Brother Zachariah and Will Herondale the thing that I am asking for them, my life's work will be to forge a blade that is capable of killing you. And I will go on making blades until one day I accomplish my goal. And I warn you, I am not only talented, I am single-minded. Feel free to ask my mother if you don't believe me."

Belial met her gaze. He blinked twice and then looked away. Sister Emilia could see, now, the way he saw her reflected in the remaining mirrors, and she quite liked, for once, how she looked.

"You are interesting," he said. "As Brother Zachariah said. But perhaps you are also dangerous. You're too small to make a suit. But a hat. You would make a fine trilby. And perhaps a pair of spats. Why shouldn't I kill you now?"

Sister Emilia stuck her chin out. She said, "Because you are bored. You are curious whether or not I will be good at my work. And if my swords fail those who wield them, you will find it good entertainment."

Belial said, "True. I will."

Emilia said, "Then our deal?"

"Done," Belial said. And was gone, leaving Sister Emilia in a room walled in mirrors, holding an *adamas* mask in one hand and in her other a sword that was quite remarkable and yet in no way the equal of the blades that she would make one day.

When she emerged onto the carnival thoroughfare, already many of the tents were gone or else simply abandoned. There were few people about, and those she saw looked dazed and dreamy, as if they had just woken up. The Mysterious Merchants' Bazaar was gone entirely, and there was not a single werewolf to be seen, although the cotton-candy machine was still spinning slowly, filaments of sugar floating in the air.

Brother Zachariah was standing in front of the empty stage where they had seen the magician and his faerie wife. "*We all play a role, and it would astonish you, I think, to know how helpful I am being,*" he said.

She realized he was quoting Belial. "I have no idea what that means," she said.

He waved his hand at the sign above the stage. ROLAND THE ASTONISHING.

"Role and," she said slowly. "It would astonish you."

Tricks and sleights. He offered me the hand of friendship. Sleight of hand. Magic tricks. I should have known sooner. I thought the magician had the look of my friend Will. But he and his wife have fled.

"You'll find them again," Sister Emilia said. "I feel quite sure."

They are Herondales, and they are in trouble, said Brother Zachariah. *So I will find them, because I must. And Belial did say something that has proved of some interest to my Brothers.*

"Go on," Sister Emilia said.

I am as I am, Brother Zachariah said. *A Silent Brother but not entirely of the Brotherhood, because for so long I was unwillingly dependent on* yin fen. *And now I am, not entirely wholeheartedly, a Silent Brother, so that I might remain alive in spite of the* yin fen *in my blood that should have killed me years ago. Brother Enoch and the others have long searched for a cure and found nothing. We had begun to think perhaps there was no cure. But Brother Enoch was extremely interested in the choice Belial offered me. He said he's already researching demonic cures associated with Belial.*

"Then if you were cured," Sister Emilia said, "you would choose not to be what you are?"

Brother Zachariah said, *Without hesitation. Though not without gratitude for what my Brothers in the Silent City have done for me. And you? Will you regret choosing a life in the Adamant Citadel?*

Sister Emilia said, "How can I know that? But no. I am being given an opportunity to become what I have always known I was meant to be. Come on. We've done what we were sent to do."

Not quite, Brother Zachariah said. *Tonight is a full moon, and we don't know whether or not the werewolves have gone back into the mountains. As long as there are mundanes here, we must wait and watch. The Praetor Lupus take a hard-line Prohibitionist stance, not to mention they crack down hard on eating mundanes, but they may still need assistance.*

"Seems a little harsh," Sister Emilia said. "The Prohibitionist stance. I get that eating people is wrong, generally."

Werewolves live by a harsh code, Brother Zachariah said. She could not tell, by looking at his face, whether or not he was joking. But she was fairly sure that he was.

He said, *Though now that you have passed your test, I know you must be anxious to return to the Adamant Citadel. I'm sorry to keep you here.*

He wasn't wrong. She longed with all her heart to go to the only place that had ever truly felt like home to her. And she knew, too, that some part of Brother Zachariah must dread returning to the Silent City. She had seen enough in the mirrors to know where his home and his heart was.

She said, "I'm not sorry to tarry here a little longer with you, Brother Zachariah. And I'm not sorry that I met you. If we never meet again, I will hope that one day a weapon made by my hand may yet prove useful to you in some way." Then she yawned. Iron Sisters, unlike Silent Brothers, required things like sleep and food.

Brother Zachariah hoisted himself up onto the edge of the stage and then patted the space beside him. *I'll keep watch. If you grow weary, sleep. No harm will come while I keep vigil.*

Sister Emilia said, "Brother Zachariah? If something strange happens tonight, if you should see something that you thought you would not see again, don't be alarmed. No harm will come of it."

What do you mean? Brother Zachariah said. *What did you and Belial discuss when I had gone?*

In the back of his mind, his Brothers murmured: *Be careful, be careful, be careful. Oh, be careful.*

Sister Emilia said, "Nothing of any great importance. But I think he is a little afraid of me now, and he should be. He offered me something so that I would not become his nemesis."

Tell me what you mean, Brother Zachariah said.

"I'll tell you later," Sister Emilia said firmly. "Right now I'm so tired I can barely talk at all."

Sister Emilia was hungry as well as tired, but she was so very tired she couldn't be bothered to eat. She would sleep first. She climbed up on the stage beside Brother Zachariah and took off her cloak and made it into a pillow. The evening was still warm, and if she grew cold, well, then she would wake up, and she and Brother Zachariah could keep watch together companionably.

She hoped that her brothers, now grown men all, were as kind and stouthearted as this man was. She fell asleep remembering how she and they had played at fighting before they were old enough to train, laughing and tumbling and vowing to be great heroes. Her dreams were very sweet, though she did not remember them in the morning when she woke.

Silent Brothers do not sleep as mortals do, but nevertheless Brother Zachariah, as he sat and watched and listened in the deserted carnival, felt as the night drew on that he was in a dream. Silent Brothers do not dream, and yet slowly the voices of Brother Enoch and the others in his head dissipated and blew away and were replaced by music. Not carnival music, but the sound of a *qinqin*. There should not have been a *qin-*

qin anywhere on the mountain above Chattanooga, and yet he heard it. Listening to the sound of it, he discovered that he was no longer Brother Zachariah at all. He was only Jem. He did not sit on a stage. Instead, he was perched on a tiled roof, and the sounds and smells and sights around him were all familiar ones. Not the Silent City. Not London. He was Jem again, and he was in the city where he had been born. Shanghai. Someone said, "Jem? Am I dreaming?"

Even before he turned his head, Jem knew who would be sitting there beside him. "Will?" he said.

And it was Will. Not Will old and tired and wasted as Jem had last seen him, and not even Will as he had been when they'd first met Tessa Gray. No, this was Will as he had been in the first few years when they had lived and trained together in the London Institute. As he had been when they made their oath and became *parabatai*. Thinking this, Jem looked at his shoulder, where his *parabatai* rune had been inscribed. The flesh there was unmarked. He saw that Will was doing the same thing, looking under his collar for the rune on his chest.

Jem said, "How is this possible?"

Will said, "This is the time between when we had pledged to become *parabatai* and when we went through the ritual. Look. See the scar here?" He showed Jem a distinctive mark on his wrist.

"You got that from an Iblis demon," Jem said. "I remember. It was two nights after we had decided. It was the first fight we had once we'd made up our minds."

"So that is *when* we are," Will said. "But what I don't know is *where* we are. Or how this is happening."

"I think," Jem said, "that a friend has made a bargain for me. I think that we are here together because the demon Belial is afraid of her, and she asked this for me. Because I would not ask for myself."

"Belial!" Will said. "Well, if he's afraid of this friend of yours, I hope I never meet her."

"I wish you could," Jem said. "But let's not waste whatever time we have talking about people you don't have any interest in. You may not know where we are, but I do. And I am afraid that the span of time we have together may not be long."

"That has always been the case with us," Will said. "But let us be grateful to your terrifying friend, because however long we have, here we are together and I see no sign of *yin fen* on you, and we are in possession of the knowledge that there was never any curse on me. For however long, there is no shadow on us."

"There is no shadow," Jem agreed. "And we are in a place that I long wished to go with you. This is Shanghai, where I was born. Remember when we used to talk about traveling here together? There were so many places I wanted to show you."

"I remember you thought very highly of a temple or two," Will said. "You promised me gardens, although why you think I care for gardens, I don't know. And there were some vistas or famous rock formations or things."

"Forget the rock formations," Jem said. "There's a dumpling place down the street, and I haven't eaten human food in half a century. Let's go see who can eat the most dumplings in the shortest amount of time. And duck! You really ought to try pressed duck! It's a great delicacy."

Jem looked at Will, suppressing a smile. His friend glared back, but at last neither of them could hold back their laughter. Will said, "There is nothing so sweet as feasting upon the bones of my enemies. Especially with you at my side."

There was a lightness in Jem's chest that he realized, finally, was joy. He saw that joy mirrored in his *parabatai*'s face. The face of the one you love is the best mirror of all. It shows you your own happiness and your own pain and it helps you to bear both, because to bear either alone is to be overwhelmed by the flood.

Jem stood up and held out his hand to Will. Without realizing it, he held his breath. Perhaps this was a dream after all, and when Jem touched him Will would vanish away again. But Will's hand was warm and solid and strong, and Jem drew him up easily. Together they began to run lightly over the tiles of the roof.

The night was very beautiful and warm, and they were both young.

A Deeper Love

By Cassandra Clare and Maureen Johnson

London, December 29, 1940

"I think first," Catarina said, "lemon cake. Oh, lemons. I think I miss them most."

Catarina Loss and Tessa Gray were walking down Ludgate Hill, just passing the Old Bailey. This was a game they sometimes played: What will you eat first when this war is over? Of all the terrible things that were going on, sometimes the most ordinary ran the deepest. Food was rationed, and the rations were small—an ounce of cheese, four thin pieces of bacon, and one egg a week. Everything came in tiny amounts. Some things simply went away, like lemons. There were oranges sometimes—Tessa saw them at the fruit-and-veg market— but they were only for children, who could have one each. The nurses were fed at the hospital, but the portions were always tiny, and never enough to keep up with all the work they performed. Tessa was lucky to have the strength she did. It was not all the physical strength of a Shadowhunter, but some trace of angelic endurance lingered within her and sustained her; she had no idea how the mundane nurses kept up.

"Or a banana," Catarina said. "I never liked them much

before, but now that they are gone, I find myself craving them. That's always the way, isn't it?"

Catarina Loss did not care about food. She barely ate at all. But she was making conversation as they walked down the street. This was what you did—you pretended life was normal, even as death rained from above. It was the London spirit. You kept to your routines as much as you could, even if you slept in a Tube station at night for shelter, or you returned home to find the neighbor's house or yours was no longer there. Businesses tried to stay open, even if all the glass blew out of the windows or a bomb went through the roof. Some would put out signs that said, MORE OPEN THAN USUAL.

You carried on. You talked about bananas and lemons.

At this point in December, London was at its darkest. The sun started going down just after three in the afternoon. Because of the air raids, London was under blackout orders every night. Blackout curtains blocked light from every window. Streetlamps were turned off. Cars dimmed their lights. People walked the streets carrying torches to find their way through the velvety darkness. All of London was shade and corner and nook, every alley blind, every wall a dark blank. It made the city mysterious and mournful.

To Tessa, it felt like London itself grieved for her Will, felt his loss, turned out every light.

Tessa Gray had not particularly enjoyed Christmas this year. It was difficult to enjoy things with the Germans raining bombs overhead whenever the whim suited them. The Blitz, as it was called, was designed to bring terror to London, to force the city to its knees. There were deadly bombs that could crush a home, leaving a pile of smoking rubble where children once slept and families laughed together. In the mornings, you would see walls missing and the inner workings of houses, exposed like a doll's house, scraps of cloth flapping against broken brick, toys and books scattered in piles of rubble. More than once she saw a bathtub hanging off the side of what remained of a house. Extraordinary things would happen, like the house where the chimney fell, smashing through the kitchen table where a family ate, shattering it but harming no one. Buses would be upturned. Rubble would fall, instantly killing one family member, leaving the other stunned and unscathed. It was a matter of chance, of inches.

There was nothing worse than being left alone, the one you loved ripped from you.

"Did you have a good visit this afternoon?" Catarina asked.

"The younger generation are still trying to talk me into leaving," Tessa replied, stepping around a hole in the pavement where part of it had been blown away. "They think I should go to New York."

"They're your children," Catarina said gently. "They want what's best for you. They don't understand."

When Will died, Tessa had known there could be no place for her among the Shadowhunters. For a time it had seemed as if there was no place for her in all the world, with so much of her heart in the cold ground. Then Magnus Bane had taken Tessa into his home when she was almost mad with grief, and when she slowly emerged, Magnus's friends Catarina Loss and Ragnor Fell encircled her.

No one understood the pain of being immortal save another immortal. She could only be grateful they had taken her in.

It was Catarina who introduced Tessa to nursing when the

war broke out. Catarina had always been a healer: of Nephilim, of Downworlders, of humans. Wherever she was needed, she went. She had nursed in the last Great War, only twenty years before, the war that was never supposed to happen again. The two of them had taken a small flat off Farringdon Street, close to the London Institute and to St. Bart's Hospital. It was not as luxurious as her previous homes—just a small, second-story walk-up with a shared bath in the hall. It was easier this way, and cozier. Tessa and Catarina shared one small bedroom, hanging a sheet down the middle for privacy. They often worked at night and slept during the day. At least the raids were only at night now—no more sirens and planes and bombs and anti-aircraft guns at noon.

The war had caused increased demonic activity—as all wars did, demons taking advantage of chaos caused by battle—which was almost overwhelming the Shadowhunters. Though it was a terrible thought to have, Tessa regarded the war as a kind of personal blessing. Here, she could be useful. One of the good things about being a nurse was that there was always something that needed doing. Always. Constant activity kept grief at bay because there was no time to think. Going to New York, sitting in safety, would be hellish. There would be nothing to do but think about her family. She did not know how to do this, how to go on agelessly as her descendants grew older than her.

She looked up at the great dome of St. Paul's Cathedral, lording over the city exactly as it had done for hundreds of years. How did it feel, seeing its city below, its sprawling child, blown to pieces?

"Tessa?" Catarina said.

"I'm fine," Tessa replied.

At that moment, a scream broke out all over the city—the air-raid siren. Moments later came the humming noise. It sounded like the approach of an army of angry bees. The Luftwaffe was overhead. The bombs would be falling soon.

"I thought we might be spared for a few more days," Catarina said grimly. "It was so nice to only have two air raids this week. I suppose even the Luftwaffe wants to celebrate the holiday."

The two quickened their steps. Then it came—that uncanny sound. As the bombs fell, they whistled. Tessa and Catarina stopped. The whistling was just above them, all around. The whistling was not the problem—the problem was when it stopped. The silence meant the bombs were less than a hundred feet overhead. That was when you waited. Were you going to be next? Where could you go when death was silent and came from the sky?

There was a clanking and a hissing sound up ahead, and the street was suddenly illuminated with spitting, phosphorescent light.

"Incendiaries," Catarina said.

Tessa and Catarina rushed forward. The incendiary bombs were canisters that looked harmless enough up close, similar to a long thermal flask. When they hit the ground, they spread fire. They were being scattered all up and down the street by the planes, highlighting the road and spitting flames at the buildings. The fire wardens began running from all directions, dampening the incendiaries as quickly as possible. Catarina bent down to one. Tessa saw a blue flash; then the bomb extinguished. Tessa ran up to another and stamped at the sparks until a fire warden poured a bucket of water over it. But now there were hundreds all over the road.

"Must get on," Catarina said. "It looks to be a long one tonight."

Passing Londoners tipped their hats. They saw what Tessa and Catarina wanted them to see—just two brave young nurses headed to the hospital, not two immortal beings trying to stem an endless tide of suffering.

On the other side of the Thames, a figure was making its way through the dark beneath the viaduct, past where the normally flourishing Borough Market was held by day. Usually, this place was heaving with activity and scraps of the day's market. Tonight, everything was muted and there was barely anything remaining on the ground. Every old cabbage and bruised piece of fruit had been plucked up by hungry people. The blackout curtains, lack of streetlights, and absence of mundanes on the streets made this corner of London foreboding. But the cloaked figure walked without hesitation, even as the air-raid siren ripped through the night. His destination was just around the corner.

Even with the war, the Shadow Market went on, though it was fragmentary. Like the mundanes with their ration cards, their limited supplies of food, of clothing, and even of bathwater, things here were in short supply. The old-book stalls had been picked through. Instead of hundreds of potions and powders, only a dozen or so graced the vendors' tables. The sparkle and the fire were nothing compared to the flames that raged on the opposite bank or the machines that dropped death from the sky, so there seemed little point in putting on light shows. The children still ran about—the young werewolves, the street children and orphans who had been Turned in the dark corners of the blackout and now roamed, seeking nourishment and parental guidance. A small vampire, Turned far too young, trailed alongside Brother Zachariah, pulling on his cloak for fun. Zachariah did not disturb him. The child looked lonely and dirty, and if it pleased him to trail a Silent Brother, then Zachariah would allow it.

"What are you?" said the little boy.

A kind of Shadowhunter, Brother Zachariah replied.

"Did you come to kill us? I heard 'at's what they do."

No. That is not what we do. Where is your family?

"Gone," the little boy said. "A bomb dropped on us, and my master came and got me."

It had been all too easy to pluck these little ones out of the wreckage of a home, take them by the hand to some pitch-black alley, and Turn them. Demon activity too was at an all-time high. After all, who could tell whether that torn limb was from someone killed by a bomb or someone ripped apart by a demon? Did it make a difference? Mundanes had their own demonic ways.

A crowd of other vampire children ran past, and the little boy ran off with them. The sky roared, thick with the sound of planes. Brother Zachariah listened to the noise of the bombing with a musician's ear. The bombs whistled when they dropped, but there was that strange punctuating silence as they neared the earth. Silences in music were as important as sound. In this case, the silences told so much of the story to come. Tonight, the bombs were falling on the other side of the river like rain—a thundering symphony with too many notes. Those bombs would be falling near the Institute, near St. Bart's Hospital, where Tessa worked. Fear for her ran through Zachariah, cold as the river cutting across the city. In these empty days since

Will's death, emotion was a rare visitor for him, but when it came to Tessa, feeling always bloomed.

"Bad one tonight," said a faerie woman with silver scaled skin who sold enchanted toy toads. They leaped about on her table, with protruding golden tongues. "Like a toad?"

She pointed at one of the toy toads. It turned blue, then red, then green, then flipped on its back and spun, before turning into a stone. Then it burst forth into toad form again and the cycle continued.

No, thank you, Zachariah said.

He turned to keep moving, but the woman spoke again.

"He's waiting for you," she said.

Who is he?

"The one you have come to meet."

For months now, he had been slowly trailing a series of contacts through the faerie world, trying to find out about the lost Herondales he had learned of at the Shadow Market and carnival in Tennessee. He had not come specifically to meet anyone tonight—he had a number of contacts who provided information as they came by it. But someone had come to meet him.

Thank you, he said politely. *Where am I to go?*

"The King's Head Yard," she said, smiling widely. Her teeth were small and pointed.

Brother Zachariah nodded. The King's Head Yard was a nearby alley—a horseshoe-shaped offshoot of Borough High Street. It was accessed through an arch between the buildings. As he approached it, he heard the sound of planes overhead, then the whistling of a payload being dropped.

Nothing to do but keep going. Zachariah crossed under the archway partway, then stopped.

I am here, he said to the darkness.

"Shadowhunter," a voice said.

From the bend at the end of the yard, a figure emerged. It was a faerie, and clearly one of the Court. He was extremely tall and almost human in appearance but for his wings, which were brown and white and spread wide, almost touching the opposite walls.

I understand you wish to speak to me, Brother Zachariah said politely.

The faerie stepped closer, and Zachariah could see a copper mask in the form of a hawk covering the top half of his face.

"You have been interfering," the faerie said.

In what, precisely? Zachariah inquired. He did not move back, but he tightened his grip on his staff.

"Things that do not concern you."

I have been making inquiries about a lost Shadowhunter family. That is very much something that concerns me.

"You come to my brethren. You ask the fey."

This was true. Since his encounter with Belial at the carnival in Tennessee, Brother Zachariah had been pursuing many leads in Faerie. He had seen, after all, a Herondale descendant with a faerie wife and child. They had fled, but it had not been him they feared. Whatever danger threatened the lost Herondale, Zachariah had learned it came from Faerie.

"What is it you know?" the faerie asked, stepping forward.

I would advise you not to come closer.

"You have no idea of the danger of what you seek. This is Faerie business. Cease your meddling in that which affects our Lands and our Lands alone."

I repeat, Zachariah said calmly, though his grip on the staff was firm now, *I ask of Shadowhunters. That is very much my business.*

"Then you do so at your peril."

A blade flashed in the faerie's hand. He swung at Zachariah, who moved at once, rolling to the ground and coming up next to the faerie, striking his arm and knocking the sword free.

The whistling of the bombs had stopped. That meant they were right overhead.

Then, they fell. Three of them clanked down on the stones at the opening of the archway and began spitting their phosphorescent flames. This distracted the faerie for just a moment, and Zachariah took the opportunity to dash around the horseshoe and out the other side. He had no desire to continue this fight, to cause problems between the Silent Brothers and the fey. Zachariah had no idea why the faerie had become so violent. Hopefully he would simply return from whence he came. Zachariah slipped onto the Borough High Street, dodging the falling cylinders. But he had barely begun his flight when the faerie was behind him. Zachariah spun, his staff ready.

I have no quarrel with you. Let us go our separate ways.

Below the hawk mask, the faerie's teeth were gritted. He sliced out with his sword, ripping the air in front of Brother Zachariah, slashing his cloak. Zachariah leaped and spun, his staff wheeling through the air to slam against the sword. As they fought, the canisters landed closer and closer, coughing fire. Neither flinched.

Brother Zachariah took care not to injure the faerie, only to block the attack. His purpose must remain secret, but the faerie was coming with increasing force. He slashed upward with his sword, meaning to cut Zachariah's throat—and Zachariah smashed it from his hands, sending it flying across the road.

Let us finish with this. Call it a fair fight ended. Walk away.

The faerie was out of breath. Blood trickled from a wound at his temple.

"As you wish," he said. "But take my warning."

He turned to go. Brother Zachariah loosened his grip on his staff for just a moment. The faerie turned back, a short blade in his hand, aimed at Zachariah's heart. With the speed of the Silent Brothers he whirled away, but he could not move fast enough. The blade sank deep into his shoulder and came out the other side.

The pain. The wound immediately began to hiss as if acid was dissolving Zachariah's flesh. Pain and numbness ran down his arm, causing him to drop his staff. He staggered back, and the faerie retrieved his sword and advanced toward him.

"You have interfered with the fey for the last time, Gregori," he said. "Our people are our people, and our enemies, our enemies. They will never be yours!"

The incendiaries landed around them now, clanking loudly against pavement and cobblestone, flashing light and licking flames at the buildings. Zachariah tried to get away, but his strength was fading. He could not run—he could only stagger drunkenly. This was no normal wound. There was poison flooding his body. The faerie was coming at him, and he would not get away.

No. Not without seeing Tessa one more time.

He looked down and saw one of the incendiaries that had fallen from the sky. This one had not detonated.

Brother Zachariah used the last of his strength to spin around, swinging out with the canister. Small bombs were still falling. Several more dropped nearby. The canister flew through the air and struck the faerie in the chest. It cracked apart, and the faerie shrieked as the iron inside was released. Zachariah fell to his knees as the iron flame burned.

The hospital was rumbling.

At St. Bart's, the upper floors of the hospital were considered too unsafe to use. The activity was all on the lower level and in the basement, where doctors and nurses ran to attend the injured and sick. The fire wardens were being brought in, their skin covered in soot, gasping for air. There were injuries from the attacks—the burns, the crushings, the people cut through with exploding glass or struck by debris. Plus all the normal business of London went on—people still had babies and became ill and had normal accidents. But the war multiplied incidents. People fell or crashed in the dark. There were heart attacks as bombs came down. There were so many people who needed help.

From the moment they arrived, Catarina and Tessa ran from one end of the hospital to the other, tending to the injured as they came in, fetching supplies, carrying bloodied bowls of water, wrapping and removing bandages. Being a Shadowhunter, Tessa could easily cope with some of the grislier aspects of the job, like the fact that no matter how hard you tried to keep your apron clean, you would be covered in blood and grime within minutes. No amount of washing got it out. No sooner would you scrub it off your arms than another patient would come in and your skin would be covered again. Through it all, the nurses strove to maintain an air of calm competence. You moved quickly but not hastily. You spoke loudly when you needed assistance, but you never screamed.

Tessa was stationed by the door, directing the orderlies as they brought in a dozen new patients. They were bringing in groups of fire wardens now, some walking wounded, others on stretchers.

"Over there," Tessa said as the orderlies carried in burn victims. "To Sister Loss."

"I've got one asking for you, Sister," said the orderly, setting down a stretcher with a figure on it wrapped tight in a gray blanket.

"Coming," Tessa said. She hurried to the stretcher and bent down. The blanket was pulled partway over the man's face.

"You're all right," Tessa said, pulling back the blanket. "You're all right now. You're at hospital. You're here at St. Bart's. . . ."

It took her a moment to realize what she was seeing. The marks on his skin were not all wounds. And his face, though covered in soot and streaked with blood, was more familiar to her than her own.

Tessa, Jem said, the echo deep inside her head like the memory of a bell ringing.

Then he went limp.

"Jem!" It couldn't be. She seized his hand, hoping she was dreaming—that the war had addled her sense of reality completely. But the slim, scarred hand in hers was familiar, even limp and without strength. This was Jem, her Jem, dressed in the bone-colored robes of a Silent Brother, the marks on his neck pulsing as his heart pumped furiously. His skin burned under her touch.

"He's in a bad way," the orderly said. "I'll fetch the doctor."

"No," Tessa said quickly. "Leave him with me."

Jem was glamoured, but he could not be examined. No mundane doctor could do anything about his injuries, and they would be shocked at his runes, his scars, even his blood.

She tore away the parchment robes. It took her only a

moment to find the source of the trauma—a massive wound in his shoulder that went clean through. The wound was black with a silvery edge, and his tunic was saturated with blood all the way down to his waist. Tessa scanned the hallway. There were so many people, she could not immediately see Catarina. She could not scream.

"Jem," she said into his ear. "I am here. I am getting help."

She stood up, as calmly as she could, and hastily made her way through the chaos of the hall, her heart beating so fast she felt like it might come up her throat and through her mouth. She found Catarina working on a burned man, her hands on his wounds. Only Tessa could see the snow-white glow emanating from under the blanket as she worked.

"Sister Loss," she said, trying to control her voice. "I need you at once."

"Just a moment," Catarina said.

"It cannot wait."

Catarina looked over her shoulder. Then the glow stopped. "You should feel better in a moment," she said to the man. "One of the other sisters will be over very soon."

"I feel better already," the man said, touching his arm in wonder.

Tessa hurried Catarina back to Jem. Catarina, seeing Tessa's taut expression, asked no questions; she only bent down and peeled the blanket back.

She looked up at Tessa. "A Shadowhunter?" Catarina said in a low voice. "Here?"

"Quickly," Tessa said. "Help me move him."

Tessa took one end of the stretcher and Catarina the other, and they moved Jem down the hallway. There was another explosion, closer. The building pulsed from the impact. The lights swung and went out for a moment, causing cries of alarm and confusion. Tessa froze in place, assuring herself that the ceiling wasn't about to come down and bury them all. After a moment, the lights came back on, and movement continued.

"Come on," Tessa said.

There was a small room at the end of the hall that was used for the nurses' tea breaks and naps, or when they could not return home because of bombings. They set Jem's stretcher gently on the empty cot on the side of the room. Jem was lying quietly, his features still, his breathing jagged. The color was draining from his skin.

"Hold the light," Catarina said. "I need to examine this."

Tessa pulled a witchlight from her pocket. It was safer and more reliable than the electric lights, but she could only use it in private. Catarina grabbed a pair of shears and cut away the cloth around the tunic to expose the wound. The veins on Jem's chest and his arm had turned black.

"What is that?" Tessa said, her voice shaking. "It looks very bad."

"I haven't seen this in a long time," Catarina said. "I think it's a cataplasm."

"What is that?"

"Nothing good," Catarina said. "Be patient."

She must be mad, Tessa thought. Be patient? How could she be patient? This was Jem, not some nameless patient under a gray blanket.

But every nameless patient was precious to someone. She forced herself to breathe more deeply.

"Take his hand," Catarina said. "It will work better if you

do it. Think of him, who he is to you. Give him your strength."

Tessa had practiced a small amount of warlock magic before, though she was not advanced. As Catarina watched, Tessa took Jem's slender hand in her own. She curled her fingers around his, his violinist's fingers, remembering the care with which he had played. The time he had composed for her. His voice echoed in her heart.

People still use the expression "zhi yin" to mean "close friends" or "soul mates," but what it really means is "understanding music." When I played, you saw what I saw. You understand my music.

Tessa smelled burned sugar. She felt Jem's lips hot against hers, the carpet underneath them, his arms holding her against his heart. *Oh, my Jem.*

His body surged against the stretcher, his back arching. He gasped, and the sound sent a shock through Tessa. Jem had been silent so long.

"Can you hear us?" Catarina asked.

I—can, came the halting reply in Tessa's mind.

"You need the Silent Brothers," Catarina said.

I cannot go to my Brothers with this.

"If you do not go to them, you will die," Catarina said.

The words hit Tessa like a blow.

It is not possible for me to go to the Bone City like this. I came here hoping you might be able to help.

"This is no time for pride," Catarina said sternly.

It is not pride, Jem said. Tessa knew this was the truth; he was the least proud person she had ever known.

"Jem!" Tessa begged. "You must go!"

Catarina started. "This is James Carstairs?" she asked.

Of course Catarina knew the name of Will Herondale's

parabatai, though she had never met him. She did not understand all that had passed between Tessa and Jem. She did not know that they had been engaged to be married. That before there was a Tessa and Will, there had been a Tessa and Jem. Tessa did not speak of these things because of Will, and then because of the absence of Will.

I have come here because it is the only place I can go, Jem said. *To speak the truth to the Brothers would be to endanger another life than mine. I will not do it.*

Tessa looked to Catarina in desperation. "He means it," she said. "He will never seek help if it means someone else will be hurt. Catarina—he cannot die. He *cannot die*."

Catarina inhaled sharply and opened the door a crack to peer into the hall.

"We will need to get him back to the flat," she said. "I can't work on him here. I don't have what I need. We will need to move quickly."

Tessa seized hold of Jem's stretcher. She understood the complications involved. They were nurses, in charge of many sick people who would be pouring in during the attack. The city was being bombed. It was on fire. Getting home was not a simple matter.

But it was what they were going to do.

The city they stepped back out into was not the same one that it had been only an hour before. The air was so hot that breathing burned the lungs. A high wall of orange jumped out of the buildings around them, and the silhouette of St. Paul's stood out in intense relief. The scene was at once terrifying and almost beautiful, like a dream image from Blake, a poet her son

James had always loved. *On what wings dare he aspire? What the hand dare seize the fire?*

But there was no time to think of things like London burning. There were two ambulances right outside on the street. Next to one, a driver was having a cigarette and talking to a fire warden.

"Charlie!" Catarina called.

The man tossed his cigarette aside and came running over.

"We need your help," she said. "This man has an infection. We can't keep him in the ward here."

"You need me to take him to St. Thomas', Sister? The going will be rough. We've got fires in almost every street."

"We can't make it that far," Catarina said. "We've got to move him quickly. Our flat is just on Farringdon Street. That will have to do for now."

"All right, Sister. Let's get him in the ambulance."

He opened the back and assisted them in getting Jem inside.

"I'll be back in one moment," Catarina said to them. "I just need to get a few supplies."

She dashed back into the hospital. Tessa climbed into the back with Jem, and Charlie got into the driver's seat.

"Don't usually take patients to nurses' flats," Charlie said, "but needs must when the devil drives. Sister Loss always looks after them. When my Mabel was having our second, she had a terrible spell. I thought we was going to lose them both. Sister Loss, bless her. She saved them both. I wouldn't have Mabel or my Eddie without them. Whatever she needs."

Tessa had heard many stories like this. Catarina was both a warlock and a mundane nurse with over a hundred years of experience. She had nursed in the last Great War. Old soldiers were always coming up to her and saying how she was "the spitting image of that nurse who saved me in the last one." But, of course, she couldn't be. That was twenty years ago, and Catarina was still so young. Catarina stood out to them because of her dark skin. They did not see a blue woman with white hair—they saw a nurse from the West Indies. She had faced considerable prejudice, but it was clear that not only was Catarina a good nurse, she was the *best* nurse in all of London. Anyone who got Catarina as a nurse was considered lucky. Even the most miserable bigot desired to live, and Catarina nursed all who came to her with equanimity. She could not save them all, but there were always a few, at least one a day, who survived something unsurvivable because Sister Loss was the one at their side. Some called her the Angel of St. Bart's.

Jem stirred and groaned lightly.

"Don't you worry, mate," Charlie called back to him. "Best nurses in the city, this lot. You couldn't be in safer hands."

Jem tried to smile—but instead he shuddered, and blood trickled from the side of his mouth. Tessa immediately wiped it away with the edge of her cloak and leaned close to him.

"You hold on, James Carstairs," she said, trying to sound brave. She gripped his hand in hers. She had forgotten how wonderful it was to hold Jem's hands—his long, graceful hands, the ones that could produce such beautiful music from the violin.

"Jem," she whispered, leaning low, "you must hold on. You must. Will needs you to. I need you to."

Jem's hand tightened on hers.

Catarina came running out of the hospital carrying a small canvas bag. She leaped into the back of the ambulance, slamming the doors behind her and snapping Tessa back to the present.

"Go, Charlie," she said.

Charlie shifted the ambulance into gear, and they started forward. Overhead, the drone of the Luftwaffe was back, like the hum of an army of bees. Catarina immediately scooted next to Jem and passed Tessa a bandage to unwind.

The ambulance juddered, and Jem was jolted on his stretcher. Tessa tented herself over him to keep him in place.

"Catarina," Tessa said, "you said this was a cataplasm. What does that mean?"

"It's a rare belladonna concentrate with demon poison added in to it," Catarina said quietly. "Until I can get the antidote, we need to try to keep it from spreading in his bloodstream, or at least slow it down. We're going to tie some tourniquets, start cutting off blood flow."

This sounded incredibly dangerous. By tying off the limbs, they could be risking their loss. But Catarina knew what she was doing.

"This will not be comfortable," Catarina said, unwinding a bandage, "but it will help. Hold him."

Tessa pressed her body down on Jem a bit more as Catarina looped the bandage around the injured arm and shoulder. She made a knot, then grabbed the ends of the bandages and pulled tight. Jem arched against Tessa's chest.

"You're all right, Jem," she said. "You're all right. We're here. I'm here. It's me. Tessa. It's me."

Tessa, he said. The word came out like a question. He writhed as Catarina wound the bandage tightly around the shoulder and arm. A mundane would not have been able to withstand it; Jem was barely able to. Sweat broke out all over his face.

"It's going to be rough going, Sisters," Charlie called back.

"They're trying to burn down St. Paul's, the bastards. I'm going to have to go around the long way. It's fires everywhere."

Charlie did not exaggerate. In front of them was a view of solid orange against the black silhouettes of burning buildings. The fires were so high that it was like there was a sun rising up from the earth, dragging day out of the ground. As they drove on, it was like they were pressing into a solid wall of heat. The wind had quickened, and now fire was meeting fire, creating walls instead of pockets. The air shimmered and cooked. Several times they turned down streets that no longer seemed to be there anymore.

"It's no good this way either," Charlie said, turning the ambulance again. "I'll have to try another way."

Then came the sharp whistling in the air. This time the pitch was different. These were not the incendiary bombs—these were the large explosives. After the fires, the idea was to kill. Charlie stopped the ambulance and craned his head to look up to see where the bomb was likely to land. They all froze, listening to the whistle go quiet.

It was a long moment. Then it came. The impact was at the other end of the street, sending the shock wave down the road and a spray of rubble into the air. Charlie started on again.

"Bastards," he said under his breath. "Bloody bastards. You all right there, Sisters?"

"We're fine," Catarina said. She had both hands on Jem's shoulder, and there was a low blue glow around the bandages. She was holding it back, whatever it was that was going through Jem's body.

They had just made another turn when there was another whistle and another silence. They stopped again. The impact was to their right this time, down at the next intersection. The ambulance rocked as the corner of a building was blown away. The ground shook. Charlie turned the ambulance away from it.

"Not going to get through this way," he said. "I'll try down Shoe Lane."

The ambulance turned once more. On the stretcher, Jem had stopped moving. Tessa could not tell if the pulsing heat was coming from the air or from Jem's body. There was fire on both sides of the street here, but the path looked almost clear to get through. There were fire wardens in the road, shooting water into a burning warehouse. Suddenly there was a creaking sound. The fire began to arc over the road.

"Blimey," Charlie said. "Hang on tight, Sisters."

The ambulance ground into reverse and started speeding backward down the alley. Tessa heard a crackling noise—uncanny, almost merry—a great tinkling. Then, all at once, the bricks of the building exploded and the building tumbled down into a mass of fire and rubble, the flames blowing up in a mighty roar. The men with the hose vanished.

"God almighty," Charlie said, grinding the ambulance to a halt. He jumped out of the driver's seat and started running for the men, two of whom were stumbling out of the flames. Catarina looked up and out the windscreen.

"Those men," she said. "The building's come down on them."

You must help them, Jem said.

Catarina looked between Jem and Tessa for a moment. Tessa felt herself full of an unbearable anxiety. She had to get Jem to safety, and yet, in front of them, men were being consumed in flame.

"I will be quick," Catarina said, and Tessa nodded.

Alone in the ambulance, Tessa looked down at Jem.

If they need you, then you must go, Jem said.

"They need Catarina," Tessa said. "You need me, and I need you. I do not leave you. No matter what happens, I do not leave you."

The ambulance was heating up like an oven, trapped as it was between multiple fires. There was no water to cool Jem's brow, so Tessa mopped it and fanned it with her hand.

After a minute, Catarina opened the back of the ambulance. She was covered in soot and water.

"I have done what I can," she said. "They will live now, as long as they reach the hospital. Charlie will have to take the ambulance."

Her eyes reflected her pain.

Yes, Jem said. Somehow he had found enough strength to rise on his elbows. *You must get them to safety. I am a Shadowhunter. I am stronger than those men.*

He had always been strong. It was not because he was a Shadowhunter. It was because he had a will fierce as starlight, burning in darkness and refusing to be put out.

Charlie brought the wounded fire wardens over, carrying one over his shoulder.

"You'll be all right, Sisters?" he said. "You can ride back with me?"

"No," Catarina said, climbing inside to help Tessa get Jem to his feet. Tessa placed herself under Jem's wounded shoulder. He winced from the movement. It was clear Jem couldn't really walk but had decided that he would do it anyway. He got his body into a standing position through sheer will. Catarina hurried to prop him up on the other side, and Tessa used her full strength to support him completely. It was strange, feeling Jem's body against hers after so long. They got out of the lane and back onto the road.

Lovely night for a walk, Jem said, clearly trying to cheer her. He was sweating all over and could no longer hold up his head. His legs had gone limp. He was like a marionette with the strings gone slack.

The buildings all around were on fire as well, but the fire was still contained inside. Tessa was covered in sweat, and the temperature was cooking them. The air was swollen with heat, and every mouthful of air scorched its way down her throat. It felt like when she first learned to change herself: the exquisite, strange pain.

The street was narrowing now to the point where they could barely walk three abreast. Catarina's and Tessa's sides scraped the hot walls. Jem's feet dragged along the ground, no longer able to take any steps. When they emerged onto Fleet Street, Tessa gasped in the relatively cool air. The sweat on her face was chilled for a moment.

"Come," Catarina said, leading them toward a bench. "Let's get him down for a moment."

They gingerly rested Jem on the empty bench. His skin was slick with sweat. Catarina pulled his shirt open to expose his chest and cool him, and Tessa could see the runes of the Silent Brothers on his skin and his veins throbbing in his throat.

"I don't know how much farther we can get him in this state," Catarina said. "The effort is too much."

Once on the bench, Jem's limbs began to jerk and twitch as the poison moved through his body once more. Catarina set to work on him again, putting her hands on the wound. Tessa scanned the road. She made out a large shadow coming in their direction, with two dimmed lights like heavily lidded eyes.

A bus. A great red double-decker London bus was making its way through the night, because nothing stopped the London buses, not even a war. They were not at a stop, but Tessa jumped into the road and waved it down. The driver opened the door and called out.

"You sisters all right?" he said. "Your friend, 'e doesn't look so good."

"He's injured," Catarina said.

"Then you get yourselves inside, Sisters," the driver said, shutting the door after they had done so, dragging Jem between them. "You've got London's best private ambulance at your service. Do you want to go to St. Bart's?"

"We've come from there. It's full. We're taking him home to care for him, and we need to go quickly."

"Then give me the address, and that's where we'll go."

Catarina shouted their address over the sound of another, slightly more distant explosion, and they got Jem over to a seat. It was instantly clear that he would not be able to hold himself sitting up, as he was too exhausted from the effort of trying to walk. They rested him on the ample floor of the bus and sat next to him on either side.

Only in London, Jem said, smiling weakly, *would a bus keep making its rounds during a massive bombing.*

"Keep calm and carry on," Catarina said, feeling Jem's pulse. "There now. We'll be at the flat in no time."

Tessa could tell from the way Catarina was becoming more and more chipper in tone that things were getting worse quickly.

The bus could not go at a high speed—it was still a London

bus on a dark night during an air raid—but it was going faster than any bus she had ever encountered. Tessa had no illusions about the safety of the bus. She had seen one of these flipped over completely after a hit, lying in the road like an elephant on its back. But they were moving, and Jem was resting on the floor. Tessa looked at the advertisements on the walls—happy images of people using Bisto gravy next to posters telling people to get their children out of London for safety.

London would not give up, and neither would Tessa.

They had another piece of good luck back at the flat. Tessa and Catarina lived in the upstairs of a small house. Their neighbors, it seemed, had gone to the shelters, so there was no one else in the house to see them dragging a bleeding man up the steps.

"The bathroom," Catarina said as they set Jem down on the dark landing. "Fill the tub with water. Lots of it. Cold. I'll get my supplies."

Tessa ran to the bathroom in the hall, praying that the water had not been disrupted by the bombing. Relief washed over her as water flowed from the tap. They were allowed to have only five inches in the bath, which was enforced by a line painted around the inside of the tub. Tessa ignored this. She opened the window wide. There was some cool air coming from the direction away from the fires. She hurried down the hall. Catarina had removed Jem's tunic, leaving his chest bare. She had taken off the bandages, and the wound was exposed and angry, the black marks tracing along his veins once again.

"Get his other side," Catarina said. Together they lifted Jem up. He was dead weight as they maneuvered him down the hall and carefully put him into the tub. Catarina positioned him so that his wounded arm and shoulder hung over the side, then reached into her apron pocket and removed two vials. She poured the contents of one into the water, turning it a light blue. Tessa knew better than to ask if Catarina thought he was going to survive. He was going to survive, because they would make sure of it. Also, you didn't ask those sorts of questions if you were concerned about the answers.

"Keep sponging him," Catarina said. "We need to keep him cool."

Tessa got down on her knees and drenched the sponge, then ran the blue-tinted water over Jem's head and chest. It smelled of a strange combination of sulfur and jasmine, and it seemed to lower his temperature. Catarina rubbed the contents of the other vial on her hands and began working at the wound and his arm and chest, massaging the spreading darkness back toward the opening. Jem's head lolled back, his breathing rough. Tessa swabbed his forehead, reassuring him all the while.

They did this for an hour. Tessa soon forgot the sound of the bombs outside, or the smoke or burning debris that drifted in. Everything was the motion of the water and the sponge, Jem's skin, his ordinarily calm face twisted in pain, then going still and slack. Both Catarina and Tessa were drenched, and there was water pooling on the floor around them.

Will, Jem said, and the voice in Tessa's head was lost but seeking. *Will, is that you?*

Tessa fought back the lump in her throat as Jem smiled at nothing. If he saw Will, let him see Will. Maybe Will was here, after all, come to help his *parabatai*.

Will, Tessa thought to herself, *if you are here, you must help. I cannot lose him too, Will. Together we will save him.*

Perhaps she imagined it, but Tessa felt something guiding her arm as she worked. She was stronger now.

Jem suddenly lurched in the water and came halfway out of the tub, his back arching into a shape that should not have been possible and sending his head under.

"Grab him," Catarina said. "Don't let him hurt himself! This is the worst of it!"

Together, and with whatever force was aiding Tessa, they grabbed Jem as he writhed, his strange, inward screams filling their heads. Because he was wet, they had to wrap themselves around his limbs to try to prevent him from flailing, from bashing his head against the tiles. He knocked Catarina loose, and she fell to the floor and smashed her head into the wall, but she came back and got her arms around his chest again. Jem's screams blended with the chaos of the night—the water splashed and the smoke blew in. Jem begged for *yin fen*. He kicked so hard that Tessa was thrown back against the sink.

Then, all at once, he stopped moving completely and fell back into the tub. He looked lifeless. Tessa crawled back across the wet floor and reached for him.

"Jem? Catarina . . ."

"He's alive," Catarina said, her chest heaving as she caught her breath. She had her fingers on his wrist. "We've done all we can do here. Let's get him into bed. We'll know soon."

The all clear rang out across London just after eleven, but there was nothing clear or safe. The Luftwaffe may have returned home, and the bombs may have stopped falling for a few hours, but the fires only increased. The wind fueled and propelled them. The air was rank with burning soot and flying scraps of debris, and London glowed.

They had moved Jem into the little bedroom. The rest of his wet clothing had to be removed. Tessa had dressed and undressed countless men at this point, and Jem was a Silent Brother, for whom intimacy was impossible. Perhaps she should have been able to do it with calm professionalism, but she could not be a nurse with Jem. She had thought once that she would see him, that they would see each other, naked on their wedding night. This was too intimate and strange—this was not how Jem would want Tessa to see him, like that, for the first time. So she left the task to Catarina, the nurse, who managed it quickly and dried Jem off. They put him in the bed and wrapped him with all the blankets in the flat. The clothes were easy enough to dry—they hung them from the window for the baking hot air of the fires. Then Catarina went into the sitting room, leaving Tessa to stay with Jem and hold his hand. It was so strange to be again in this position of standing by the bed of the man she loved, waiting, hoping. Jem was—Jem. Exactly as he had been all those years ago, except for the marks of the Silent Brothers. He was Jem, the boy with the violin. Her Jem. Age had not consumed him, as it had her Will, but he might be taken from her all the same.

Tessa reached up to her jade pendant, hidden beneath her collar. She sat and waited and listened to the roar and the wail outside as she held his hand.

I am here, James, she said in her mind. *I am here, and I will always be here.*

Tessa let go of Jem's hand only to occasionally go to the window to make sure the fires did not come too close. There was a halo of orange all around. The fires were only a few streets away. It was strangely beautiful, this terrible blaze. The city was burning; hundreds of years of history, ancient beams and books were alight.

"They mean to burn us out this time," Catarina said, coming up behind her friend. Tessa had not heard her enter. "This ring of fire, it goes around St. Paul's. They want the cathedral to burn. They want to break our spirits."

"Well," Tessa said, pulling the curtain closed, "they won't succeed."

"Why don't we go and make a cup of tea?" Catarina said. "He'll be sleeping for some time."

"No. I need to be here when he wakes."

Catarina looked at her friend's face.

"He means a great deal to you," she said.

"Jem—Brother Zachariah—and I have always been close."

"You love him," Catarina said. It was not a question.

Tessa squeezed a handful of curtain in her fist. They stood in silence for a moment. Catarina rubbed her friend's arm consolingly.

"I'll make the tea," she said. "I'll even let you have the last biscuits in the tin."

Biscuits?

Tessa whirled around. Jem was sitting up. She and Catarina hurried to him. Catarina began checking his pulse, his skin. Tessa looked at his face, his dear and familiar face. Jem was back; he was here.

Her Jem.

"It is healing," Catarina said. "You'll need to rest, but you will live. It was a narrow escape, though."

Which is why I came to the best nurses in London, Jem said.

"Perhaps you can explain that wound you have?" Catarina said. "I know where it comes from. Why were you attacked with a faerie weapon?"

I was looking for information, Jem said, shifting himself painfully to sit up a bit higher. *My inquiries were not appreciated.*

"Clearly, if you were attacked with a cataplasm. That is intended to kill. It does not wound. It is usually not survivable. Your Silent Brother markings gave you some protection, but . . ."

Catarina felt his pulse again.

But? Jem said curiously.

"I did not believe you would make it through the night," she said simply.

Tessa blinked. She'd known it was serious, but the way Catarina said it hit her physically.

"You should perhaps avoid making those inquiries again," Catarina said, putting the blankets back over Jem. "I'll go and make the tea."

She left the room quietly, closing the door behind her, leaving Tessa and Jem together in the darkness.

The raid seems worse than any before tonight, Jem finally said. *Sometimes I think the mundanes will do more harm to each other than any demon could ever do to them.*

Tessa felt a wave of emotion go through her—everything from the night burst to the surface, and she sank her head into the side of Jem's bed and wept. Jem sat up and pulled her close, and she rested her head on his chest, now warm, his heart beating strong.

"You might have died," Tessa said. "I might have lost you, too."

Tessa, he said. *Tessa, it's me. I am here. I am not gone.*

"Jem," she finally said. "Where have you been? It's been so long since . . ."

She pulled herself up and rubbed the tears from her cheeks. She still couldn't say the words "since Will died." Since that day she sat next to him on the bed and he drifted gently to sleep and never woke again. Jem had been there then, of course, but over the last three years she saw him less and less. They still met at Blackfriars Bridge, but otherwise he stayed away.

I thought it best to keep away from you. I am a Silent Brother, he said, and his voice in her head was quiet. *I am no use to you.*

"What do you mean?" Tessa asked helplessly. "It is always better for me to be with you."

Being what I am, how can I comfort you? asked Jem.

"If you cannot," said Tessa, "there is nobody in this world who can."

She had known that always. Magnus and Catarina had both tried to speak to her tactfully of immortal lives and other loves, but if she lived until the sun died, there would never be any other for her besides Will and Jem, those two twin souls, the only souls she had ever loved.

I do not know what comfort a creature like me could bring, said Jem. *If I could die to bring him back, I would, but he is gone, and with his loss the world seems even more lost to me. I fight for every drop of emotion I have, but at the same time, Tessa, I cannot see you lonely and not wish to be with you. I am not what I was. I did not want to cause you more pain.*

"The whole world seems to have gone mad," she said, tears burning in her eyes. "Will is gone from me, and you are gone from me, or so I have long thought. And yet tonight, I realized—I could still lose you, Jem. I could lose the hope, the slim hope of the possibility that someday . . ."

The words hung in the air. They were words they never spoke to each other aloud, not before Will died and not after. She had taken the part of her heart that loved Jem wildly, violently, and locked it up in a box: she had loved Will, and Jem had been her best friend, and they had never, ever spoken of what might happen if he were no longer a Silent Brother. If somehow the curse of that cold fate could be lifted. If his silence were gone, and he became human again, able to live and breathe and feel. Then what? What would they do?

I know what you are thinking. His voice in her mind was soft. His skin under her hands was so warm. She knew it was fever, but she told herself it was not. She lifted her face and looked into his, the cruel runes shutting his beloved eyes forever, the unchanged planes of his countenance. *I think of it too. What if it ended? What if it were possible for us? A future? What would we do?*

"I would seize that future," she said. "I would go with you anywhere. Even if the world was burning, if the Silent Brothers hunted us to the ends of the earth, I would be happy, if I was with you."

She could not quite hear him in her head, but she could feel him: the edge of a jumble of emotions, his longing now as desperate as it had been when they had fallen together onto the carpet of the music room, the night she had begged him to marry her as soon as possible.

He caught her in his arms. He was a Silent Brother, a Gregori, a Watcher, barely human. And yet he felt human enough—his lean chest hot against her skin as she tilted her face up. His lips met hers, soft and so sweet it made her ache. It had been so many, many years, but this was still the same.

Almost the same. *I am not what I was.*

Almost the fire of lost nights, the sound of his passionate music in her ears. She put her arms around his slim shoulders and clung to him fiercely. She could love enough for both of them. Any part of Jem was better than all of any other man alive.

His musician's hands drew over her face, over her hair, over her shoulders, as though he was seizing a last chance to memorize what he could never touch again. Even as she kissed him and insisted desperately to herself that it was possible, she knew it was not.

Tessa, he said. *Even when I cannot see, you are so beautiful.*

Then he grasped her shoulders in his beautiful hands and gently put her away from him.

I am sorry, my darling, he told her. *That was not fair of me, or well done. When I am with you, I want to forget what I am, but I cannot change it. A Silent Brother can have no wife, no love.*

Tessa's heart was pounding, her skin blazing like the fires all over London. She had not felt desire like this since Will. She knew she would never feel it for anyone else; only Will or Jem. "Don't go away from me," she whispered. "Don't stop talking to me. Don't retreat into silence. Will you tell me how you were injured?" she asked, grasping his hand. He drew it against his heart. She could feel it hammering through his rib cage. "Please. Jem, what were you doing?"

Jem sighed.

I was looking for lost Herondales, he said.

"Lost Herondales?"

This was from Catarina, who stood in the bedroom doorway,

holding a tray with two cups of tea. The tray rattled in her hands, as shaken as Tessa felt. She had not even thought of Catarina's presence.

Catarina steadied her grip and quickly set the tray down on the dresser. Jem's eyebrow quirked up.

Yes, Jem said. *Do you know something about them?*

Catarina was still visibly shaken. She didn't answer.

"Catarina?" Tessa asked.

"You have heard of Tobias Herondale," she said.

Of course, Jem replied. *His story is infamous. He ran from a battle and his fellow Shadowhunters were killed.*

"That is the story," Catarina said. "The reality was that Tobias was under a spell, made to believe that his wife and unborn child were in danger. He ran to help them. His fear was for their safety, but nevertheless, he broke the Law. When he could not be found, the Clave punished Tobias's wife in his stead. They killed her, but not before I helped her birth the child. I enchanted her so that it appeared she was still with child when she was executed. In reality, she had a son. His name was Ephraim."

She sighed and leaned against the wall, knotting her hands together.

"I took Ephraim to America and raised him there. He never knew what he was or who he was. He was a happy boy, a good boy. He was *my* boy."

"You had a son?' Tessa asked.

"I never told you," Catarina replied, looking down. "I should have. It's just . . . it was so long ago now. But it was a wonderful period in my life. For a time, there was no chaos. There was no fighting. We were a family. I did only one thing to connect him to his secret heritage—I gave him a necklace in the shape of a heron. I couldn't allow his Shadowhunter lineage to be blotted out completely. But, of course, he grew up. He had a family of his own. And his family had their own families. I stayed the same and gradually faded out of their lives. It is what we immortals must do. One of his descendants was a boy named Roland. He became a magician, and he was famous in Downworld. I tried to warn him away from using magic, but he wouldn't listen. We had a terrible fight and parted badly. I tried to find him, but he was gone. I've never been able to find any trace of him. I drove him away when I tried to save him."

No, Jem said. *That is not why he ran away. He married a woman who was a fugitive. Roland went into hiding to protect her.*

Catarina looked up at him.

"What?" she said.

I was in America a short while ago with an Iron Sister, he said, *to retrieve some* adamas. *While there, we encountered a Shadow Market connected to a carnival. It was run by a Greater Demon. We confronted him, and he told us that there were Herondales lost in the world and that they were in danger and that they were very close by. He said that they were hiding from an enemy neither mortal nor demon. Also at this market, I saw a faerie woman with a mortal man. They had a child. The man was called Roland.*

Tessa was stunned by the rush of information coming from all sides, but she was caught by the thought of a man throwing away his whole life to run with the woman he loved, giving everything he had to shield her and counting it as nothing. That sounded like a Herondale.

"He was alive?" Catarina said. "Roland? At a carnival?"

When I realized what was happening, I tried to track him down, but I was unable to find him. Please know that it was not you he was running from. The Greater Demon told me that they were being chased and that they were in great danger. Now I know that to be true. The faerie who came to me tonight—he meant to kill me. The forces looking for the Herondales are neither mortal nor demon— they are fey, and the fey mean to keep something secret.

"So . . . I did not chase him away?" Catarina said. "All this time . . . Roland . . ."

Catarina shook herself and regained her composure. She picked up the tea tray and brought it over to the bed, setting it on the edge.

"Drink your tea," she said. "I used the last of our ration of milk and the biscuits."

You know that Silent Brothers do not drink, Jem said.

Catarina gave him a sad smile. "I thought you might still find comfort in holding the warm cup."

She wiped her eyes covertly and turned and left the room.

You did not know of this? Jem said.

"She never said," Tessa replied. "So many problems are caused by unnecessary secrets."

Jem turned his face away and ran his finger along the edge of the teacup. She caught at his hand. If that was all she could have, she would hold on to it.

"Why have you kept so far away?" Tessa said. "We have both been grieving Will. Why do so separately?"

I am a Silent Brother, and Silent Brothers cannot—

Jem cut himself off. Tessa clasped his hand to the point where she might have broken it.

"You are Jem—my Jem. Always my Jem."

I am Brother Zachariah, Jem returned.

"So be it!" said Tessa. "You are Brother Zachariah, and my

Jem. You are a Silent Brother. That does not mean you are not dear to me as you always were, and you always will be. Do you think anything could separate us? Are either of us so weak as that? After all we have seen and all we have done? I spend every day grateful that you exist and are in the world. And as long as you live, we keep Will alive."

She saw the impact these words had on Jem. Being a Silent Brother meant destroying some parts of you that were human, burning them away, but Jem was still there.

"We have so much time, Jem. You must promise me that we will not spend it apart. Do not keep away from me. Make me a part of this quest as well. I can help. You must be more careful."

I would not put you in danger, he said.

At this Tessa laughed—a true, ringing laugh.

"Danger?" she said. "Jem, I am immortal. And look outside. Look at the city burning. The only thing I am frightened of is being without those I love."

At last she felt the pressure of his fingers, holding her hand back.

Outside, London burned. Inside, in this moment, all was well.

The morning came, cold and gray, with the smell of the still-burning fires in the air. London woke, shook itself off, picked up its brooms and buckets, and began the daily act of repair. The blackout curtains were opened to the morning air. People went to work. The buses ran, and the kettles boiled; the shops opened. Fear had not won. Death and fire and war had not won.

Tessa had fallen asleep around dawn, sitting by Jem's side, holding his hand, her head leaning on the wall. When she stirred awake, she found that the bed was empty. The blankets had been neatly pulled back up and the clothes were gone from the sill.

"Jem," Tessa said, frantic.

Catarina was asleep in their little sitting room, her head basketed in her arms and resting on their kitchen table.

"He is gone," Tessa said. "Did you see him go?"

"No," Catarina said, rubbing her eyes.

Tessa returned to the bedroom and looked around. Had it all been a dream? Had the war driven her mad? As she turned, she saw a folded note on the dresser that said *TESSA*. She opened it:

> *My Tessa,*
> *There will be no separation between us.*
> *Where you are, I am. Where we are, Will is.*
> *Whatever else I may be, I remain always,*
> > *Your Jem*

Brother Zachariah walked through London. The city was gray with night, its buildings reduced to broken remnants of what they had once been, until it seemed a city made of ash and bone. Perhaps all cities would become the Silent City, one day.

He was able to conceal some things from his Brothers, even though they had ready access to his mind. They did not know all his secrets, but they knew enough. Tonight every voice in his mind was hushed, overwhelmed by what he had felt and what he had almost done.

He was bitterly ashamed of what he had said this night. Tessa was still grieving Will. They shared that grief, and they loved each other. She did still love him. He believed that. But she could not feel what she had felt for him once. She had not, thank the Angel, lived as he had lived, in bones and silence and on memories of love. She'd had Will, and loved him so long, and now Will was lost. He worried that he had taken advantage of her misery. She might well cling to what was familiar in a world gone mad and strange.

But she was so brave, his Tessa, carving out a new life now the old life was lost. She'd done it once already, as a girl coming from America. He had felt it as a bond between them long ago, that they had both come across the seas to find a new home. He had thought they could find a new home with each other.

He knew now that had been a dream, but what had been dreams for him could be real for Tessa. She was immortal and valiant. She would live again in this new world, and build a whole new life. Perhaps she would love again, if she could find a man who would measure up to Will, though in almost a hundred years Zachariah had not known any who could. Tessa deserved the richest life and the greatest love imaginable.

Tessa deserved more than a being who could never truly be a man again, who could not love her with a whole heart. Even though he loved her with all the broken fragments of heart he had left, it was not enough. She deserved more than he had to offer.

He should never have reached for her that way.

Nevertheless, there was a selfish joy within him, a warmth that he could carry even into the deathlike coldness of the City of Bones. She had kissed him and clung to him. For one shining night, he had held her in his arms again.

Tessa, Tessa, Tessa, he thought. She could never be his again, but he was hers forever. That was enough to live on.

* ✳ *

That evening, Catarina and Tessa walked in the direction of St. Bart's.

"A bacon sandwich," Catarina said. "Piled so high you can barely hold it. And thick with so much butter the bacon slides off the bread. That's what I'm having first. How about you?"

Tessa smiled and shone her torch down the pavement, stepping over a bit of rubble. Around them, there were shells of buildings. Everything around had been reduced to charred brick and ash. But already London was picking up, pushing the debris back. The dark was like an embrace. All of London was under a blanket together, holding each other close.

"An ice cream," Tessa said. "With strawberries. Loads and loads of strawberries."

"Oh, I like that," Catarina said. "I'm changing mine."

A man walking toward them tipped his hat.

"Evening, Sisters," he said. "You see that?"

He gestured up at St. Paul's Cathedral, the great building that had sat guarding over London for hundreds of years.

"They wanted to take it down last night, but they didn't, did they?" The man smiled. "No, they didn't. They can't break us. You have a good evening, Sisters. You keep well."

The man walked on, and Tessa looked up at the cathedral. Everything around it was gone, but it had been saved—impossibly, improbably saved from thousands of bombs. London would not let it die, and it had lived.

She touched the jade pendant around her neck.

The Wicked Ones

By Cassandra Clare and Robin Wasserman

Paris, 1989

It was said among the Shadowhunters that one could not know true beauty until one had seen the gleaming towers of Alicante. It was said that no city on earth could rival its wonders. It was said that no Shadowhunter could feel truly at home anywhere else.

If anyone had asked Céline Montclaire her opinion on the subject, she would have said: obviously these Shadowhunters had never been to Paris.

She would have rhapsodized about gothic spires spearing the clouds, cobblestone streets shimmering with rain, sunlight dancing on the Seine, and, *bien sûr*, the infinite varieties of cheese. She would have pointed out that Paris had been home to Baudelaire and Rimbaud, Monet and Gauguin, Descartes and Voltaire, that this was the city that had birthed a new way of speaking, seeing, thinking, *being*—drawing even the most mundane of mundanes a little closer to the angels.

In every way, Paris was *la ville lumière*. The City of Light. *If you ask me*, Céline would have said, *nothing could be more beautiful than that.*

But no one ever asked. As a general rule, no one asked Céline Montclaire's opinion on anything.

Until now.

"You sure there's not some kind of rune to keep these foul beasts away?" Stephen Herondale said as a thunderous flutter of wings descended. He ducked, whacked blindly at his feathered foe.

The flock of pigeons quickly passed, without dealing any mortal blows. Céline waved off a couple of stragglers, and Stephen breathed a sigh of relief.

"My hero," he said.

Céline felt her cheeks warm alarmingly. She had a terrible blushing problem. Especially when she was in the presence of Stephen Herondale. "The great Herondale warrior afraid of pigeons?" she teased, hoping he wouldn't hear the quaver in her voice.

"Not afraid. Simply exhibiting a prudent amount of caution in the face of a potentially demonic creature."

"Demon pigeons?"

"I look upon them with great suspicion," Stephen said with as much dignity as a pigeon-phobe could muster. He tapped the longsword hanging by his hip. "And this great warrior stands at the ready to do what needs be done."

As he spoke, another flock of pigeons took flight from the cobblestones, and for a moment all was wings and feathers and Stephen's rather high-pitched squeal.

Céline laughed. "Yes, I can see you're fearless in the face of danger. If not in the beak of danger."

Stephen glared fiercely at her. Her pulse quickened. Had she overstepped? Then he winked.

Sometimes she wanted him so much she felt like her heart might explode.

"You sure we're still going in the right direction?" he said. "I feel like we're walking in circles."

"Trust me," she said.

Stephen clapped a hand to his heart. "*Bien sûr*, mademoiselle."

Unless you counted the starring role he played in her daydreams, Céline hadn't seen Stephen since he'd graduated from the Academy four years before. Back then, he'd barely noticed her. He was too busy with his training, his girlfriend, and his friends in the Circle to give much thought to the slip of a girl whose eyes tracked his every move. But now, Céline thought, her cheeks burning again, they were practically equals. Yes, she was seventeen, still a student, while he was twenty-two, not just a full-fledged adult but Valentine Morgenstern's most trusted lieutenant in the Circle—the elite group of young Shadowhunters sworn to reform the Clave and return it to its pure and ancient glory. But Céline was finally a member of the Circle too, handpicked by Valentine himself.

Valentine had been a student at the Academy alongside Stephen and the other founding members of the Circle—but unlike the rest of them, he'd never seemed quite young. Most of the students and teachers at the Academy had thought of Valentine's crowd as nothing but a harmless clique, odd only in that it preferred late-night policy debates to partying. Even then, Céline understood that this was exactly how Valentine wanted to appear: harmless. Those who paid attention knew better. He was a fierce warrior, with an even fiercer mind— once he fixed his inky black gaze on a goal, nothing would stop him from achieving it. He'd composed his Circle of young

Shadowhunters he knew to be as capable as they were loyal. Only the best of them, he'd told her that day he'd approached her at a particularly boring lecture on Downworlder history. "Every member of the Circle is *exceptional*," he'd said. "Including, if you accept my offer, you." No one had ever called her exceptional before.

Ever since then, she'd felt different. Strong. *Special*. And it must have been true, because even though she still had one more year at the Academy, here she was, spending her summer vacation on an official mission with Stephen Herondale. Stephen was one of the greatest fighters of his generation, and now—owing to Lucian Graymark's unfortunate werewolf situation—Valentine's most trusted deputy. But Céline was the one who knew Paris, its streets and its secrets. It was the perfect moment to show Stephen that she'd changed, that she was exceptional. That he couldn't do this without her.

Those had, in fact, been his exact words. *I couldn't do this without you, Céline.*

She loved the way her name sounded on his tongue. She loved every detail of him: the blue eyes that sparkled like the sea of the Côte d'Azur. The white-blond hair that glowed like the golden rotunda of the Palais Garnier. The curve of his neck, the tautness of his muscles, the smooth lines of his body like something carved by Rodin, a model of human perfection. Somehow he'd gotten even more handsome since she saw him last.

He'd also gotten married.

She tried not to think about that.

"Can we pick up the pace?" Robert Lightwood grumbled. "The sooner we get this done, the sooner we can get back to civilization. And air-conditioning."

Robert was something else she tried not to think about. His grouchy presence made it substantially more difficult to pretend she and Stephen were taking a romantic stroll through the moonlight.

"The faster we go, the more you'll sweat," Stephen pointed out. "And trust me, no one wants that." Paris in August was approximately ten degrees hotter than Hell. Even after dark, the air felt like a blanket soaked in hot soup. For the sake of discretion, they'd traded their Shadowhunter gear for mundane fashion, choosing long sleeves to cover up their runes. The white T-shirt Céline had selected for Stephen was already soaked through. This was not exactly unfortunate.

Robert just grunted. He was different than Céline remembered him from the Academy. Back then, he'd been a little stiff and curt, but never deliberately cruel. Now, though, there was something in his eyes she didn't like. Something icy. It reminded her too much of her father.

According to Stephen, Robert had had some kind of falling-out with his *parabatai* and was understandably cranky. *It's just Robert being Robert*, Stephen had said. *Great fighter but a bit of a drama queen. Nothing to worry about.*

Céline always worried.

They trudged up the final hill of Rue Mouffetard. By day, this was one of Paris's most bustling market streets, bursting with fresh produce, colorful scarves, falafel vendors and gelato stands, and obnoxious tourists. At night, its storefronts were shuttered and silent. Paris was a market town, but all of its markets went to sleep after dark—all except one.

Céline hurried them around a corner, down another narrow, winding road. "We're almost there." She tried to keep the anticipation out of her voice. Robert and Stephen had made it very clear that the Circle did not approve of Shadow Markets. Downworlders mingling with mundanes, illicit goods changing hands, secrets swapped and sold? According to Valentine, this was all the unseemly consequence of the laxness and corruption of the Clave. When the Circle took power, Stephen had assured her eagerly, the Shadow Markets would be shut down for good.

Céline had been in the Circle for only a few months, but she'd already learned this lesson: if Valentine hated something, it was her duty to hate it too.

She was trying her best.

There was no Law that a Shadow Market had to be located on a site rich with dark energy, marinated in the blood of a violent past—but it helped.

Paris had no shortage of possibilities. It was a city of ghosts, most of them angry. Revolution after revolution, blood-spattered barricades and heads rolling from the guillotine, the September Massacres, the Bloody Week, the burning of the Tuileries, the Terror . . . As a child, Céline had spent many sleepless nights wandering the city, summoning visions of its greatest cruelties. She liked to imagine she could hear screams echoing through the centuries. They made her feel less alone.

This, she knew, was not a normal childhood hobby.

Céline's had not been a normal childhood. She discovered this only when she arrived at the Academy, where for the first time she'd met Shadowhunters her own age. That first day, the other students had chattered about their idyllic lives in Idris, galloping horses across the Brocelind Plain; their idyllic lives in London, New York, Tokyo, training under the kind eye of loving parents and Institute tutors; their idyllic lives anywhere and everywhere. After a while Céline stopped listening and drifted out unnoticed, too bitterly jealous to stay. Too embarrassed by the prospect that someone might make her tell her own story. After all, she'd grown up on her parents' Provence estate, surrounded by apple orchards, vineyards, rolling fields of lavender: by all appearances, *la belle epoque*.

Céline knew her parents loved her, because they told her so repeatedly.

We're only doing this because we love you, her mother would say before locking her in the basement.

We're only doing this because we love you, her father would say before lashing her with the whip.

We're only doing this because we love you, when they set the Dragonidae demon on her; when they dumped her for the night, eight years old and weaponless, in a werewolf-ridden wood; when they taught her the bloody consequences of weakness or clumsiness or fear.

The first time she ran away to Paris, she was eight years old. Young enough to think she could escape for good. She'd found her way to the Arènes de Lutèce, the remains of a Roman amphitheater from the first century AD. It was, perhaps, the city's oldest blood-soaked ruin. Two thousand years before, gladiators had warred to the death before a cheering, bloodthirsty crowd, until the arena—and its crowd—were overtaken by an equally bloodthirsty barbarian horde. For a time, it had been a cemetery; now it was a tourist trap, yet another heap of stones for bored schoolchildren to ignore. By day, at least. Under the midnight moon, it came alive with Downworlders, a bacchanalia of faerie fruits and wines, gargoyles enchanted by warlock magic, waltzing werewolves, vampires in berets painting portraits in blood, an ifrit accordionist who could make you weep yourself to death. It was the Paris Shadow Market, and from the moment Céline first saw it, she felt herself finally home.

That first trip, she'd spent two nights there, haunting the booths, befriending a shy werewolf cub, sating her gnawing hunger with the Nutella crepe that a Silent Brother had purchased for her, no questions asked. She'd napped beneath the tablecloth of a vampire's jewelry stand; she'd whirled with horned children in an improvised faerie revel; she'd finally discovered what it meant to be happy. On the third night, the Shadowhunters of the Paris Institute tracked her down and returned her home.

That was when she learned—not for the last time—the consequences of running away.

We love you too much to lose you.

That night, Céline had curled fetal in the corner of the basement, back still bloody, and thought, *So this is how it feels to be loved too much.*

Their mission was straightforward. First, track down the warlock Dominique du Froid's booth at the Paris Shadow Market. Second, find some evidence of her shady business dealings with two rogue Shadowhunters.

"I have reason to believe they've been trading Downworlder blood and parts to her in return for illegal services," Valentine had told them. He needed proof. It was up to Céline, Stephen, and Robert to find some.

"*Quietly,*" Valentine had cautioned. "I don't want her

tipping off her associates." Valentine made the word "associates" sound like a vulgarity. For him, it was: Downworlders were bad enough, but Shadowhunters allowing themselves to be corrupted by a Downworlder? That was unforgivable.

Step one proved simple. Dominique du Froid was easy to find. She'd conjured her name in neon lights, right out of thin air. Literally—the letters glowed brightly, three feet above her booth, with a neon arrow pointing down. DOMINIQUE DU FROID, LES SOLDES, TOUJOURS!

"Just like a warlock," Robert said sourly. "Always for sale."

"Always *on* sale," Céline corrected, too quietly for him to hear.

The booth turned out to be an elaborate tent with display tables and a curtained-off area in the back. It was crammed with tacky jewelry and colorful potions—none quite as tacky or as colorful as Dominique herself. Her hair was dyed in platinum-blond and hot-pink stripes, half of it scooped into a side ponytail. The other half was crimped and hair-sprayed to a hard sheen. She wore a ripped lace shirt, a black leather miniskirt, purple fingerless gloves, and what looked like a significant portion of her jewelry inventory around her neck. Her warlock mark, a long, feathered pink tail, was slung over her shoulders like a boa.

"It's like an Eidolon demon tried turning into Cyndi Lauper and accidentally got stuck midway through," Céline joked.

"Huh?" Robert said. "Is that another warlock?"

Stephen smirked. "Yeah, Robert. Another warlock. The Clave executed her 'cause she just wanted to have fun."

Céline and Stephen laughed together, and Robert's obvious fury at being mocked only made them laugh harder. Like most Shadowhunters, Céline had grown up entirely ignorant of mundane pop culture. But Stephen showed up at the Academy full of arcane knowledge about bands, books, songs, movies that no one had ever heard of. Once he'd joined the Circle, he'd dropped his love of the Sex Pistols just as quickly as he'd traded his leather jacket and frayed denim for the dull black uniform that Valentine favored. Still, Céline had spent the last couple of years studying mundane TV, just in case.

I can be whatever you want me to be, she thought, wishing she had the nerve to *say* it.

Céline knew Amatis, Stephen's wife. At least, she knew enough. Amatis was sharp-tongued and stuck-up. She was opinionated, argumentative, stubborn, and not even that pretty. There were also rumors that she still secretly associated with her werewolf brother. Céline didn't much care about that—she had nothing against Downworlders. But she had plenty against Amatis, who obviously didn't appreciate what she had. Stephen needed someone who would admire him, agree with him, support him. Someone like Céline. If only she could make him see that for himself.

They surveilled the warlock for a couple of hours. Dominique du Froid was constantly leaving her booth unattended, scurrying off to gossip or trade with other sellers. It was almost like she wanted someone to rifle through her belongings.

Stephen yawned theatrically. "I was hoping for slightly more of a challenge. But let's get this done and get out of here. This place stinks of Downworlders. I already feel like I need a shower."

"*Ouais, c'est terrible,*" Céline lied.

The next time Dominique left her booth, Stephen tailed her. Robert slipped into the booth's curtained-off area to poke around for evidence of dirty dealings. Céline was left to play lookout, browsing the booth next to Dominique's, where she could signal Robert if Dominique unexpectedly came back.

Of course they'd assigned her the most boring job, the one that required nothing but shopping for jewelry. They thought she was useless.

Céline did as she was told, feigning interest in the hideous display of enchanted rings, chunky gold chains, charm bracelets jangling with Greater Demons carved in brass and pewter. Then she spotted something that actually did interest her: a Silent Brother, gliding toward the booth in that disconcertingly inhuman way they all had of moving. She watched out of the corner of her eye as the robed Shadowhunter studied the jewelry display with great care. What could someone like him possibly be looking for in a place like this?

The scruffy preteen werewolf manning the booth had barely acknowledged Céline's presence. But he scurried straight over to the Silent Brother, eyes wide with fear. "You can't be poking around here," he said. "My boss doesn't like doing business with your kind."

Aren't you a bit young to have a boss?

The words reverberated in Céline's mind, and she wondered for a moment whether the Silent Brother wanted her to overhear. But that seemed unlikely—she was standing several feet away, and there was no reason for him to have noticed her.

"Parents threw me out when I got bitten, so it's either work or go hungry," the kid said. He shrugged. "And I like food. Which is why you got to get out of here before the boss comes back and thinks I'm selling to a Shadowhunter."

I am in search of a piece of jewelry.

"Look, man, there's nothing here you can't get somewhere

else, better and cheaper. This stuff is all junk."

Yes, that I can see. But I am looking for something particular, something I've been told I can find here only. A silver necklace, with a pendant in the shape of a heron.

The word "heron" pricked Céline's ear. It was such a specific request. And it was something so suited to a Herondale.

"Uh, yeah, I don't know how you heard about that, but it's possible we've got one of those back here. I told you, though, I can't sell to—"

What if I doubled the price?

"You don't even know what the price is."

No, I do not. And I imagine you won't get a better offer, given that the necklace is not on display for customers.

"Yeah, I pointed that out myself, but . . ." He leaned forward and lowered his voice. Céline tried not to make it too obvious she was straining to hear. "Boss doesn't want his wife to know he's selling it. Said he just needs to put the word out, and a buyer will find us."

And now a buyer has. Imagine how pleased your employer will be when you tell him it sold for more than his asking price.

"I guess he never needs to know who bought it. . . ."

He will not hear it from me.

The kid considered this for a moment, then ducked beneath the counter for a moment and reappeared dangling a silver pendant. Céline suppressed a gasp. It was a delicately shaped heron, sparkling in the moonlight, the perfect gift for a young Herondale proud of his heritage. She closed her eyes, letting herself drift into an alternate reality, one in which she was allowed to give Stephen gifts. Imagining fastening the pendant around his neck, nuzzling his soft skin, breathing him in.

Imagining him saying, *I love it. Almost as much as I love you.*

It is beautiful, is it not?

Céline flinched at the voice of the Silent Brother in her head. Of course he couldn't know what she'd been thinking. But nonetheless, her cheeks burned with shame. The kid had retreated to the back of the booth to count his money. The Silent Brother had now fixed his blind gaze on her.

He was different from the other Silent Brothers she'd seen, his face young—even handsome. His jet-black hair was marked with a streak of white, and his eyes and mouth were sealed but not sewn shut. Runes sliced viciously across each cheek. Céline was reminded how envious she had once been of the Silent Brotherhood. They had scars like she had scars; they endured great pain like she endured great pain. But their scars gave them power; their pain felt like nothing, because they had no feeling. You could not be a Silent Brother if you were a girl. This had never seemed very fair to Céline. Women were, however, allowed to join the Iron Sisters. Céline had liked the idea when she was younger, but now she felt no desire to live cloistered on a volcanic plain, with nothing to do but craft weapons of *adamas.* The very thought of it made her claustrophobic.

I am sorry to startle you. But I noted your interest in the pendant.

"It's . . . it just, it reminded me of someone."

Someone you care about a great deal, I sense.

"Yeah. I guess."

Is that someone perhaps a Herondale?

"Yes, and he's wonderful." The words slipped out accidentally, but there was an unexpected joy in saying them out loud. She'd never let herself do so before—not in front of someone else. Not even alone.

That was the thing about Silent Brothers. Being with them wasn't quite like being with someone else *or* like being alone. Confiding in a Silent Brother was like confiding in no one, she thought, because who was he going to tell?

"Stephen Herondale," she said, softly but firmly. "I'm in love with Stephen Herondale."

There was a jolt of power in saying the words, almost as if speaking her claim aloud made it a little more real.

The love of a Herondale can be a great gift.

"Yeah, it's awesome," she said, bitterly enough that even the Silent Brother noticed her tone.

I have upset you.

"No, it's just . . . I said *I* love *him*. He barely knows I'm alive."

Ah.

It was stupid, hoping for sympathy from a Silent Brother. Like hoping for sympathy from a rock. His face remained completely impassive. But the voice that spoke in her head was gentle. She let herself believe it was even a little kind.

That must be difficult.

If Céline had been another type of girl, the type with friends or sisters or a mother who spoke to her with anything but icy disdain, she might have told someone else about Stephen. She might have spent hours dissecting his tone, the way he sometimes seemed to flirt with her, the way he'd once touched her on the shoulder in gratitude when she lent him a dagger. Maybe talking about it would have blunted the pain of loving him; maybe she even would have talked herself *out* of loving him. Talking about Stephen might have become commonplace, like talking about the weather. Background noise.

But Céline had no one to talk to. All she had were her secrets, and the longer she kept them, the more they hurt.

"He's never going to love me," she said. "All I've ever wanted was to be near him, but now he's right here, and I can't have him, and in a way that's even worse. I'm just . . . I just . . . it just hurts so much."

I sometimes think there is nothing more painful than love denied. To love someone you cannot have, to stand beside your heart's desire and be unable to take them in your arms. A love that cannot be requited. I can think of nothing more painful than that.

It was impossible that a Silent Brother could understand how she felt. And yet . . .

He sounded as if he understood exactly how she felt.

"I wish I could be more like you," she admitted.

In what sense?

"You know, just shut off my feelings? Feel nothing. For anybody."

There was a long pause, and she wondered if she'd offended him. Was that even possible? Finally, his cool, steady voice spoke again.

This is a wish you should dispense with. Feeling is what makes us human. Even the most difficult feelings. Perhaps especially those. Love, loss, longing—this is what it means to be truly alive.

"But . . . you're a Silent Brother. You're not supposed to feel any of those things, right?"

I . . . There was another long pause. *I remember feeling them. That is sometimes as close as I can get.*

"And you're still alive, as far as I can tell."

Sometimes that, too, is difficult to remember.

If she didn't know any better, she would think he had sighed.

The Silent Brother she met on her first trip to the Shadow

Market had been kind like this. When he bought her the crepe, he hadn't asked her where her parents were or why she was wandering the crowds alone or why her eyes were red from crying. He only knelt and pinned his blind eyes on hers. *The world is a hard thing to face alone*, he said inside her mind. *You do not have to.*

Then he did what Silent Brothers did best and fell silent. She knew, even as a child, that he was waiting for her to tell him what she needed. That if she asked for help, he might even offer it.

No one could help her. Even as a child, she knew that, too. The Montclaires were a respected, powerful Shadowhunter family. Her parents had the ear of the Consul. If she told the Brother who she was, he would only bring her home. If she told him what waited for her there, what her parents were *really* like, he probably wouldn't believe her. He might even tell her parents she was spreading lies about them. And there would be consequences.

She'd thanked him for the crepe and skittered away.

She'd endured so many years since then. After this summer, she would return to the Academy for her final year, and graduate; she would never have to live in her parents' house again. She was almost free. She didn't need anyone's help.

But the world was still a hard thing to face alone.

And she was so, so lonely.

"Maybe the pain of loving someone is a fact of life and all, but do you really think that, like, *all* pain is? You don't think it would be better if you could just stop hurting?"

Is something hurting you?

"I . . ." She summoned her nerve. She could do it. She almost believed that. She could tell this stranger about the cold house. About the parents who seemed to notice her only when she did something wrong. About the consequences, when she did. "The thing is—"

She broke off abruptly as the Silent Brother turned away. His closed eyes seemed to be tracking a man in a black trench coat hurrying toward him. The man stopped short when he caught sight of the Silent Brother. His face abruptly drained of color. Then he spun on his heel and hustled away. Most Downworlders were skittish around Shadowhunters these days—news of the Circle's exploits had gotten around. But this looked almost personal.

"Do you *know* that guy?"

I apologize, I must attend to this.

Silent Brothers did not display emotion, and, as far as Céline knew, they didn't feel it. But if she didn't know any better, she would say this Silent Brother was feeling something very deeply. Fear, maybe, or excitement—or that strange combination of the two that descended just before a fight.

"Okay, I just—"

But the Silent Brother was already gone. She was alone again. And thank the Angel for that, she thought. It had been careless, even toying with the idea of dredging her dark truths into the light. How foolish, how weak, wanting to be heard. Wanting to be truly *seen* by anyone, much less a man with his eyes fused shut. Her parents always said she was stupid and weak. Maybe they were right.

Brother Zachariah wove through the crowded Shadow Market, careful to keep a few feet of distance between him and his target. It was a strange game they were playing. The man, who went by the name of Jack Crow, certainly knew that Zachariah was following him. And Brother Zachariah could have picked up his speed and overtaken the man at any point. But for whatever reason, Crow didn't want to stop, and Brother Zachariah didn't want to make him. So Crow strode across the arena and into the dense warren of streets just beyond its gates.

Brother Zachariah followed.

He was sorry to have left the girl so abruptly. He felt a certain kinship with her. They'd both given a piece of their hearts to a Herondale. And they both loved someone they could not have.

Of course, Brother Zachariah's love was a pale imitation of the real, raw, human thing. He loved through a scrim, and every year it got harder to remember what lay beyond. To remember how it had felt to *long* for Tessa the way a living, breathing human longed. How it had felt to *need* her. Zachariah no longer truly needed anything. Not food, not sleep, not even, much as he sometimes tried to summon it in himself, Tessa. His love persisted, but it was blunted. The girl's love had a jagged edge, and talking to her had helped him remember.

She had wanted his help too, he could tell. The most human part of him was tempted to stay by her side. She'd seemed so fragile—and so determined to seem otherwise. It touched his heart. But Brother Zachariah's heart was encased in stone.

He tried to tell himself otherwise. After all, the very fact of his presence here was evidence of his still-human heart. He'd been hunting for decades—because of Will, because of Tessa, because a part of him was still Jem, the Shadowhunter boy who had loved them both.

Still loves them both, Brother Zachariah reminded himself. Present tense.

The heron pendant had confirmed his suspicions. This was definitely the man he'd been seeking. Zachariah couldn't let him get away.

Crow ducked into a narrow cobblestone alley. Brother Zachariah followed, tense and alert. He sensed their slow-motion chase was nearing its end. And indeed, the alley was a dead end. Crow whirled around to face Zachariah, a knife in his hand. He was still young, barely into his twenties, with a proud face and a shock of blond hair.

Brother Zachariah had a weapon and was quite good at using it. But he made no move to draw his staff. This man could never be a threat to him.

"Okay, Shadowhunter, you wanted me, you got me," Crow said, feet braced and knife ready, clearly expecting an attack.

Brother Zachariah studied his face, searching for something familiar. But there was nothing. Nothing but the pretense of brash courage. With his closed eyes, Zachariah could see beneath such facades. He could see fear.

There was a rustling behind him. Then a woman's voice.

"You know what they say, Shadowhunter. Be careful what you wish for."

Brother Zachariah turned, slowly. Here was a surprise. A young woman—even younger than Crow—stood in the mouth of the alley. She was almost ethereally beautiful, with shining blond hair and the kind of ruby lips and cobalt eyes that had inspired millennia of bad poetry. She was smiling sweetly. She was aiming a crossbow directly at Brother Zachariah's heart.

He felt a jolt of fear. Not because of the knife or the crossbow; he had nothing to fear from these two. He would prefer not to fight at all, but if necessary he could disarm them harmlessly.

They weren't equipped to protect themselves. That was the problem.

The fear stemmed from the realization that he had achieved his goal. This search was the one thing that still bound him to Tessa, to Will, to his former self. What if today he lost his only remaining tie to Jem Carstairs? What if this, today, was his last truly human act?

"Come on, Shadowhunter," the woman said, coming closer but keeping the crossbow steady. "Spit it out. If you're very lucky, maybe we'll let you live."

I don't want to fight you. From their reaction, he could tell they hadn't expected the voice in their head. These two knew enough to recognize a Shadowhunter—but apparently they didn't know as much as they thought. *I have been looking for you, Jack Crow.*

"Yeah, so I heard. Someone should have warned you, people who come looking for me tend to regret it."

I mean you no harm. I only want to deliver a message. It is about who you are and where you came from. You might find this difficult to believe, but—

"Yeah, yeah, I'm a Shadowhunter too." Crow shrugged. "Now tell me something I don't know."

"You here to buy or to shoplift?"

Céline dropped the potion bottle. It shattered on the ground, releasing a puff of noxious blue smoke.

After the Silent Brother had ditched her for the hot guy in the trench coat, the werewolf kid had shut down the booth. He glared at Céline until she accepted it was time to move on. So she'd meandered over to Dominique du Froid's booth, trying to look innocuous. Which worked fine, until the warlock herself appeared, seemingly out of nowhere.

"Or just here to cause havoc?" Dominique said in French.

Céline cursed silently. She'd had *one* job, a humiliatingly easy one at that, and she'd still managed to fail. Stephen was nowhere in sight, and Robert was still rummaging through the warlock's tent.

"I was waiting for you to come back," Céline said loudly and in English, so Robert would be sure to hear. "Thank goodness you finally did. *I'm melting in this heat.*" She said that last part even louder. It was a prearranged signal, just in case. Translation: get out, *now*. Hopefully she could keep the warlock distracted long enough that he could slip out unseen.

Where was Stephen?

"*Bien sûr.*" The warlock had a terrible accent, French by way of Southern California. Céline wondered if warlocks could surf. "And what is it you're looking for, mademoiselle?"

"A love potion." It was the first thing that popped into her head. Maybe because she'd just spotted Stephen, hurrying toward them—while trying very much to look like he wasn't hurrying. Céline wondered how Dominique had managed to give him the slip in the first place, and if she'd done so on purpose.

"A love potion, eh?" The warlock followed her gaze and made an approving noise. "Not bad, though a little beefy for my taste. The better the body, the worse the mind, I always find. But maybe you prefer dumb and pretty. *Chacun à son goût*, eh?"

"Um, *oui*, dumb and pretty, sure. So—" What was Robert *doing* back there, anyway? Céline hoped he'd managed to slip out without her seeing him, but she couldn't take the risk. "Can you help me?"

"Love is a little beyond my pay grade, *chérie*. Anyone around here who tells you different is lying. But I can offer you . . ."

She fell silent as Stephen arrived, looking slightly harried. "Everything okay here?"

He shot Céline a concerned look. Her heart pounded; he was worried about her. She nodded. "Totally fine. We were just—"

"Your friend here wanted me to sell her a potion to make you fall in love with her," the warlock said. Céline thought she might drop dead on the spot. "I was about to tell her I could only offer her the next best thing." She pulled what looked like a can of hair spray from beneath the booth and sprayed a puff of it in Stephen's face. His expression went slack.

"What did you do?" Céline cried. "And why did you *say* that?"

"Oh, relax. Trust me, in this state, he won't care what anyone says. Watch."

Stephen was staring at Céline like he'd never seen her before. He reached out a hand and touched her cheek, gently, his expression wondering. He looked at her like he was thinking, *Could you be* real?

"Turns out your little blond friend here has a nasty case of demon pox," Dominique told Stephen. Céline decided she was not, in fact, going to drop dead; she was going to murder the warlock.

"Demon pox is so sexy," Stephen said. "Will there be warts?" He batted his eyes at Céline. "You would look beautiful with warts."

"See?" the warlock said. "I fixed him for you."

"What did you *do*?"

"It's not obvious? I did what you asked for. Well, it's a cheap approximation of what you asked for, but what else is the Shadow Market for?"

Céline didn't know what to say. She was furious on Stephen's behalf.

On her own behalf, she was . . . something else. Something she should not have been.

"Did anyone ever tell you that you're beautiful when you're confused?" Stephen gushed. He gave her a moony grin. "Of course, you're also beautiful when you're angry, and when you're sad, and when you're happy, and when you're laughing, and when you're . . ."

"What?"

"When you're kissing me," he said. "But that one's just a theory. Do you want to test it out?"

"Stephen, I'm not sure you really know—"

Then he was kissing her.

Stephen Herondale was kissing her.

Stephen Herondale's lips were on her lips, his hands were on her waist, caressing her back, cupping her cheeks. Stephen Herondale's fingers were threading through her hair.

Stephen Herondale was holding her tight, tighter, as if he wanted more of her than he could have, as if he wanted all of her.

She tried to hold herself at a distance. This was not real, she reminded herself. This was not him. But it felt real. It felt like Stephen Herondale, warm in her arms, wanting her, and her resistance gave way.

For one eternal moment, she was lost to bliss.

"Enjoy it while you can. It'll wear off in an hour or so."

Dominique du Froid's voice yanked her back to reality—the reality in which Stephen was married to someone else. Céline forced herself to pull away. He let out a tiny whimper and looked like he was going to cry.

"First taste is free. You want permanent, you have to pay," the warlock said. "But I suppose I could give you the Shadowhunter discount."

Céline froze. "How did you know I was a Shadowhunter?"

"With your grace and beauty, how could you be anything else?" Stephen said. Céline ignored him. Something was very wrong here. Her runes were covered; her clothing was convincingly mundane; her weapons were hidden. There was nothing to mark her true identity.

"Or perhaps you'd like to buy two doses," the warlock said. "One for this schmuck, and one for the schmuck behind the curtain. Not quite as handsome, of course, but those uptight ones can be a lot of fun once they let loose. . . ."

Céline's hand crept toward her hidden dagger.

"You look surprised, Céline," the warlock said. "Did you honestly think I didn't know you three stooges were watching me? Did you think I would just leave my booth without a security system? I guess lover boy's not the only thing dumb but pretty around here."

"How do you know my name?"

The warlock threw back her head and laughed. Her molars gleamed with gold. "Every Downworlder in Paris knows about poor Céline Montclaire, wandering the city like a murderous little Éponine. We all feel a little sorry for you."

Céline lived with a steady, secret simmer of rage, but now she felt it boiling over.

"I mean, I can't afford to have Shadowhunters poking around in my business, so I'm still going to have to take care of you, but I'll feel sorry for you as you die."

Céline drew her dagger just as a flock of Halphas demons exploded from the tent. The winged beasts swooped toward her and Stephen, razor-sharp talons extended, beaks open to unleash an unearthly screech.

"Demon pigeons!" Stephen shouted in disgust, his long-sword in his hand. The blade flashed silver in the starlight as he sliced and slashed through thick, scaly wings.

Céline danced and dodged two birdlike demons, fending them off with her dagger as she pulled out two seraph blades with her free hand. "*Zuphlas*," she whispered. "*Jophiel*." As the blades began to glow, she flung them in opposite directions. Each flew true, straight into a demon's throat. Both Halphas demons exploded in a cloud of bloody feathers and ichor. Céline was already in motion, leaping through the warlock's curtain. "Robert!" she cried.

He was locked inside what looked like a gigantic antique birdcage, its floor coated with Halphas feathers—as was he. He looked unharmed. And *very* unhappy.

Céline broke through the lock as quickly as she could, and the two of them rejoined Stephen, who had managed to dispatch several of the demons, though a handful of them swooped off the ground to safety, looping and diving through the night sky. Dominique had opened a Portal and was about to leap through it. Robert seized her by the throat, then slammed the blunt end of his sword down on her head with a resounding thud. She dropped to the ground, out cold.

"So much for stealth," he said.

"Céline, you're wounded!" Stephen said, sounding horrified.

Céline realized a demonic beak had torn a chunk out of her

calf. The blood was seeping through her jeans. She had barely felt it, but as the adrenaline of battle faded away, a sharp, stabbing pain took its place.

Stephen already had his stele in his hand, eager to apply an *iratze*. "You're even more beautiful when you're bleeding," he said.

Céline shook her head and backed away. "I can do it myself."

"But it would be my honor to heal your perfect skin," Stephen protested.

"Did he get hit on the head?" Robert asked.

Céline was too embarrassed to explain. Fortunately, the cawing of Halphas demons echoed in the distance, followed by a woman's scream. "You two watch the warlock," she said. "I'll deal with the rest of the demons before they eat anyone." She took off before Robert could ask any more questions.

"I'll miss you!" Stephen called after her. "You're so cute when you're bloodthirsty!"

More than a hundred and fifty years before, the Shadowhunter Tobias Herondale had been convicted of cowardice, a crime punishable by death. The Law, in those days, was not just hard, it was merciless. Tobias went mad and took flight, so he could not be tried and executed for his crimes, so in his absence, the Clave meted his punishment out on his wife, Eva. Death to her. Death to the Herondale child she carried.

This, at least, was the story.

Many decades ago, Zachariah had learned the truth behind this tale. He had met the warlock who saved Eva's child—and then, after the mother's death, raised that child as her own.

That child had sired a child, who had sired a child, and so

forth: a secret line of Herondales, lost to the Shadowhunter world. Until now.

The surviving member of this line was in grave danger. For a long time, that was all Brother Zachariah knew. For Tessa, for Will, he had dedicated himself to learning more. He had followed bread crumbs, run headlong into dead ends, and nearly died at the hand of a faerie who wanted the lost Herondale to stay that way. Or worse, Zachariah feared.

The lost descendant of Tobias Herondale had fallen in love with a faerie. Their child—and all their child's children—were part Shadowhunter, part fey.

Which meant Zachariah wasn't the only one seeking. He strongly suspected, however, he was the only seeker who meant no harm. If an emissary of Faerie was willing to attack not just a Shadowhunter but a Silent Brother—willing to break the Accords in the most egregious of ways—simply to stop his search, then surely the search was imperative. Surely the danger was mortal.

Decades of quiet inquiries had led here, to the Paris Shadow Market, to a booth run by the man rumored to have in his possession a precious heron-shaped pendant, a Herondale heirloom. The man named Crow, who most assumed to be a mundane with the Sight, known as savvy but untrustworthy, a man all too satisfied by life in the shadows.

Zachariah had learned the whereabouts of the pendant first—it was a Parisian warlock who'd heard about his search and contacted him with confirmation. She told him his suspicions were correct: the owner of the pendant, whatever he wanted to call himself, was a Herondale.

Which, apparently, was old news to everyone but Zachariah himself.

You've known about your heritage all this time? And yet you never revealed yourself?

"Sweetheart, I think you can put down the crossbow," Crow told the woman. "The psychic monk doesn't seem like he means us any harm."

She lowered the weapon, though she didn't look very happy about it.

Thank you.

"And maybe you should leave us alone to talk," Crow added.

"I don't think that's a good idea—"

"Rosemary, trust me. I got this."

The woman, who must have been his wife, sighed. It was the sound of someone who understood stubbornness and had long ago given up trying to fight it. "Fine. But you . . ." She poked Brother Zachariah with the crossbow, hard enough he could feel it through his thick robes. "Anything happens to him, and I will hunt you down and make you pay."

I have no intention of letting anything happen to either of you. That's why I've come.

"Yeah, whatever." She took Crow in her arms. The two embraced for a long moment. Zachariah had often heard the expression "holding on for dear life," but rarely had he seen it enacted. The couple clung to each other like it was the only way to survive.

He remembered loving someone like that. He remembered the impossibility of saying good-bye. The woman whispered something to Crow, then hoisted her crossbow and disappeared into the Paris night.

"We're newlyweds, and she's a little overprotective," Crow said. "You know how it is."

I'm afraid I do not.

Crow looked him up and down, and Brother Zachariah wondered what this man saw. Whatever it was, he seemed unimpressed. "Yeah, I guess you wouldn't."

I have been looking for you for a long time, longer than you can imagine.

"Look, I'm sorry you wasted your time, but I don't want anything to do with you people."

I fear you don't realize the danger you're in. I am not the only one looking for you—

"But you're the only one who can protect me, right? 'Come with me if you want to live,' and all that? Yeah, I've seen that movie. Not interested in living it."

He was plenty sure of himself, Brother Zachariah thought, and felt the strange urge to smile. Maybe there was a trace of the familiar here after all.

"A man like me, he makes his fair share of enemies. I've been looking out for myself my whole life, and I don't see any reason I—"

Whatever he said next was drowned out by an unholy screeching. A giant birdlike demon swooped down, speared Crow's coat with its razor-sharp beak, and lifted him into the air.

Brother Zachariah seized one of the seraph blades he had brought along, just in case. *Mebahiah*, he named it, and flung it at the birdlike demon. The blade embedded itself in the feathered sternum, and the demon exploded midair. Crow tumbled several feet to the ground, landing in a noisy heap of feathers and ichor. Zachariah rushed over to help the man to his feet, but these efforts were rebuffed.

Crow examined the large, ragged hole in his trench coat

with disgust. "That was brand-new!"

It is indeed a very nice coat. Or . . . it was. Zachariah refrained from pointing out the good fortune that the Halphas demon hadn't ripped a hole through anything more valuable. Like his rib cage.

"So is that the danger you came to warn me about? Saving my new coat from a demon seagull?"

It struck me as more of a demon pigeon.

Crow brushed himself off. He darted several suspicious looks at the sky, as if expecting another attack. "Listen, Mr. . . ."

Brother. Brother Zachariah.

"Right, okay, bro, I can see that a guy like you could come in handy in a fight. And if you're that determined to protect me from some big, scary danger, I guess I won't fight you on it."

Brother Zachariah was surprised by the sudden change of heart. Perhaps nearly getting pecked to death by a demon pigeon had that effect on people.

I'd like to take you somewhere safe.

"Sure. Fine. Give me a few hours to tie up some loose ends, and Rosemary and I will meet you on the Pont des Arts at dawn. We'll do whatever you want. Promise."

I can accompany you, as you tie these ends.

"Listen, *brother*, the kinds of ends I'm talking about, they don't take kindly to Shadowhunters poking around in their business. If you catch my drift."

Your drift sounds mildly criminal.

"You want to make a citizen's arrest?"

I am concerned only with your safety.

"I made it twenty-two years without your help. I think I can make it another six hours, don't you?"

Brother Zachariah had invested decades into this search.

It seemed wildly unwise to let this man slip away, with only a promise that he would return. Especially given what he'd learned about the man's reputation. It didn't exactly inspire confidence in his word.

"Look, I know what you're thinking, and I know I can't stop you from following me. So I'm just asking you flat out: You want me to trust you? Then you try trusting me. And I'm swearing, on whatever you need me to, that your precious lost Shadowhunter will be on that bridge waiting for you at dawn."

Against his better judgment, Brother Zachariah nodded.

Go.

Céline had no taste for torture. Not that this was what they would call it, whatever they did to the warlock to get her to talk. Valentine had taught his Circle to be careful with their words. Robert and Stephen would "interrogate" Dominique du Froid, using whatever methods they deemed requisite. When they got the answers they needed—names of her Shadowhunter contacts, details of crimes committed—they would deliver her and an inventory of her sins to Valentine.

The warlock was bound to a folding chair in the cheap flat they were using as a home base.

The warlock was unconscious, blood trickling from the shallow wound on her forehead.

This was how Robert and Stephen referred to her, not by name but as "the warlock," as if she were more thing than person.

Valentine had wanted them to conduct this investigation without alerting the warlock to their presence. It was only midnight on their first day in Paris, and they'd already screwed everything up. "If we bring him some answers, he can't be too mad," Stephen said. It sounded more like wish than prediction.

Stephen had stopped commenting on the gamine beauty of Céline's legs and the addictive qualities of her porcelain skin. He claimed not to remember the effects of the warlock's potion, but his glance strayed to Céline every time he thought she wasn't looking. She couldn't help wondering.

What if he did remember?

What if, having finally touched her, held her, kissed her, he'd discovered a new desire in himself?

He was still married to Amatis, of course; even if he desired Céline—maybe even, a little bit, loved Céline—there was nothing to be done about it.

But what if?

"Is anyone else hungry?" Céline said.

"Am I ever not hungry?" Stephen said. He slapped the warlock sharply. She stirred but did not wake.

Céline backed toward the door. "Why don't I go find us something to eat, while you're . . . taking care of this?"

Robert yanked the warlock's hair back, hard. She yelped, and her eyes flew open. "Shouldn't take long."

"Great." Céline hoped they couldn't tell how desperate she was to get out of the apartment. She didn't have the stomach for this kind of thing, but she couldn't have them report that back to Valentine. She'd worked too hard to gain his respect.

"Hey, you're limping," Stephen said. "You need another *iratze*?"

He was worried about her. She told herself not to read anything into it. "It doesn't even hurt anymore," she lied. "I'm fine."

She'd applied the healing rune half-heartedly, and it had

not completely closed her wound. She preferred, sometimes, to feel the pain.

When she was a child, her parents had often refused her *iratzes* after training sessions, especially when her injuries were caused by her own mistakes. *Let the pain remind you to do better next time,* they told her. All these years later, she was still making so many mistakes.

Céline was halfway down the precarious staircase when she realized she'd forgotten her wallet. She tromped painfully back up, then hesitated outside the door, stopped by the sound of her name.

"Me and Céline?" she heard Stephen say.

Feeling slightly ridiculous, Céline withdrew her stele and drew a careful rune on the door. Their amplified voices came through loud and clear.

Stephen laughed. "You've got to be kidding me."

"It sounded like a pretty good kiss. . . ."

"I was under the influence!"

"Still. She's pretty, don't you think?"

There was an excruciating pause. "I don't know, I never really thought about it."

"You do realize that marriage doesn't mean you're never allowed to *look* at another woman, right?"

"It's not that," Stephen said. "It's . . ."

"The way she follows you around like a drooling puppy?"

"That doesn't help," Stephen acknowledged. "She's just such a *child*. Like, no matter how old she gets, she's always going to need someone else telling her what to do."

"I'll give you that," Robert said. "But Valentine seems convinced there's something more to her."

"Nobody's right all the time," Stephen said, and now they were both laughing. "Not even him."

"Don't let him hear you say that!"

Céline didn't realize she was in motion until she felt the rain on her face. She collapsed against the cool stone of the building's facade, wishing she could melt into it. To turn herself to stone; to shut down her nerves, her senses, her heart; to feel *nothing* . . . if only.

Their laughter echoed in her ears.

She was a joke.

She was pathetic.

She was someone Stephen had never thought about, never cared about, never wanted. Would never want, under any circumstances.

She was a pathetic creature. A child. A mistake.

The sidewalks were empty. The streets shimmered with rain. The searchlight beacon atop the Eiffel Tower had gone to sleep, along with the rest of the city. Céline felt utterly alone. Her leg throbbed. Her tears would not stop. Her heart screamed. She had nowhere to go but could not go back upstairs, back to that room, to that laughter. She set off blindly into the Paris night.

Céline was at home in the dark, slumbering streets. She wandered for hours. Through the Marais and past the hulking Pompidou, crossing from the Right Bank to the Left and back again. She visited with the gargoyles of Notre Dame, those hideous stone demons clinging to Gothic spires, awaiting their chance to devour the faithful. It seemed unfair that the city was so full of stone creatures who could feel nothing, and here she was, feeling so unbearably much.

She was in the Tuileries—more bloody ghosts, more creatures carved of stone—when she spotted the trail of ichor. She was still a Shadowhunter, and she was a Shadowhunter in desperate need of distraction, so she followed it. She caught up with the Shax demon in the Opera district but stayed in the shadows, wanting to see what it was up to. Shax demons were trackers, used to hunt people who didn't want to be found. And this demon was definitely tracking something.

Céline tracked it in turn.

She tracked it through the slumbering courtyards of the Louvre. It was oozing ichor from a wound, but it wasn't moving like a creature slinking off to nurse its wounds. Its giant pincers skittered at the cobblestones as it hesitated at corners, deciding which way to turn. This was a predator, tracking its prey.

The demon paused in the archway of the Louvre, at the foot of the Pont des Arts. The small pedestrian bridge stretched across the Seine, its railings crowded with lovers' locks. It was said that if a couple attached a lock to the Pont des Arts, their love would last forever. The bridge was almost deserted at this hour, except for one young couple, locked in an embrace. Completely oblivious to the Shax demon slithering out of the shadows, pincers clicking together in eager anticipation.

Céline always carried a misericord blade. Its narrow point was exactly what she needed to penetrate the insectoid demon's carapace.

She hoped.

"*Gadreel*," Céline whispered, naming a seraph blade. She crept behind the Shax demon, as steady and silent as it was. She, too, could be a predator. In one smooth, sure motion, she stabbed the misericord straight through the carapace, then slid the seraph blade into the wound she'd opened.

The demon dissolved.

It had all happened so swiftly, so quietly, that the couple on the bridge didn't even break from their embrace. They were too intent on each other to realize how close they'd come to being a demon's late-night snack. Céline lingered, trying to imagine it: standing on the bridge with someone who loved her, a man gazing so intently into her eyes that he wouldn't have noticed the world ending.

But Céline's imagination gave out. Reality had caged her in. As long as she thought Stephen hadn't noticed her, she could fantasize about what might happen if he ever did.

Now she knew. She could not unknow.

Céline wiped and sheathed her blades, then crept closer to the couple, close enough to hear what they were saying. She was glamoured, so there was no danger in doing a little eavesdropping, but she tried to keep herself hidden in case more demons appeared. What words did a man say to the woman he loved, when he thought no one else could hear? She might never find out, if she waited for someone to say them to her.

"I hate to say I told you so," the woman said, "but . . ."

"Who knew he'd be so willing to trust a warlock?"

"Who knew anyone would believe *you* were the long-lost descendant of some noble Shadowhunter line?" she said, then laughed. "Oh wait, I knew. Admit it, deep down, you knew it would work. You just didn't want it to."

"Of course I didn't want it to." He touched her cheek, impossibly gently. "I hate this. I hate leaving you here." Céline realized with a slight shock that she recognized him. This was the man the Silent Brother had chased after at the Market.

"It's not for long. And it's for the best, Jack, I promise."

"You'll come find me in L.A. as soon as it's taken care of? You swear?"

"In the Shadow Market. At our old place. I swear. As soon as I can be sure the trail's gone cold." She kissed him, long and hard. When she pressed her hand to his cheek, Céline spotted the glint of a wedding band.

"Rosemary—"

"I don't want you anywhere near these people. It's not safe."

"But it's safe for you?"

"You know I'm right," she said.

The man hung his head and tucked his hands into the pockets of his trench coat. It looked expensive, except for the giant gaping hole torn through the left side. "Yeah."

"You ready?"

He nodded, and she pulled a small bottle from her bag. "This better work the way it's supposed to." She handed it to her husband, who uncorked it, swallowed its contents, and tossed it into the river.

A moment later, he clutched his hands to his face and began to scream.

Céline panicked. It wasn't her place to interfere, but she couldn't just stand here and watch as this woman murdered her—

"Jack, Jack, it's okay, you're okay."

She clung to him as the man moaned and shuddered, and, finally, slumped quietly into her arms. "I think it worked," he said.

When they backed away from each other, Céline gasped. Even in the dim light of the streetlights, she could see that his face had transformed. He had been a blond with sparkling green eyes and sharp, chiseled features, around the age of Stephen and nearly as handsome. Now he looked ten years older, his face carved with worry lines, his hair mud colored, his smile crooked.

"Hideous," the woman named Rosemary said approvingly. Then she kissed him again, just as desperately as before, as if nothing had changed. "Now go."

"You sure?"

"As sure as I am that I love you."

The man fled into the night, his coat melting into the darkness.

"And ditch the trench!" Rosemary called after him. "It's too obvious!"

"Never!" he shouted back, and then he was gone.

Rosemary sagged against the bridge and buried her face in her hands. So she didn't see the gargoyle behind her blink its eyes and swivel its stone snout in her direction.

Céline suddenly remembered: the Pont des Arts *had* no gargoyles. This was a flesh-and-blood Achaieral demon, and it looked hungry.

With a furious roar, the monstrous shadow peeled itself off the bridge and unfolded a set of huge, batlike wings that blotted out the night. It opened its jaw wide and bared razor-like teeth, then lunged straight for Rosemary's throat. With shocking speed, Rosemary hefted a sword and slashed. The demon screeched in pain, raking its talons against the metal blade with enough force to knock it from the woman's hands. Rosemary stumbled to the ground, and the demon seized its moment. It leaped onto her chest, immobilizing her beneath its massive wings, and hissed. Teeth neared flesh.

"*Sariel*," Céline whispered, and stabbed a seraph blade through the demon's neck. It yowled with pain and whirled toward her, its innards bursting through its hide even as it tried, in its last remaining moments, to attack.

Rosemary heaved her sword and sliced off the creature's head, seconds before head and torso exploded into a cloud of dust. Satisfied, she collapsed backward, the wound in her shoulder bleeding freely.

Céline could tell how much it hurt—and how determined the woman was to reveal no pain. She knelt by her side. Rosemary flinched away. "Let me see—I can help."

"I would never ask for help from a Shadowhunter," the woman said bitterly.

"You didn't exactly ask. And you're welcome."

The woman sighed, then examined her bloody wound. She touched it gingerly, winced. "As long as you're here, you want to give me an *iratze*?"

It was obvious the woman was no mundane. Even a mundane with the Sight couldn't have fought the way she did. But that didn't mean she could withstand an *iratze*. No one but a Shadowhunter could.

"Look, I don't really have the time to explain it, and I can't exactly go to the hospital and tell them I got gnawed on by a demon, can I?"

"If you know about *iratzes*, you know that only a Shadowhunter can bear a rune," Céline said.

"I know." Rosemary met her gaze steadily.

She didn't bear the Voyance rune. But the way she had moved, the way she had fought . . .

"Have you borne a rune before?" Céline asked hesitantly.

Rosemary smirked. "What do you think?"

"Who *are* you?"

"No one you need to worry about. You going to help or not?"

Céline drew her stele. Applying a rune to anyone who wasn't a Shadowhunter meant probable death, certain agony. She took a deep breath, then carefully applied stele to skin.

Rosemary let out a relieved sigh.

"Are you going to tell me who sent a Shax demon after you?" Céline said. "And whether it was the same person who made sure an Achaieral demon was here to finish the job?"

"No. You going to tell me why you're wandering around in the middle of the night looking like someone just drowned your pet rock in the Seine?"

"No."

"Okay, then. And thank you."

"That guy who was here with you before . . ."

"You mean the one you didn't see and won't say anything about, ever, if you know what's good for you?"

"You love him, and he loves you, right?" Céline asked.

"I guess he must, because there are some dangerous people out there looking for me," Rosemary said. "And he's done his best to make sure they think they're looking for him instead."

"I don't understand."

"And you don't have to. But yeah. He loves me. I love him. Why?"

"I just . . ." She wanted to ask what that was like, how it felt. She wanted, also, to extend the conversation. She was afraid to be alone again, stranded on this bridge between the endless black of river and sky. "I just want to make sure you have someone to take care of you."

"We take care of each other. That's how it works. Speaking of which . . ." She gave Céline an appraising look. "I'm in your debt now, for helping me out with the demon. And for keeping my secret."

"I didn't say I would—"

"You will. And I don't believe in debts, so let me do you a favor."

"I don't need anything," Céline said, meaning, *I don't need anything anyone can give me.*

"I keep my eyes open, and I see what's happening in the Shadowhunter world. You need more than you think you do. Most of all, you need to stay away from Valentine Morgenstern."

Céline stiffened. "What do you know about Valentine?"

"I know that you're just his type, young and impressionable, and I know that he can't be trusted. I pay attention. You should too. He's not telling you everything. I know that." She looked over Céline's shoulder, and her eyes widened. "Someone's coming. You should get out of here."

Céline turned around. A Silent Brother was gliding along the Left Bank, nearing the edge of the bridge. There was no way of knowing if it was the same one she'd met in the Shadow Market, but she couldn't risk running into him again. Not after what she'd told him. It was too humiliating.

"Remember," Rosemary said. "Valentine is not to be trusted."

"And why should I trust *you*?"

"No reason at all," Rosemary said. Without another word, she strode down the bridge toward the Silent Brother.

The sky was pinking. The endless night had finally given way to dawn.

I had expected to find your husband on this bridge. But even as he formed the words, Brother Zachariah sensed their untruth.

He had trusted a man he knew could not be trusted. He had let his sympathies for the Herondale line, his desire to believe there remained some bond between the Carstairs and the Herondales—even though this man was barely a Herondale and Zachariah was barely a Carstairs—cloud his judgment. And now it was Jack Crow who might bear the consequences.

"He's not coming. And you're never going to see him again, Shadowhunter, so I suggest you not bother to look."

I understand that the Shadowhunters have given your family every reason not to trust us, but—

"Don't take it personally. I don't trust anyone," she said. "It's how I've managed to stay alive."

She was stubborn and rude, and Brother Zachariah couldn't help but like her.

"I mean, if I *was* going to trust someone, it wouldn't be a cult of violent fundamentalists who get a kick out of executing their own . . . but like I said, I don't trust anyone."

Except Jack Crow.

"That's not his name anymore."

Whatever name he chooses, he will always be a Herondale.

She laughed, and when she did, her face took on a strangely familiar cast. Familiar in the way that Jack Crow's had never been. "You don't know nearly as much as you think you do, Shadowhunter."

Brother Zachariah reached into his robe and pulled out the heron necklace he'd bought from the Shadow Market. The necklace, he remembered, that Crow had sold without his wife's permission or knowledge. As a man might do if it were not truly his to sell. The pendant glittered in the dawn light. Zachariah marked her surprise and offered the chain.

She opened her palm and allowed him to place the pendant gently in her possession. Something deep in her seemed to settle as her hand wrapped around the heron charm—as if she had lost some essential piece of her soul, and now it was returned to her.

"A pigeon?" She raised her eyebrows.

A heron. Perhaps you recognize it?

"Why would I?"

Because I purchased it from your husband.

Her lips were pressed together in a thin, tight line. Her hand had formed a fist around the chain. It was clear the child at the booth had spoken the truth: she didn't know the pendant had been for sale.

"Then why give it to me?"

She could pretend a lack of interest, but Zachariah wondered what she would say if he asked for it back. He suspected he would have a fight on his hands.

Because I have a feeling it belongs to you—and to your family.

She stiffened, and Brother Zachariah marked the minute twitch of her hand, as if instinctively reaching for a weapon. She had sharp instincts, but also self-control—and arrogance, grace, and loyalty, and the capacity for great love, and a laugh that could light up the sky.

He had come to Paris looking for the lost Herondale.

And he had fou d her.

"I don't know what you're talking about."

You are the Herondale. Not your husband. You. The lost heir to a noble line of warriors.

"I'm nobody," she snapped. "Nobody of interest to you, at least."

I could reach into your mind and confirm the truth.

She flinched. Zachariah didn't have to read her mind to understand her panic, or her welling self-doubt as she scrambled to figure out how he had seen through the ruse.

But I would not trespass on your secrets. I want only to help you.

"My parents told me everything I need to know about the Shadowhunters," she said, and Brother Zachariah understood this was as close to an admission as he was going to get. "Your precious little Clave. Your *Law*." She spit out that last word like it was poison.

I am not here as a representative of the Clave. They have no idea I've come to you—or even that you exist. I have my own reasons for finding you, for wanting to protect you.

"And they are?"

I would not trespass on your secrets, and I would ask that you not trespass on mine. Know only that I owe a great debt to your family. The bonds holding me to the Herondales run deeper than blood.

"Well, that's nice of you and all, but no one asked you to pay any debts," Rosemary said. "Jack and I are doing just fine, taking care of each other, and that's what we'll keep doing."

It was clever of you to make it seem as if your husband was the one I sought, but—

"It was clever of *Jack*. People underestimate him. And they pay for it."

—but, if I could penetrate your ruse, others who seek you may as well. And they are more dangerous than you know.

"These 'others' you talk about butchered my parents." Rosemary's face betrayed no expression. "Jack and I have been on the run for years. Trust me, I know exactly how dangerous this is. And I know exactly how dangerous it is to trust a stranger, even a stranger with psychic ninja powers and a deeply weird fashion sense."

One of the things Brother Zachariah had learned in the Silent Brotherhood was the power of acceptance. Sometimes it was stronger to recognize an unwinnable fight and accept defeat— the better to begin laying groundwork for the next battle.

Though this was not a battle, he reminded himself. You could not war for a person's trust; you could only earn it.

Your heron necklace now has an enchantment on it. If you encounter trouble you cannot face on your own, you need only summon me, and I will come.

"If you think you can track us through this thing—"

Your husband suggested that the only way to earn trust is by offering it. I will not try to find you if you prefer not to be found. But with this pendant, you can always find me. I trust you will summon me for help, if and when you need it. Please trust that I will always answer.

"And who are you, exactly?"

You may call me Brother Zachariah.

"I could, but if I end up in this hypothetical situation where I need my life saved by some bloodthirsty monk, I'd rather know his actual name."

I was once . . . It had been so long. He almost didn't feel entitled to the name. But there was a deep, nearly human pleasure in allowing himself to claim it. *I was once known as James Carstairs. Jem.*

"So who will *you* summon when you encounter trouble you can't face on your own, Jem?" She fastened the pendant around her neck, and Zachariah felt a sliver of relief. At least he'd accomplished that much.

I don't anticipate that.

"Then you're not paying attention."

She touched him on the shoulder then, unexpectedly, and with unexpected gentleness.

"Thank you for trying," she said. "It's a start."

Then he was watching her walk away.

Brother Zachariah watched the water stream beneath the bridge. He thought about that other bridge, in another city, where once a year he returned to remember the man he'd once been and the dreams that man had once had.

At the far end of the Pont des Arts, a young street musician opened a violin case and raised the instrument to his chin. For a moment, Zachariah thought he was imagining it— that he had conjured up a fantasy of his former self. But as he drew closer—because he could not stay away—he realized the musician was a girl. She was young, no more than fourteen or fifteen, her hair swept up beneath a newsboy cap, a neat, old-fashioned bow tie at the collar of her white blouse.

She bowed the strings and began to play a haunting melody. Brother Zachariah recognized it: a Bartók violin concerto that had been written well after Jem Carstairs had put down his violin.

Silent Brothers played no music. They didn't listen to music either, not in the ordinary way. But even with their senses sealed off to mortal pleasures, they still heard.

Jem heard.

He was glamoured; the musician must have assumed she was alone. There was no audience for her music, no possibility of payment. She wasn't playing for spare change but for her own pleasure. She faced the water, the sky. This was a song to welcome the sun.

Distantly, he remembered the soft pressure of the chin rest. He remembered his fingertips capering across the strings. He remembered the dance of the bow.

He remembered how, sometimes, it had felt like the music was playing him.

There was no music in the Silent City; there was no sun, no dawn. There was only dark. There was only quiet.

Paris was a city that luxuriated in the senses—food, wine, art, romance. Everywhere was a reminder of what he'd lost, the pleasures of a world no longer his. He had learned to live with the loss. It was harder, when he immersed himself in the world like this, but it was bearable.

This was something else, though.

The nothing he felt, as he listened to the melody, watched the bow waltz up and down the strings—the great hollow it opened inside him, echoing only with the past? That made him feel utterly, dismally inhuman.

The longing he felt, to truly hear, to want, to *feel*? That made him feel almost alive.

Come home, the Brothers whispered in his mind. *It is time.*

Over the years, as he'd gained more control, Brother Zachariah had learned how to isolate himself from the voices of his Brothers when need be. It was a strange thing, the Brotherhood. Most assumed it was a lonely, solitary life—and it was, indeed, solitary. But he was never truly alone. The Brotherhood was always there, on the edge of his awareness, watching, waiting. Brother Zachariah needed only extend a hand, and the Brotherhood would reclaim him.

Soon, he promised them. *But not yet. I have more business here.*

He was more Silent Brother than not. But he was still less

Silent Brother than the others. It was a strange, liminal space, one that allowed him a modicum of privacy—and a desire for it that his Brothers had long since abandoned. Zachariah shut himself off from them for the moment. He felt a deep regret over his failure here, but it was good, it was *human*, to feel regret, and he wanted to savor it, all on his own.

Or maybe not all on his own.

There was, in fact, one more piece of business before he could return to the Silent City. He needed to explain himself to the one person who cared as much about the Herondales as he did.

He needed Tessa.

Céline didn't go to Valentine's apartment intending to break in. That would have been madness. And anyway, after a night and day of blindly wandering the city, she was too sleep deprived to form clear intentions of anything. She simply followed a whim. She wanted the certainty that settled over her in Valentine's presence, the power he had to make her believe. Not just in him but in herself.

After her strange encounter on the bridge, she'd considered going back to the flat in the Marais. She knew Stephen and Robert should be apprised of the unexpected demon activity, the possibility of a rogue Shadowhunter causing trouble and spreading suspicion about the Circle.

She couldn't face them. Let them worry about what had become of her. Or not worry. She no longer cared.

At least, she was trying very hard not to care.

She'd spent the day in the Louvre, haunting galleries that none of the tourists cared to see, old Etruscan masks and

Mesopotamian coins. She'd spent hours there when she was younger, blending in with the hordes of schoolchildren. It was easy, when you were a child, to go unseen.

The challenge, Céline understood now, was to be seen—and once seen, to endure judgment.

She couldn't stop thinking about the couple on the bridge, the way they'd gazed at each other. The way they'd touched each other, with so much care and so much need. Nor could she stop thinking about the woman's warning about Valentine. Céline was certain she could trust Valentine with her life.

But if she'd been so wrong about Stephen, how could she know for sure she was right about anything?

Valentine was staying in opulent quarters in the sixth arrondissement, down the street from a famous chocolatier and a *mercerie* where the custom hats cost more than most people spent on rent. She knocked loudly. When no one answered, it was easy enough to pick the lock.

I am breaking into Valentine Morgenstern's apartment, she thought, bewildered by herself. It didn't seem quite real.

The apartment was elegant, almost regal, walls draped with gold fleurs-de-lis, furniture covered with velvet. Plush rugs dotted the gleaming hardwood floors. Heavy golden curtains dimmed the light. The room's only anachronism was a large glass case in the center, inside of which lay Dominique du Froid, bound, beaten, and unconscious.

Before she could decide what to do, there was the sound of a key rattling in the lock. The doorknob turned. Without thinking, Céline dove behind the thick curtains. She held herself very, very still.

From her hiding spot, she couldn't see Valentine pacing

back and forth across the living room. But she could hear everything she needed to.

"Wake up," he snapped.

There was a pause, a rustling, and then a woman's yelp of pain.

"Halphas demons?" he said, sounding halfway between amused and enraged. "Really?"

"You told me to make it look real," Dominique whined.

"Yes, I told you to make it *look* real—not endanger them."

"You also told me you'd pay, but here I am, in some kind of cage. With an empty wallet. And a couple unseemly lumps on my head."

Valentine sighed heavily, as if this were all an irritating imposition on his time. "You told them exactly what we agreed upon, yes? And signed the confession?"

"Isn't that what the little brats told you when they dumped me here? So how about you pay me for my services, and we can forget this ever happened."

"Gladly."

There was a strange sound, one that Céline couldn't place. Then a smell, one that she could: burnt flesh.

Valentine cleared his throat. "You can come out now, Céline."

She froze. Didn't so much catch her breath as lose the ability to breathe.

"Not very good at subterfuge lately, are we? Come on now, show yourself." He clapped his hands together sharply, as if summoning a pet. "No more games."

Céline stepped out from behind the curtains, feeling like a fool.

"You knew I was here? The whole time?"

"You would be surprised what all I know, Céline." Valentine smiled coldly. As always, he was dressed in all black, which made his white-blond hair seem to glow with pale fire. Céline supposed that by objective standards, Valentine was just as handsome as Stephen, but it was impossible to think of him that way. He was handsome the way a statue was handsome: perfectly sculpted, unyielding as stone. Sometimes at the Academy, Céline would watch him with Jocelyn, wondering at the way a single touch from her could melt his ice. Once Céline had come upon them in an embrace and had watched from the shadows as they lost themselves in each other. When they broke from the kiss, Valentine had raised a hand to Jocelyn's cheek in an impossibly tender touch, and his expression, as he gazed at his first and only love, was almost human.

There was no trace of that in him now. He opened his arms wide, as if welcoming her to make herself at home in the opulent living room. The cage at the center was empty, except for a smoldering pile of black lace and leather. Dominique du Froid was gone.

Valentine followed her gaze.

"She was a criminal," he said. "I simply expedited the inevitable sentence."

There were rumors about Valentine, about the change that had come over him when his father was killed. Dark whispers about the cruelties he carried out not just on trespassing Downworlders but on anyone who crossed him. Anyone who *questioned* him.

"You look worried, Céline. Even . . . afraid."

"No," she said quickly.

"It's almost as if you think breaking into my apartment to spy on me might draw some kind of nasty consequence."

"I wasn't spying, I was just—"

He favored her with a smile then, so warm, so sunny, that she felt ridiculous for having been so afraid. "Would you settle for tea? And maybe some biscuits. You look like you haven't eaten in a year."

He set out a bounty: not just tea and biscuits but a sliced baguette, fresh chèvre and a small pot of honey, and a bowl of blueberries that tasted like they'd just been plucked from the branch. Céline hadn't known she was hungry until the taste of honey hit her tongue. She realized she was ravenous.

They made polite Paris small talk: their favorite cafés, their preferred picnic spots, the best crepe stand, the relative merits of the Orsay and the Pompidou. Then Valentine took a hearty bite of cheese-smeared baguette and said, almost cheerfully, "You know, of course, that the others think you're weak and not particularly bright."

Céline almost choked on a blueberry.

"If it were up to most of the Circle, you wouldn't be in it. Fortunately, this isn't a democracy. They think they know you, Céline, but they don't know the half of it, do they?"

Slowly, she shook her head. No one knew her, not really.

"I, on the other hand, believed in you. I trusted you. And you repay this trust with suspicion?"

"I really didn't—"

"Of course you had no suspicions. You just thought you'd pay a social call. Behind my curtains. While I was out."

"Okay. *Oui.* I was suspicious."

"See? You are smart." That smile again, warm and approving,

like she'd fulfilled his intentions. "And what is it you've discovered about me, with your intrepid investigation?"

There was no point in pretense. And Céline was almost as curious as she was terrified. So she told the truth, as she'd surmised it. "Dominique du Froid wasn't in business with two Shadowhunters. She was in business with you. You're trying to set someone up, and you're using us to do it."

"Us?"

"Me. Robert. Stephen."

"Robert and Stephen, yes. I'm indeed using them. But you? You're here, aren't you? You're getting the full story."

"I am?"

"If you want it . . ."

Céline had not had the kind of parents who read her fairy tales. But she'd read enough of them herself to know the cardinal rule of these stories: be careful what you wish for.

And like every Shadowhunter, she knew: all the stories are true.

"I want to know," she said.

He told her she was right. He was framing two Shadowhunters, innocent of these crimes but guilty of a much larger one—standing in the Circle's way. "They're bogged down in tradition, they're beholden to the Clave's corruption. And they're dead set on destroying me. So I acted first." He'd used the warlock to plant evidence, he admitted. Now he would use Stephen and Robert as witnesses to her confession. "Since she is, unfortunately, no longer able to testify."

"What about the Mortal Sword?" Céline asked. "Aren't you worried what will happen when the accused Shadowhunters are interrogated?"

Valentine tsked, as if disappointed that she hadn't jumped to the correct conclusion. "It's very unfortunate, they'll never make it that far. I happen to know these two Shadowhunters will make an escape attempt during their transport to the Silent City. They'll be killed in the ensuing chaos. Tragic."

The words sat heavy between them. Céline tried to process it. Valentine wasn't just setting up two Shadowhunters, two *innocent* Shadowhunters. He was planning to murder them in cold blood. This was an unthinkable crime, for which the Law would demand death.

"Why are you telling me this?" she said, trying to keep her voice from trembling. "What makes you think I won't turn you in? Unless . . ."

Unless he had no intention of letting her leave this apartment alive.

A man who could kill two Shadowhunters in cold blood could presumably kill a third. Everything in her said that she should leap to her feet, draw her weapon, fight her way out of here, run straight to the Paris Institute, tell them everything. Stop this—stop *him*—before he went any further. Valentine watched her calmly, palms up on the table, as if to say, *Your move.*

She didn't move.

The Verlac family, who ran the Paris Institute, were friends with her parents. More than once, a Verlac had sought out her hiding place and dumped her back home. That first time, she'd pleaded for asylum at the Institute, where all Shadowhunters were supposedly guaranteed a safe home. Céline was told she was too young to make such requests, too young to know what "safe" meant. She was told her parents loved her and she should stop causing them so much trouble.

She owed these people nothing.

Valentine, on the other hand, had singled her out. Given her a mission, a family. She owed him everything.

He leaned toward her, reached out his hand. She willed herself not to flinch. He touched her neck, lightly, where the Achaieral demon had scratched her. "You're hurt."

"It's nothing," she said.

"And you were limping."

"I'm fine."

"If you need another *iratze*—"

"I'm *fine*."

He nodded, like she'd confirmed a suspicion. "Yes. You prefer it this way, don't you."

"What way?"

"In pain."

Now Céline flinched. "I do not," she insisted. "That would be sick."

"But do you know *why* you prefer it? Why you chase the pain?"

She had never understood this about herself. Only knew it, in the deep, wordless way you knew your most essential truth.

There was something about pain that made her feel more solid, more real. More in control. Sometimes the pain felt like the only thing she *could* control.

"You covet pain, because you know it makes you strong," Valentine said. It felt like he had given name to her nameless soul. "You know why I understand you better than the rest of them? Because we're the same. We learned early, didn't we? Cruelty, harshness, pain: no one shielded us from the realities of life, and that made us strong. Most people, they're ruled by fear. They flee the specter of pain, and that makes them weak. You and I, Céline, we know the only way through is to *face* pain. To invite the cruelty of the world—and master it."

Céline had never thought of herself this way, hard and strong. She'd certainly never dared think of herself as anything like Valentine.

"That's why I wanted you in the Circle. Robert, Stephen, the others? They're still just boys. Children playing at adult games. They haven't yet been tested—they will be, but not yet. You and I, though? We're special. We haven't been children for a long time."

No one had ever called her strong. No one had called her special.

"Things are accelerating," Valentine said. "I need to know who's with me and who's not. So you can see why I told you the truth about this"—he gestured to the singed heap of warlock clothes—"situation."

"It's a test," she guessed. "A loyalty test."

"It's an opportunity," he corrected her. "To invite you into my confidence, and reward you for yours. My proposal: you stay silent about what you've learned here and allow events to proceed as I intend, and I will deliver you Stephen Herondale on a silver platter."

"What? I—I don't—I—"

"I told you, Céline. I know things. I know you. And I can give you what you want, if you really want it."

Be careful what you wish for, she thought again. But oh, she wished for Stephen. Even knowing what he thought of her, even with his mocking laughter ringing in her ears, even believing what Valentine said, that she was strong and Stephen was weak, even knowing what she knew to be true, that Stephen did not love her and never would, she wished for him. Always and forever.

"Or you can leave this apartment, run to the Clave, tell them whatever story you like. Save these two 'innocent' Shadowhunters—and lose the only family who's ever truly cared about you," Valentine said. "The choice is yours."

Tessa Gray breathed in the city that had once, briefly but indelibly, been her home. How many nights had she stood on this same bridge, gazing at the hulking shadow of Notre Dame, the rippling waters of the Seine, the proud scaffolding of the Eiffel Tower—all of it, Paris's heartbreaking beauty, blurred by her ceaseless tears. How many nights had she searched the river for her ageless reflection, imagining the seconds, days, years, centuries she might live, and every one of them in a world without Will.

No, not imagining.

Because it had been unimaginable.

Unimaginable, but here she was, more than fifty years later, still living. Still without him. Heart forever broken yet still beating, still strong.

Still capable of love.

She'd fled to Paris after he died, stayed until she was strong enough to face her future, and hadn't been back since. On the face of things, the city hadn't changed. But then, on the face of things, neither had she. You couldn't trust the face of things to show you their truth. You didn't have to be a shape-shifter to know that.

I'm so sorry, Tessa. I had her, and I let her go.

Even after all these years, she wasn't used to it, this cold version of Jem's voice speaking inside her mind, at once so intimate and so far away. His hand rested on the railing bare inches from hers. She could have touched him. He wouldn't pull away, not from her. But his skin would be so cold, so dry, like stone.

Everything about him like stone.

"You found her—that's what we set out to do, right? This was never about bringing the lost Herondale back to the Shadow-hunter world or choosing a path for her."

There was comfort in the familiar weight of the jade pendant around her neck, warm against her chest. She still wore it, every day, as she had since the day Jem gave it to her, more than a century before. He didn't know.

What you say is true, but still . . . it does not seem right for a Herondale to be in danger while we do nothing. I fear I failed you, Tessa. That I have failed him.

Between her and Jem, there was only ever one *him*.

"We found her, for Will. And you know Will would want her to choose for herself. Just like he did."

If he had still been wholly Jem, she would have put her arms around him. She would have let him feel, in her embrace, her breath, her heartbeat, how impossible it was for him to fail either her or Will.

But he was both Jem and not Jem. Both himself and unfathomably other, and she could only stand beside him, assure him with useless words that he had done enough.

He'd warned her once what would happen, as he became less himself, more Silent Brother—promised her that the transformation would never be complete. *When I no longer see the world with my human eyes, I will still be in some part the Jem you knew,* he had said. *I will see you with the eyes of my heart.*

When she looked at him now, his sealed eyes and lips, his cold face, when she breathed in his inhuman smell, like paper, like stone, like nothing that had ever lived or loved, she tried to remember this. She tried to believe that some part of him was still in there, seeing her, and longing to be seen.

It got harder every year. There had been moments, over the decades, when the Jem she remembered truly broke through. Once, during one of the mundane world's innumerable wars, they had even stolen a kiss—and almost more. Jem had pushed her away before things could go too far. After that, he'd held himself more distant from Tessa, almost as if afraid of what might happen if he let himself near the brink. That embrace, which she thought about almost every day, was more than forty years ago now—and every year, he seemed a little less Jem, a little less human. She feared he was forgetting himself, piece by piece.

She could not lose him. Not him, too.

She would be his memory.

I met a girl here, he said, *in love with a Herondale.*

She imagined she could hear a faint smile in his voice.

"Did she remind you of anyone?" Tessa teased.

Her love seemed to cause her great pain. I would have liked to help her.

It was one of the things she loved about him, his abiding desire to help anyone in need. This was something the Silent Brotherhood could not strip away.

"I used to come to this bridge all the time, you know, when I lived in Paris. After Will."

It is very peaceful here. And very beautiful.

She wanted to tell him that wasn't it. She hadn't come

for the peace or the beauty—she'd come because this bridge reminded her of Blackfriars Bridge, the bridge that belonged to her and Jem. She'd come because standing here, suspended between land and water, her hands tight on the iron railing, her face raised to the sky, reminded her of Jem. The bridge reminded her that there was still someone in the world that she loved. That even if half of her heart was gone forever, the other half was still here. Unreachable, maybe, but *here*.

She wanted to tell him, but she couldn't. It wouldn't be fair. It would be asking something of Jem that he couldn't deliver, and the world had already asked far too much of him.

"He would have hated it, the idea of a Herondale out there somewhere who thinks she can't trust the Shadowhunters. Who thinks *we're* the villains."

He might well have understood.

It was true. Will himself had been raised to distrust the Shadowhunters. He knew, better than most, how harshly the Clave treated those who turned their backs on it. He would have been enraged to learn about this lost branch of his family, at the thought of the Clave attempting to execute a mother and child for a father's sins. Tessa feared for the safety of this lost Herondale, but just as much, she longed to persuade her that some Shadowhunters could be trusted. She wanted to make this young woman understand that they weren't all hard and unfeeling: that some of them were like Will.

"I get so angry at them sometimes, the Shadowhunters who came before us, the mistakes they made. Think how many lives have been ruined by the choices of an earlier generation." She was thinking of Tobias Herondale, but also Axel Mortmain, whose parents had been murdered in front of him, and Aloysius Starkweather, who'd paid for that sin with his granddaughter's life. She was thinking, even, of her own brother, whose mother had refused to claim him as her own. Who might have found his way to being a better man had he been better loved.

It would be unjust to blame the past for choices made in the present. Nor can we justify present choices by invoking the sins of the past. You and I know that, better than most.

Jem, too, had seen his parents murdered in front of him. Jem had endured a life of pain, but he'd never let himself be warped by it—never turned to revenge or vindictiveness. And Tessa had been conceived as a demonic tool, literally. She could have chosen to accept this fate; she could have chosen to flee the Shadow World altogether, return to the mundane life she'd once known and pretend she did not see the darkness. Or she could have claimed that darkness as her own.

She'd chosen a different path. They both had.

We always have a choice, Jem said, and for once, the voice in her mind sounded like him, warm and close. *It's not always the choice we would want, but it's a choice nonetheless. The past happens to us. But we choose our future. We can only hope that our lost Herondale ultimately chooses to save herself.*

"That's the best hope for any of us, I suppose."

Jem slid his hand across the railing and rested it atop hers. It was, as she knew it would be, cold. Inhuman.

But it was also Jem: flesh and blood, undeniably alive. And where there was life, there was hope. Maybe not now, not yet, but someday, they could still have their future. She chose to believe it.

* ✳ *

The Saint-Germain-des-Prés Church was founded in 558 AD. The original abbey was built on the ruins of an ancient Roman temple, then destroyed two centuries later in a Norman siege. Rebuilt in the tenth century AD, the church has now endured, in one form or another, for a millennium. The Merovingian kings are buried in its tombs, as is the torn-out heart of John II Casimir Vasa and the headless body of René Descartes.

Most mornings the abbey saw a steady trickle of tourists and observant locals wandering through its apse, lighting candles, bowing heads, whispering prayers to whoever might be listening. But this particular drizzly August morning, a sign on the door indicated the church was closed to the public. Inside, the Paris Conclave had assembled. Shadowhunters from all across France listened solemnly to charges lodged against two of their own.

Jules and Lisette Montclaire stood silently, heads bowed, as Robert Lightwood and Stephen Herondale testified to their crimes.

Their daughter, Céline Montclaire, was not called on to speak. She had, of course, not been present for the warlock's revelation of her parents' crimes.

The scene played out as if Valentine had scripted it himself, and like everyone else present, Céline did exactly as Valentine intended: nothing.

Inside, she was at war with herself. Furious at Valentine for making her complicit in her parents' destruction; furious with herself for sitting silently as their fates were sealed; more furious at her own instinct for mercy. After all, her parents had never shown any to her. Her parents had done their best to teach her that mercy was weakness, and cruelty was strength. So she steeled herself to be strong. Told herself this wasn't personal; this was about protecting the Circle. If Valentine believed this was the righteous way forward, then this was the only way forward.

She watched her parents quaver with fear under the steely eye of the Inquisitor, and she remembered the two of them backing away from her, ignoring her cries, closing her into darkness—and she said nothing. She sat very still, head lowered, and endured. They had taught her that, too.

The Shadowhunters of France all knew Céline, or thought they did: that sweet and obedient daughter of the Provençal countryside. They knew how devoted she was to her parents. Such a dutiful daughter. She would, of course, inherit their estate.

Céline bore the weight of the stares with dignity. She did not acknowledge the pitying looks. She kept her eyes on the floor when the judgment was issued and so did not see the horror on her parents' faces. She did not watch them placed in the custody of the Silent Brothers, to be transported to the Silent City. She did not expect them to survive long enough to face the Mortal Sword.

She did not speak to Robert or Stephen, and let them believe this was because they had just consigned her parents to death.

Valentine caught up with Céline just outside the church. He offered her a Nutella crepe. "From the stand across from Les Deux Magots," he said. "Your favorite, right?"

She shrugged but took what he had to offer. The first bite—warm chocolate hazelnut, sweet pastry—was as perfect as ever and made her feel like a child again.

Sometimes it was difficult to believe she had ever been young.

"You could have told me," she said.

"And ruin the surprise?"

"Those are my parents."

"Indeed."

"And you've killed them."

"They're still alive, last I checked," Valentine said. "They could probably stay that way, with a word from you. But I didn't hear it."

"You took a pretty big risk, not telling me the whole story. Expecting me to let you . . . to let them go."

"Did I?" he said. "Or did I simply know you well enough to know exactly what you would choose? To know I was doing you a favor."

He met her eyes. She could not look away. For the first time, she didn't want to.

"You don't have to admit it, Céline. Just know that I know. You're not alone in that."

He *saw* her; he understood. It was as if a muscle she'd been clenching her entire life finally released.

"A deal's a deal, though," he said. "Even if you got more than you bargained for. Stephen is all yours—assuming that's still what you want?"

"How exactly would you make that happen?" she asked, clear now on what Valentine was capable of. "You wouldn't . . . you wouldn't hurt him, would you?"

Valentine looked disappointed in her. "Stephen is my closest friend, my most trusted lieutenant. The fact that you could even ask that makes me question your loyalty, Céline. Do you want me questioning your loyalty?"

She shook her head.

Then that warm, buttery smile broke over his face again. She couldn't tell whether this was the real Valentine breaking through or the mask dropping back over his face. "On the other hand, it would be foolish of you not to ask. And as we've discussed, there's nothing foolish in you. No matter what people might think. So, your answer: no. I swear to you, on the Angel, I will cause Stephen no harm in the enactment of this agreement."

"And no threat of harm?"

"Do you think so little of yourself that you assume a man would need to be threatened with harm before he could love you?"

She didn't answer. She didn't need to: he could surely read it all over her face.

"Stephen is with the wrong woman," Valentine told her, almost gently. "Deep down, he knows that. I'll simply make this as clear to him as it is to us, and the rest will be as easy as falling off a cliff. You need only relax and let gravity do its work. Don't be afraid to reach for the things you really want, Céline. It's beneath you."

What she really wanted . . .

It wasn't too late to speak up, to save her parents.

Or she could keep her word and keep his secret. She could let her parents pay for what they'd done to her. For the lattice of scars on her skin and her heart. For the ice in her blood. If she was the kind of daughter who could consign her parents to death, then they had no one to blame but themselves.

But that didn't mean she had to accept the entire bargain. Even if she stayed silent, she could walk away: away from Valentine, now that she knew what he was capable of. Away from Stephen, now that she knew what he thought of her. She could close the door on the past, start again. She could choose a life without pain, without suffering or fear.

But who would she be without pain?

What was strength, if not the endurance of suffering?

There is nothing more painful than love denied, the strange Silent Brother had told her. *A love that cannot be requited. I can think of nothing more painful than that.*

If Valentine said he could give her Stephen Herondale, he meant it. Céline did not doubt this. He could do anything, and that included finding a way to force Stephen Herondale into her life and her arms. But even Valentine could not make Stephen love her.

To have Stephen would mean *not* having him—it would mean knowing in every moment, every embrace, that he wanted someone else. It would mean a lifetime of longing for the one thing she could not have. The Silent Brother was wise and spoke the truth. There could be no greater pain than that.

"Take your time," Valentine said. "It's a big choice."

"I don't need time," she told Valentine. "I want it. I want Stephen."

It didn't feel like choosing, because it was the only choice she had.

Son of the Dawn

By Cassandra Clare and Sarah Rees Brennan

New York City, 2000

Every world contains other worlds within it. People wander through all the worlds they can find, searching for their homes.

Some humans thought their world was the only world there was. Little did they know of other worlds as close to their own as the next room, or of the demons trying to find a door through to them, and the Shadowhunters who barred those doors.

Still less did they know of Downworld, the community of magical creatures who shared their world and carved out their own little space therein.

Every community needs a heart. There had to be a common area where everyone could gather, to trade for goods and secrets, to find love and riches. There were Shadow Markets, where Downworlders and those with the Sight met, all over the world. Usually they were held outside.

Even magic was a little different in New York.

The abandoned theater on Canal Street had stood since the 1920s, silent witness to but not part of the blaze of activity that was the city. Humans who did not have the Sight passed by its terra-cotta facade in a hurry about their own affairs. If they spared the theater a look, they thought it as dark and still as ever.

They could not see the haze of faerie light that turned the gutted amphitheater and bare concrete halls to gold. Brother Zachariah could.

He walked, a creature of silence and darkness, through halls with sunshine-yellow tiles, panels of gold and red blazing on the ceiling above him. There were busts grimy with age set in alcoves along the walls, but for tonight faeries had coaxed flowers and ivy to twine around them. Werewolves had set little twinkling charms depicting the moon and stars in the boarded windows, lending brightness to the decayed red curtains still hanging in the arched frames. There were lamps with casements that reminded Brother Zachariah of a time long ago, when he and all the world had been different. In one vast echoing theater room there hung a chandelier that had not worked in years, but tonight warlock magic had suffused each bulb with a different-colored flame. Like burning jewels, amethyst and ruby, sapphire and opal, their light created a private world that seemed both new and old, and restored the theater to all its former glory. Some worlds lasted only one night.

If the Market had the power to lend him warmth and illumination for only a night, Brother Zachariah would have taken it.

A persistent faerie woman had tried to sell him a love charm four times. Zachariah wished such a charm would work on him. Creatures as inhuman as he did not sleep, but sometimes he lay down and rested, hoping for something like peace. It never came. He spent his long nights feeling love slip through his fingers, more a memory by now than a feeling.

Brother Zachariah did not belong to Downworld. He was a Shadowhunter, and not only a Shadowhunter but one of the cloaked and hooded Brotherhood dedicated to arcane secrets and the dead, sworn and runed to silence and withdrawal from any world. Even his own kind often feared the Silent Brothers, and Downworlders usually avoided any Shadowhunter, but the Downworlders were used to the presence of this particular Shadowhunter at Markets now. Brother Zachariah had been coming to Shadow Markets for a hundred years, on a long quest that even he had begun to believe would be fruitless. Yet he continued searching. Brother Zachariah had little enough, but one thing he did have was time, and he had always tried to be patient.

Tonight, though, he had already been disappointed. The warlock Ragnor Fell had no word for him. None of his few other contacts, painstakingly gathered over the decades, had attended this Market. He was lingering not because he was enjoying this Shadow Market but because he remembered enjoying Markets once.

They had felt like an escape, but Brother Zachariah hardly remembered the wish to escape from the City of Bones, where he belonged. Always in the back of his mind, cold as a tide waiting to wash all other things away, were the voices of his Brothers.

They were urging him home.

Brother Zachariah turned under the glitter of diamond-paned windows. He was leaving the Market, making his way through the laughing, bargaining crowd, when he heard a woman's voice saying his name.

"Tell me again why we want this Brother Zachariah. The normal Nephilim are bad enough. Angel in the veins, stick up the butts, and I bet with Silent Brothers it's a whole staff. We definitely can't take him out for karaoke."

The woman was speaking in English, but a boy's voice

replied to her in Spanish: "Quiet. I see him."

It was a pair of vampires, and as he turned, the boy lifted a hand to attract Zachariah's attention. The vampire with his hand up looked fifteen years old at most, and the other like a young woman about nineteen, but that told Zachariah nothing. Zachariah still looked young too.

It was unusual for a strange Downworlder to want his attention.

"Brother Zachariah?" asked the boy. "I came here to meet you."

The woman whistled. "Now I see why we might want him. Helloooo, Brother *Mackariah*."

Did you? Brother Zachariah asked the boy. He felt what would once have been surprise and now was at least intrigue. *Can I be of any use to you?*

"I certainly hope so," said the vampire. "I am Raphael Santiago, second in command of the New York clan, and I dislike useless people."

The woman waved her hand. "I'm Lily Chen. He's always this way."

Brother Zachariah studied the pair with new interest. The woman had hair streaked neon yellow and wore a scarlet qipao that suited her, and despite her own remark she was smiling at her companion's words. The boy's hair was curly, his face sweet, and his air disdainful. There was a burn scar at the base of his throat, where a cross might lie.

I believe we have a mutual friend, said Brother Zachariah.

"I don't think so," said Raphael Santiago. "I don't have friends."

"Oh, thank you very much," said the woman at his side.

"You, Lily," said Raphael coldly, "are my subordinate." He turned back to Brother Zachariah. "I assume you refer to the warlock Magnus Bane. He is a colleague who always has more dealings with Shadowhunters than I approve of."

Zachariah wondered if Lily spoke Mandarin. The Silent Brothers, speaking mind to mind, had no need for language, but sometimes Zachariah missed his. There had been nights—in the Silent City it was always night—when he could not remember his own name, but he could remember the sound of his mother or his father or his betrothed speaking Mandarin. His betrothed had learned some of the language for him, in the time when he had thought he would live to marry her. He would not have minded talking with Lily longer, but he did not particularly like her companion's attitude.

Since you do not appear to care for Shadowhunters, and you have little interest in our mutual connection, Brother Zachariah observed, *why approach me?*

"I wished to talk to a Shadowhunter," said Raphael.

Why not go to your Institute?

Raphael's lips curled back from his fangs in a sneer. Nobody sneered like a vampire, and this vampire was particularly adept. "My Institute, as you call it, belongs to people who are . . . how do I put this tactfully . . . bigots and murderers."

A faerie selling ribbons with glamour twined in them passed by, trailing blue and purple banners.

The way you put that was not particularly tactful, Brother Zachariah felt bound to point out.

"No," said Raphael thoughtfully. "I am not gifted in that arena. New York has always been a place of heightened Down-worlder activity. The lights of this city work on people as if we are all werewolves howling for an electric moon. A warlock tried to destroy the world here once, before my time. The leader of my clan made a disastrous experiment with drugs here, *against* my advice, and made the city her slaughter ground. The werewolves' fatal struggles for leadership are far more frequent in New York than anywhere else. The Whitelaws of the New York Institute understood us, and we them. The Whitelaws died defending Downworlders from the people who now occupy their Institute. Of course the Clave did not consult us when they made us the punishment of the Lightwoods. We do not have any dealings with the New York Institute now."

Raphael's voice was uncompromising, and Brother Zachariah thought he should be concerned. Zachariah had fought in the Uprising, when a band of renegade youths rose up against their own leaders and against peace with Downworld. He had been told the story of Valentine's Circle hunting werewolves in New York City, and the Whitelaws getting in their way, resulting in a tragedy that even that group of angry Downworlder-hating youths had not intended. He had not approved of the Lightwoods and Hodge Starkweather being banished to the New York Institute, but the word was that the Lightwoods had settled down with their three children and were truly remorseful for their past actions.

The pain and power struggles of the world seemed very far away, in the Silent City.

It had not occurred to Zachariah that the Downworlders would resent the Lightwoods so much they might decline their aid even when Shadowhunter help was truly needed. Perhaps it should have.

Downworlders and Shadowhunters have a long, complicated history full of pain, and much of the pain has been the fault of the Nephilim, Brother Zachariah admitted. *Yet through the ages, they have found a way to work together. I know that when they followed Valentine Morgenstern, the Lightwoods did terrible things, but if they are truly repentant, could you not forgive them?*

"Being a damned soul, I have no moral objection to the Lightwoods," said Raphael in deeply moralistic tones. "I do have strong objections to my head being cut off. Given the least excuse, the Lightwoods would lay waste to my clan."

The only woman Zachariah had ever loved was a warlock. He had seen her weep over the Circle and its effects. Brother Zachariah had no reason to support the Lightwoods, but everyone deserved a second chance if they wanted that chance enough.

And one of Robert Lightwood's ancestors had been a woman called Cecily Herondale.

Say they would not, suggested Brother Zachariah. *Would it not be preferable to reestablish relations with the Institute rather than hope to catch a Silent Brother at the Shadow Market?*

"Of course it would," said Raphael. "I fully recognize this is not an ideal situation. This is not the first stratagem I have been forced to employ when I required an audience with Shadowhunters. Five years ago I had coffee with a visiting Ashdown."

He and his companion shared a shudder of distaste.

"I absolutely hate the Ashdowns," remarked Lily. "They are so tedious. I believe that if I fed on one of them I would nod off halfway through."

Raphael gave her a warning look.

"Not that I would ever dream of nonconsensually drinking the blood of any Shadowhunter, because it would violate the Accords!" Lily informed Brother Zachariah in a loud voice. "The Accords are deeply important to me."

Raphael shut his eyes, a briefly pained expression crossing his face, but after an instant he opened them and nodded.

"So how about it, Brother Lipsmackariah, will you help us out?" Lily asked brightly.

A cold weight of disapproval made itself known from his silent brethren, like stones being pressed against his mind. Zachariah was allowed a great deal of latitude for a Silent Brother, but his frequent visits to the Shadow Markets and his annual meeting with a lady on Blackfriars Bridge were already testing the limits of what could be allowed.

If he began consorting with Downworlders on issues that could be handled perfectly well by an Institute, Brother Zachariah's privileges were in danger of being suspended.

He could not risk missing that meeting. Anything but that.

The Silent Brothers are forbidden to interfere with the affairs of the outside world. Whatever your problem is, said Brother Zachariah, *I strongly urge you to consult with your Institute.*

He bowed his head and began to turn away.

"My problem is werewolves smuggling *yin fen* into New York," Raphael called after him. "Ever heard of *yin fen*?"

The bells and songs of the Shadow Market seemed to go quiet.

Brother Zachariah turned sharply back to the two vampires. Raphael Santiago stared at him with glittering eyes, which left Zachariah in no doubt that Raphael knew a good deal about the Silent Brother's own history.

"Ah," said the vampire. "I see you have."

Zachariah usually tried to preserve memories of his mortal life, but now he had to make an effort to banish the intruding horror of waking up as a child with all he loved dead, and silver fire burning in his veins.

Where did you hear about the yin fen?

"I don't intend to tell you," said Raphael. "Nor do I intend to let that stuff be freely available in my city. A large quantity of *yin fen* is on its way to the city, on board a ship carrying cargo from Shanghai, Ho Chi Minh, Vienna, and Idris itself. The ship unloads at the New York Passenger Ship Terminal. Will you help me or not?"

Raphael had already mentioned the leader of his clan performing disastrous experiments with drugs. Zachariah's guess was that many potential customers in Downworld were talking about the shipment of *yin fen* at the Market. The fact that a Downworlder with conservative views had heard about it was sheer luck.

I will help you, said Brother Zachariah. *But we must consult with the New York Institute. If you wish, I can go with you to the Institute and explain matters. The Lightwoods will appreciate the information, and you offering it. This is an opportunity to improve relations between the Institute and all the Downworlders in New York.*

Raphael did not look convinced, but after a moment he nodded.

"You will go with me?" he asked. "You will not fail? They would not listen to a vampire, but I suppose it is possible they will listen to a Silent Brother."

I will do whatever I can, said Brother Zachariah.

Cunning crept into Raphael's voice. "And if they don't help me, if they or even the Clave refuse to believe me, then what will you do?"

Then I will still help you, said Brother Zachariah, ignoring the chill howl of his brethren in his mind and thinking of Tessa's clear eyes.

He dreaded being forbidden to meet with Tessa this year, but when he did meet her, he wanted to face her with no stain upon him. He could not let any child suffer what he had suffered, not if he could prevent it.

Zachariah was not able to feel all he had felt when he was mortal, but Tessa could still feel. He could not let her be disappointed in him. She was the last star he had to steer by.

"I'll come to the Institute with you," Lily volunteered.

"You will do no such thing," snapped Raphael. "It is not safe. Remember, the Circle attacked Magnus Bane."

The ice in Raphael's voice could have laid the whole of New York City under frost for a week in midsummer. He eyed Brother Zachariah with disfavor.

"Magnus invented your Portals, not that he receives any credit for it from Shadowhunters. He is one of the most powerful warlocks in the world, and so tenderhearted he rushes to the aid of vicious killers. He is the best Downworld has to offer. If the Circle targeted him, they would cut down any one of us."

"Would've been a damn shame," Lily confirmed. "Magnus throws an amazing rager, too."

"I wouldn't know," said Raphael, casting a look of distaste on the joyful riot of the Market. "I do not enjoy people. Or gatherings."

A werewolf wearing an enchanted papier-mâché full-moon head shoved past Raphael, shouting, "Awoooo!" Raphael turned to look at him, and the werewolf backed away with his hands up, mumbling, "Uh, sorry. My mistake."

Despite slight fellow feeling with the werewolf, Brother Zachariah unbent a little at the vampire's words regarding Magnus, evidence that he was not entirely awful.

I understand that you value Magnus highly. So do I. Once he aided someone very dear to—

"No, I don't!" Raphael interrupted. "And I don't care about your story. Don't tell him I said any of that. I can have opinions on my colleagues. It does not mean I have personal feelings about them."

"Hey, my man, great to see you," said Ragnor Fell, passing by.

Raphael paused to fist-bump the green warlock before Ragnor disappeared among the stalls and sounds and many-colored lights of the Market. Lily and Brother Zachariah regarded him.

"He's another colleague!" Raphael protested.

I like Ragnor, said Brother Zachariah.

"Good for you," snapped Raphael. "Revel in your hobby of liking and trusting everyone. It sounds as appealing to me as sunbathing."

Zachariah felt he had become acquainted with another reason, besides Magnus's evil vampire ex, why Magnus always seemed to develop a migraine when people mentioned the vampire clan of New York in his presence. Brother Zachariah, Lily, and Raphael strolled through the Market.

"Love charm for the handsomest Silent Brother?" asked the faerie woman for the fifth time, leering through her dandelion-clock hair. Sometimes one could wish the Shadow Market had not become quite so comfortable with him.

He remembered this woman, he thought, dimly recollecting her hurting a golden-haired child. It had been so long ago. He had cared very much at the time.

Lily snorted. "I hardly think Brother Beast-with-two-backs-ariah needs a love charm."

Thank you, but no, Brother Zachariah told the faerie woman. *I'm very flattered, though Brother Enoch is a fine figure of a man.*

In Zachariah's head, Brother Enoch was annoyed at being the subject of a joke.

"Or perhaps you and the lady would enjoy some phoenix tears for a night of burning pass—" She went suddenly silent, and the whole stall scuttled away across the bare concrete floor on little chicken feet. "Oops, never mind! Didn't see you there, Raphael."

Raphael's thin eyebrows went up and down like a guillotine.

"More of a buzzkill than the Silent Brother," murmured Lily. "Oh, the shame."

Raphael looked smug. The gleam and whirl of the Shadow Market shone with pale radiance in Brother Zachariah's eyes. He did not like the thought of *yin fen* spreading like silver wildfire in another city, killing fast as flame or slowly as choking smoke. If it was coming, he had to stop it. This trip to the Market had been useful after all. If he could not feel, he could act.

Perhaps tomorrow night the Lightwoods will earn your trust, said Brother Zachariah as he and the vampires stepped out into the mundane bustle of Canal Street.

Raphael said, "Unlikely."

I have found it always better to hope than despair, said Brother Zachariah mildly. *I will wait for you outside the Institute.*

Behind them, enchanted lights shimmered and the sound of faerie music rang through the halls of the theater. A mundane woman turned to face the building. Glittering blue light fell in a strange beam across her unseeing eyes.

The two vampires were heading east, but partway up the

street, Raphael turned back to where Brother Zachariah stood. In the night, away from Market lights, the vampire's scar was white and his eyes were black. His eyes saw too much.

"Hope is for fools. I will meet you tomorrow night, but remember this, Silent Brother," he said. "Hate like that does not fade. The work of the Circle is not done yet. The Morgenstern legacy will claim more victims. I do not intend to be one of them."

Wait, said Brother Zachariah. *Do you happen to know why the ship is unloading its cargo at the Passenger Ship Terminal?*

Raphael shrugged. "I told you the ship was carrying cargo from Idris. I believe some Shadowhunter brat is on board."

Brother Zachariah walked away from the Market alone, thinking of a child on a ship with deadly cargo, and the potential of more victims.

Isabelle Lightwood was not accustomed to feeling nervous about anything, but anyone might be apprehensive when faced with the prospect of a new addition to the family.

This was not like before Max was born, when Isabelle and Alec had laid bets on whether it would be a boy or a girl, and afterward Mom and Dad trusted them enough to let them take turns holding him, the smallest and tenderest bundle imaginable.

A boy older than Isabelle was being dumped on their doorstep and was supposed to live with them. Jonathan Wayland, the son of Dad's *parabatai*, Michael Wayland. Far away in Idris, Michael Wayland had died, and Jonathan needed a home.

For herself, Isabelle was a little excited. She liked adventure and company. If Jonathan Wayland was as much fun and as good a fighter as Aline Penhallow, who came to visit sometimes with her mother, Isabelle would be glad to have him.

Except there was not just Isabelle to consider.

Her parents had been fighting over Jonathan Wayland ever since the news of Michael's death came. Isabelle gathered Mom had not liked Michael Wayland. She was not sure Dad had liked him much either. Isabelle herself had never met Michael Wayland. She had never even known that Dad had a *parabatai*. Neither Mom nor Dad ever talked about when they were young, except that Mom had once said they made many mistakes. Isabelle sometimes wondered whether they had been mixed up in the same trouble as their tutor, Hodge. Her friend Aline said Hodge was a criminal.

Whatever her parents had or had not done, Isabelle did not think her mother wanted Jonathan Wayland to be a reminder of her mistakes in her own home.

Dad did not seem happy when he talked about his *parabatai*, but he did seem determined that Jonathan would come to live with them. Jonathan had nowhere else to go, Dad insisted, and he belonged with them. That was what being *parabatai* meant. Once when she was eavesdropping on them shouting, Isabelle heard Dad say, "I owe Michael this."

Mom agreed to let Jonathan come for a trial period, but now that the shouting had died down, she was not really speaking to Dad. Isabelle was worried about both her parents, and especially her mom.

Isabelle also had to consider her brother.

Alec did not like new people. Whenever new Shadowhunters arrived from Idris, Alec would mysteriously slope off. Once Isabelle had found him lurking behind a large vase, claiming he got lost trying to find the training room.

Jonathan Wayland was taking a ship to New York. He should be in the Institute by the morning after next.

Isabelle was in the training room, practicing with a whip and pondering the problem of Jonathan Wayland, when she heard rushing footsteps, and Alec poked his head around the door. His blue eyes were sparkling.

"Isabelle!" he said. "Come quickly! There's a Silent Brother meeting with Mom and Dad in the Sanctuary. And a *vampire*!"

Isabelle ran to her room to get out of her gear and into a dress. The Silent Brothers were fancy company, almost as if the Consul had come to visit.

By the time she got downstairs, Alec was already in the Sanctuary observing the proceedings, and her parents were deep in conversation with the Silent Brother. Isabelle heard her mom say something to the Silent Brother that sounded like "Yogurt! Unbelievable!"

Maybe not "yogurt." Maybe it was a different word.

"On the ship with Michael's son!" Dad said.

It couldn't be "yogurt," unless Jonathan Wayland had a very serious allergy to dairy.

The Silent Brother was a lot less scary than Isabelle had been expecting. His mouth and eyes weren't stitched shut like they were on other Silent Brothers, only closed in a peaceful way that made it look like he was sleeping. In fact, from what Isabelle could see beneath the hood, he resembled one of the mundie singers she had seen in posters around the city. From the way Robert was nodding at him and Maryse was leaning toward him in her chair, Isabelle could see they were getting along.

The vampire was not conversing with their parents. He was

leaning against one of the walls, arms crossed, and glaring at the floor. He did not seem as if he was interested in getting along with anyone. He looked like a kid, hardly older than they were, and he would have been almost as handsome as the Silent Brother if not for his sour expression. He was wearing a black leather jacket to go with his scowl. Isabelle wished she could see the fangs.

"Can I offer you a coffee?" Maryse said to the vampire in a cool, stilted tone.

"I do not drink . . . coffee," said the vampire.

"Odd," said Maryse. "I heard you had a delightful coffee with Catherine Ashdown."

The vampire shrugged. Isabelle knew vampires were dead and soulless and all, but she did not see why they had to be rude.

She nudged Alec in the ribs. "Get a load of the vampire. Can you believe that?"

"I know!" Alec whispered back. "Isn't he *amazing*?"

"What?" Isabelle said, grabbing Alec's elbow.

Alec did not glance at her. He was studying the vampire. Isabelle started to get the same uneasy feeling that she got whenever she noticed Alec looking at the same posters of mundie singers that she did. Alec always got red and angry when she saw him looking. Isabelle sometimes thought it would be nice to talk about the singers, the way she'd heard mundie girls doing, but she knew Alec wouldn't want to. Once Mom had asked them what they were looking at, and Alec had looked afraid.

"Don't go near him," Isabelle urged. "I think vampires are gross."

Isabelle was used to being able to whisper to her brother in a crowd. The vampire turned his head slightly, and Isabelle remembered vampires did not have pathetic hearing like mundanes. The vampire could definitely hear her.

This nasty realization caused Isabelle to relax her hold on Alec. She watched in horror as he pulled away from her and advanced with nervous determination toward the vampire. Not wanting to be left out, Isabelle trailed a few steps behind him.

"Hello," said Alec. "It's, um, very nice to meet you."

The vampire boy gave him a thousand-yard stare that suggested a thousand yards was too close up and the vampire wished he were enjoying blissful solitude in the far reaches of space. "Hello."

"I'm Alexander Lightwood," said Alec.

Grimacing as if the introduction were vital information being tortured out of him, the vampire said: "I am Raphael."

When he made that face, Isabelle did see the fangs. They were not as cool as she had hoped.

"I'm basically twelve," continued Alec, who was totally eleven. "You don't look a lot older than me. But I know it's different with vampires. I guess you kind of stay the same age you stop at, though, right? Like you're fifteen, but you've been fifteen for a hundred years. How long have you been fifteen?"

Raphael said flatly, "I'm sixty-three."

"Oh," said Alec. "Oh. Oh, that's cool."

He advanced several steps toward the vampire. Raphael did not take a step back, but he looked like he wanted to.

"Also," Alec added shyly, "your jacket is cool."

"Why are you talking to my *children*?" Mom asked sharply.

She was already up from her chair opposite the Silent

Brother, and as she spoke she seized hold of Alec and Isabelle. Her fingers pinched, she was holding them so hard, and fear seemed to travel to Isabelle through her mother's touch, even though she had not been afraid before.

The vampire had not been looking at them as if he thought they would be delicious at all. Maybe that was how he lured you in, though, Isabelle considered. Maybe Alec was just ensorcelled by vampire wiles. It would be nice to be able to blame the Downworlder for making Isabelle worry.

The Silent Brother rose from his chair and glided to join them. Isabelle heard the vampire whisper to the Silent Brother, and she was pretty sure he said, "This is my nightmare."

Isabelle stuck her tongue out at him. Raphael's lip curled the tiniest fraction farther from his fangs. Alec did glance at Isabelle then, to make sure she was not scared. Isabelle wasn't scared of much, but Alec was always fussing.

Raphael came here out of concern for a Shadowhunter child, said the Silent Brother.

"No, I didn't," Raphael sneered. "Better watch your children. I once killed a whole gang of boys not much older than your boy here. Shall I take this as a refusal to help with the shipment? I am deeply shocked. Well, we tried. Time to go, Brother Zachariah."

"Wait," said Robert. "Of course we will help. I will meet you at the drop-off point in New Jersey."

Naturally her dad would help, Isabelle thought indignantly. This vampire was an idiot. Whatever mistakes they might have made when they were really young, her parents ran this whole Institute and had killed lots and lots of evil demons. Anyone sensible would know you could always count on her dad.

"You can consult with us on other Shadowhunter matters

at any time," her mom added, but she did not let go of Alec and Isabelle until the vampire and Brother Zachariah had left the Institute.

Isabelle had thought the visit would be exciting, but she had ended up feeling more apprehensive than ever. She wished that Jonathan Wayland was not coming.

Guests were terrible, and Isabelle never wanted any more.

The plan was to stow away aboard ship undetected, apprehend the smugglers, and dispose of the *yin fen*. The child would never have to know about any of it.

It was almost nice to be in one of the sleek Shadowhunter boats again. Brother Zachariah had been in the multihulled trimarans as a child on lakes in Idris, and once his *parabatai* had stolen one and they had rowed it down the Thames. Now he, an edgy Robert Lightwood, and two vampires had used one to navigate the black nighttime waters of the Delaware River, coming down from the port of Camden. Lily kept complaining that they were practically in Philadelphia, until the boat drew close to the tall cargo ship. DAWN TRADER was painted in dark blue letters against its gray side. They waited for their moment, then Robert threw a grappling hook.

Brother Zachariah, Raphael, Lily, and Robert Lightwood made it onto the boat and into a deserted cabin. This journey, short and stealthy though it was, left them with the impression that there was no mundane crew on board at all. Hiding there, they counted the voices of the smugglers and realized there were far more than had been reported.

"Oh no, Brother Hop-in-the-sack-ariah," Lily whispered. "I think we're going to have to fight them."

She looked very cheerful about the prospect. As she spoke, she winked and pulled her feathered flapper's headband from her yellow-streaked hair.

"It's actually from the 1920s, so I don't want to damage it," she explained, and nodded to Raphael. "I've had it longer than I've had him. He's from the 1950s. Jazz baby and greaser teen take on the world."

Raphael rolled his eyes. "Desist with the nicknames. They are getting worse."

Lily laughed. "I will not. Once you go Zachariah, you never go backariah."

Raphael and Robert Lightwood both looked appalled, but Zachariah did not mind the nicknames. He did not hear laughter often.

What worried him was the child.

We cannot allow Jonathan to be scared or hurt, he said.

Robert was nodding and the vampires looking supremely unconcerned, when a boy's voice came from outside the door.

"I'm not frightened of anything," he said.

Jonathan Wayland, Zachariah presumed.

"Then why are you asking about the Lightwoods?" asked a woman's voice. She sounded irritated. "They're taking you in. They won't be unkind to you."

"I was only curious," said Jonathan.

He was clearly doing his best to sound airy and aloof, and his best was not bad. His voice almost swaggered. Brother Zachariah thought it would have convinced most people.

"Robert Lightwood's got some influence in the Clave," remarked the woman. "Solid man. I'm sure he's ready to be a father to you."

"I had a father," said Jonathan, cold as the night wind.

The woman was silent. Across the cabin, Robert Lightwood's head was bowed.

"But the mother," said Jonathan, a touch tentative. "What's Mrs. Lightwood like?"

"Maryse? I barely know her," the woman replied. "She's already got three kids. Four's a lot to handle."

"I'm not a kid," said Jonathan. "I won't bother her." He paused and observed, "There are a lot of werewolves aboard this ship."

"Ugh, kids raised in Idris are exhausting," said the woman. "Werewolves are a fact of life, unfortunately. Creatures are everywhere. Go to bed, Jonathan."

They listened as another cabin door shut and a lock was shot home.

"Now," said Robert Lightwood. "Vampires, starboard. Brother Zachariah and I, port. Contain the werewolves by any means necessary, then locate the *yin fen*."

They spilled out onto the deck. It was a rough night, the wind pulling Zachariah's hood down farther, the deck jerking beneath their feet. Zachariah could not open his lips to taste the salt in the air.

New York was a glimmer on the horizon, shining like the lights of the Shadow Market in the dark. They could not allow the *yin fen* to hit the city.

There were a couple of werewolves on the deck. One was in wolf form, and Zachariah could see a tinge of silver in his fur. The other had lost color in his fingertips. Zachariah wondered if they knew that they were dying. He remembered, too vividly, how it had felt when the *yin fen* was killing him.

Sometimes it was good to be without feeling. Sometimes being human hurt too much, and Zachariah could not afford pity now.

Brother Zachariah slammed his staff against one of their heads, and when he turned, Robert Lightwood had already dealt with the other. They stood braced, listening to the howl of the wind and the surge of the sea, waiting for the others to come from belowdecks. Then Zachariah heard the sounds from the other side of the ship.

Stay where you are, he told Robert. *I will go to the vampires.*

Brother Zachariah had to fight his way to them. There were even more werewolves than he had guessed. Across their heads, he could see Raphael and Lily, leaping as if they were insubstantial as shadows, teeth shining in the moonlight.

He could see the werewolves' teeth too. Zachariah shoved one werewolf over the side of the ship and knocked out another one's teeth in the same swing, then had to dodge a swipe of claws that almost sent Zachariah over himself. There were so many of them.

It was with vague surprise that Zachariah thought this could be the end. There should have been something more than surprise to the idea, but all he knew was the hollowness he had felt walking through the Market and the sound of his Brothers' voices, colder than the sea. He did not care about these vampires. He did not care about himself.

The roar of a werewolf sounded in his ear, and behind it came the crash of a wave. Brother Zachariah's arms ached from wielding the staff. It should all have ended a long time ago, anyway. He could scarcely remember a reason why he fought.

Across the deck a werewolf, almost fully shifted, whirled a

clawed fist directly at Lily's heart. She already had her hands locked around another werewolf's neck. She did not have a chance to defend herself.

A door swung open, and a Shadowhunter woman ran out into the path of the werewolves. She was not ready. A wolf tore her throat out, and as Zachariah tried to get to her, a werewolf slammed against his back. The staff fell from his nerveless fingers. A second werewolf piled onto him, claws digging into his shoulders, bearing him down to his knees. Another climbed on, and Zachariah's head slammed onto the wood. The dark rose before him. His Brothers' voices could be gone, along with the crash of the sea and all the light of the world that no longer touched him.

The dead woman's eyes stared into his face, a last empty gleam before the dark consumed all. It seemed as if he were as empty as she. Why had he ever fought?

Only he remembered. He would not allow himself to forget. *Tessa*, he thought. *Will.*

Despair was never stronger than the thought of them. He could not betray them by giving up.

They are Will and Tessa, and you were Ke Jian Ming. You were James Carstairs. You were Jem.

Brother Zachariah drew a dagger from his belt. He fought to his feet, sending two of the werewolves sprawling and backhanding the third through the open cabin door. He looked to Lily.

Raphael was standing in front of her. His arm was flung out to shield her, his blood a macabre scarlet splash across the deck. Human blood was black at night, but vampire blood never looked anything but red. Lily screamed his name.

Brother Zachariah needed his staff. It was rolling across the wood of the deck, silver in the moonlight and rattling like bones. Its carving leaped out, shadow dark against the silver, as the staff rolled to the feet of a boy who had just stepped out into this space of chaos and blood.

The boy who must be Jonathan Wayland stared around him, at Brother Zachariah, at the wolves, at the woman with her throat ripped out. A werewolf woman was bearing down on him. The boy was too young to even bear warriors' runes.

Brother Zachariah knew he was not going to be fast enough.

The boy turned his head, hair bright gold in the silver moonshine, and picked up Zachariah's staff. Small and slim, the most fragile of barriers possible against darkness, he charged at the snarling teeth and bared claws. He struck her down.

Two more went for the boy, but Zachariah killed one, and the boy spun and struck the other. When he twisted in the air, Zachariah thought not of shadows, as he had with the vampires, but of light.

When the boy landed on the deck, feet spread wide and staff twirling between his hands, he was laughing. It was not a child's sweet laugh, but a wild exuberant sound that rang out stronger than sea or sky or silent voices. He sounded young, and defiant, and joyful, and a little mad.

Brother Zachariah had thought earlier in the night that he did not hear laughter often. It had been an achingly long time since he had heard a laugh like that.

He stabbed another werewolf running for the boy, and another, throwing his body between the boy and the wolves. One got past his guard and swiped at the boy, and Zachariah heard him make a small sound between his locked teeth.

Are you all right? he asked.

"Yes!" the boy shouted. Brother Zachariah could hear him panting at his back.

Never fear, said Brother Zachariah. *I am fighting with you.*

Zachariah's blood ran colder than the sea, and his heart hammered until he heard Robert Lightwood and Lily coming to their aid.

Once the remaining werewolves were subdued, Robert took Jonathan with him to the bridge. Zachariah turned his attention to the vampires. Raphael had taken off his leather jacket. Lily had ripped part of her shirt off and was tying the material around his arm. She was crying.

"Raphael," she said. "Raphael, you shouldn't have done it."

"Sustained a wound that will heal in a night in preference to losing a valuable member of the clan?" Raphael asked. "I acted to benefit myself. I generally do."

"You'd better," Lily muttered, wiping tears savagely with the back of her hand. "What would I do if something happened to you?"

"Something practical, I hope," said Raphael. "Please salvage material from one of the many dead werewolves next time. And stop embarrassing the clan in front of Shadowhunters."

Lily followed Raphael's line of vision, over her shoulder to Brother Zachariah. There was blood smudged and mixed with her blurred eyeliner, but she gave him a cheeky fanged smile.

"Maybe I wanted to rip my shirt for Brother Let-him-see-my-rack-ariah."

Raphael lifted his eyes to heaven. Since he was not looking at her, Lily could look at him. She did. Brother Zachariah saw her lift a hand, her fingernails painted red and gold, and almost touch his curly hair. Her hand moved as if she might stroke the shadows over his head, then curled into a fist. She did not permit herself the luxury.

Raphael motioned her away and got to his feet.

"Let's go find the *yin fen*."

It was not difficult to locate. It was in a large box in a cabin belowdecks. Lily and Brother Zachariah carried the box up between them, Lily clearly ready to make a scene if Raphael tried to help.

Zachariah pried open the lid of the box. Even after all these years, seeing the glimmer of *yin fen* in the moonlight made his stomach lurch and turn, as if the sight pitched him onto a boat on a different sea, one in which he could never keep his balance.

Lily moved to tip the box over the side and let it be swallowed by the hungry waters.

"No, Lily!" said Raphael. "I will not have drug-addled mermaids infesting the rivers of my city. What if we end up with glowing silver alligators in the sewers? Nobody will be surprised, but I will know it is your fault, and I will be extremely disappointed in you."

"You never let me have any fun," Lily grumbled.

"I never let anyone have any fun," said Raphael, and looked smug.

Brother Zachariah stared into the box full of silver powder. It had meant the difference between quick and slow death to him once. He set the fire using a rune known only to the Silent Brothers, a rune meant to burn away harmful magic. Life and death were nothing but ashes in the air.

Thank you for telling me about the yin fen, he told Raphael.

"From my perspective, I took advantage of your weakness over the stuff," said Raphael. "You used to take it to keep yourself alive once, as I understand it. Didn't work, I see. Anyway, your emotional state is no concern of mine, and my city is safe. Mission accomplished."

He wiped his hands, gleaming with blood, over the lapping waves.

Does your leader know anything about this mission? Zachariah asked Lily.

She was watching Raphael.

"Of course," she said. "My leader told you all about it. Didn't he?"

"Lily! That is stupidity and treason." Raphael's voice was chill as the sea breeze. "If I was ordered to execute you for it, make no mistake, I would do so. I would not hesitate."

Lily bit her lip and tried to pass off how hurt she clearly was. "Oh, but I have a good feeling about Brother Zacharide-him-like-a-bad-pony. He won't tell."

"Is there a place here for a vampire to be stowed away safely from the sunrise?" Raphael asked.

Brother Zachariah had not considered that the protracted fight with the werewolves meant the sun was close to rising. Raphael glanced at him sharply when he did not answer.

"Is there only room for one? Lily needs to be secured. I am responsible for her."

Lily turned her face away so Raphael did not see her expression, but Zachariah saw it. He recognized her expression from a time when he had been able to feel that way himself. She looked sick with love.

There was room for both vampires in the cargo hold. On their way to examine the hold, Lily almost tripped over the dead Shadowhunter woman.

"Oooh, Raphael!" she exclaimed brightly. "It's Catherine Ashdown!"

It was like the faint cold spray of seawater, to see how utterly indifferent she was to human life. Brother Zachariah saw her belatedly recall his presence.

"Oh no," she added in not terribly convincing tones. "What a senseless tragedy."

"Go to the hold, Lily," Raphael commanded.

Will you not both go? asked Brother Zachariah.

"I prefer to wait as long as I can before dawn to test myself," said Raphael.

Lily sighed. "He's Catholic. So very, very Catholic."

Her hand moved restlessly by her side, as if she wanted to reach out and pull Raphael along with her. Instead, she used it to give Zachariah another little wave, the same one she had given when they first met.

"Brother Sixpackariah," she said. "It's been a pleasure."

And for me, said Brother Zachariah, and listened to her skip lightly down the stairs.

She had, at least, given him the woman's name. Brother Zachariah could take her back to her family and the City of Bones, where she could rest and he could not.

He knelt down by the dead woman's side and closed her staring eyes.

Ave atque vale, *Catherine Ashdown,* he murmured.

He rose to find Raphael still by his side, though not looking at him or the dead woman. Raphael's eyes rested on the black sea touched with moonlight, the black sky edged with the faintest line of silver.

I am glad to have met you both, Zachariah added.

"I can't imagine why," said Raphael. "Those names Lily came up with were very bad."

People do not joke with the Silent Brothers often.

The prospect of not being joked around with made Raphael look wistful. "It must be nice to be a Silent Brother. Aside from the fact that Shadowhunters are annoying and pathetic. And I don't know that she was joking. I'd watch yourself next time you're in New York."

Of course she was joking, said Brother Zachariah. *She is in love with you.*

Raphael's face twisted. "Why do Shadowhunters always want to talk about feelings? Why can nobody ever be a professional? For your information, I do not have any interest in romance of any kind and never will. Now can you drop this revolting subject?"

I can, said Brother Zachariah. *Perhaps you would like to talk about the gang of boys you claim to have killed?*

"I've killed many people," said Raphael distantly.

A group of children? said Zachariah. *In your city? Did this happen in the 1950s?*

Maryse Lightwood might have been fooled. Brother Zachariah was familiar with what it looked like when someone blamed and hated themselves for what had happened to those they loved.

"There was a vampire hunting children on the streets where my brothers played," Raphael said, his voice still distant. "I led my gang to his lair to stop him. None of us survived."

Brother Zachariah tried to be gentle.

When a vampire is newborn, they cannot control themselves.

"I was the leader," said Raphael, his steely voice brooking no argument. "I was responsible. Well. We did stop the vampire, and my family lived to grow up."

All but one, Brother Zachariah thought.

"I generally do accomplish what I set my mind on," said Raphael.

That is extremely clear, said Brother Zachariah.

He listened to the sound of the waves hitting the side of the boat, carrying them to the city. On the night of the Market he had been detached from the city and everyone in it, and certainly he had felt nothing for a vampire determined to feel nothing himself.

But then had come a laugh, and the sound had woken things inside him that he had feared dead. Once woken to the world, Zachariah did not want to be blind to any of it.

You saved people today. The Shadowhunters saved people, even though they did not save you when you were a child trying to fight monsters.

Raphael twitched as if this implication of why he disliked Shadowhunters was a fly landing on him.

"Few are saved," said Raphael. "Nobody is spared. Somebody tried to save me once, and I will pay him back one day. I don't choose to owe another debt, or for anyone to owe me. We all got what we wanted. The Shadowhunters and I are done."

There might always be another time for help or cooperation, said Brother Zachariah. *The Lightwoods are trying. Consider letting the other Downworlders know you survived dealing with them.*

Raphael made a noncommittal sound.

There are more kinds of love than stars, said Brother Zachariah. *If you do not feel one, there are many others. You know what it is to care for family and friends. What we keep sacred keeps us safe. Consider that by trying to cut yourself off from the possibility of being hurt, you shut the door on love and live in darkness.*

Raphael staggered over to the rail and pretended to vomit. Then he straightened up.

"Oh wait, I'm a vampire and we don't get seasick," he said. "I got nauseous for a second. Can't think why. I heard Silent Brothers were withdrawn. I was looking forward to withdrawn!"

I am not a typical Silent Brother, observed Brother Zachariah.

"Just my luck I got the touchy-feely Silent Brother. Can I request a different one in the future?"

So you think there might be a time when your path crosses with Shadowhunters again?

Raphael made a disgusted noise and turned away from the sea. His face was pallid as moonlight, ice white as the cheek of a child long dead.

"I am going belowdecks. Unless, of course, you have any other brilliant suggestions?"

Brother Zachariah nodded. The shadow of his hood fell across the scar of a cross on the vampire's throat.

Have faith, Raphael. I know you remember how.

With the vampires safely hidden below and Robert Lightwood steering the ship toward Manhattan, Brother Zachariah took on the task of cleaning up the deck, moving the bodies out of sight. He'd call on his Brothers to help him attend to them, and to the survivors, who were currently secured in one of the cabins. Enoch and the others might not approve of his decision to help Raphael, but they would still fulfill their mandate to keep the Shadow World hidden and safe.

Once Brother Zachariah had finished, all there was to do was wait for the ship to carry them to the city. Then he would have to return to his own city. He took a seat and waited, enjoying the sensation of the light of a new day on his face.

It had been a long time since he felt the light, and longer since he could truly enjoy the simple pleasure of it.

He sat near the bridge, where he could see Robert and young Jonathan Wayland in the morning light.

"You're sure you're all right?" Robert said.

"Yes," said Jonathan.

"You don't look much like Michael," Robert added awkwardly.

"No," said Jonathan. "I always wished I did."

Zachariah could see the boy's thin back. He seemed braced to be a disappointment.

Robert said, "I am sure you're a good boy."

Jonathan did not look sure. Robert saved himself from awkwardness by conspicuously examining the controls.

The boy left the bridge, graceful despite the lurch of the boat and how weary he must be. Zachariah was startled when young Jonathan advanced across the deck to where Zachariah himself sat.

Brother Zachariah pulled his hood close around his face. Some Shadowhunters were disquieted by a Silent Brother who did not appear exactly as the rest did, though the Silent Brothers looked fearsome enough. He did not want to distress the boy, either way.

Jonathan carried Brother Zachariah's staff back to him, balanced flat as a tightrope along his palms, and laid the staff with a respectful bow on Zachariah's knees. The boy moved with military discipline unusual in one so young, even among Shadowhunters. Brother Zachariah had not known Michael Wayland, but he guessed he must have been a harsh man.

"Brother Enoch?" the boy guessed.

No, said Brother Zachariah. He knew Enoch's memories as his own. Enoch had given the boy his first Mark, though his memories were gray with lack of interest. Brother Zachariah briefly wished he could have been the Silent Brother who oversaw the rite of passage for this child.

"No," the boy repeated slowly. "I should've known. You moved differently. I just thought it might be, since you rolled your staff to me."

He bowed his head. It struck Zachariah as a sorry thing, that the child would not have expected even the smallest mercy from a stranger.

"Thank you for letting me use it," Jonathan added.

I am glad it was useful, returned Brother Zachariah.

The boy's glance up at his face was shocking, the flare of twin suns in what was still almost night. They were not the eyes of a soldier but a warrior. Brother Zachariah had known both, and he knew the difference.

The boy took a step back, nervous and agile, but stopped with his chin high. Apparently he had a question.

Zachariah was not expecting the one he asked.

"What do the initials mean? On your staff. Do all Silent Brothers have them?"

They looked together at the staff. The letters were worn by time and Zachariah's own flesh, but they had been struck deep into the wood in the precise places where Zachariah would put his hands on them when he fought. So, in a way, they would always be fighting together.

The letters were *W* and *H.*

No, said Brother Zachariah. *I am the only one. I carved them into the staff on my first night in the City of Bones.*

"Were they your initials?" the boy asked, his voice low and a little timid. "Back when you were a Shadowhunter, like me?"

Brother Zachariah still considered himself a Shadowhunter, but Jonathan clearly did not mean any offense.

No, said Jem, because he was always James Carstairs when he spoke of what was dearest to him. *Not mine. My* parabatai's.

W and *H.* William Herondale. Will.

The boy looked struck yet wary at the same time. There was a certain guardedness about him, as if he was suspicious of whatever Jem might say before he even had the chance to say it.

"My father says—said—a *parabatai* can be a great weakness."

Jonathan said the word "weakness" with horror. Jem wondered what a man who had drilled a boy to fight like that might have considered weakness.

Jem did not choose to insult an orphan boy's dead father, so he arranged his thoughts carefully. This boy was so alone. He remembered how precious that new link could be, especially when you had no other. It could be the last bridge that connected you to a lost life.

He remembered traveling across the sea, having lost his family, not knowing that he was going to his best friend.

I suppose they can be a weakness, he answered. *It depends on who your* parabatai *is. I carved his initials here because I always fought best with him.*

Jonathan Wayland, the child who fought like a warrior angel, looked intrigued.

"I think—my father was sorry he had a *parabatai*," he said. "Now I have to go and live with the man my father was sorry about. I don't want to be weak, and I don't want to be sorry. I want to be the best."

If you pretend to feel nothing, the pretense may become true, said Jem. *That would be a pity.*

His *parabatai* had tried to feel nothing, for a time. Except what he felt for Jem. It had almost destroyed Will. And every day, Jem pretended to feel something, to be kind, to fix what was broken, to remember names and voices almost forgotten, and hoped that would become truth.

The boy frowned. "Why would it be a pity?"

We battle hardest when that which is dearer to us than our own lives is at stake, said Jem. *A parabatai is both blade and shield. You belong together and to each other not because you are the same but because your different shapes fit together to be a greater whole, a greater warrior for a higher purpose. I always believed we were not merely at our best together but beyond the best either of us could be apart.*

A slow smile broke across the boy's face, like sunrise bursting as a bright surprise upon the water.

"I'd like that," said Jonathan Wayland, adding quickly, "To be a great warrior."

He flung his head back in a sudden, hasty assumption of arrogance, as if he and Jem might both have imagined he meant that he would like to belong to someone.

This boy, hell-bent on fighting rather than finding a family. The Lightwoods guarding against a vampire, when they could have extended some trust. The vampire, holding every friend at bay. All of them had their wounds, but Jem could not help resenting them, for even the privilege of feeling hurt.

All these people were struggling not to feel, trying to freeze their hearts inside their chests until the cold fractured and broke them. While Jem would have given every cold tomorrow he had for one more day with a warm heart, to love them as he once had.

Except Jonathan was a child, still trying to make a distant father proud even when death had made the distance between them impossible. Jem should be kind.

He thought of the boy's speed, his fearless strike with an unfamiliar weapon on a strange and bloody night.

I'm sure you will be a great warrior, said Jem.

Jonathan Wayland ducked his shaggy golden head to hide the faint color in his cheeks.

The boy's forlornness made Jem recall too vividly the night he had carved those initials into his staff, a long, cold night with all the icy strangeness of the Silent Brothers new in his head. He had not wanted to die, but he would have chosen death rather than the awful severing from love and warmth. If only he could have had a death in Tessa's arms, holding Will's hand. He had been robbed of his death.

It seemed impossible to stay anything like human, in among the bones and endless dark.

When the alien cacophony of the Silent Brothers threatened to engulf all that he had been, Jem held fast to his lifelines. There had been none stronger than that one, and only one other so strong. His *parabatai*'s name had been a shout into the abyss, a cry that always received an answer. Even in the Silent City, even with the silent howl insisting that Jem's life was no longer his own but a shared life. No longer my thoughts, but our thoughts. No longer my will, but our will.

He would not accept that parting. *My Will.* Those words meant something different to Jem than to anyone else, meant: my defiance against encroaching dark. My rebellion. Mine, forever.

Jonathan scuffed his shoe against the deck and peered up at Jem, and Jem realized he was trying to see his face beneath the hood. Jem drew the hood, and the shadows, close. Even though he had been rebuffed, Jonathan Wayland offered him a small smile.

Jem had not looked for any kindness from this hurt child. It made Jem think that Jonathan Wayland might grow up to be more than a great warrior.

Maybe Jonathan would have a *parabatai* one day, to teach him the kind of man he wanted to be.

This is the link stronger than any magic, Jem had told himself that night, knife in hand, cutting deep. *This is the bond I chose.*

He had made his mark. He had taken the name Zachariah, which meant "remember." *Remember him,* Jem had willed himself. *Remember them. Remember why. Remember the only answer to the only question. Do not forget.*

When he looked again, Jonathan Wayland was gone. He wished he could thank the child, for helping him remember.

Isabelle had never been to the New York Passenger Ship Terminal before. She was not very impressed. The terminal was like a glass-and-metal snake, and they had to sit in its belly and wait. The ships were like warehouses on the water, when Isabelle had been picturing a boat from Idris as like a pirate ship.

It had been dark when they woke, and it was barely dawn now, and freezing. Alec was huddled in his hoodie against the wind blowing off the blue water, and Max was fussing at their mother, cranky about being up so early. Basically both her brothers were cranky, and Isabelle did not know what to expect.

She saw her father walk down the gangway with a boy beside him. The dawn drew a line of thin gold over the water. The wind made little white capelets for every wave in the river and played with the gold locks of the boy's hair. The boy's back was straight and slim as a rapier. He was wearing dark, close clothes that looked almost like gear. And there was blood on them. He had actually been part of the fighting. Dad and Mom had not let her or Alec fight even one tiny demon yet!

Isabelle turned to Alec, confident he would share her sense of deep betrayal at this unfairness, and found him staring at the new arrival with wide eyes as though beholding a revelation with the morning.

"Wow," Alec breathed.

"What about that vampire?" Isabelle demanded, outraged.

Alec said, "What vampire?"

Mom hushed them.

Jonathan Wayland had gold hair and gold eyes, and those eyes had no depths but only shiny reflective surface, showing as little as if they were metal doors slammed down on a temple. He did not even smile as he came to a stop in front of them.

Bring back that Silent Brother, was Isabelle's feeling.

She looked to her mother, but Mom was staring at this new boy with an odd expression on her face.

The boy was looking back at her. "I'm Jonathan," he told her intently.

"Hello, Jonathan," said Isabelle's mother. "I am Maryse. It's nice to meet you."

She reached out and touched the boy's hair. Jonathan flinched but held himself still, and Maryse smoothed back the shining gold waves the wind had ruffled.

"I think we need to get you a haircut," Mom said.

It was such a Mom thing to say, it made Isabelle smile at the same time as she rolled her eyes. Actually, the boy Jonathan did need a haircut. The ends of his hair were spilling over his collar, untidy as if whoever had cut it last—too long ago—had not cared enough to do a good job. He had the faint air of a stray animal, fur rough and one breath away from a snarl, though that did not make sense for a kid.

Mom winked. "Then you will be even more handsome."

"Is that even possible?" Jonathan asked dryly.

Alec laughed. Jonathan looked surprised, as if he had not noticed Alec before then. Isabelle did not think he had paid attention to any of them except her mother.

"Say hello to Jonathan, kids," said Isabelle's dad.

Max stared up at Jonathan in awe. He dropped his stuffed rabbit on the cement floor, shuffled forward, and hugged Jonathan's leg. Jonathan flinched again, though this time it was more of an instinctive rear back, until the genius figured out he was not being attacked by a two-year-old.

"Hello, Jonathing," said Max, muffled in the material of Jonathan's trousers.

Jonathan patted Max on the back, very tentatively.

Isabelle's brothers were *so* not showing sibling solidarity on the issue of Jonathan Wayland. It was worse when they got home and made awkward small talk even though everybody really wanted to go back to bed.

"Jonathing can sleep in my room because we love each other," Max proposed.

"Jonathan has his own room. Say 'Sleep well, Jonathan,'" said Maryse. "You can see Jonathan after we've all had a little more rest."

Isabelle went to her own room, but she was still buzzing with excitement and could not sleep. She was painting her toenails when she heard the tiny creak of a door down the hall.

Isabelle leaped up, the toenails of one foot painted sparkly black and the other foot still encased in a fuzzy pink sock, and ran to the door. She edged it open a fraction and poked her head out, and caught Alec doing the same thing from his own room. They both watched the silhouette of Jonathan Wayland creeping down the corridor. Isabelle made a complicated series of gestures to determine whether Alec wanted to follow him together.

Alec stared at her in total bafflement. Isabelle loved her big brother, but sometimes she despaired about their future demon-hunting endeavors. He was so bad at remembering her cool military-style signals.

She gave up and they both hurried after Jonathan, who did not know the layout of the Institute and could only retrace his steps to the kitchen.

Which was where they found him. Jonathan had his shirt pulled up, and he was dabbing a wet dish towel along the red cut running up his side.

"By the Angel," said Alec. "You're hurt. Why didn't you say?"

Isabelle hit Alec in the arm for not being stealthy.

Jonathan stared at them, guilt written across his face as if he had been stealing from the cookie jar rather than injured.

"Don't tell your parents," he said.

Alec left Isabelle's side and ran to Jonathan. He examined the cut, then shepherded Jonathan toward a stool, making him sit down. Isabelle was unsurprised. Alec always fussed when she or Max fell down.

"It's shallow," Alec said after a moment, "but our parents really would want to know. Mom could put an *iratze* on—or something—"

"No! It's better for your parents not to know it happened at all. It was just bad luck one of them got me. I'm a good fighter," Jonathan protested sharply.

He was so vehement it was almost alarming. If he hadn't been ten years old, Isabelle would have thought he was worried they might send him away for being an inadequate soldier.

"You're obviously great," said Alec. "You just need someone to have your back."

He put his hand lightly on Jonathan's shoulder as he spoke. It was a small gesture Isabelle would not even have noted, except for the fact that she had never seen Alec reach out like that to anyone who was not family and that Jonathan Wayland went perfectly still at his touch, as if he was afraid the tiniest movement would scare Alec away.

"Does it hurt a lot?" Alec added sympathetically.

"No," Jonathan Wayland whispered.

Isabelle thought it was perfectly clear Jonathan Wayland would claim having his leg cut off did not hurt, but Alec was an honest soul.

"Okay," said her brother. "Let me grab a few things from the infirmary. Let's deal with this together."

Alec nodded in an encouraging fashion and went to fetch supplies from the infirmary, leaving Isabelle and this weird bleeding boy alone together.

"So you and your brother seem . . . really close," Jonathan said.

Isabelle blinked. "Sure."

What a concept, being close to your family. Isabelle refrained from being sarcastic, as Jonathan was both unwell and a guest.

"So . . . I guess you're going to be *parabatai*," Jonathan ventured.

"Oh, no, I don't think so," said Isabelle. "Being *parabatai* is a little old-fashioned, isn't it? Besides, I don't like the idea of giving up my independence. Before I am my parents' daughter or my brothers' sister, I am my own. I'm already a lot of people's something. I don't need to be anyone else's anything, not for a long time. You know?"

Jonathan smiled. He had a chipped tooth. Isabelle wondered how that had happened, and hoped it had been chipped in an awesome fight. "I don't know. I'm not really anyone's anything."

Isabelle bit her lip. She had never realized before that she took feeling secure for granted.

Jonathan had glanced at Isabelle as he spoke, but immediately after he returned to watching the door through which Alec had disappeared.

Isabelle could not help observing that Jonathan Wayland had lived in their home for less than three hours, and he was already trying to lock down a *parabatai*.

Then he slouched further into his chair, resuming his too-cool-for-the-Institute attitude, and she forgot the thought in annoyance that Jonathan was such a show-off. She, Isabelle, was the only show-off this Institute needed.

She and Jonathan stared each other down until Alec returned.

"Oh—would you rather I put on the bandages or do you want to do it yourself?"

Jonathan's face was opaque. "I can do it myself. I don't need anything."

"Oh," Alec said unhappily.

Isabelle could not tell if Jonathan's expressionless face was to ward them off or protect himself, but he was hurt. Alec was still shy with strangers, and Jonathan was a closed-off human being, so they were going to be awkward even though Isabelle could tell they both really liked each other. Isabelle sighed. Boys were hopeless, and she had to take charge of this situation.

"Hold still, idiot," she ordered Jonathan, seized ointment from Alec's hands, and began to smear it over Jonathan's cut. "I am going to be a ministering angel."

"Um," said Alec. "That's a lot of ointment."

It did look a little like when you squeezed the center of the tube of toothpaste too hard, but Isabelle felt you did not get results without being willing to make a mess.

"It's fine," said Jonathan quickly. "It's great. Thank you, Isabelle."

Isabelle glanced up and grinned at him. Alec efficiently unwound a bandage. Having gotten them started, Isabelle stepped back. Her parents would object if she accidentally turned their guest into a mummy.

"What's going on?" said Robert Lightwood's voice from the door. "Jonathan! You said you were not hurt."

When Isabelle looked, she saw both her mom and dad standing at the threshold of the kitchen, arms folded and eyes narrowed. She imagined they would have objections to her and Alec playing doctor with the new kid. Strong objections.

"We were just patching Jonathan up," Alec announced anxiously, ranging himself in front of Jonathan's stool. "No big deal."

"It was my fault I got hurt," said Jonathan. "I know excuses are for incompetents. It won't happen again."

"It won't?" asked her mother. "All warriors get wounded sometimes. Planning to run away and become a Silent Brother?"

Jonathan Wayland shrugged. "I applied to the Iron Sisters, but they sent me a hurtful and sexist refusal."

Everyone laughed. Jonathan looked briefly startled again, then pleased, before he shut away his expressions as if slamming a lid down on a treasure chest. Isabelle's mother was the one who went and gave Jonathan an *iratze*, while her father stayed by the door.

"Jonathan?" Maryse remarked. "Does anyone ever call you anything else?"

"No," said Jonathan. "My father used to tell a joke about having another Jonathan, if I wasn't good enough."

Isabelle did not think that was much of a joke.

"I always think that naming one of our kids Jonathan is like the mundanes calling kids Jebediah," said Isabelle's mother.

"John," said her father. "Mundanes often call their kids John."

"Do they?" asked Maryse, and shrugged. "I could have sworn it was Jebediah."

"My middle name is Christopher," said Jonathan. "You can—you can call me Christopher if you like."

Maryse and Isabelle exchanged a speaking look. She and her mother had always been able to communicate like this. Isabelle thought it was because they were the only girls, and special to each other. She could not imagine her mother telling her anything she would not want to hear.

"We're not going to *rename* you," said Maryse sadly.

Isabelle was not sure if her mother was sad that Jonathan thought they would do that, give him a different name as if he were a pet, or sad that he would have let them.

What Isabelle was sure about was that her mother was watching Jonathan in the same way she had watched Max when he was still learning to walk, and there would be no more discussion of a trial period. Jonathan was obviously here to stay.

"Maybe a nickname," Maryse proposed. "What would you think of Jace?"

He was silent for a moment, observing Isabelle's mother carefully from the corner of his eye. At last he offered her a smile, faint and cool as the light in early morning, but growing warm with hope.

Jonathan Wayland said, "I think Jace will work."

As a boy was introduced to a family, and vampires slept cold but curled together in the hold of a ship, Brother Zachariah walked through a city not his own. The people hurrying by could not see him, but he saw the light in their eyes as if it had been made new. The blare of car horns and scream of tires from yellow cabs and the chatter of many voices in many tongues formed a long, living song. Brother Zachariah could not sing the song, but he could listen.

This was not the first time this had happened to him, seeing a trace of what had been in what was. The coloring was entirely different. The boy did not really have anything to do with Will. Jem knew that. Jem—for in the moments he remembered Will, he was always Jem—was used to seeing his lost and dearest Shadowhunter in a thousand Shadowhunter faces and gestures, the turn of a head or the note of a voice. Never the beloved head, never the long-silent voice, but sometimes, more and more rarely, something close.

Jem's hand was firmly clasped around his staff. He had not paid attention to the carving beneath his palm like this for many a long, cold day.

This is a reminder of my faith. If there is any part of him that can be with me, and I believe there is, then he is at hand. Nothing can part us. He allowed himself a smile. His mouth could not open, but he could still smile. He could still speak to Will, though he could no longer hear any answer.

Life is not a boat, bearing us far away on a cruel, relentless tide from all we love. You are not lost to me on some forever distant shore. Life is a wheel.

From the river, he could hear mermaids. All the sparks of the city by morning were kindling a new fire. A new day was born.

If life is a wheel, it will bring you back to me. All I must do is keep faith.

Even when having a heart seemed hard past bearing, it was

better than the alternative. Even when Brother Zachariah felt he was losing the struggle, losing everything he had been, there was hope.

Sometimes you seem very far away from me, my parabatai.

Light on water had not rivaled the boy's blazing contradiction of a smile, somehow both indomitable and too easily hurt. He was a child going to a new home, as Will and the boy Zachariah had been had once traveled in lonely sorrow to the place where they would find each other. Jem hoped Jonathan would find happiness.

Jem smiled back at a boy long gone.

Sometimes, Will, he said, *you seem very close.*

The Land I Lost

By Cassandra Clare and Sarah Rees Brennan

J

New York, 2012

The sky was soft gray with evening, stars not yet out. Alec
Lightwood was napping because he and his *parabatai* had
been out fighting Croucher demons all last night, and Jace
Herondale, famed among the Nephilim as a master strategist,
apparently thought "about a dozen demons" was a fair estimate
for "definitely thirty-seven demons." Alec had gone around
counting them out of spite.

"Give yourself a break, Should-Be-Sleeping Beauty," Magnus
had told him. "I need to make a potion, and Max is scheduled
for his evening temptation."

Alec woke in a nest of lavender-and-green silk sheets. Under
the door of the bedroom, eerie silver lights played. There was
a smell of sulfur, and the hiss of a demon, and the sound of
beloved voices. Alec smiled against his pillow.

Just as he was about to roll out of bed, letters of fire appeared
on the wall.

*Alec, we need your help. For years we have searched for a
family in peril and the truth behind why they are in danger.*

We believe we have found a lead in the Shadow Market of Buenos Aires.

But there is unrest between the Shadowhunters and Downworlders of this city. This Shadow Market is guarded like a throne room, run by a werewolf known as the Queen of the Market. She says her doors are closed to every soul associated with the Nephilim. Every soul, except for Alexander Lightwood, who she says she has need of. We need to enter the Shadow Market. Lives are at stake.

Will you open the doors for us? Will you come?

—Jem and Tessa

Alec stared at the letter for a long moment. Then he sighed, fished a sweater up from the floor, and weaved his way out of their bedroom, still half-asleep.

In their main room, Magnus stood with one elbow casually propped against their mantel, decanting a vial of turquoise liquid into a jar of black powder. His green-gold eyes were narrowed with focus. The dark worn floorboards and the woven silk rug alike were littered with their son Max's toys. Max himself was sitting on the rug, wearing a sailor suit with elaborate navy ribbons to match his hair, tightly embracing Chairman Meow.

"You are my meow friend," he told the Chairman solemnly, squeezing him.

"Meow," Chairman Meow protested. He'd lived a life of torment since Max learned to walk.

The pentagram had been drawn a safe distance away from the rug. Silvery light and mist rose from within the pentagram, shrouding its inhabitant in shimmering fog. The demon's long, writhing shadow fell dark against their green wallpaper and family pictures.

Magnus raised an eyebrow. "Ease up," he suggested to the pentagram. "It's like someone loaned overly enthusiastic kids a dry-ice machine for their high-school production of *Demon Oklahoma!* in here."

Alec grinned. The silvery mist dissipated enough to see the demon Elyaas in the pentagram, his tentacles drooping in a sulky fashion.

"Child," he hissed to Max. "You know not of what dark lineage you come. You are naturally inclined to evil. Join me, infernal foundling, in my revels—"

"My *bapa* is Ultra Magnus," Max announced proudly. "And Daddy is a Shadowhunter."

Alec thought Max had gotten the name Ultra Magnus from one of his toys. Magnus seemed to like it.

"Don't interrupt me when I'm promising you dark demonic delights," the demon Elyaas said fussily. "Why are you always interrupting me?"

Max brightened at the word "demonic."

"Uncle Jace says we will kill all the demins," he reported with joy. "All the demins!"

"Well, have you considered that your uncle Jace is a hurtful person?" said the demon. "Always rudely stabbing everyone, and sarcastic."

Max scowled. "Love Uncle Jace. Hate demins."

With his free hand, Magnus picked up a marker and drew another blueberry on the whiteboard to show Max had successfully resisted today's demonic wiles. Ten blueberries, and Max got a reward of his choosing.

Alec crossed the floor to where Magnus stood considering the whiteboard. Carefully, since Magnus was still holding a bubbling jar, he slid his arms around Magnus's waist, linking his hands together over the embossed buckle of Magnus's belt. The T-shirt Magnus was wearing had a dramatic scoop neckline, so Alec put his face down in the smooth bare expanse of skin and breathed in the smell of sandalwood and spell ingredients.

"Hi," he mumbled.

Magnus reached back with his free hand, and Alec felt the slight sweet pull of rings in his hair. "Hi, yourself. Couldn't sleep?"

"I slept," Alec protested. "Listen, I have some news."

He filled Magnus in on the message Jem Carstairs and Tessa Gray had sent: the family they were searching for, the Shadow Market they could not enter without his help. As Alec spoke, Magnus gave a little sigh and leaned against him, one of the small unconscious gestures that meant the most to Alec. It reminded him of the first day he'd ever touched Magnus, drawn close to and kissed another man, someone even taller than he was, his body lean and lithe and right against Alec's. At the time, he'd thought he felt dizzy with relief and joy because he was finally touching someone he wanted to be touched by, when he'd thought he might never have that. Now he thought he'd felt that way because it was Magnus: that even then, he'd known. Now the gesture spoke of all the days since the first.

When he felt Magnus relax against him, he felt like he could relax too.

Whatever this strange task Jem and Tessa needed him for, he could do it. Then he would come home.

As Alec fell silent, Chairman Meow made a break for

freedom from Max's loving stranglehold, streaking across the floor, through the door Alec had left open, and into Alec and Magnus's bedroom, where Alec suspected he would be hiding under the bed for the rest of the night. Max stared sadly after the cat, then looked up and grinned, his teeth tiny pearls. He launched himself at Alec as if he had not seen him for several weeks. Alec always got the same enthusiastic greeting, whether he was back from a trip, back from patrolling, or had simply been in the other room for five minutes.

"Hey, Daddy!"

Alec took a knee and opened his arms to scoop Max up. "Hey, my baby."

He stood with Max curled against his chest, a warm soft bundle of ribbons and round limbs, Max's gurgling laughter in his ears. When Max was tiny, Alec used to marvel at how neatly his little body fit into the crook of Alec's arm. He'd scarcely been able to imagine Max getting bigger. He needn't have worried. Whatever size his kid was, he was always a perfect fit for Alec to hold.

Alec tugged at the front of Max's sailor suit. "That's a lot of ribbons there, buddy."

Max nodded sadly. "Too much ribbons."

"What happened to your sweater?"

"That's a fine question, Alexander. Allow me to unfold to you the tale. Max rolled his sweater in the cat litter," Magnus related. "So he could 'look like Daddy.' Thus he must wear the sailor suit of shame. I don't make the rules. Oh wait, yes, I do."

He waved a reproving finger at Max, who laughed again and tried to grab for the glitter of rings.

"It's really inspiring to see you crazy kids making it work," chipped in Elyaas the tentacle demon. "I don't have much luck with romance. Everyone I meet is treacherous and heartless. Well, we are demons. Comes with the territory."

Magnus had insisted warlocks needed to know what summoning demons entailed. He said that the more comfortable Max was with them, the less likely he was to be tricked or terrified when he summoned his first. Hence the temptation lessons. Elyaas was not so bad, as demons went, which meant he was still terrible. As Max had passed the pentagram, Alec had seen the wicked silver curve of one tentacle moving hungrily close to the edge lest Max make a false move.

Alec looked at Elyaas with narrowed eyes.

"Don't imagine I ever forget what you are," Alec said grimly. "I'm watching you."

Elyaas held up all his tentacles in surrender, scooting to the other side of the pentagram. "It was a reflex! I didn't mean anything by it."

"Demins," said Max darkly.

Magnus banished Elyaas with a snap of his fingers and a murmur, then turned back to Alec.

"So, they're asking for you in Buenos Aires," said Magnus.

"Yeah," said Alec. "I don't know why anyone at the Market wants me specifically, as opposed to any other Shadowhunter."

Magnus laughed. "I can see why someone might."

"Okay, other than that." Alec grinned. "I don't speak Spanish."

Magnus could speak Spanish. Alec wished that Magnus could go with him, but one of them always tried to stay home with Max. Once, when Max was still a baby, there had been a terrible time when they were both forced to leave him. Neither of them wanted to repeat it.

Alec was trying to learn Spanish, as well as several other

languages. The Speak in Tongues rune didn't last and seemed like cheating. Downworlders from all over the world came to New York to consult with them these days, and Alec wanted to be able to talk with them properly. First on the list of languages he was trying to learn was Indonesian, for Magnus.

Unfortunately, Alec wasn't great at languages. He was able to read them, but when he was talking he found words difficult, no matter the tongue. Max had picked up more words in various languages than Alec.

"It's fine," Magnus had commented once. "I never knew any Lightwood but one who was good at languages."

"Which one?" Alec had asked.

"His name was Thomas," Magnus said. "Tall as a tree. Very shy."

"Not a green-eyed monster like the other Lightwoods you've mentioned?"

"Oh," said Magnus. "There was a bit of the monster in him."

Magnus had elbowed him and laughed. Alec remembered a time when Magnus never talked about the past, when Alec thought it meant he was doing something wrong or Magnus didn't care. Now he understood it was only that Magnus had been hurt before and was afraid Alec would hurt him too.

"I thought I might bring Lily," he told Magnus. "She can speak Spanish. And I thought it might cheer her up. She likes Jem."

Nobody at any Market would question Lily's presence. Everybody had heard of the Downworlder-Shadowhunter Alliance by now, and it was well known that members of the Alliance helped each other out.

Magnus raised his eyebrows. "Oh, I know Lily likes Jem. I've heard the nicknames."

Max looked back and forth at their expressions, his face bright.

"Bring back brother orra sister?" Max hoped.

They had talked with Max about the idea of another kid, as they had talked to each other. Neither of them had expected Max would take to the idea so much. Max asked about the brother or the sister every time one of them left the house: last Tuesday Magnus had forestalled the question by yelling, "Not getting a baby, going to Sephora. There are no babies at Sephora!" and bolting. One day at the park, Max had seized a pram with a mundane baby in it. Luckily, he'd been glamoured at the time, and the mundane mother thought it was a rogue gust of wind rather than Alec's little rogue.

It would be nice for Max to have someone to grow up with. It would be nice to have another baby, with Magnus. Still, Alec remembered when he'd first held Max, how the world and Alec's heart had gone quiet and certain. Alec was waiting to be sure again.

Alec's pause left Max obviously thinking there was room for negotiation here.

"Bring back brother anna sister anna dinosaur?" asked Max. Alec blamed Max's attitude on his aunt Isabelle, who kept telling him his bedtime was never.

They were saved by Jace's signal, a faerie-leaf folded plane striking the glass of the window.

Alec gave Max a little kiss, in the midst of his curls but avoiding his horns. "No, I'm going on a mission."

"I come with you," Max proposed. "I be a Shadowhunter."

Max said that a lot too, for which Alec blamed Max's uncle Jace. Alec looked appealingly at Magnus over Max's head.

"Come to Papa, bluebottle," said Magnus, and Max went unsuspectingly to his open arms.

"Go get Lily," said Magnus. "I'll have a Portal set up for you."

Max shrieked his outrage. "Down!"

Magnus put him down gently. Alec paused at the door to catch one last glimpse of them. Magnus glanced up at him, touched his own heart with his ringed hand, and made a little flicking gesture. Alec grinned and opened his own hand to see the tiny blue spark of magic burning briefly there.

"Hate you, Daddy," Max said, and sulked.

"That's a shame," said Alec. "I love you both," he added quickly, and closed the door on his own embarrassment.

The words were seldom easy for him to say, but he tried to say them whenever he was going on a mission. Just in case they were the last words.

Jace was waiting for him on the sidewalk, leaning against a sad-looking city tree, flipping a knife from palm to palm.

As Alec reached the sidewalk, there was a sound from above. Alec looked up to see Magnus, but instead he saw Max's round face. Alec assumed Max wanted to get a glimpse of his magnificent uncle Jace. Then he saw Max was looking at him, big blue eyes mournful. He put his hand on the front of his sailor suit, then gestured to Alec the same way Magnus had, as if Max could do magic already.

Alec pretended to see a magic spark in his hand and put the magic kiss in his pocket. Then he gave Max a last wave as he and Jace headed down the street.

"What was that about?" Jace asked.

"He wanted to come patrolling."

Jace's face softened. "My good boy! He should—"

"No!" said Alec. "And nobody will let you have your own kid until you stop putting other people's kids in bags meant for axes and trying to smuggle them out on patrol."

"I almost got away with it, due to my supernatural speed and unmatched cunning," Jace claimed.

"No, you didn't," said Alec. "That bag was wriggling."

Jace shrugged philosophically. "Ready for another round of heroically defending the world from evil? Or if it's a slow night, pranking Simon?"

"Actually, I can't," said Alec, and explained the message from Jem and Tessa.

"I'll come with you," Jace offered instantly.

"And leave Clary to run the Institute alone?" asked Alec. "A week before her exhibition?"

Jace looked shaken by the force of this argument.

"You're not letting Clary down. Lily and I can deal with whatever's going on," said Alec. "Besides, it's not like Jem and Tessa can't handle themselves. We'll be a team."

"Fine," said Jace reluctantly. "I guess three other fighters are an acceptable substitute for me."

Alec thumped him swiftly on the shoulder with a fist, and Jace smiled.

"Well," he said. "To the Hotel Dumort."

From the outside the hotel's facade was grimy, the graffitied sign the dark brown of old blood.

Since Lily Chen had become the leader of the vampires of New York, she'd redecorated on the inside. Alec and Jace opened splintered double doors on a shining hall. The flight of stairs and the balcony above them had a glittering rail, gilt-painted iron fretwork depicting snakes and roses. Lily liked things to look like the 1920s, which she said was the best decade. The decor wasn't the only thing that had changed; now there were hipsters in the know, and though Alec didn't understand the allure himself, there was a waiting list to be a party victim.

A pair of legs was sticking out from under the curving flight of stairs. Alec strode over and peered into the shadowy alcove, seeing a man wearing suspenders, a blood-smudged shirt, and a grin.

"Hi," Alec said. "Just checking. Is this a voluntary situation?"

The man blinked. "Oh yes. I signed the consent form!"

"There's a consent form now?" Jace murmured.

"I told them they didn't have to do that," Alec murmured back.

"My fabulous fanged lady friend said I should sign it, otherwise the Clave would get stern with her. Are *you* the Clave?"

"No," said Alec.

"But Hetty said that if I didn't sign the consent form, the Clave would look at her with those disappointed blue eyes. Your eyes are very blue."

"And very disappointed," said Alec sternly.

"Are you bothering Alec?" demanded a vampire girl, running out of the double doors that led to the parlor. "Don't bother Alec."

"Oh dear," said the man in delighted tones. "Is my mortal soul doomed? Are you about to visit your undead wrath upon me?"

Hetty snarled, and dived under the stairs with a giggle. Alec averted his eyes and headed for the parlor, Jace falling in behind him. Jace let Alec take point when it came to the vampires. As head of the New York Institute, Jace reprimanding a vampire might sound like a threat. Jace and Alec had talked over how to make the city welcoming to all Downworlders, now that New

York was a refuge in the times of the Cold Peace.

Through the parlor doors came the sound of music: not Lily's usual jazz but a pounding mix that sounded like rap and jazz combined. Inside the parlor were tufted chairs, a gleaming piano, and an elaborate set of turntables and wires. Bat Velasquez the werewolf DJ was sitting cross-legged on a plush velvet sofa, fiddling with dials.

In other cities, vampires and werewolves didn't get along. Things were different in New York.

Elliott, second in command of the vampire clan, was dancing around in a happy circle by himself. His arms and dreadlocks waved to the beat like plants underwater.

"Is Lily up?" asked Alec.

Elliott suddenly looked hunted. "Not yet. We had a bit of a late morning yesterday. There was an incident. Well, more a disaster."

"What caused this disaster?"

"Well," Elliott said. "Me, like usual. But this time it really wasn't my fault! It was a total and complete accident that could have happened to anyone. You see, I have this regular selkie Thursday-night booty call."

Selkies were water faeries who shed their sealskins to assume human form. They were fairly rare.

Alec subjected him to a judgmental stare. "So this disaster could have happened to anyone with a regular selkie booty call."

"Yeah, exactly," said Elliott. "Or, like, regular booty calls with two different selkies. One of them found the other's sealskin in my wardrobe. There was a scene. You know how it is with selkies."

Alec, Jace, and Bat shook their heads.

"Only one tiny wall fell down, but now Lily's all mad."

Lily had made Elliott her second in command because they were friends, not because Elliott had any aptitude for leadership. Sometimes Alec worried about the New York vampire clan.

Bat said, "This guy. Why do you have to suggest threesomes to everybody? Why are vampires like this?"

Elliott shrugged. "Vampires love threesomes. Live long, get decadent. We aren't all the same, of course." His face brightened with a pleasant memory. "The boss used to get very cross about decadence. But really, I'm ready to settle down. I think you and I and Maia—"

"My *abuela* wouldn't like you," Bat said firmly. "My *abuela* loves Maia. Maia's learning Spanish for her."

Bat's slightly raspy voice went low and warm whenever he talked about Maia, the leader of the werewolves, and his girlfriend. Alec couldn't blame him. Alec never worried about the werewolves. Maia always had everything under control.

"Speaking of Spanish," Alec said, "I'm going to Buenos Aires, and I'm asking Lily to come with me, since she's fluent. By the time Lily gets back, she'll have cooled off."

Elliott nodded. "A trip would be good for her," he said, his voice unusually serious. "She hasn't been doing well lately. She misses the boss. Well, we all do, but it's different for Lily. It takes us like this sometimes." He glanced at Alec and clarified: "Immortals. We're used to seeing each other off and on through the centuries. Years go by, then someone's back, and it's just the way it was before. Because we stay the same, though the world doesn't. When someone dies, it takes us a while to process. You think to yourself: I wonder when I'll see him again. Then you remember, and it's a shock every time. You have to keep reminding yourself, until you believe it: I'll never see him again."

There was an achingly sad note in Elliott's voice. Alec nodded. He knew how it would be, one day, when Magnus had to think "never again" about him.

He knew how strong someone had to be, to withstand the loneliness of immortality.

"Also, honestly, Lily could use some help with the clan."

"You could help her," said Alec. "If you were just a bit more responsible . . ."

Elliott shook his head. "Not gonna happen. Hey, Mr. Head of the Institute, you're a leader! How about it? I make you a vampire, you help lead the clan, you stay gorgeous forever."

"That would be a gift to future generations," Jace remarked thoughtfully. "But no."

"Elliott!" Alec snapped. "Stop offering to make people immortal! We have spoken about this!"

Elliott nodded, looking abashed but smiling a tiny smile. From outside and above, a voice drifted down.

"I hear someone bossing people around! Alec?"

One of the most worrying things about the vampire clan was that speaking to them reasonably didn't work at all, but they were delighted to be told off. Raphael Santiago had really left a mark on these people.

Alec walked over and peered out the open doors. Lily was standing on the balcony, wearing rumpled pink pajamas with drawings of snakes and the words RISE AND STRIKE on them. She looked tired.

"Yeah," he said. "Hey. Jem asked me to come to Buenos Aires and help him out. Do you want to come with?"

Lily lit up. "Do I want to come on a bro road trip with you, rushing to the aid of gorgeous damsel-in-distress Jem I'd-love-to-climb-'em Carstairs?"

"So, yes."

Lily's smile was wide enough to show fangs. "Hell yes."

She darted away from the balcony. Alec noted the door she went through, and climbed the stairs. He waited a bit, leaning against the rail, then tapped on the door.

"Come in!"

He didn't come in, but he opened the door. The room inside was narrow as a cell, with stripped floorboards and walls bare except for a cross on a hook. This was the only room in the Hotel Dumort Lily hadn't redecorated. She was sleeping in Raphael's room again.

Lily was wearing a leather jacket that had been Raphael's too. Alec watched as she fluffed her hot-pink-streaked hair, then kissed the cross for luck and headed out. Christian vampires were burned by a cross, but Lily was a Buddhist. The cross meant nothing to her, except that it had been Raphael's.

"Do you . . ." Alec coughed. "Do you want to talk?"

Lily tipped her head back to stare all the way up at him. "About feelings? Do we do that?"

"Preferably not," said Alec, which made her smile. "But we could."

"Nah," Lily answered. "Let's go on a road trip and see hotties instead! Where's that idiot Elliott?"

She ran lightly down the stairs to the parlor, and Alec followed her.

"Elliott, I'm leaving you in charge of the clan!" said Lily. "Bat, I'm stealing your girl!"

Bat shook his head. "Why are vampires like this?" he murmured again.

Lily grinned. "For administrative purposes. Maia's running the Downworlder-Shadowhunter Alliance until we get back."

"I don't want to be in charge of the clan," Elliott wailed. "Please be a vampire and lead us, Jace! Please!"

"I used to walk in here and have to fight for my life as the place fell down around me," Jace mused. "Now it's all velvet cushions and insistent offers of immortal beauty."

"It's just one tiny bite," Elliott coaxed him. "You'll like it."

"Nobody likes getting all their blood sucked out, Elliott," Alec said severely.

Both the vampires in the room smiled because he was telling them off, then looked upset because of what he was saying.

"You only think that because Simon did it wrong," Lily argued. "I've pointed out to him many times that he messed up everything for all of us."

"Simon did fine," Jace muttered.

"I didn't like it," said Alec. "I won't talk about this again. Let's get going."

"Ah yes." Lily brightened. "I'm very curious to see how the hottest Shadowhunter in the world is doing."

"I'm great," said Jace.

Lily tapped her foot. "Nobody's talking about you, Jason. Have you heard the phrase 'tall, dark, and handsome'?"

"Sounds like an old-fashioned saying," said Jace. "Sounds like something people used to say before I was born."

He grinned at Lily, who grinned back at him. Jace didn't just pull the pigtails of people he had crushes on. He pulled the pigtails of everyone in the world he liked. This was something

Simon still had not figured out over the years.

"There are a lot of hot Shadowhunters," said Elliott. "That's the point of them, isn't it?"

"No," said Alec. "We fight demons."

"Oh," said Elliott. "Right."

"I don't mean to brag. I'm just saying that if they made a book of hot Shadowhunters, my illustration would be on every page," Jace said serenely.

"Nope," said Lily. "It would be filled with pictures of the Carstairs family."

Alec said, "Are you talking about Emma?"

Lily frowned. "Who's Emma?"

"Emma Carstairs," said Jace helpfully. "She's Clary's pen pal who lives in L.A. Sometimes I write postscripts to Clary's letters and tell Emma handy knife tricks. Emma's very good."

Emma was a single-minded force of destruction, which of course Jace liked. Jace fished out his phone and showed Lily a recent picture of Emma that Emma had sent Clary. Emma was holding her sword on a beach and laughing.

Lily breathed, "Cortana."

Alec glanced at her sharply.

"I don't know Emma," Lily said. "But I'd like to. I don't normally go for blonds, but she's hot. Bless the Come-and-Stare family. They never fail me. On that note, I'm off to admire the views in Buenos Aires."

"Jem is *married*, you know," said Alec.

"Don't leave me in charge!" Elliott begged. "You can't trust me! It's a terrible mistake!"

Lily ignored them both, but she caught Alec studying her as they left the hotel.

"Don't look so worried," she said. "Elliott probably won't burn the city down. When I get back, everybody will be so grateful that they'll do everything I say. Leaving that fool in charge is part of my leadership strategy."

Alec nodded and didn't say that he was worried about her.

There had been a time when Alec was unsettled by vampires, but Lily had always so clearly needed someone, and Alec had wanted to be there for her. They'd been teammates running the Alliance with Maia for long enough now that Lily felt like Aline Penhallow, a friend close enough to be family.

The thought of Aline sent a familiar pang through Alec. Aline had gone into exile on Wrangel Island to be with her wife, Helen. They had lived in that stony wasteland for years, just because Helen had faerie blood.

Whenever Alec thought of Helen and Aline, he wanted to change everything about the way the Clave worked and bring them home.

It wasn't only Aline and Helen. He felt that way about all the warlocks and vampires and werewolves and faeries who streamed to New York to talk to the Alliance because they couldn't go to their Institutes. Every day, he felt the same urge he'd felt on his first mission, when he saw Jace and Isabelle charge into a fight. *Protect them*, he'd thought desperately, and lunged for his bow.

Alec squared his shoulders. Worrying wouldn't help anyone. He couldn't save everybody, but he could help people, and now he intended to help Jem and Tessa.

Brother Zachariah walked through the Silent City, down corridors lined with bones. The ground was marked with the relentless passage of the Silent Brothers' feet, of his own feet, moving in their accustomed path day after silent day, year after dark, endless year. He could not get out. Soon he would forget how it had ever been to live and love in the light. Every skull grinning at him from the wall was a thing more human than he.

Until the darkness he'd thought inescapable was obliterated by consuming fire. The silver fire of *yin fen* had burned in him once, the worst burning the world had to offer, but this golden fire was remorseless as heaven. He felt as if he were being torn apart, every burning atom of him weighed in the balance by a cruel god, and every piece found wanting.

Even in the midst of agony, there was some small measure of relief. This was the end, he told himself desperately, and was desperately thankful. At last this was the end, after all that misery and darkness. He would die before his humanity was entirely crushed out. Finally, there might be rest. He might see his *parabatai* again.

Except with the thought of Will came the thought of another. He thought of soft cool air drifting from the river, and her sweet serious face, unchanging as his own heart. With the thought of Will, he knew what Will would say. He could hear him, as if even the veil of death were burning between them and Will was shouting in his ear. *Jem, Jem. James Carstairs. You can't leave Tessa on her own. I know you better than you know yourself. I always did. I know you would never give up. Jem, hold on.*

He would not dishonor love by letting go. In the end, he chose to endure any pain rather than do that. Through the fire, as through the darkness, he held on.

And impossibly, through fire and darkness and time, he survived.

Jem woke gasping. He was in a warm bed, with his wife in his arms.

Tessa was still sleeping, on white sheets in the small white-washed room they were renting in the small lodging house. She murmured as Jem watched her, a soft string of incomprehensible words. She talked in her sleep, and every sound was a comfort. More than a century ago, he'd wondered how it would be to wake up with Tessa. He'd dreamed of it.

Now he knew.

Jem listened to her sweet sleepy murmurs, and watched the rise and fall of the white sheet with her breathing, and his body eased.

Tessa's curling lashes stirred on her cheeks.

"Jem?" she asked, and her hand found his arm, palm sliding down his skin.

"I'm sorry," Jem said. "I didn't mean to disturb you."

"Don't be sorry." Tessa smiled sleepily.

Jem leaned over to the pillow beside his and kissed his wife's eyes closed, then watched them open again, clear and cool as river water. He kissed her cheek, the eloquent curve of her mouth, her chin, and trailed his open mouth hungrily down the line of her throat.

"Tessa, Tessa," he murmured. *"Wŏ yào nĭ."*

I want you.

Tessa said, "Yes."

Jem lifted the sheet and kissed the line of her collarbone, loving the taste of her soft sleep-warm skin, loving every atom of her. He laid a trail of kisses for himself to follow all the way down her body. When he drew his mouth down the tender skin of her stomach, her hands slipped into his hair and fastened tightly there, anchoring him, encouraging him on. Her voice, no longer soft, made the walls ring with his name.

She was all around him. All horror and pain was washed away.

Jem and Tessa lay facing one another on the bed, their hands entwined, their voices hushed. They could whisper and laugh all night together, and often had: it was one of Jem's great joys, just to lie with Tessa and talk for hours.

But that required quiet and peace, which was not to be had tonight. Light exploded through their dim room, and Jem bolted upright, shielding Tessa from any possible threat.

Words of shimmering blue and silver had appeared on the wall. Tessa sat up, tucking the sheet around her. "Message from Magnus," she said, twisting her hair up into a knot at the back of her head.

The message said that Alec and Lily Chen were on their way to help. Once they had stowed their belongings at the Buenos Aires Institute, they would meet Tessa and Jem outside the walls of the Shadow Market.

Jem met Tessa's gaze and read his own alarm in her eyes.

"Oh no," said Tessa. Jem was already scrambling off the bed, searching for their clothes. "We have to find them. We have to stop them. They *can't* go to the Institute."

The Buenos Aires Institute was located in the town of San Andrés de Giles. To mundane eyes, the Institute looked like a large crypt standing in an abandoned cemetery, in a profusion of ghost-pale wildflowers.

To Alec's eyes, it looked worse. It was a tall edifice, painted a dull rust color, but one wing of the building was a charred ruin. Alec had known the Institute was damaged during the Dark War, but he'd thought it would have been repaired long before.

Lily sniffed the air. "They mixed blood in the paint."

The Institute looked abandoned, except for the fact there was a guard at the door. Even that made Alec's eyes narrow. Shadowhunters didn't typically keep watch on their own Institutes, unless it was a time of war.

He nodded to Lily, and they moved forward to meet the Shadowhunters of Buenos Aires. The guard at the door looked a few years younger than Alec. His face was hard, his black eyebrows drawn sharply together, and he was squinting at them suspiciously.

"Um," said Alec. "*Bonjour?* Wait, that's French."

Lily smiled a sunny fanged smile at the guard. "Let me handle this."

"I can speak English," the guard told Alec hastily.

"Great," said Alec. "I'm from the New York Institute. My name is—"

The guard's dark eyes went wide. "You're Alexander Lightwood!"

Alec blinked. "That's me."

"I was in the Inquisitor's office once," the guard confided shyly. "He has a tapestry of you hanging up in there."

"Yeah," said Alec. "I know."

"That's how I know what you look like. I'm so thrilled to meet you. I mean, it's such an honor. Oh no, what am I doing? I'm Joaquín Acosta Romero. It's a pleasure."

Joaquín held out his hand for Alec to shake. When Alec shook it, he felt the younger man vibrating slightly with excitement. He cast a panicked glance toward Lily, who grinned and mouthed "cute" at him.

"This is Lily, who is no help," said Alec.

"Oh yes, oh, pleased to meet you, too," said Joaquín. "Wow, come in."

Lily smiled sweetly, showing her fangs. "I can't."

"Oh, right! I'm sorry. I'll show you around to the back entrance. There's a door to the Sanctuary there."

Magnus had enchanted the New York Institute so Downworlders could walk in certain places there, but most Institutes still kept them out of all but the Sanctuary rooms. Alec was pleased to see Joaquín flash a smile at Lily that seemed genuine and welcoming.

"Thanks," said Alec. "We're meeting friends on a mission, but I hoped we could stow our bags now so we can come back to sleep later. We can set up cots in the Sanctuary."

Joaquín led them down a dark cobwebbed alley. Alec thought of the wing that was rubble. Possibly this Institute wouldn't have cots.

"Um, will your friend—will she need a coffin?" asked Joaquín. "I don't think we have coffins. I mean, I'm sure I could find one somewhere! The head of our Institute is, um, very careful about visitors, but I'm certain he can't object to a guest who is coming with Alec Lightwood."

"I don't need a coffin," said Lily. "Just a windowless room. It's no problem."

"You can address her when you're talking about her," said Alec mildly.

Joaquín cast an anxious look at Alec, then an even more anxious look at Lily. "Of course! I'm sorry. I don't have much experience talking to—"

"Vampires?" asked Lily sweetly.

"Women," said Joaquín.

"It's true I'm five fabulous feet of pure woman," Lily mused.

Joaquín coughed. "Well, I don't know any vampires, either. My mother died in the Dark War. A lot of us did. And afterward, most of the women left. Mr. Breakspear says that women aren't suited to the rigor of a tightly run Institute."

He peered anxiously at Alec, as if checking in on Alec's opinion on this.

"Clary Fairchild is one of the heads of my Institute," said Alec curtly. "Jia Penhallow is the leader of all Shadowhunters. Anyone who says women are weak is afraid they're too strong."

Joaquín nodded several times in rapid succession, though Alec wasn't sure if it was agreement or pure nerves.

"I haven't been to any other Institutes. I was born in the Institute when it was located in the city of Buenos Aires, near the Casa Rosada."

"I was wondering why the Buenos Aires Institute was here, and not in the city," said Alec.

"Our old Institute was leveled in the Dark War," Joaquín explained. "Not many of us got out, and we took refuge in the nearest remaining Institute. Together, we were able to defend this place, though you can see the building was damaged by the Endarkened. I still remember the old Institute, and its red arched roof against the blue sky, how beautiful it was, when my parents were alive and the world was different. Now this is the only Institute Buenos Aires has. We used to talk about going back, but . . . we don't anymore. The head of our Institute says we're not ready and corruption is everywhere, but I still want to try. When I turned eighteen, I was hoping I could go to another Institute on my travel year and see how other Institutes worked, maybe even meet a girl, but the head of our Institute said I couldn't be spared. Not when the Downworlders in our Shadow Market are so dangerous."

Joaquín hung his head. Alec was trying to phrase a question that wouldn't shock the boy further, about why this was such a harsh posting. About what exactly was going on with the Buenos Aires Institute. But before he could, they reached the end of the alley and passed through the battered door to the Sanctuary of the Institute. Inside it looked like a church that had suffered a blast, the long windows boarded up, the floor blackened.

There was a man in the center of the charred floor, holding forth to a group of silent Shadowhunter men. He looked about forty, his fair hair already turning silver, and he was the only one in the room wearing gear that was not patched or worn.

"That's Clive Breakspear, the head of our Institute," said Joaquín. "Sir, we have a visitor. It's Alexander Lightwood."

He said something in Spanish, which judging by the repetition of Alec's name, Alec thought was the same thing, then glanced around as if expecting an enthusiastic response. He didn't receive one. Several of the men in the circle seemed immediately wary.

Clive Breakspear did not look wary at all.

"So you're Alec Lightwood," said the head of the Buenos Aires Institute slowly. "Then this must be your Downworlder whore."

There was a terrible silence.

It was broken by Lily, who blinked and said, "Excuse me? Have you been living in a hole? Are you not aware Alec is dating famous warlock Magnus Bane and is not interested in ladies of any persuasion?"

There was a rush of whispers. Alec didn't think everyone was stunned by this information. They were stunned that Lily would say it, as if they expected him to be ashamed.

"Let's be clear on this matter. This is my friend Lily, the head of the New York vampire clan." Alec put his hand on his seraph blade, and the whispers hushed. "Think very carefully," said Alec, "about how you wish to speak of her. Or of Magnus Bane."

He almost said "my fiancé," but it was an awkward word. Once he'd said "my betrothed" and felt like a total idiot. He longed sometimes, with an almost physical ache, just to say "my husband" and have it be true.

"I'm here on a mission," Alec continued. "I thought I could rely on the hospitality of the Institute and my fellow Shadow-hunters. I see I was wrong."

He cast a look around the room. Several of the men could not meet his eyes.

"What mission?" demanded Clive Breakspear.

"One that requires discretion."

Alec regarded him steadily, until Clive Breakspear flushed and looked away.

"You can stay here," he agreed grudgingly. "The Down-worlder cannot."

"Like I want to," Lily sneered. "I don't stay in places where the decor isn't ten out of ten, and this place is a minus fourteen thousand. Okay, Alec, let's make a plan for where we will meet up after I find a nice windowless hotel room. Do you want to—"

"What are you talking about?" Alec demanded. "If they won't have you, I won't stay here. To hell with this place. I'm going with you."

Lily's face went soft, for the space of time it took to blink. Then she patted his arm and said, "Of course you are."

She sniffed disdainfully and spun on her heel. Clive Breakspear barreled toward her.

"I have some questions for you, Downworlder."

Alec caught his arm and stepped in front of Lily. "Are you sure about that?"

They were outnumbered, but Alec was the Inquisitor's son, Jace Herondale's *parabatai*. He was protected in a way many others were not. That meant he had to use whatever he had, for those who had no protection.

After a long moment, Breakspear stepped back.

Alec wished he could've thought of a really scathing exit line, but those weren't his specialty. He and Lily just left, Joaquín chasing after them.

"By the Angel," Joaquín said. "I didn't expect that—I didn't think—I'm so sorry."

"It's not the first Institute I haven't been welcome in," said Alec.

Especially if he was with Magnus. It didn't happen often, but a couple of Institutes before now had tried to separate them or suggested that they shouldn't have come together. Alec always made clear what he thought of that.

"I'm so sorry," Joaquín repeated helplessly.

Alec nodded to him; then Alec and Lily went out into the night. Alec stood with the blasted building at their backs and breathed in one long, deep breath.

"Shadowhunters are trash," Lily announced.

Alec gave her a look.

"Present company excepted. And Jem," said Lily. "I'm having a terrible time in Buenos Aires, and I don't eat, but I'm in the mood for a delicious bowl of Jembalaya."

"He's married!" Alec pointed out once again.

"Please stop reminding me. She smells like books. I may be immortal, but life is too short to spend reading." Lily paused for an instant, then added quietly, "Raphael liked her. She and Ragnor Fell and Raphael used to have little meetings and tell each other secrets."

Alec understood the tension in her voice now. Lily was slightly wary of Magnus too, of anyone not in her clan whom she thought Raphael Santiago might have loved.

"I told Jem we'd meet him outside the Shadow Market," said Alec, effectively distracting Lily. "We can just carry our bags until we find a place to stay. For now let's see about this place that has the Buenos Aires Institute running scared, where only I can go."

Alec went to the New York Shadow Market on Canal Street with Magnus and Max often, but the first time at a new Shadow Market as a Shadowhunter could be tricky.

The Buenos Aires Shadow Market looked more than tricky. Barbed wire was hung on every plank. The smooth sun-bleached wood and snarled loops of barbed wire were an impenetrable stretch of silver. There was a large metal door in front of them, more suited to a prison than a market, and a werewolf's eyes shone behind a metal grille. He snapped something at them.

"He said 'No Shadowhunters,'" Lily interpreted cheerfully.

There was a line of Downworlders behind them, staring and murmuring. Alec felt a shadow of the old discomfort at being the focus of attention, and a sudden doubt about the information Jem had provided.

"I'm Alec Lightwood," he said. "I hear that I'm allowed in."

There was a stir behind his back, a brief silence, and then a rush of different-sounding whispers, like listening to a tide turn.

"You could just be another lying Nephilim," the werewolf snarled, switching to English. "Can you *prove* you're Alec Lightwood?"

Alec said, "I can."

He took his hands out of his pockets and held up the right one to the grille so the werewolf could see it plainly: scarred skin, calluses from his bow, the dark lines of his Voyance rune, and moonlight striking and holding on the bright band of his family ring with its etched pattern of flames.

Another set of eyes appeared at the grille, this pair a faerie's, pupil-less and green as woodland lakes fathoms deep. She said something soft in Spanish.

"She says the magic in your ring is very strong," Lily reported at his shoulder. "Too strong. She says that kind of power comes from the very heart of Hell."

Alec knew that was true. There was not only one charm in this ring but spell after spell: magic for protection and deflection, magic to guide his arrows and blades, all the power at Magnus's command poured into the metal. There was everything Magnus had been able to think of, to act as Alec's armor and ensure Alec would return home safe to him. Most important, there was the look on Magnus's face when he returned the ring, now symbolizing Alec's family in two ways, to Alec. That was when Magnus had assured him that he believed they would be married one day.

"I know where this kind of power comes from." Alec raised his voice so that the whole murmuring crowd could hear. "I'm

Alec Lightwood. Magnus Bane wove this enchantment for me."

The werewolf guard held open the door to the Shadow Market.

Alec and Lily walked into a barbed-wire tunnel. Alec could hear the sounds and glimpse the lights of a Market, but the tunnel split off in two directions. The guard took them to the left, away from light and sound, into a shed lined with wards and metal. The room was lit by a single lantern that hung from the ceiling. Broken weapons were fixed on the walls, and there was a roughly hewn circular platform in the center of the room, and on that platform a huge chair. There were crossed axes on the back of that chair, and a row of glittering spikes ran along the top. A slender faerie girl, with a crown of thorns and a wistful face, was sitting cross-legged at the foot of the throne.

Upon the throne was a young woman who looked about Alec's age. She was wearing jeans and a flannel shirt, her legs swung carelessly over the throne's arm, the row of spikes glinting above her light hair. This must be the woman Jem had written about, the werewolf Queen of the Market.

She saw Alec and her face went blank. Then she started to smile and said in English but with a distinct French accent, "Alec! It's really you. I can't believe it!"

This was very awkward.

"Sorry," said Alec. "Have we met?"

The werewolf swung her legs to the floor, leaning forward. "I'm Juliette."

"I'm not Romeo," said Lily. "But you are cute, so tell us more about yourself in your sexy accent."

"Um, who are you?" asked Juliette.

"Lily Chen," said Lily.

"Head of the New York vampire clan," added Alec.

"Oh, of course," said Juliette. "From the Alliance! Thank you for coming with Alec to help us. It's a real privilege to meet you."

Lily beamed. "I know, right?"

Juliette's eyes went back to Alec. The way she was looking at him, wide-eyed and startled, did ring a faint bell.

"And this is my daughter Rose," said Juliette the werewolf, her hands firm on the young faerie's shoulders.

Alec didn't recognize the woman, but he recognized that tone of voice. He knew how it was to lay claim to what you loved, all the more insistently because people doubted the love that belonged to you. Alec wasn't sure what to say, so he did one of his favorite things. He produced his phone and found a really good picture, walked up to the dais, and showed it to them both.

"This is my son, Max."

Juliette and Rose leaned forward. Alec saw the werewolf's eyes flicker, saw the moment where it registered with Juliette that Max was a warlock.

"Oh." Juliette's voice was soft. "He's beautiful."

"I think so," said Alec shyly, and showed them a few more pictures. Alec found it difficult to select the best pictures. So many of them were great. It was hard to take a bad picture of Max.

Juliette gave the adolescent faerie a push between the shoulder blades.

"Go get your brother and sister," she urged. "Quick."

Rose sprang to her feet, faerie light, cast a shy sidelong glance at Alec, and ran out.

"You know me," said Alec. "How?"

"You saved my life," Juliette said. "Five years ago, when

demons attacked the Orient Express."

"Oh," said Alec.

His and Magnus's first vacation. He tried not to think of the less pleasant aspects of that trip, but he remembered the train, the warm falling water and the shine of demons' eyes, the screaming wind and the abyss below. He'd been terrified for Magnus that night.

"You fought demons on the Orient Express?" Lily asked with interest.

"I fight demons in lots of places," said Alec. "It was all very normal."

"I'd never seen anything like it in my life," Juliette told Lily enthusiastically. "There were so many demons! They broke the windows. I thought I was about to be killed. Then Alec took out every demon he saw. He was soaking wet, and he wasn't wearing a shirt."

Alec didn't see how that was relevant.

"Very normal," he repeated. "Except normally I wear a shirt."

Lily's eyes were dancing with glee. "What a wild time you seem to have on holiday, Alec."

"I had a totally standard and boring time," Alec told her.

"Sounds like it."

"And I was at that party in Venice," Juliette continued. "When the mansion collapsed."

"I was there too!" said Lily. "Raphael was super sad to be at a party; it was hilarious. I made out with so many people, it was a personal record. I think one of them was a hot blonde! Was it you?"

Juliette blinked. "Er, no. I don't really . . . make out with girls."

Lily shrugged. "Sorry you're wasting your life."

"I don't either," Alec commented mildly.

Juliette nodded. "I remember Magnus at that party too. He was trying to help."

Alec heard his own voice go low and tender, entirely out of his control. "He always does."

There was a clatter of feet behind them. Rose the faerie girl had returned. There were two more kids hand in hand with her now, another faerie girl with the sturdy build of a goblin and a dark-skinned warlock boy with a fox tail. They ran up to the chair and clustered about Juliette. The girl looked about ten, and the boy no more than six.

"Kids," said Juliette, "this is Alec Lightwood, whom I've told you about. Alec, these are my kids."

"Hi," said Alec.

The kids stared.

"When you saved me on the Orient Express," said Juliette, "I asked how I could repay you, and you said you'd seen a faerie child alone in the Paris Shadow Market. You asked me if I could look out for her. I'd never spoken to a Shadowhunter before. I didn't think they were like you. I was—surprised you asked me that. So when I got back to Paris, I went looking for her. My Rosey and I have been together ever since."

She ruffled Rose's wispy hair around her crown of thorns. Rose flushed green.

"*Maman.* Do not embarrass me in front of Alec Lightwood!"

The Paris Shadow Market Alec and Magnus had visited on their first vacation together had been Alec's first Market ever. The Downworlders hadn't been used to him then, and he hadn't been used to them. He did recall the faerie child he'd seen there:

how skinny she'd been, and how sorry he'd been for her.

She'd been about the same age as his baby brother, whom Max was named for. Unlike his brother, she had lived to be older.

"Rose," Alec said. "How grown up you are now."

Rose beamed.

"We were happy together in Paris, you and I, weren't we, *ma petite?*" Juliette asked Rose, sounding wistful. "I thought the end of the war with Valentine would be an end to all wars. But then there was another war, and so many Shadowhunters died, and so many faeries, too. And the Cold Peace began."

She fixed her eyes on Alec. The light from the lantern above the throne caught her eyes, like headlights catching the eyes of a wolf.

"I heard about you and Magnus, and the Downworlder-Shadowhunter Alliance you set up. You were both helping people. I wanted to do that too. I heard about people hunting faeries in Belgium, and I got my youngest girl out."

Rose's hands closed on the goblin girl's shoulders. Alec recognized that gesture too: the constant worry of the oldest in the family, the knowledge that you were responsible for the younger ones.

"Then I heard about Buenos Aires," said Juliette. "The Institute in the city was crushed in the Dark War. Most of the Downworlders fled the city before the Institute fell. The Downworlders of the Shadow Market ran here, and for a time cooperated with the surviving Shadowhunters, but then the Clave sent a new leader to the Institute. Breakspear was supposed to help, but Shadow Markets in Europe began to hear dark rumors. I came to see if there was anything I could do. At the time, I thought we could work with the Shadowhunters, rebuild the Institute in the city of Buenos Aires, and make sure the Shadow Market could return safely. It didn't work out that way. I've lost all hope for the Shadowhunters of this Institute."

The little boy lifted his arms to her, and Juliette picked him up, cuddling him on her knee. The boy watched Alec, sucking thoughtfully on the tip of his fox tail.

"There were a lot of children orphaned in the war," said Juliette. "The Shadow Market here became a refuge for unwanted children. A haphazard kind of orphanage, among the stalls and lights and magic. The Market became a community, because we needed one, a Market that never ceased. People live inside these walls. My baby was left here, because he manifested his warlock mark so young."

"So did Max," said Alec.

"There are so many kids." Juliette closed her eyes.

"What's wrong with this Institute?" Alec asked. "Why hasn't someone reached out to the Clave?"

"We did," Juliette returned. "It was useless. Breakspear has powerful friends. He made sure the message went right to a man called Horace Dearborn. Do you know him?"

Alec's eyes narrowed. "I know him."

The aftereffects of too many wars and the constant pressure of the Cold Peace provided opportunities for a certain kind of person. Horace Dearborn was one of the type who flourished on unrest and fear.

"After the Institute was destroyed by the Endarkened," said Juliette, "Clive Breakspear arrived here with that man Dearborn's name behind him, like a vulture glutting himself on the remains. The word is, his Shadowhunters take missions for money. Like—if someone wanted a rival dead, Breakspear's

Shadowhunters would see it done. They don't hunt demons. They don't hunt Downworlders who break the Law. They hunt us all."

Alec's stomach turned. "They're mercenaries."

"The decent Shadowhunters left, when they couldn't make any difference to the way things were done," said Juliette. "I don't think they talked. I think they were ashamed. This Market, with all the kids in it—the Market wasn't safe. It seemed like the leaders were being picked off, so people would be more vulnerable. They didn't try for me. I've got friends in Paris and in Brussels who would raise a howl if I disappeared. So I ordered wards and fences put up. I let people call me a queen. I tried to seem as strong as I could, so they wouldn't come at us. But things are getting worse, not better. Female werewolves are disappearing."

"Killed?" asked Alec.

"I don't know," said Juliette. "We thought they were running at first, but there are too many. Mothers who wouldn't have left their families. Girls as young as my Rosey. Some people say they've seen a strange warlock about. I have no idea what's happening to those women, but I knew I couldn't trust anyone at the Institute to find out. I won't risk trusting any Shadowhunter. Except you. I put out the word I wanted you. I wasn't sure you would come, but here you are."

She lifted her face imploringly to Alec's. The Queen of the Shadow Market looked, in that moment, as young as the kids clustered around her.

"Will you help me? One more time?"

"As many times as you need me," said Alec. "I'll find those women. I'll find out who's doing this. I'll stop them. You have my word."

He hesitated, remembering Jem and Tessa's mission.

"I have friends here, besides Lily. A warlock woman and a man who used to be a Silent Brother, with a white streak in his hair. Can they enter the Market? I swear to you they can be trusted."

"I think I know who you mean," Juliette said. "They were asking for admittance a few nights back, weren't they? I heard the man was handsome."

"Boy, did you hear right," said Lily.

Juliette's smile spread. "There really are some very handsome Nephilim around."

"Uh, I guess," said Alec. "I don't really think about Jem that way."

"How can you be good at archery, when you're so blind?" Lily demanded.

Alec rolled his eyes. "Thanks, Juliette. I'll let you know as soon as I find something out."

Juliette said softly, "I'm glad you're here."

"I won't leave until I've helped you," said Alec, then glanced at the kids, who were still staring. "Um. Bye, kids. It was very nice to meet you."

He nodded to them awkwardly, then made his way back toward the lights and music of the Market.

"Okay," he told Lily as they walked. "Let's take a quick look around the Market, ask some questions before we meet Jem and Tessa."

"Let's drop by the faerie fruit gin stall!" Lily suggested.

Alec said, "No."

"We can't be all business all the time," said Lily, who was seldom all business for five minutes. "So, who do you think is hot?" When Alec stared at her, she said, "We're on a bro road trip! We're meant to share secrets. You said not Jem. So who?"

Alec shook his head at a faerie trying to sell them charmed bracelets, though she insisted they were real charms and really charming. When Alec asked about the disappearances, the faerie's eyes widened, but she didn't know any more than Juliette.

"Magnus is hot," Alec said finally, as they went on their way.

Lily rolled her eyes. "Wow, you and Monogamous Bane make me tired. He's even dumber than you are."

"He's not dumb."

"An immortal who sets his soft heart on one person?" Lily bit her lip, fangs pressing down too hard. "That's dumb."

"Lily," said Alec, but Lily was shaking her head and proceeding, her voice firmly light.

"Leaving aside your destined honey lamb and all, I know there was Jace. Is it just guys with golden eyes?" asked Lily. "That is a very particular taste you have there, friend. It really narrows the playing field. So no other crushes besides Jace? Even a teeny tiny one when you were young?"

"Why are you leering like you know something I don't?" Alec asked warily.

Lily giggled.

There was a lot of noise happening behind one of the stalls. Alec turned his head toward it automatically, but also because he didn't know how to explain that specific crushes hadn't been the problem. It had been a relief, in a way, to pretend even to himself that a crush on Jace was the thing that was making him miserable.

Even when he was a kid, he'd found his attention caught by posters of mundane men in the streets of New York, or found himself drawn to guys visiting the Institute, listening from behind his vase to their stories of demon-hunting and thinking they were cool. He'd had unfocused childish daydreams, created hazy bright dreamlands featuring boys, and then he'd lost the dream with his childhood. He'd been too young to understand himself, and then he hadn't been. He heard the way Shadowhunter visitors sneered, how his dad hinted at the subject as if it were too awful even to be said outright, when saying things outright was the only way Alec knew how to say them. Alec felt guilty every time he had to pull his eyes off another boy, even just a curious look, and then there had been Magnus, and he hadn't been able to look away from him at all.

The noise from behind the stall was growing closer.

A lot of noise, very close to the ground.

The orphans of the Buenos Aires Shadow Market exploded from behind a stall where a werewolf was selling stew. There were kids everywhere, Downworlders of every kind, and all of them seemed to be trying to get his attention, shouting out names, requests, jokes. The main language was Spanish, but Alec heard a few others, and was immediately confused about which words belonged to which language. Multicolored lights swung on dozens of faces. He turned his head, overwhelmed, not able to make out any face or voice in the chaos.

"Hey," he said, stooping over the kids and pulling food out of his duffel bag. "Hey, is anybody hungry? Take these."

"Gross, are those energy bars?" Lily demanded. "Way to pile misery on orphans!"

Alec took out his wallet and began to give the kids money. Magnus was always magically making cash appear there, in case of emergencies. Alec wouldn't spend it on himself.

Lily was laughing. She liked kids, though sometimes she

pretended she didn't. Then she froze. For a moment her bright black eyes went flat and dead. Alec stood up straight.

"You, kid." Lily's voice was trembling. "What did you say your name was?"

She shook her head and repeated the question in Spanish. Alec followed her line of sight to one particular child in the crowd.

The other children were jostling each other, pressed up against each other and the stalls, but there was a small circle of space around this boy. Now that he had their attention, he wasn't shouting. His curly head was tipped back so he could study them, and he was doing so with narrowed, very dark eyes. His extremely critical air had to be Alec's imagination. The kid looked about six years old.

The boy answered Lily, his voice calm: "Rafael."

"Rafael," Lily whispered. "Right."

Rafael's face was one of the youngest in that crowd of heartbreakingly young faces, but there was a chilling air of self-possession about him. He advanced, and Alec wasn't surprised to see the other kids move out of his path. He carried distance with him.

Alec's own eyes narrowed. He couldn't tell what kind of Downworlder this kid was, but there was something about the way he moved.

Rafael said something else in Spanish. From the imperious tilt at the end of the sentence, it was a question or a demand. Alec looked helplessly at Lily. She nodded, visibly gathering her composure.

"The kid said . . ." She cleared her throat. "He says: 'Are you a Shadowhunter? Not like the ones at the Institute. Are you a *real* Shadowhunter?'"

Alec blinked. Rafael's eyes were fixed on his face.

Alec knelt on the ground amid the bright riot of the Shadow Market, so he could look into those dark intent eyes.

"Yes," said Alec. "I'm a Shadowhunter. Tell me how I can help you."

Lily translated. Rafael shook his curly head, expression even cooler, as if Alec had failed some sort of test. He snapped out several more lines of Spanish.

"He says he doesn't want help," said Lily. "He says he over-heard you ask about the women who vanished."

"So the kid can understand some English?" asked Alec, hopeful.

Rafael rolled his eyes and said something else in Spanish.

Lily grinned. "He says no, not at all. He has information, but he doesn't want to talk here."

Alec frowned. *"Boludo,"* he repeated. "He said that. What does that word mean?"

Lily grinned. "It means he thinks you're a nice man!"

It hadn't sounded nice. Alec squinted at Rafael. Rafael gave him a blank stare back.

"All right," Alec said slowly. "Who's taking care of you? Let's go to them, and we can talk together."

The night was dark, especially under the awning of a stall, but Alec was pretty sure Rafael rolled his eyes. He transferred his attention from Alec, whom he clearly found to be hopeless, and looked to Lily.

"He says that he takes care of himself," said Lily.

"But he can't be more than six!" said Alec.

"He says he's five," Lily said, her brows knitted as she lis-tened and translated slowly. "His parents died in the Dark War, when the Institute fell, and then there was a werewolf woman who looked after a bunch of kids. But she's gone now. He says nobody else wants him."

She must be one of the women who disappeared, Alec thought grimly. That thought was lost in the rush of horror when he realized what Lily was saying.

"His parents died when the Institute fell?" Alec repeated. Every cell in his body sparked with shock. *"Is this boy a Shadowhunter?"*

"Would it be worse to find a Shadowhunter child like this?" Lily asked, her voice cold.

"Yes," Alec snarled back. "Not because Downworlder kids deserve this. My kid's a Downworlder. No kid deserves this. But you heard Juliette. Everybody's doing the best they can. Shadowhunters fall in battle every day, and homes are found for orphans. There is a system in place for Shadowhunter children. The Shadowhunters should be doing better than this. The Law is meant to protect the most helpless among us. What is *wrong* with this Institute?"

"As you're using your stern voice, I guess we're going to find out," Lily remarked, sounding chipper again.

Alec was still looking at Rafael with dismay so profound it felt almost like despair. He saw now that Rafael looked dirtier, and less cared for, than any other child in the crowd. Alec had learned the Law at his mother's knee, at his father's, from his tutor and every book in the library at the Institute back home. It had made sense to him when he was young, when very little made sense to him. The Shadowhunters' sacred duty, for all time: to stand unseen against the darkness, to defend at any cost.

Now he was older, and he knew how complicated the world could be. It still hurt like an unexpected blow when he saw that shining ideal tarnished. If he were in charge of it all—

But they didn't live in that world.

"Come with me for now," Alec told the Nephilim child. "I'll take care of you."

If Rafael really was alone, Alec could take Rafael to the New York Institute or to Alicante. He wasn't going to leave him here where he looked so friendless and neglected. He reached out, arms open, to pick Rafael up and carry him away.

Rafael bolted backward with the speed of a wild animal. He gave Alec a filthy look, as if he might bite if Alec tried that again.

Alec drew his arms back and lifted his hands in a gesture of surrender. "All right," he said. "Sorry. But will you come with us? We want to hear your information. We want to help."

Lily translated. Rafael, still watching Alec warily, nodded. Alec rose and offered Rafael his hand. Rafael eyed the hand with disbelief, shaking his head and muttering something. Alec was almost sure it was that word again. He looked Rafael over. The kid's clothes were stained and torn, he was much too thin, and he was barefoot. There were dark circles of exhaustion under his eyes. Alec didn't even know where they were going to sleep.

"Okay," he said at last. "We have to buy him some shoes."

He walked out of the throng of kids, with Lily at his side and Rafael orbiting them like a wary moon.

"Maybe I can help you, Shadowhunter," called out a faerie woman with dandelion hair from a stall.

Alec started forward, then stopped. Lily had caught his arm in a grip like iron.

"Don't go near that woman," she whispered. "I'll explain later."

Alec nodded and went on, despite the call of the faerie

woman to come buy. Juliette had been right: this Market was a community, with huts and wagons surrounding the stalls. It was the biggest Market Alec had ever seen.

Alec found a faerie cobbler who seemed nice enough, though even the smallest pair of boots he had were too big. Alec took them anyway. He asked the cobbler, who spoke English, if anyone was taking care of Rafael. Surely, no matter what the kid said, someone must care.

After a moment the cobbler shook his head. "When the werewolf woman who looked after the orphans vanished, the other kids were given homes by my people. But, no offense meant, faeries won't take in a Shadowhunter."

Not with the Cold Peace breeding hatred between Shadowhunters and faeries. The laws were all wrong, and children were paying the price.

"Also, that child hates everybody," said the faerie cobbler. "Watch out. He bites."

They were almost at the wire tunnel leading to the exit of the Shadow Market now. This far out from the center of the Market there were fallen walls, more signs of a place crushed by war and then left to decay.

"Hey," Alec told Rafael. "Come here a second. *Mach dir keine Sorgen*—"

"You're telling him not to worry in German," Lily reported gleefully.

Alec sighed and knelt in the gray dust, among the rubble, gesturing for Rafael to sit on a piece of the fallen wall. The child eyed Alec and the boots in his hand with an air of extreme mistrust. Then he plunked himself down and let Alec slip his feet into the too-large boots.

The kid's feet were small, his soles black with filth. Alec swallowed, and drew the laces on the boots as tight as he could, so they would stay on and Rafael could walk properly.

Rafael stood as soon as Alec was done tying his laces. Alec stood as well.

"Come on," he said.

Rafael's dark, measuring gaze was on Alec again. He stood perfectly still, for a long moment.

Then he lifted both his arms in a commanding gesture. Alec was so used to that gesture from Max that he moved without even thinking and scooped Rafael up in his arms.

It was nothing like carrying Max, small and plump, always laughing and cuddling. Rafael was much too thin. Alec could feel the knobbly bones of his back. Rafael held himself very stiffly, as though he was undergoing an unpleasant ordeal. It was like holding a small statue, if you felt desperately sorry for the statue and unsure what to do.

"Carrying you means the boots are pointless," murmured Alec. "But that's all right. I'm glad you're coming with us. You're safe now. I have you."

"*No te entiendo*," said Rafael's small clear voice in his ear, then after a thoughtful pause: "*Boludo.*"

Alec was sure of two things: that word was not a nice word, and this kid didn't like him at all.

Jem and Tessa were standing at the gates of the Shadow Market when they saw him. They'd hoped to catch Alec and Lily before they reached the Buenos Aires Institute. Finding no sign of them, they'd worried Breakspear had detained them, but a warlock acquaintance of Tessa's had sent word that a

Shadowhunter had been let into the Market.

Now they were worried the Queen of the Market had detained them. Jem was conferring with Tessa when the gates opened. Against barbed wire and starlight they saw a tall man, his black head bowed and his tender blue eyes fixed on the child in his arms. *Will*, thought Jem, and grasped Tessa's hand tight. Whatever he felt, it was worse for her.

Alec looked up and said, sounding relieved, "Tessa."

"What a handsome end to a long night," Lily said delightedly. "If it isn't the former Brother Snackariah."

"Lily!" Alec exclaimed.

But Tessa, still holding Jem's hand, gave Jem a highly amused look and smiled her gradual, beautiful smile. "It's Raphael's Lily," she said. "How nice to see you. Forgive me, I feel like I know you better than I do. He talked about you often."

Lily's grin fractured as if someone had dropped a mirror.

"What did he say about me?" she asked in a small voice.

"He said you were more efficient and intelligent than most of the clan, who were morons."

It sounded very cold to Jem, but that had been Raphael's way. Lily's smile returned, warm as a flame held between cupped hands. It reminded Jem of the way she'd looked when they first met. He had not known then that Tessa had sent Raphael to him for help. He'd done his best then, and now Lily was a friend.

"Thank you both for coming to help us," said Jem. "Who is the child?"

Alec explained the events of the night—being turned away from the Buenos Aires Institute, learning of the disappearances, and the discovery of Rafael, the child the Institute had abandoned.

"I'm sorry you went to the Institute at all," Jem said. "We should have warned you, but I haven't been a Shadowhunter in a long time. I didn't realize that your first instinct would be to go there. Our lodging house has rooms available, and at least one of them is windowless. Come with us."

Alec carried the child with the ease of long habit. One hand remained free to grab a weapon, and he walked easily through the streets with the small precious weight. Jem, long out of practice, wouldn't have been able to do it himself. He'd held Tessa's children, James and Lucie, when they were little, but that had been more than a century ago. Not many people wanted a Silent Brother close to their child, unless that child was near death.

They walked through the streets, past houses painted in flamboyant hues—flame scarlet, sea blue, crocodile green— the streets lined with jacaranda and olive trees. At last they reached their lodgings, the low whitewashed building turned blue by the first signs of dawn. Jem pushed open the circular red door and requested more rooms from their landlady, one without a window.

Jem and Tessa had already secured the use of the little courtyard at the center of the lodging house, a group of small stone pillars open to the sky, circled with the soft violet-blue of bougainvillea. They gathered there, Alec placing Rafael carefully down on the stone bench beside him. Rafael scooted to the other edge of the bench. He hung his head and was silent when Tessa spoke to him softly in Spanish, asking him for any information about the missing women. Jem hadn't heard about them before, but now that he knew, it was clear they had to help. Rosemary Herondale might be in danger, but so were these werewolf women. Jem wanted to do whatever he could for them.

Returning to speech had been strange for Jem, but Tessa had learned many languages and taught him everything she could. Jem tried asking Rafael too, but Rafael shook his head sullenly.

Lily was sitting cross-legged on the ground, one elbow propped on Alec's knee, to be near the child. She tilted her head toward Rafael and asked him if he would please get on with it, because the sun was rising and she'd have to go to bed soon.

Rafael reached out and patted the bright pink streak in Lily's hair.

"*Bonita*," he said, face still solemn.

The poor child didn't smile much, Jem thought. Of course, neither did Alec, who was looking miserable and determined about the missing women.

Lily, who smiled very easily, did so now. "Aw, cute baby," she said in Spanish. "Do you want to call me Aunt Lily?"

Rafael shook his head. Lily looked undaunted.

"I have a trick," she offered, and snapped her fangs in Rafael's direction.

Rafael looked absolutely appalled.

"What are you guys saying?" asked Alec worriedly. "Why is he looking like that? Why did you do that?"

"Max loves it when I do that!" said Lily, and added in Spanish, "I didn't mean to scare you."

"Wasn't scared," Rafael responded in Spanish. "That was stupid."

"What did he say?" Alec asked.

"He said that was an awesome trick and he really enjoyed it," Lily reported.

Alec raised a skeptical eyebrow in her direction. Rafael pressed close to Alec. Tessa joined Lily on the ground. Tessa talked to Rafael gently, and Lily teased him, and together they got the full story, Lily translating for Alec as they went. Alec's face went more and more grim as he heard the story.

"Rafael knows he's a Shadowhunter, and he's trying to learn—"

Rafael, who Jem thought understood more English than he was letting on, interrupted to correct Lily.

"Excuse me," Lily said. "He's trying to train. He spies on the other Shadowhunters, so he knows what to do. He's small, and he makes sure they don't see him. While he was spying on them, he saw a Shadowhunter creeping off down a lane. He met a warlock at the door of a big house. Rafael got as close as he could, and he heard women inside."

"Can you describe the Shadowhunter you saw?" asked Alec, and Jem translated for him.

"I think you can do it," Jem added to the child encouragingly. "You see so much."

Rafael gave Jem a dark look, as though he disliked praise. He spent a few more moments in furious thought, kicking his too-big boots over the edge of the stone bench, then reached into the pocket of his tattered trousers and placed a slim wallet in Alec's hands.

"Oh." Alec looked startled. "You stole this from the Shadowhunter you saw?"

Rafael nodded.

"That's great. I mean . . ." Alec paused. "It's good that you're helping us, but it's very bad to steal wallets generally. Don't do it again."

"*No te entiendo*," Rafael announced firmly.

He said that he didn't understand Alec, and his tone suggested that he wasn't planning to understand Alec on this topic anytime soon.

"Don't say the other word," Alec said quickly.

"What other word?" Jem asked.

"Don't ask," said Alec, and opened the wallet.

Shadowhunters did not carry mundane forms of identification like passports or ID cards, but they carried other things. Alec took out a weapons requisition document marked with the Breakspear family symbol.

"Clive Breakspear," Alec said slowly. "The head of the Institute. Juliette said that these Shadowhunters act as mercenaries. What if this warlock hired them?"

"We have to find out what's happening," said Jem. "And stop it."

Alec set his jaw. "Rafael can show us the house after he gets some rest," he said. "Tomorrow night we'll go back to the Shadow Market. We'll try to find the information you're looking for and tell the Queen of the Market what, if anything, we've discovered."

Rafael nodded, then held his hand out for the wallet. Alec shook his head.

"What is this secret you want to know about?" Lily asked Jem.

"Lily, it's a secret," Alec said reprovingly.

There were crickets chirping in an odd beautiful melody beyond the walls.

"I trust you both," Jem said slowly. "You came here to help

us. I trust this will go no further. I'm looking for someone who needs my help. There's a hidden line of Shadowhunters I became aware of in the 1930s."

Lily shook her head. "The 1930s were such a disappointment. Every year, they insisted on not being the 1920s."

Will had died in the 1930s, and Tessa had been in agony. Jem had not liked the 1930s much either.

"This family has been hunted for decades," said Jem. "I don't know why. I learned how they split off from the Nephilim, but I still didn't know why faeries are hunting them. I met one of them, but she refused my help and ran away. Since then, I have looked for them, and friends I trust have asked discreetly around the Shadow Markets. The year I met you there, Lily, I was searching for Ragnor Fell, to find out what he could tell me. I want to know why they are being hunted, so that I can help them. Whoever their enemies are, they are mine, too."

Because the Carstairs owe the Herondales.

"I asked in the Spiral Labyrinth as well," said Tessa. "There was never any word. Until suddenly we heard that someone was telling stories to the children of this Market, stories of love and revenge and misery. We heard a whisper of the name Herondale."

She said the name that had once been hers very softly. Alec jumped as if someone had shouted it in his ear.

Neither Jem nor Tessa mentioned Catarina Loss, who had carried the first lost Herondale child over the seas and raised him on strange shores. That wasn't their secret to tell. Jem trusted Alec, but he was still a Shadowhunter, and his father was the Inquisitor. Jem and Tessa were both well aware of the sentence the Law would pass on Catarina for her act of love and mercy.

"I'll ask Juliette," said Alec. "I'll find out whatever I can. I won't go home until I've helped you."

"Thank you," Jem said.

"Now Rafael has to go to bed," said Alec.

"We have a nice little room for you," Tessa told Rafael in Spanish, her voice soft and encouraging. Rafael shook his head. "Do you not want to be alone?" Tessa asked. "That's fine too. You can sleep with me and Jem."

When Tessa reached out her hands, Rafael turned his face into Alec's bicep and screamed. Tessa drew back at the long mutinous howl. Alec automatically put his arm around the child.

"Lily's vulnerable during the day," he said. "I'd rather stay with her. Will you be all right in the windowless room, Rafael?"

Lily translated. Rafael nodded emphatically.

Jem showed them the way. At the door, he caught Alec's arm before he could follow Lily and Rafael.

"I appreciate this," said Jem. "I truly do. Please don't tell Jace yet."

Jem still thought about Jace, that fierce helpless child he'd met on a dark sea, and the young man burning with heavenly fire. He'd imagined a hundred scenarios where he did better by Jace. If he'd been the Silent Brother who cared for Jace after his father left him, if he'd spent more time with Jace, if Jace had been just slightly older, the age Will had been when Jem first met him . . . maybe Jem would have known.

But what could he have done for Jace, even if he had known?

"I don't want Jace to think he has family somewhere he won't get to know," said Jem. "Blood is not love, but it offers a chance for love. He never had the chance to know Céline Montclaire or Stephen Herondale. I don't want him to feel he is missing another chance."

Jace was happy in New York, though Jem had not helped him be so. He had his love and his *parabatai* and his Institute. If Jem couldn't help him, at least he did not want to hurt him.

Jem still thought about Céline Montclaire, too. If he hadn't been a Silent Brother, with his heart turning to stone in his breast, perhaps he would have understood how much trouble she was in. Perhaps he could have found a way to help her.

He didn't call Céline Jace's mother, because Jem had seen how Jace looked at Maryse Lightwood. Maryse was Jace's mother.

Many years ago, when Jem was still a child, his uncle Elias had come to the London Institute and offered to take him away. "After all," he'd said, "we are family."

"You should go," Will had said stormily to Jem. "I don't care."

Will had slammed the door on his way out, declaring he was off on a wild adventure. After Elias departed, Jem had found Will sitting in the dark in the music room, staring at Jem's violin. He'd sat down on the floor beside Will.

"Entreat me not to leave thee, idiot," Jem had said, and Will had put his head down on Jem's shoulder. Jem had felt him trembling with the effort not to laugh or cry, and known Will wanted to do both.

Blood was not love.

But Jem didn't forget that Céline had never had the chance to be Jace's mother. Life was full of broken hearts and missed chances, but Jem could try to redress some of the wrong done Céline by the world. He could do his best for Jace.

Alec was studying Jem intently.

"I won't tell Jace," he said. "Not yet. Not if you tell him soon."

"I hope I will," said Jem.

"Can I ask you something?" said Alec abruptly. "The Buenos Aires Institute is corrupted, and the Cold Peace is fraying our bonds with Downworlders. You could do a lot of good, if you were with us. Why did you stop being a Shadowhunter?"

"I am with you," said Jem. "Do I have to be a Shadowhunter to be that?"

"No," said Alec. "But I don't understand—why you don't want to be one anymore."

"Don't you?" Jem asked. "You have a *parabatai*. Once, so did I. Can you imagine fighting without him?"

Alec was holding on to the doorframe, and as Jem watched, his knuckles went white.

"I have Tessa, so I have more joy every day than some do in their whole lives. Far more than I deserve. I have seen the world with my wife by my side, and we have our tasks to make life meaningful. We all have different ways to serve. She has the secrets from the Spiral Labyrinth, and I those of the Silent Brothers, and we have combined our knowledge and saved lives that I believe couldn't have been saved by any other means. I do want to help, and I will. But not as a Shadowhunter. I will never be that again."

Alec looked at Jem, those blue eyes wide and sorrowful. He looked like Will, but he wasn't Will, any more than Jace was. None of them could ever be Will.

"When you fight, you should fight with your whole heart," said Jem softly. "I don't have the heart for life among the Nephilim, for that particular fight, not any longer. Too much of my heart is in a grave."

"I'm sorry," Alec said awkwardly. "I do understand."

"There's nothing to be sorry for," Jem told him.

He went back to his room, where Tessa was waiting, a book open in her lap. She looked up when he came in, and she smiled. There was no smile like hers in the world.

"Everything all right?" she asked.

He looked down at her and said, "Yes."

Tessa shut her book and reached up to him. She was kneeling on the bed and he was standing beside it, and the world was filled with missed chances and heartbreak, but then there was Tessa.

Tessa kissed him, and he felt her grin against his mouth. "Brother Snackariah," she murmured. "Come here."

The room might be windowless, but there was a brown jar crowded with red flowers on the table, and two white single beds. Lily had tossed her leather jacket onto the bed closest to the wall.

Rafael was sitting on the other bed, turning over a metallic object thoughtfully in his hands. Alec suddenly understood why he had agreed to be carried.

"What's that you have there, sweetie?" Lily asked as Alec came in.

"What he has is my phone," said Alec. "Which he *stole*."

In Rafael's hands, Alec's phone buzzed. Alec reached for it, but Rafael moved casually out of reach. He didn't seem terribly concerned that Alec had grabbed for him. He was staring at the phone.

Alec reached for the phone again, then stopped, caught off guard. As Rafael studied the phone, the sullen line of his mouth twitched, then slowly curved into a smile. The smile, slow and warm and sweet, altered his whole face.

Alec's hand dropped. Rafael turned a suddenly bright countenance up to him and chirped a question. Even his voice sounded different when he was happy.

"I don't understand you," Alec said helplessly.

Rafael waved the phone in Alec's face to illustrate his point. Alec looked at the screen and kept looking. He'd had a sick unsteady feeling in his chest since he realized what the Shadowhunters might be doing here, but the world felt steady again now.

Magnus had sent a photo with the caption BLUEBIRD AND I HOME FROM A WILD AND DANGEROUS MISSION WITH A SWING SET.

Magnus was leaning against their front door. Max was laughing, all dimples, the way he did whenever Magnus did magic to amuse him. There were blue and golden lights streaming all around them, and huge iridescent bubbles that seemed made of light too. Magnus was smiling a small fond smile, the black spikes of his hair wreathed with radiant ribbons of magic.

Alec had asked Magnus to send him pictures whenever he was away, after their first mission when Max was a baby. To remind Alec what he was fighting for.

Lily cleared her throat. "The kid asked: 'Who is that cool man?'"

"Oh," said Alec, kneeling by the bed. "Oh, that's—that's Magnus. His name is Magnus Bane. He's my—I'm his—he and I are going to get married."

One day they would.

Alec wasn't sure why it felt important to tell this child.

Lily translated. Rafael looked from the phone to Alec's face, then back again, his brow furrowed in clear surprise. Alec waited, and listened apprehensively as Rafael said something Alec couldn't understand. He'd heard kids say terrible things before now. Adults poured poison in their minds, and then it came out of their mouths.

Lily laughed.

"He said," she reported with unholy joy, "'What is that cool man doing with you?'"

Alec said, "Rafael, give me back my phone."

"Let him have it for a bit while he goes to sleep," said Lily, who was one of the reasons Max was spoiled.

Alec glanced over and found Lily wearing an unusually serious look.

"Come here to me a minute," she said. "I promised to tell you why I didn't want you to go near that faerie woman at the Shadow Market. I have a story I want you to hear, that I think might help Jem. I don't want to tell anybody but you."

Alec let Rafael keep the phone. In return, Rafael let Alec tuck him into bed. Alec took the chair by the door and placed it by Lily's bed. They waited until Rafael's eyes fell shut, with Alec's phone on the pillow beside him.

Lily studied the striped pillow on her bed as if it were fascinating.

"Are you hungry?" Alec asked at last. "If you—need blood, you can take mine."

Lily glanced up, her face startled. "No. I don't want that. You're not for that."

Alec tried not to show how relieved he was. Lily looked back down at the pillow and squared her shoulders.

"Remember when you asked me if I was a jazz baby, and I said to call me *the* jazz baby?"

"I'm still not going to do that."

"I still think you should," Lily argued. "But that's . . . not what I meant. The 1920s were my favorite decade, but . . . I may have been misleading you about my age." She grinned. "It's a lady's prerogative."

"Okay," Alec said, not sure where this was going. "So—how old are you, then?"

"I was born in 1885," said Lily. "I think. My mother was a Japanese peasant girl, and she was—sold to my father, a rich Chinese merchant."

"Sold!" said Alec. "That's not—"

"It wasn't legal," Lily said in a tight voice. "But it happened. They lived together for a few years, in Hong Kong, where he worked. I was born there. My mother thought my father would take us back home with him. She taught me to speak the way he would want and dress the way he would want, like a Chinese lady. She loved him. He got tired of her. He left, and before he left, he sold us off. I grew up in a place called the House of Eternal Pearl."

She looked up from the pillow.

"I don't have to tell you, do I?" she asked. "What kind of place it was, where women were sold, and men came and went?"

"Lily," Alec breathed, in horror.

Lily shook her black-and-pink head defiantly. "They called it the House of Eternal Pearl because—some men want women to be young and beautiful forever. Pearls are created from a center of dirt that can't be washed away. In the cellar without windows, in the heart of that house, were chained women.

Those women were cold and lovely forever. They would never age and would do anything for blood. They were for the richest men, they fetched the highest prices, and they had to be fed. My mother grew too old, so they fed her to the vampires. And that night, I crept down and I made a deal with one of them. I promised if she Turned me, I'd free us all. She kept her side of the bargain, but I didn't keep mine." Lily studied the toes of her pointed boots. "I woke up and killed a lot of people. I don't mean that I drank from somebody, though I did that, too. I burned the place to the ground. Nobody got out, not the men, not the women. Nobody but me. I didn't care about anybody but myself."

Alec moved his chair closer to her, but Lily drew her legs up onto the bed, making herself as small as possible.

"Nobody knows all that," she said. "A few people know a little. Magnus knows I wasn't made in the 1920s, but he could tell that I didn't want to say. He never asked for any of my secrets."

"No," said Alec. "He wouldn't."

Magnus knew all about painful secrets. Alec had learned.

"Raphael bribed somebody to find out," said Lily. "I don't know who, or how much he paid. He could have asked me, but he wasn't like that. I only knew that he knew because he was sweet to me for a few nights. In his way. We never talked about it. I've never told anybody. Not until you."

"I won't tell anybody," Alec promised.

The corner of Lily's mouth lifted. "I know you won't, Alec."

Some of the tension went out of her thin shoulders.

"I told you so you'd understand what happened next," she said. "I couldn't stay in Hong Kong. I came to London, I think it was 1903, and I met Shadowhunters for the first time."

"Shadowhunters!" said Alec.

He understood why Downworlders said the word with fear sometimes. Already he couldn't bear what had happened to Lily. He didn't want to hear about Shadowhunters doing anything worse to his friend.

But Lily was smiling now, just a little. "I noticed one in particular, a girl with hair the color of blood in shadows. I barely knew what Shadowhunters were, but she was brave and kind. She protected people. Her name was Cordelia Carstairs. I asked around about Shadowhunters. I heard about a faerie woman with a grudge against all Shadowhunters, particularly against one family. We saw her at the Shadow Market tonight. Tell Jem to ask the woman with dandelion hair about the Herondales. She knows something."

Lily fell silent. Alec knew he had to say something, but he didn't know how. "Thanks, Lily," he said at last. "Not for the information. Thanks for telling me."

Lily smiled, as though she didn't think what Alec had said was too dumb. "After London I traveled on and met Camille Belcourt in Russia. Camille was fun. She was bright and heartless and hard to hurt. I wanted to be like her. When Camille traveled to New York and became head of the vampire clan there, I went with her."

Lily bowed her head. After a long moment sunk in memory, she looked up.

"Want to know something dumb? When Camille and I reached New York after the Great War," she said brightly, "I looked around for Shadowhunters. Wasn't that stupid? Most Shadowhunters are not like you or Jem or Cordelia. I encountered Nephilim who made it very clear the angelic warriors were not sent to shield a creature like me. I didn't care about anybody, and nobody cared about me, and that was how it was, for decades and decades. It was really fun."

"Was it?" Alec asked.

He kept his voice noncommittal. She sounded so brittle.

"The twenties in New York were the brightest time for both of us, when the whole world seemed as frenzied as we were. Decades later Camille was still trying to replicate them, and so was I, but even I thought Camille went too far sometimes. There was an emptiness in her she was always trying to fill. She'd permit her vampires to do anything. Once, in the 1950s, she let a very old vampire called Louis Karnstein stay at the hotel. He preyed on children. I thought he was disgusting, but I didn't care much. I was very good at not caring by then."

Lily shrugged and laughed. The sound was not convincing.

"Maybe I hoped the Shadowhunters would come, but they didn't. Someone else came instead. A pack of scruffy mundane boys who wanted to defend their streets from the monster. They all died, except one. He always did what he set out to do. He killed the monster. He was my Raphael."

Lily stroked the leather jacket where it lay in a heap on her bed.

"Before he killed the monster, Raphael was made into a vampire himself. Your Magnus came to Raphael's aid, but I didn't. Raphael could have died then, and I would never have even known. I met Raphael later. He came upon a bunch of us feeding in an alley and gave us a terrible lecture. He was so solemn, I thought he was funny. I didn't take him seriously at all. But when he came to live at the hotel, I was pleased. Because hey, it seemed like more fun. Who doesn't want more fun? There was nothing else in the world."

Magnus had told Alec this story, though Magnus had never painted himself as anyone's savior. It was strange to hear it from Lily, and stranger to hear knowing how the story ended.

"Raphael asked for better security at the hotel on his second day of living there. He argued that a pack of mundane kids had been able to break in and kill one of our own. Camille laughed at him. Then we were attacked by a rogue band of werewolves, and Raphael's security measures were put in place. Guards were posted, and Raphael always took his turn guarding the hotel, even once he was second in command and didn't have to. He took the first watch, on the first day and night. I remember him showing me plans of the hotel, every weak point, the ways he'd figured out how to best defend ourselves. He had it all worked out, though he'd been with us less than a week. He left to take up his post, and as he went he said, 'Sleep, Lily. I'll watch the doors.' I never slept peacefully before then. I didn't know how to rest and trust I was safe. I slept that day as I'd never slept before."

Lily stared at the vase of flowers, bright red as vampire blood. Alec didn't think she was seeing them.

"Later it turned out that Raphael hired the werewolves to attack us so that we would implement the safety precautions he wanted," Lily added in pragmatic tones. "He was extremely set on having his own way. Also, he was a total asshat."

"That is clear to me," said Alec.

Lily laughed again. She got up from the bed, gripping Alec's shoulder for a moment as she passed, then she began to pace the little room as if it were a cage.

"Raphael was always there, from then on. Camille would demote him from being second in command now and then, to annoy him. It didn't matter. He never wavered, no matter what anyone else did. I thought he'd be there forever. Then he was taken. I told myself I had to hold it together, form an alliance with the werewolves, hold the line against madness. Just until Raphael came back. Only Raphael never came back."

Lily drew a hand over her eyes. She went to Rafael's bedside, passing her tearstained hand lightly over his curly hair.

"Well," she said. "I was happy for fifty-four years. That's more than most people get. Now there's the clan to look after, like Raphael would've wanted. The night we knew he was gone, and every night since, I watch my vampires in the home he guarded. I watch the mundanes in the streets he loved. Every one of them looks like a child I should help, a possibility for a future I wasn't able to imagine. Every one of them seems precious, worth defending, worth the world. Every one of them is Raphael."

The child stirred, as if he were being called. Lily pulled her hand away.

It was day, after a long night.

Alec rose and guided her, a hand on her trembling shoulder, to the bed. He pulled a sheet over her as if she were Rafael. Then he positioned the chair between Lily and Rafael and the entrance, and took his place there.

"Sleep, Lily," Alec said gently. "I'll watch the doors."

Alec didn't rest well. His mind was churning with thoughts of Lily's story, the Buenos Aires Institute's corruption, lost Herondales and werewolves, and Jem and Tessa's quest.

He was used to waking up in dark silk sheets and strong arms. He missed home.

Rafael slept in, not stirring until afternoon. Alec suspected that the orphans of the Shadow Market had all developed nocturnal tendencies. When Rafael woke, Alec took him out to the courtyard, where he sat on the stone bench moodily eating an energy bar. Alec thought he was sulking because Alec had taken back his phone.

"Has anyone ever given you a nickname?" he asked Rafael. "Do people ever call you Rafe?"

Rafael gave him a blank look. Alec worried he hadn't conveyed his meaning.

"Rafa," Rafael said finally.

He finished one energy bar and held his hand out for another. Alec gave it to him.

"Rafa?" Alec tried. "Do you want me to call you that? Are you getting any of this? I'm sorry I can't speak Spanish."

Rafael made a face, as if to say what he thought of being called Rafa.

"Okay," said Alec. "I won't call you that. Just Rafael, then?"

The boy gave Alec a massively unimpressed look. *Here this fool goes again*, his air suggested, *talking to me when I cannot understand him.*

Jem and Tessa joined them in the courtyard, ready for Rafael to lead them to the house he'd seen.

"I'll stay and guard Lily," said Tessa, reading Alec's mind. "Don't worry about her. I have wards up, and even if somebody came, I've got it covered."

She made a tiny gesture. Gray glowing magic, like the shine of light on river water or the sheen of pearls in shadow, twined about her fingers. Alec smiled his gratitude at Tessa. Until he was sure about what was happening with this warlock and these Shadowhunters, he didn't want anybody undefended.

"Don't you worry about me, either," Tessa told Jem, settling her magic-bright fingers into his black-and-white hair, drawing him down for a good-bye kiss.

"I won't," Jem told her. "I know my wife can take care of herself."

My wife, Jem said, his voice sounding casual and delighted in that mutual possession: the bargain made between them in the sight of everyone they loved.

Alec had heard a poem read at weddings: *My true love has my heart, and I have his. Never was a fairer bargain made.* Love that was permanent in the eyes of all the world, demanding respect, blazoning the certain knowledge Alec had when he woke every morning. Nobody else for me, until the day I die: having everyone else know that. Jem and Tessa had that, as Helen and Aline had it. But a Shadowhunter couldn't marry a Downworlder in gold. A Shadowhunter was forbidden to wear the wedding rune for a Downworlder, and he wouldn't insult Magnus with a ceremony the Nephilim saw as lesser. He and Magnus had agreed to wait until the Law was changed.

Alec couldn't help the tiny sting of jealousy.

His phone buzzed in his pocket, and Rafael perked up. Magnus had sent Alec a picture of Max sleeping, using Chairman Meow as his pillow. Rafael glared, obviously disappointed Magnus was not in the picture.

Alec was slightly disappointed about that himself.

The afternoon was hot, the streets mostly deserted. The house where the warlock lived was down several winding streets, some cobbled and some dirt. Most of the houses on the curving roads were small, painted bright yellow or brick red or snowy white, but the warlock's house that Rafael pointed out was a huge gray building on the end of a street. A figure was approaching the door—a Shadowhunter. Alec and Jem exchanged a grim look. Alec recognized him as one of Breakspear's men from the Institute. He pulled Jem and Rafael into an alleyway.

"Stay with Jem a minute," he told Rafael, and tossed a grappling hook to the roof of a neighboring house.

Alec climbed up and made his way across the sloping terracotta tile until he was across from the gray building. There were bars on the windows, and the enchantments Magnus had put on his ring allowed him to sense wards with enormous accuracy. The place was heavily warded. Alec crouched down behind a chimney and swiftly drew runes for Clarity and Awareness on his arms.

With increased ability, he could hear noises from behind those walls. There were a lot of people in that house. Shuffling feet, muffled conversation. Alec was able to pick out a few distinct words.

". . . next delivery from Breakspear will be at midnight tonight . . ."

He heard another noise, much closer up, and twisted to see Rafael and Jem coming toward him across the roof.

Jem offered a small rueful smile. "He slipped away from me and climbed a drainpipe."

Jem was hovering at Rafael's back, obviously nervous about touching him. Alec saw how Rafael had managed to slip away.

"Can you sense those wards?" Alec asked, and Jem nodded. Alec knew Tessa had taught him ways to use and discern magic, even though Jem no longer had all the power of a Silent Brother or a Shadowhunter. "Can Tessa handle them?"

"Tessa can handle anything," Jem said proudly.

"I said to stay down there with Jem," Alec told Rafael.

Rafael gave him a look that was at once uncomprehending and insulting, and then his big boots slipped on the ridged terra-cotta tiles. Jem caught him before he hit the tile, and set him upright. If Rafael kept walking like this, he was going to skin his knees.

"You have to walk differently on roofs," Alec told him. He took Rafael's hands in his, showing him how. "Like this, because they slope. Do it like me."

It was oddly nice, to teach a child these things. He'd had all sorts of plans to teach his little brother, when he got older, but his baby brother hadn't lived to be older.

"When will you give your parents a real grandchild?" he'd heard Irina Cartwright ask Isabelle after a Clave meeting.

"By the Angel," said Isabelle. "Is Max imaginary?"

Irina paused, then laughed. "A Shadowhunter child, to teach our ways. Nobody would give those people a Shadowhunter child. Imagine a warlock around one of our little ones! And that kind of behavior. Children are so impressionable. It wouldn't be right."

Isabelle went for her whip. Alec dragged his sister back.

"You Lightwood kids are out of control and out of your minds," muttered Irina.

Jace had appeared beside Alec and Isabelle, and given Irina a radiant smile. "Yes, we are."

Alec had told himself that it was all right. It was a comfort, sometimes, when he was most worried about his friends, to consider that both Magnus and Max were warlocks. They didn't have to fight demons.

Rafael mimicked how Alec was walking with careful precision. He was going to be good one day, Alec thought. Whoever got to raise him would be proud.

"Well done, Rafe," he said. He hadn't meant the nickname to come out: it just had, but Rafael glanced at him and smiled. They fell silent, crouching down as the Shadowhunter departed the warlock's house. Jem raised his eyebrows at Alec, who shook his head.

Once the man was gone, they helped Rafe down from the roof.

"I wonder how far the corruption goes in this Institute," Jem said soberly.

"We'll know soon enough," Alec said. "I heard that mercenary say 'the next delivery from Breakspear will be at midnight tonight.' If he's delivering women, we need to save them and stop the Shadowhunters as well as the warlock. We need to catch them all at once, and there are a lot of people inside. We don't know how many might be prisoners and how many are guards. We need reinforcements, and there's someone I want to talk to about that before we go back to Tessa and Lily. I have to believe not all the Shadowhunters in this city are traitors."

Jem nodded. As they left the alley, Alec described the faerie woman he and Lily had seen, her withered-apple face and dandelion hair. "Lily said she might have information about the family you're searching for."

Jem's expression darkened. "I've encountered her before. I'll know who she is when I see her at the Market. And I will make sure she talks." His face was cold and grim for a moment. Then he glanced toward Alec. "How is Lily?"

"Um." Alec tried to work out if he'd let something slip.

"You're worried for your friend," Jem said. "Perhaps you are more worried for her, because how she feels makes you think of how Magnus will feel, one day." Jem's eyes were as dark as the Silent City, and as sad. "I know."

Alec wouldn't have been able to put any of that into words himself. There was only the nameless shadow on Magnus's face sometimes, the echo of old loneliness, and Alec's yearning to protect him always and knowledge he could not.

"You were nearly immortal. Is there any way to make it—easier?"

"I lived a long time," said Jem, "but I lived in a cage of bones and silence, feeling my heart turn to ashes. I can't explain what it was like."

Alec thought of growing up in the Institute, crushed under the weight of his father's expectations as if they were stones, trying to teach himself not to look, not to speak, not to dare try and be happy.

"Maybe I know," he said. "Not—entirely. Not for a hundred years, obviously. But—maybe a little."

He worried he was presuming, but Jem smiled as if he understood.

"It's different, for my Tessa and your Magnus. They were born what they are, and we love them for it. They live forever in a changing world, and still have the courage to find it beautiful. We all want to shield our best beloved from whatever danger or sorrow comes," he said. "But we have to trust them too. We have to believe that they will have the strength to live on and laugh again. We fear for them, but we should believe in them past fear."

Alec bowed his head and said, "I do."

A block from the Buenos Aires Institute, Alec's phone

buzzed again. Clary had sent him a message.

A few months ago, they'd left Max with Maryse and gone out on the town. Simon's old band was playing at Pandemonium and Simon had agreed to sub in for their missing bass player, as he occasionally did. Alec, Magnus, Jace, Clary, and Isabelle had all gone to listen. Simon's friend Eric had written a song called "My Heart Is an Overripe Melon Bursting for You," and that song was the worst.

Alec didn't like to dance, unless it was with Magnus. Even then, he preferred the music not be terrible. Magnus, Jace, and Isabelle went to dance, the brightest points in the crowd. Alec enjoyed watching Magnus for a while, his chin propped on his hands. Then he grew tired of the assault on his ears. He caught Clary's eye. She was sitting bolt upright in her chair, only wincing occasionally.

"This is fine," Clary told him, nodding bravely.

"This is terrible," said Alec. "Let's go for tacos."

Simon was only just offstage by the time they got back, drinking from a bottle of water and asking everybody what they'd thought of the set.

"You were very sexy up there," Isabelle was saying, sparkling up at Simon, as Alec and Clary arrived.

Simon smiled a crooked smile. "Really?"

Jace said, "No."

"You were so great!" Clary exclaimed, dashing up to Simon. "Wow, I don't know what other word there could be. You were great. The band was great."

Clary was a true and noble *parabatai*, but Simon was a sharp guy and had known her a long time. His eyes traveled from Clary's guilty face to Alec's.

"You went for tacos *again?*" Simon lamented.

Alec grinned. "They were great."

He went over to Magnus, sliding an arm around his waist. Since they were going to a club, Magnus had swept silver glitter under his golden eyes, and he looked like starshine and moonlight.

"I know you were dancing," Alec said in his ear. "But that band was terrible, right?"

"I can dance to anything," Magnus murmured back, "but I have personally heard Mozart play. Also the Sex Pistols in their best days. I can confirm Simon's band is beyond terrible."

Alec's friends were gathered all around him, and his family, and it was one of those moments when he remembered the desperate loneliness of when he was younger, hopelessly torn between fearing for what he might never have and what he might lose. Alec secured his hold on Magnus's waist and felt a small incredulous starburst of happiness in his chest: that he could have all this.

"Tacos again next time?" Alec had whispered as they left, and Clary nodded behind Simon's back.

That was how Alec had come to love her, after resenting her so much at first: in the greatest or smallest of ways, Clary never failed.

She hadn't failed him now. She'd sent a picture saying WE HAVE BEEN IMPRISONED BY THE DREAD PIRATE MAX! Alec suspected this was a joke he didn't understand.

Clary was at an odd angle taking the selfie, but he could see Magnus and Max well enough. Magnus had dashed brilliant blue color through the front of his hair. Max was holding on to Magnus's spiky blue locks and Clary's red curls with one hand each and looking supremely self-satisfied. Magnus was laughing.

"Oh, look," said Alec softly, and showed Rafael the picture.

Rafael snatched the phone, then skipped away to contemplate the photo further.

Alec let him keep it for now. He and Jem stopped at the door of the Buenos Aires Institute. As Alec had hoped, Joaquín was guarding the door again. He greeted Alec happily, then gave the faint scars on Jem's face a startled glance.

"Are you the Silent Brother whom the heavenly fire changed?" he asked eagerly. "The one who—"

"Ran off and married a warlock, yes," said Jem. Somewhere in his quiet voice and his smile, there was an edge of shining defiance.

"I'm sure she's very nice," said Joaquín hastily.

"She is," Alec confirmed.

"I don't know many Downworlders," Joaquín said apologetically. "Though I met Alec's friend yesterday! She also seemed . . . nice. There are a lot of nice Downworlders, I'm sure! Just not in our city. They say the Queen of the Shadow Market is a terrifying tyrant."

Alec thought of Juliette with her kids gathered around her.

"I didn't think so."

Joaquín looked at him with wide eyes. "I bet you're not afraid of anything, though."

"Some things," said Alec. "Failing. You know there's something wrong with your Institute, don't you? I want to believe you're not part of it, but you have to know something is very wrong."

Joaquín avoided Alec's gaze, and as he did he caught sight of Rafael for the first time. Rafael was hanging back, clutching Alec's phone.

"That's little Rafael," said Joaquín.

Rafael blinked up at him and corrected, in his small stern voice: "Rafe."

"You know him?" asked Alec. "Then you knew there was a Shadowhunter child living in the Shadow Market. It's the duty of Nephilim to care for war orphans."

"I—" Joaquín faltered. "I tried. But he won't let anyone near him. It was like he didn't want to be helped."

"Everyone wants to be helped," said Alec.

Joaquín was already kneeling down, offering Rafael a brightly wrapped piece of candy. Rafe eyed him, then came cautiously forward, snatched the candy, and retreated behind Alec's legs.

Alec understood being young and scared, but there came a time where you had to choose to be brave.

"Here's an address," he said, offering a scrap of paper. "If you want to find out what's really happening at your Institute, meet me there tonight. Bring reinforcements—only the people you trust."

Joaquín didn't meet Alec's eyes, but he accepted the piece of paper. Alec walked away, with Jem and Rafael on either side of him.

"Do you think he will come?" Jem asked.

"I hope so," said Alec. "We have to trust people, right? Like you were saying. Not just people we love. We have to believe in people, and we have to defend them. As many people as possible, so we can be stronger." He swallowed. "I have a confession to make. I'm—jealous of you."

Jem's face was genuinely startled. Then he smiled.

"I'm a little jealous of you, too."

"Of me?" Alec asked, startled.

Jem nodded toward Rafael and the picture of Magnus and Max in Rafael's hands. "I have Tessa, so I have the world. And I have loved going all through the world with her. But there are times I think about—a place that could be home. My *parabatai*. A child."

All the things Alec had. Alec felt as he had last night, putting on Rafael's boots over his battered feet: stricken, but knowing this was not his pain.

He hesitated. "Couldn't you and Tessa have a child?"

"I could never ask her," said Jem. "She had children once. They were beautiful, and they are gone. Children are meant to be our immortality, but what if you live forever and your child does not? I saw how she had to rip herself away from them. I saw what it cost her. I will not ask her to suffer like that again."

Rafe held up his hands to be carried. Alec swung him up in his arms. Warlock hearts beat differently, and Alec was used to feeling the sound of Magnus's and Max's hearts, infinitely steady and reassuring. It was odd, holding a child with a mortal heartbeat, but Alec was getting used to the new rhythm.

The evening sun was scorching on whitewashed walls of the street they were heading down. Their shadows were long behind them, but the town was still bright, and Alec saw for the first time that it could be lovely.

Occasionally he despaired: that the world couldn't be changed, or even that it wouldn't change fast enough. He was not immortal, and didn't want to be, but there were times he was afraid he wouldn't live long enough, that he'd never have the chance to take Magnus's hands in front of everyone they loved and make a sacred promise.

At those times, there was an image Alec held against

exhaustion or surrender, a reminder to always keep fighting.

When he was gone, when he was dust and ashes, Magnus would still be walking through this world. If the world was changed for the better, then that unknowable future would be better for Magnus. Alec could imagine that on some scorching-hot day like this, on a strange street in a strange land, Magnus might see something good that reminded him of Alec, some way that the world was changed because Alec had lived. Alec couldn't imagine what the world would be like then.

But he could imagine, in some faraway future, the face he loved best.

Jem filled Tessa in on what they had seen and who they were searching for in the Shadow Market.

Lily caught Jem's glance at her as he explained. "What are you looking at, you delicious peanut-butter-and-Jem sandwich?"

Tessa snorted behind Jem.

"I've got more names," Lily told her, encouraged. "They just come to me. Want to hear them?"

"Not really," said Jem.

"Definitely not!" snapped Alec.

"Yes," said Tessa. "Yes, I really do."

Lily regaled her with many names on their way to the Shadow Market. Tessa's laughter was like a song to Jem, but he was glad when they reached the Shadow Market, though the place was a barbed-wire fortress and the door had been barred against them last time.

The door was not barred against them tonight.

Jem was accustomed to Shadow Markets by now, after years searching through them for answers about demons and

Herondales. He was also used to being somewhat conspicuous among the people of the Market.

Tonight, though, everyone was looking at Alec and Lily. The Queen of the Shadow Market, a rather lovely and dignified young woman, came out among the stalls to greet them personally. Alec drew her aside to tell her of their plans for the evening and to ask for her help. The Queen smiled and agreed.

"They're from the *Alliance*," he heard one teenage werewolf whisper to another, in awed tones.

Alec bowed his head and fussed over Rafe. Alec seemed slightly abashed by the attention.

Jem met Tessa's eyes and smiled. They had seen other generations pass, shining bright and hopeful, but Alec's was something new.

Alec paused to talk to a faerie girl in her teens. "Rose, have you seen a fey woman with dandelion hair at the Market tonight?"

"You must mean Mother Hawthorn," said Rose. "She's always here. She tells stories to the children. Loves children. Hates everybody else. If you're looking for her, stick around the kids. She's sure to come."

So they headed toward a campfire where most of the children were congregated. A faerie was playing the bandonion at this fire. Jem smiled to hear the music.

Rafe clung to Alec's shirt and glared jealously around. The other kids seemed intimidated by his scowl.

A teenage warlock girl was doing magic tricks, creating shadow puppets in the smoke of the fire. Tessa whispered helpful hints in the girl's ear. Even Rafe laughed, all the sullenness gone from his face. He was only a child, leaning into Alec's side, learning to be happy.

"He says she is very good," Lily translated for Alec. "He likes magic, but most of the powerful warlocks left ages ago. He wants to know if the cool man can do that."

Alec took out his phone to show Rafael a video of Magnus and a witchlight.

"Look, it turns red," Alec said, and Rafe instantly seized the phone. "No, we don't grab! We stop stealing. I have to text Magnus back sometime, and I can't if you keep stealing my phone."

Alec glanced through the leaping iridescent flames at Jem.

"I was actually wondering if you could give me some advice," he said. "I mean, you were saying all that stuff earlier. Like—romantic stuff. You always know what to say."

"Me?" Jem asked, startled. "No, I've never thought of myself as very good with words. I like music. It's easier to express what you feel with music."

"Alec is right," said Tessa.

Jem blinked. "He is?"

"At some of the worst and darkest times in my life, you have always known what to say to comfort me," said Tessa. "I had one of my darkest moments when we were young, and we had only known each other a little while. You came to me and said words that I carried with me like a light. That was one of the moments that made me fall in love with you."

She lifted her hand to his face, her fingers tracing the scars there. Jem dropped a kiss on her wrist.

"If my words comforted you, we are even," he said. "Your voice is the music I love best in all the world."

"You see," Alec muttered darkly to Lily.

"We do love an eloquent babe," said Lily.

Tessa leaned close to Jem and whispered in the language she'd learned for him: "Wǒ ài nǐ."

And at that moment, looking into her eyes, Jem caught a flash of movement and then stillness in the dark. The faerie woman with the dandelion hair had been coming toward the children, pushing her little cart full of poisons. She stopped at the sight of Jem. She recognized him, as he did her.

"Mother Hawthorn," said the warlock girl Tessa had talked to. "Have you come to tell us a story?"

"Yes," said Jem. He rose to his feet and advanced on her. "We want to hear a story. We want to hear why you hate the Herondales."

Mother Hawthorn's eyes widened. Her eyes were colorless and pupil-less, as if her eye sockets were filled with water. For a moment Jem thought she would run, and he tensed to spring after her. Tessa and Alec were ready to come for her as well. Jem had waited too long to wait another moment.

Then Mother Hawthorn looked around at the children and shrugged her thin shoulders.

"Ah well," she said. "I have waited more than a century to boast of a trick. I suppose it doesn't matter now. Let me tell you the story of the First Heir."

They found a solitary campfire, with no children to hear a dark tale save Rafael, solemn faced and silent in the protective curve of Alec's arm. Jem sat down with his friends and his best beloved to listen. Light and shadows danced a long dance together, and by the strange fireside of the Shadow Market, an old woman wove a tale of Faerie.

"The Seelie Court and the Unseelie have always been at war, but there are times in war that wear the mask of peace. There was even a time that the King of the Unseelie Court and the Queen of the Seelie Court made a secret truce and had a union to seal it. They conceived a child together and agreed that one day that child would inherit both the Seelie and Unseelie thrones, and unite all Faerie. The King wished all his sons to be raised as pitiless warriors, and he believed this First Heir would be the greatest of them all. Since the child would have no mother in the Unseelie Court, he engaged my services, and I thought myself honored. I have always been fond of children. Once they called me the great faerie midwife.

"The King of the Unseelie Court had not expected a daughter, but when the child was born, a daughter she was. She was given into my hands in the Unseelie Court on the day she came into the world, and from that day to this day, the light of her eyes was the only light I wished for.

"The Unseelie King was displeased with his daughter, and the Seelie Queen was enraged that he would not, being displeased, give her back. There came a prophecy from our soothsayers that the day the First Heir reached for their full power, all of Faerie would fall under shadow. The King was murderously angry, and the Queen was terrified, and all the shades and shadows and rushing waters in my land seemed to threaten the girl that I loved. The war between Seelie and Unseelie raged all the more fiercely for the brief peace, and the faerie folk whispered that the First Heir was cursed. And so she fled, fearing for her life.

"I did not call her the First Heir. Her name was Auraline, and she was the loveliest thing that ever walked.

"She took refuge in the mortal world, and she found it

beautiful. She was always searching for the beauty in life, and it always made her sad to find ugliness instead. She liked to go to the Shadow Market and mingle with the Downworlders and mundanes who did not know of her birth and would not call her cursed.

"After visiting the Shadow Market for many decades, she met a magician there who made her laugh.

"He called himself Roland the Astonishing, Roland the Extraordinary, Roland the Incredible, as if he were something special, when she was the unique one. I hated that insolent boy from the moment I laid eyes on him.

"When he was not calling himself one of his foolish magician's names, he called himself Roland Loss, but that was another lie."

"No," Tessa said very softly. "It wasn't."

Nobody heard her but Jem.

"There was a warlock woman he said he loved as a mother, but Roland was no warlock, nor a mundane with the Sight. He was something far more deadly than that. I learned this warlock's secret. She took a Shadowhunter child across the seas to America and raised him, pretending he was not Nephilim. Roland was descended from that child: Roland was drawn to our world because his blood called him to it. That boy's true name was Roland Herondale.

"Roland suspected enough of his heritage, and he paid to learn more at the Market. He told Auraline all his secrets. He said he couldn't go to the Nephilim and be one of them, lest it endanger the warlock woman he loved like a second mother. He said instead he would become the greatest magician in the world.

"Auraline lost all caution. She told him of the prophecy and the danger attached to it.

"Roland said they were both lost children, and they could be lost together. He said he didn't mind being lost, if he could be lost with her. She swore the same. He lured her away from my side. He told her to come live with him in the mortal world. He doomed her and called it love.

"They ran away together, and the King's fury was a fire that would have consumed a forest. He wanted the prophecy kept secret, which meant he needed Auraline back under his thumb or killed. He sent his trusted messengers to every corner of the world hunting her, even the bloodthirsty Riders of Mannan. He had all the worst eyes of Faerie looking for her. I kept watch for her myself, and love made my eyes the sharpest. I found her a dozen times, though I never told the King where she was. I will never forgive him for turning against her. I followed them and watched them together, my shining First Heir and that awful boy. Oh, how she loved him, and oh, how I hated him.

"I was at a Shadow Market not long after Roland and Auraline went away together, and there I saw another angel boy, proud as God. He told me of his high position among the Nephilim, and I knew that his *parabatai* was another Herondale. I played a cruel trick on him. I hope he paid for his arrogance in blood."

"Matthew," whispered Tessa, the name sounding unfamiliar in her mouth, spoken for the first time in years.

Matthew Fairchild had been *parabatai* to Tessa's son, James Herondale. Jem had known that this faerie had tricked Matthew to do a terrible deed, but he had thought it was only spite, not revenge.

Even this faerie woman's voice sounded tired. Jem remembered feeling that way, near the end of his days as a Silent Brother. He remembered being that hollow.

"But what does that matter now?" asked the woman, as if speaking to herself. "What did it matter then? Long years passed. Auraline spent decade after decade with her magician in the filth of the mundane world, my girl born to a golden throne. They were together all the days of his life. Auraline shared what she could of her faerie power with Roland, and he stayed young longer, and lived longer, than most of their filthy kind could. She wasted her magic, like someone prolonging the life of a flower: they can only make the flower last for a little more time, before it withers. At last Roland grew old, and older, in the way of mortals, until he reached an end, and Auraline met the end with him. A faerie can choose the season of their own death. I knew how it would be, when I first beheld them together. I saw her death in his laughing eyes.

"My Auraline. When Roland Herondale died, she laid down her golden head on the pillow next to her mortal love and never rose again. Their child wept for them both and threw flowers on their grave. Auraline could have lived for century after century, but she was hunted to the point of desperation, and she threw her life away for a foolish mortal love.

"Their child wept, but I never wept. My eyes stayed dry as the dust and dead flowers on their grave. I hated Roland from the day he took her from me. I hate all Nephilim for *her* sake, and the Herondales most of their kind. Whatever the Shadowhunters touch is brought to destruction. Auraline's child had a child. There is still a First Heir in the world. When the First Heir rises, in all the awful glory bought by the blood of Seelie and Unseelie and Nephilim, I hope destruction comes to the Shadowhunters as well as Faerie. I hope the whole world is lost."

Jem thought of Roland and Auraline's descendant Rosemary and the man she'd loved. They might have a child by now. The curse the faeries had talked about had already claimed lives. This danger was far greater than he had ever suspected. Jem had to protect Rosemary from the Unseelie King and the Riders who brought death. If there was a child, Jem had to save that child. Jem had already failed to save so many.

Jem rose and left Mother Hawthorn. He went to the barbed-wire edge of the Market, moving desperately fast, as if he could race back into the past and save those he had lost there.

When he stopped, Tessa caught him. She held him in her arms, and when he stopped trembling, she drew his head down to hers.

"Jem, my Jem. It's all right. I thought it was a very beautiful story," she said.

"*What?*"

"Not her story," said Tessa. "Not the story of her warped sight and terrible choices. I can see the story behind hers. The story of Auraline and Roland."

"But all the people who were hurt," Jem murmured. "The children we loved."

"My James knew the power of a love story, as well as I do," said Tessa. "No matter how dark and hopeless the world seemed, Lucie could always find beauty in a story. I know what they would have thought."

"I'm sorry," said Jem instantly.

He hadn't meant to make Tessa speak of her children. He knew how much losing them had hurt her. Every time he dreamed of a child, he remembered the pain she had endured, and knew he could never ask her to lose more. She was enough for him: she always would be.

"Auraline grew up in horror. She felt cursed. And he was lost and wandering. They seemed destined for misery. Only they found each other, Jem. They were together and happy, all the days of their lives. Her story is just like mine, because I found you."

Tessa's smile lit the night. She always brought hope when he was in despair, as she had brought words when everything within him was silence. Jem put his arms around her and held on tightly.

"I hope you learned what you needed to learn tonight," Alec told Jem and Tessa when they reached their rooms.

Jem had looked upset when he bolted from the fireside, but he and Tessa had seemed different when they returned.

"I hope they're all right," Alec said quietly to Lily when Jem and Tessa went off to prepare for their midnight visit to the warlock's house.

"Of course Tessa's fine," said Lily. "You do realize she gets to go to the Jem-nasium anytime she wants?"

"I'm never talking to you again if those names don't stop," Alec told her, gathering his arrows and tucking daggers and seraph blades into his weapons belt. He found himself thinking of the heartbroken way Jem said *parabatai*. It made him remember the shadow that hung over his father, the wound where a *parabatai* should be. It made him think of Jace. Ever since he could remember, Alec had loved and felt responsible for his family. There had never been any choice, but with Jace it was different. Jace, his *parabatai*, the first person who'd ever chosen him. The first time Alec had decided to choose someone back, to take on another responsibility. The first choice, opening the door to all the others.

Alec took a deep breath and tapped out MISS U into his phone.

He immediately received back MISS U TOO and let himself take a breath, the ache in his chest easier now. Jace was there, waiting for him in New York with the rest of his family. Talking about feelings wasn't so bad.

Then he received another text.

R U OK?

In rapid succession, Alec received several more texts.

R U IN SOME KIND OF TROUBLE?

DID U GET HIT IN UR HEAD!

Then he got a text from Clary.

WHY DID JACE GET A TEXT FROM YOU AND LOOK VERY PLEASED BUT THEN SUDDENLY VERY WORRIED? IS SOMETHING GOING ON?

Talking about feelings was the worst. Once you did it, everybody immediately wanted you to do it more.

Alec typed out a grouchy I'M FINE and then called out cautiously, "Rafe?"

Rafael popped immediately up from his bed.

"Would you like the phone back?" asked Alec. "Here it is. Take it. Don't worry if any more texts arrive. Just show me if there are any more pictures."

He didn't know how much Rafael understood of what he said. He suspected not much, but Rafe certainly understood the gesture of Alec offering his phone. He held out his hands eagerly.

"You're a good kid, Rafe," said Alec. "Take that phone away."

* ✳ *

"Are we going to smuggle our way into the house in laundry carts?" Lily asked Alec excitedly.

Alec blinked at her. "No, we're not. What laundry carts? I'm a straightforward person. I'm going to knock on the door."

He stood with Lily on the cobbled street before that great gray house. Jem and Tessa were waiting on the roof. Alec had literally used rope to tie Rafe to Jem's wrist.

"I know Rafe stole your phone," said Lily, "but who stole your sense of adventure?"

Alec waited, and the door opened. A warlock blinked up at him. He looked as if he was in his early thirties, a businessman with close-cropped blond hair and no visible warlock mark until he opened his mouth and Alec saw his forked tongue.

"Oh, hello," he said. "Are you another of Clive Breakspear's men?"

Alec said, "I'm Alec Lightwood."

The warlock's face cleared. "I see! I've heard of you." He winked. "Fond of warlocks, aren't you?"

"Some of them," said Alec.

"Want your cut, I expect?"

"That's right."

"No problem," the warlock told him. "You and your vampire friend should come in, and I'll explain what I'll want in return. I think the vampire will be very amused. They don't like werewolves, do they?"

"I don't like most people," Lily said helpfully. "But I do love murder!"

The warlock waved his hand to let them through the wards, and led them through a hexagonal hall with a ceiling carved in a shape like a plaster jelly mold. The green quartz of the floor shone like jade. There were no signs of ruin or decay here. The warlock obviously had money.

There were several doors, all painted white, set in the many walls. The warlock chose one and led Alec and Lily down rough-hewn stone steps into the dark. The smell hit Alec before the sight did.

There was a long stone passage, with flaming torches on the walls and with grooves on either side for filth and blood. Along the passageway were rows of cages. Eyes shone from behind the bars, catching the firelight in the same way Juliette's eyes had shone from her throne in the Shadow Market. Some cages were empty. In others were huddled shapes that were not moving.

"So you've been taking werewolf women, and hiring the Shadowhunters to help you," said Alec.

The warlock nodded with a cheery smile.

"Why werewolves?" Alec asked grimly.

"Well, warlocks and vampires can't bear children, and faeries find it difficult," said the warlock in a practical tone. "But the werewolves whelp more easily, and there's a great deal of animal strength. Everybody says that Downworlders can't bear warlock children, that their bodies always reject them, but I thought of putting a little magic in the mix. People whisper about a warlock born from a Shadowhunter woman, and that's probably a myth, but it got me thinking. Imagine the power a warlock might have, with a werewolf mother and a demon father." He shrugged. "Seems worth trying. Of course, you do use up the werewolf women at a terrible rate."

"How many have died?" Lily asked casually. Her expression was unreadable.

"Oh, a few," the warlock admitted genially. "I'm always in need of a fresh supply, so I'm happy to pay you to snatch more. But these experiments haven't been going as well as I'd like. Nothing has worked yet. You're, uh, close to Magnus Bane, aren't you? I'm probably the most powerful warlock you'll ever meet, but I hear he's pretty good too. If you can get him to come on in an assisting capacity, you'll be very well rewarded. So will he. I think you'll both be very happy."

Alec said, "Yeah, I hope so."

It wasn't the first time someone had assumed Magnus was for sale. It wasn't the first time someone had assumed that because Alec was connected to Magnus, Alec was sullied.

That used to make Alec angry. It still did, but he'd learned to use it.

The warlock turned his back to Alec, surveying the cages as if selecting a product from a market stall. "So, what do you say?" he asked idly. "Do we have a deal?"

"I don't know yet," said Alec. "You don't know my price."

The warlock laughed. "What is it?"

Alec scythed the warlock's feet out from under him, so he fell to his knees. He drew his seraph blade and held it to the man's throat.

"All the women go free," he said. "And you are under arrest."

Alec realized why the warlock was burning torches, and not using witchlight or electricity, when a torch tumbled out of the wall and onto the straw. Lily, who was kneeling to speak to someone behind the bars, rolled hastily away from the flames. She came up to her feet with fangs out. Alec had to leap to stamp out the fire.

The warlock was good, Alec thought, as the world went orange with not just fire but magic, crisscrossing from the bars, blinding Alec with its light.

Then another light sliced through the orange wires of magic, pearly gray, cutting through all darkness. Tessa Gray, daughter of a Prince of Hell, stood at the foot of the stairs with her hands glowing.

Tessa's magic was all around him. Alec had learned how to sense magic over the years, learned to move with it and fight with it as another weapon on his side. This wasn't the singing power he was used to, well-known and well-beloved as his bow, but it felt friendly. He let Tessa's magic wrap around him, cooling and protecting, as he ducked through the fiery sparks of power back to the warlock.

"The most powerful warlock I've ever seen?" Alec snarled. "She cut through your wards like tissue paper. And my man would eat you for *breakfast*."

He made a mistake, because he was overconfident. He didn't hear Tessa's stifled sound, and he didn't see the shadow moving as he swept his blade toward the warlock.

Clive Breakspear's seraph blade met his. Alec met Breakspear's furious eyes. He looked to Tessa, struggling with three Shadowhunters with Jem coming to help her, Lily with another Shadowhunter prowling toward her, and he glanced toward the warlock, who was making every torch fall. Alec was used to being able to see the whole battle, fighting at a distance.

Too late, he saw the blade in Clive Breakspear's free hand, aimed for his heart.

Rafael barreled out of the shadows and sank his teeth deep into Breakspear's wrist. The blade dropped to the stone.

The man roared, and with all the Nephilim strength that should be used to shield the defenseless, he hurled Rafael's body into the cage bars. There was a sickening crack.

Alec shouted: *"No!"*

He backhanded Clive Breakspear in the face. The warlock dashed a torch at his feet, and Alec stepped over the flames and seized him by the throat, then lifted him like a doll and smashed the warlock's skull against Breakspear's forehead. The warlock's eyes rolled back, but Breakspear screamed in outrage and charged at Alec. There was still a seraph blade shining in his hand, so Alec broke that hand, then used his hold on it to force the corrupt Shadowhunter to his knees. Alec stood over them, panting so hard his chest felt as if it would split apart. He wanted to kill them both.

Only Rafael was here. Magnus and Max were at home, waiting for him. Tessa, Jem, and Lily had made short work of the Shadowhunters attacking them. Alec turned to Tessa now.

"Will you enchant ropes to hold them?" he asked. "They have to stand trial."

Tessa moved forward. So did Lily. Alec knew the situation was desperate because Lily didn't make a joke about murdering them. Alec was too close to the edge. He was afraid he would have taken her up on it.

He went to the place where Rafael lay, his body a small wretched shape thrown into the dirt. Alec pulled Rafe into his arms, feeling his throat close up. He understood now what he had found here in Buenos Aires. He understood now that it might be too late.

Rafael's grubby face was still. He was barely breathing. Jem came to kneel beside them.

"I'm so sorry. He slipped the rope, and I came in for him, but—but—"

"It isn't your fault," Alec said numbly.

Jem said, "Give him to me."

Alec stared at Jem, then bundled Rafe into his arms.

"Take care of him," he said. "Please."

Jem took Rafe and ran toward Tessa, and together they rushed up the stone steps. There was still orange magic in the air, and the flames had caught in earnest. Smoke was rising fast, in a thick choking cloud.

One of the werewolf women reached out a thin hand and clutched the bars.

"Help us!"

Alec took an axe with an electrum head from his belt and struck open the lock on her cage. "That's what I'm here to do." He paused. "Um, Lily, are there keys on that warlock?"

"Yep," said Lily. "Just grabbed them. I'll open the doors with the keys, and you can keep doing your cool dramatic axe thing."

"Fine," said Alec.

The werewolf woman who had spoken to him bolted out the door as soon as she was free. The woman in the next cage was unconscious. Alec walked into the cage and knelt beside her, and that was when he heard the sounds of a fight breaking out at the top of the stairs.

He picked the woman up and ran for the stairs.

Tessa and Jem were in the hall, almost at the doors. The burning house was crawling with Shadowhunters. Jem couldn't fight, because he was holding Rafael. Tessa was doing her best to clear a way for them, but Rafael needed Tessa's help too.

One man shouted, "Where's our leader?"

"You call *that* a leader?" Alec shouted back. He looked at the woman in his arms, then held her out so the Shadowhunters of the Buenos Aires Institute could see. "He helped a warlock do this. He crushed a child's body against a wall. Is that what you want to lead you? Is that what you want to *be?*"

Several Shadowhunters turned to him in total puzzlement. Lily quickly shouted out a translation.

Joaquín stepped forward.

Lily said quietly, "He told them to stand down."

The man who'd shouted for his leader hit Joaquín across the mouth. Another Shadowhunter shouted in startled fury and produced a whip, defending Joaquín.

Alec ran his eyes over the crowd. Some of the Shadowhunters looked uncertain, but Shadowhunters were soldiers. Too many of them were intent on following whatever orders they had been given, fighting Joaquín and Alec and whoever else stood in their way, to get to an unworthy leader. They were blocking Jem and Tessa's way. They were keeping Rafe from help.

The doors of the burning house burst open. The Queen of the Shadow Market stood outlined against the smoke.

"Get to Alec!" Juliette shouted, and a dozen Downworlders sprang.

Juliette cleared a path. Jem and Tessa slipped out the door. Rafe was out of this place of filth and smoke. Alec fought toward Juliette.

"*Mon Dieu,*" she breathed when she saw the woman in Alec's arms.

She made a gesture, and a warlock jumped to take the unconscious werewolf out into the night.

"There are more women down there," Alec said. "I'll get them. Some of the Shadowhunters are on our side."

Juliette nodded. "Which ones?"

Alec turned to see Joaquín, fighting two Shadowhunters at once. The man with the whip who'd come to help him was down.

"That one," said Alec. "And whoever else he tells you."

Juliette set her jaw and began to transform to her wolf shape, striding across the green-quartz floor to Joaquín's side. She tapped one of the men fighting him on the shoulder. When he turned, she ripped out his throat with one clawed hand.

"Maybe take them alive!" said Alec. "Not that guy, obviously."

Joaquín was staring at Juliette with eyes gone enormous. Alec remembered that Joaquín had heard tales of horror about the Queen of the Shadow Market. Juliette, with blood on her hands and firelight in her snarled hair, might not be doing a lot to dispel that image.

"Don't hurt her!" Alec cried. "She's with us."

"Oh good," said Joaquín.

Juliette squinted at him suspiciously through the smoke. "You're not evil?"

"Trying not to be," said Joaquín.

"*Bien*," said Juliette. "Show me who to kill. I mean . . . take alive if possible."

Alec left them to it. He spun around and raced back down the stairs, Lily at his heels. The smoke was thick in the passage below by now. Alec saw there were Shadowhunters there already, getting Clive Breakspear and his warlock confederate out. Alec's lip curled. "If your loyalty is to the Clave, put a watch on them. They're going to stand trial."

He and Lily opened the remaining doors. The women who

could move on their own did. Too many could not. Alec picked up one woman after another and carried them out. Lily helped women who needed support to walk. Alec gave the women to the Downworlders of the Shadow Market whenever he could, so he was able to get back to the basement faster. He reached the top of the stairs with another woman and saw the hall was deserted, taken over by smoke and falling masonry. Everyone had fled the death trap this building had become.

Alec bundled the woman into Lily's arms. Lily was small enough that it was difficult, but she was strong enough to bear her weight.

"Take her. I have to get the others."

"I don't want to go!" Lily shouted over the crackling fire. "I don't ever want to abandon anybody again!"

"You won't. Lily, go."

Lily stumbled for the door under her heavy burden, sobbing. Alec turned back. The smoke had turned the whole world into a gray hell. He couldn't see or breathe.

A hand caught his shoulder. Joaquín stood behind him.

"You can't go down there!" he panted. "I'm so sorry about those women, but they're—"

Alec said icily, "Downworlders?"

"It's too dangerous. And you—you have a lot to go back to."

Magnus and Max. If Alec closed his eyes, he could see them with absolute clarity. But he knew he had to be worthy of going back to them.

Joaquín was still holding on to him. Alec shrugged him off, and not gently.

"I will not leave one woman down there, abused and forgotten," he said. "Not *one*. No real Shadowhunter would."

He looked over his shoulder at Joaquín as he was going down the steps into hell.

"You can leave," said Alec. "If you do, you can still call yourself a Shadowhunter. But will you be one?"

Rafael lay on the cobbled street as Jem and Tessa hovered over him. Jem used every silent enchantment he had learned among the Silent Brothers. Tessa whispered every healing spell she had learned in the Spiral Labyrinth. Jem could tell, from long, bitter experience, that there was too much broken and bruised within that small body.

There was a fire burning and a battle raging. Jem could not pay attention to any of it, could not bring himself to care about anything but the child under his hands.

"Dittany, Jem," Tessa whispered desperately. "I need dittany."

Jem climbed to his feet, searching the crowd. There were so many from the Shadow Market here, there was surely one who could help. His gaze fell on Mother Hawthorn, with starlight on her dandelion hair.

She met his eyes and made to run. Jem was fast as a Shadowhunter still, when he had to be. He was at her side in a moment, catching her wrist.

"Do you have dittany?"

"If I do," snarled Mother Hawthorn, "why should I give it to you?"

"I know what you did, more than a century ago," he said. "I know better than you do. The trick you played, causing one Shadowhunter to poison another? It poisoned an unborn child. Does that amuse you?"

The faerie's mouth went slack.

"That child died, because of you," said Jem. "Now there is another child who needs help. I could take the herb from you. I will if I have to. But I'm giving you the chance to make another choice."

"It's too late!" said Mother Hawthorn, and Jem knew she was thinking of Auraline.

"Yes," said Jem, merciless. "It's too late to save the ones we lost. But this child is not lost yet. This choice is not lost yet. Choose."

Mother Hawthorn turned her face away, her mouth set in bitter lines. But she reached inside the worn pouch at her belt and put the herb into his hand.

Jem took it and raced back to Tessa. Rafael's body was arching under her hands. The dittany flared to life at her touch, and Jem joined his hands with Tessa's, joined his voice with hers as they spoke in all the languages they had ever taught each other. Their words were a song, their linked hands magic, and they poured everything they knew, together, into the child.

Rafael's eyes opened. There was a flash of Tessa's pearlescent magic in his dark irises, then it was lost. The child sat up, looking perfectly all right, well and whole and somewhat annoyed. He gazed into their distraught faces and asked, in clipped Spanish, "Where is he?"

"He's in there," Lily answered.

The narrow cobbled street was full of members of the Shadow Market seeing to the werewolf victims or herding Shadowhunters, with some different, deeply nervous-looking Shadowhunters tentatively assisting or trying to put out the flames. Lily was not doing any of that. She stared at the house with her arms crossed and her eyes dark with tears.

As they watched, part of the roof collapsed. Rafe started

forward. Tessa lunged and seized him, holding him as he strained against her grip. Jem stood.

"No, Jem," said Tessa. "Take the child. Let me go in."

Jem tried to take Rafe, but he was fighting them both. Then Rafe went still. Jem twisted around to see what the child was looking at.

What everybody was looking at. There was a ripple in the crowd, then a hush. Jem did not think any of the Shadow Market or the Institute would forget what had happened here tonight.

From the swirling smoke, out of the collapsing building, came two Shadowhunters with werewolves in their arms. They walked tall, their faces grim, and people parted to let them pass.

The women had been saved, and the child. Jem felt new resolution rise in him. Tessa was right. If Rosemary could be saved, he would save her. If there was a child, he and Tessa would stand between that child and the Riders and the King.

Alec carried the werewolf he bore to Tessa, who immediately began enchanting the smoke from her lungs. Then he dropped to his knees in front of Rafe.

"Hey, my baby," said Alec. "Are you all right?"

Rafael might not have entirely understood the language, but anyone could have understood the message of Alec on his knees in the rubble, the love and concern on his face. Rafael nodded, dust drifting from his curly hair, and walked into Alec's open arms. Alec folded the little boy against his chest.

"Thank you both," Alec said to Tessa and Jem. "You're heroes."

"You're welcome," said Jem.

"You're a moron," said Lily, and put her face in her hands.

Alec rose and patted her awkwardly on the back, Rafe

held in the circle of his other arm. He turned to Juliette, who had called one of her warlocks over to see to the werewolf in Joaquín's arms.

"You got them all out." Juliette smiled at them both, her expression wondering, as if she were as young as Rafe and seeing magic for the first time. "You did it."

"The werewolf woman who was looking after Rafe," said Alec. "Is she . . . here?"

Juliette looked at the ashes drifting on the cobbled streets. The fire was dying, now that Tessa could spare magic to cool the flames, but the house was a ruin.

"No," said Juliette. "My girls tell me she was one of the first to die."

"I'm sorry," Alec told her, then his voice changed as he addressed Rafe. "Rafe, I have to ask you something," he said. "*Solomillo*—"

"Steak?" Lily smirked.

"Dammit," said Alec. "Sorry, Rafe. But will you come back with me to New York? You can—I have to talk to—if you don't like it there, you don't have to—"

Rafe watched him stumble over his words.

"I can't understand you, fool," he said sweetly in Spanish, and tucked his head down under Alec's chin, his arms going around Alec's neck.

"Okay," said Alec. "Good. I think."

Tessa walked away from the burned-out building. There were several warlocks in the crowd watching her with awe, Jem noted proudly. She strode over to the bound warlock and the head of the Buenos Aires Institute.

"Shall we ask Magnus to open a Portal for them?" she asked.

"Not just yet," said Alec.

There was a change in his demeanor, his shoulders going back, his face stern. If it weren't for the child in his arms, he might have been fearsome.

Alec Lightwood, leader of the Alliance, said, "First, I want a word."

Alec looked around at the assembled faces. His breathing felt as if it were tearing his throat and his eyes were still stinging, but he was holding Rafe, so everything was perfectly all right.

Except for the fact that he had no idea what to say. He couldn't know how many of the Shadowhunters had cooperated with the capture and torture of these women. He suspected most of them had gone along with their leader's orders, but he didn't know how responsible that made them. If he arrested everybody, then the Institute would be left an empty ruin. The people here were owed protection.

"Clive Breakspear, the head of the Buenos Aires Institute, broke the Accords and will pay for it," he said at last, and paused. "Lily, can you translate for me?"

"Absolutely, yes," Lily said promptly, and began to do so.

Alec listened to her talk, watched the faces of the people listening, and saw a few smirks. Alec listened more intently and picked up a word.

"*Boludo*," Alec said to Jem. "What does that mean?"

Jem coughed. "It's not . . . a polite word."

"I knew it," Alec said. "Lily, stop translating! Sorry, Jem, could you translate instead?"

Jem nodded. "I'll do my best."

"The head of your Institute has brought shame on us all,"

Alec told the Shadowhunters. "I could bring everybody here to Alicante. I could have every one of you put to the trial of the Sword. I know you were left after the war, to rebuild as best you could, and instead of leading you, this man brought more ruin. But the Law says that I should make each of you pay."

Alec thought of Helen and Mark Blackthorn, cut off from their family by the Cold Peace. He thought of the way Magnus had sunk his face into his hands, despairing, when the Cold Peace was passed. Alec never wanted to see that despair again. Every day since that day, he'd tried to work out ways that they could all live united.

"What happened in that house should sicken any Shadowhunter," said Alec. "We have to earn back the trust of everyone we have wronged. Joaquín, you will know the names of every man who was in Breakspear's inner circle. They will go with their leader to stand trial. For the rest, it is time for a new leader and a new chance to live as Nephilim should."

He glanced at Joaquín, who was wiping tears from his eyes. Alec frowned at him and mouthed, "What?"

"Oh, it's j-just the way Jem is translating," Joaquín explained. "I mean, your speech is good too, very stern, it makes me want to do everything you say. And Jem is basically repeating it, but it's the way he puts things, you know? It's beautiful."

"Uh-huh," Alec said.

Joaquín grabbed his free hand. "You be the new head of the Institute."

"No, I will not," Alec snapped.

People were always trying to make him head of Institutes, and it made Alec tired. He couldn't change enough, if he took that kind of position. He had more important things to do.

"No," repeated Alec, less grouchily but no less firmly. "I'm not Clive Breakspear. I'm here to help you, not to take over. When you saw what was happening, you told your men to stand down. You should act as the head of your own Institute until the Consul can consider your case."

Joaquín stood amazed. Alec nodded at him.

"You can work with the Shadow Market to rebuild," he said. "I can provide you with resources."

"So can I," said Juliette.

Joaquín stared at her, then swung his head back to Alec.

"The Queen of the Shadow Market," said Alec. "Do you think you will be able to cooperate with her?"

Juliette gave Joaquín a hostile look. There was still a suggestion of wolfish teeth in her mouth. Joaquín reached out, as if to point to the blood on Juliette's hands, and Alec wondered for a nasty moment if the hatred between the Nephilim and the Downworlders in this place ran too deep.

Joaquín lifted Juliette's hand to his lips and kissed it.

"I did not know," he breathed, "that the Queen of the Shadow Market was so beautiful."

Alec realized abruptly that he'd gotten everything wrong. Juliette mouthed several shocked demands for explanation, and several more French expletives, at Alec over Joaquín's bowed head.

"Shadowhunters go *so hard*." Lily cackled.

"Okay, fine, glad we're entering into the spirit of cooperation," said Alec, and turned back to the crowd. "This Nephilim child is now under the protection of the New York Institute," he said. "Let's say this was a very standard and normal adoption.

Let's say that though the head of your Institute was corrupt, you survived under a bad leader and kept your honor. You hold Breakspear here until he can be tried. I will, of course, be returning here often to finalize details of the adoption, and I'll see what is happening. I want to believe in my fellow Shadowhunters. Don't let me down."

He had no doubt Jem would make that sound better in Spanish. He turned back to Juliette, who had succeeded with difficulty in freeing her hand and was retreating several steps under Joaquín's rapt gaze.

"I should be getting back to my kids!" she said, gesturing to the three kids. Rosey gave Alec a little wave.

"Oh," said Joaquín, a world of devastation in the syllable, then he seemed to notice the lack of anyone else with the kids. "Has it been very difficult, ruling the Shadow Market as a single mother?" he asked with sudden transparent hope.

"Well, none of this has exactly been easy!" said Juliette.

Joaquín beamed at her. "That's wonderful."

"What?" said Juliette.

Joaquín was already heading toward the kids, on an obvious mission to endear himself to them. Alec hoped he had a lot of candies.

Juliette demanded, "Did he inhale a lot of smoke in there?"

"Probably," said Alec.

"Shadowhunters get very set on things," said Lily. "Very set. Do you enjoy intensely serious romantic commitment?"

"I don't know his name," Juliette pointed out. She sneaked a self-conscious look over at Joaquín, whose endearing of himself seemed to be going very well. He had Juliette's warlock boy up on his shoulders.

"His name's Joaquín," Alec said helpfully.

Juliette smiled. "I suppose I do like some Shadowhunters. It's always a pleasure, Alec Lightwood. Thanks for everything."

"It was nothing," said Alec.

Juliette strolled over to her kids, calling out to them to stop bothering the head of the Institute.

Alec looked around at the smoke drifting up to the stars and the people in the streets all talking to each other without barriers. His eyes fell on Tessa and Jem.

"Is it time to go home?" Tessa asked.

Alec bit his lip, then nodded. "I'll text Magnus and ask him to open a Portal."

There was an official protocol for adopting Shadowhunter children. He knew that he and Rafael would have to go back and forth from Buenos Aires several times, but this trip home would be worth it, even if it did not last long. Alec wanted to take Rafael home as soon as he could.

He was tired, and he wanted to sleep in his own bed.

"I don't suppose you have any ideas for how I can explain all this to Magnus?" he asked Jem.

"I think you'll find all the words you need, Alec," said Jem.

"Thanks, that's very helpful."

Jem smiled. "You even found a way to make the boy who doesn't like anybody like you. Thanks for all your help, Alec."

Alec wished he could help more, but he knew that at least for now he had done his part. They all had to trust each other, and he did trust his friends. If there was a Herondale in danger, they could not ask for better protection than Jem and Tessa.

"I didn't do much, but it was good to see you both. Good luck with the Herondale."

Jem nodded. "Thank you. I think we might need it."

The Portal was open, and shimmering.

"Bye, Jem," said Lily.

"Oh, no nickname?" Jem sounded pleased. "Bye, Lily."

Alec studied Rafe's face. "Do you like me?" he asked.

Rafe beamed and shook his head, then secured his arms more tightly around Alec's neck.

"Oh, fine, *that* you understand," Alec grumbled. "Come on. Let's go home."

They stepped out of the Portal into the electric starriness of a New York night. Alec could see his apartment down the street, the shimmer of a witchlight behind pale blue curtains. He checked his watch: it was past Max's bedtime. Max fought bedtime like it was a demon, so Magnus was probably reading him a fifth story or singing him a third song.

Every brown-and-white facade, every tree surrounded by wire on the cracked sidewalk, was dear to him. Alec used to think, when he was younger and felt as if he might die amid the crushing expectations and stone walls of the Institute, that he might feel better if he could live among the glass towers of Alicante. He hadn't known home was across the city, waiting for him.

He set Rafe on the steps of their building and hopped him up one step, then swung him up another, for sheer joy. He opened the door to home.

"Alec," boomed a voice behind him.

Alec jumped. Lily swiftly thrust Rafael behind the protection of Alec's front door and spun, lip curling from her needle-sharp teeth.

Alec turned as well, very slowly. He wasn't scared. He knew that voice.

"Alec," said Robert Lightwood. "We need to talk."

"Okay, Dad," said Alec. "Lily, I need to explain everything to Magnus, so could you watch Rafe for a second?"

Lily nodded, still giving Robert the evil eye. There was a pause.

"Hello, Lily," Robert added gruffly.

"Who the hell are you?" asked Lily.

"My dad," said Alec. "The Inquisitor. The second most important person in the Clave. Someone you have met at least twenty-six times."

"I don't recall," said Lily.

Alec's incredulous look was mirrored on his father's face.

"Lily," said Robert. "I know you know me."

"Never gonna, don't wanna." Lily shut the door of Alec's apartment building in his father's face.

There was an awkward silence.

"Sorry about that," said Alec finally, jogging down the steps to join his father on the sidewalk.

"All your other vampires like me," muttered Robert.

Alec blinked. "My other vampires?"

"Your friend Elliott reaches out whenever Lily leaves him in charge," explained Robert. "He says he feels in need of Lightwood guidance. I visited the Hotel Dumort while you were away, and the vampires had a little dinner just for me, and they all talked to me about you. Elliott gave me his phone number, I presume so I can call him in case of emergencies. Elliott's always charming to me."

Alec didn't know how to break it to his dad that Elliott was shamelessly hitting on him.

"Huh," said Alec.

"How is Magnus? Doing well? Dressing, uh, uniquely?"

"Still gorgeous," said Alec defiantly. "Yeah."

His father looked abashed. Alec wasn't comfortable talking about how he felt, but he wasn't ashamed, and nobody was going to make him be ashamed ever again. He didn't know why his father never stopped poking at him, with the obsessive curiosity of a child poking at a scab.

When he was younger, his dad used to joke insistently about Alec and girls. It was too painful to respond to those comments. Alec talked less and less.

He remembered the day he'd walked out of the Institute to find Magnus. He'd met Magnus twice and couldn't forget him. The Institute lay behind him, its stark outlines cutting the sky. He'd been breathless and terrified, with one thought very clear in his mind.

Is this how you want to live your whole life?

Then he'd gone to Magnus's place and asked him out.

Alec couldn't bear the idea of one of his kids ever feeling trapped in their own home. He knew his dad hadn't meant to do that. But he had.

"How's my little M&M?" asked Robert.

Max's middle name was Michael, after Robert's long-dead *parabatai*.

Usually that was Alec's cue to take out his phone and show his dad all the new pictures of Max he possessed, but he was in a hurry today.

"He's the best," Alec said. "Is there something you need, Dad?"

"I heard some rumors about the Buenos Aires Institute," said Robert. "I heard you were there."

"Right," said Alec. "Clive Breakspear, the head of the Institute, had his Shadowhunters acting as mercenaries. They'll need to stand trial. But I encouraged a change in leadership. The Buenos Aires Institute is going to be all right."

"This is why I needed to talk to you, Alec," said Robert.

Alec studied the cracks in the sidewalk and tried to think of a way to explain everything that would implicate nobody else.

"Do you know, the positions of Consul and Inquisitor often stay within the same families? I've been thinking about what happens when the time comes for me to retire."

Alec stared at a weed growing through the cracks in the sidewalk. "I don't think Jace wants to be Inquisitor, Dad."

"Alec," said Robert. "I'm not talking to Jace. I'm talking to you."

Alec jolted. *"What?"*

He looked up from the sidewalk. His father was smiling at him as if he meant it.

Alec remembered his own words. *The Inquisitor. The second most important person in the Clave.*

Alec allowed himself a moment to dream. Being Inquisitor, and having a hand in the making of the Law itself. Being able to get Aline and Helen back. Being able to put some sort of dent in the Cold Peace. Being able, Alec thought with slow-dawning hope, to get married.

Having his dad believe that Alec could do it. Alec knew his dad loved him, but that wasn't the same as his dad believing in him. He hadn't known that before.

"I'm not saying it would be easy," said Robert. "But several members of the Clave have mentioned it as a possibility. You know how popular you are with Downworlders."

"Not really," mumbled Alec.

"A few more people in the Clave are coming around," said Robert. "I have that tapestry up of you, and I take care to mention your name often."

"Here I thought it was up because you love me."

Robert blinked at him, as if he was wounded by the joke. "Alec. It—it is. But I want this for you too. That's what I came here to ask. Do you want it for yourself?"

Alec thought of the power to change the Law from a sword that hurt people into a shield to defend them.

"Yeah," said Alec. "But you have to be sure you want me to have it, Dad. People won't be happy with me taking it, and once I have it, I'm going to split the Clave apart."

"You are?" Robert asked, his voice faint.

"Because I have to," said Alec. "Because everything has to change. For everybody's sake. And for Magnus and our kids."

Robert blinked. "Your what?"

"Oh, by the Angel," said Alec. "Please don't ask me any questions! I have to go! I have to talk to Magnus right away."

Robert said, "I am very confused."

"I really have to go," said Alec. "Thanks, Dad. I mean it. Come for dinner again soon, all right? We'll talk more about the Inquisitor thing then."

"All right," said Robert. "I'd like that. When I had dinner with you three a few weeks ago? I don't remember the last time I had such a happy day."

Alec remembered how difficult it had been during Robert's visit to keep the conversation going, how only Max prattling at his grandpa's knee had broken the frequent silences. It broke Alec's heart to think Robert had thought of that strained awkward dinner as happiness.

"Come over anytime," said Alec. "Max loves seeing his grandpa. And—thank you, Dad. Thanks for believing in me. Sorry if I caused you a lot of paperwork tonight."

"You saved lives tonight, Alec," said Robert.

He took an awkward step toward Alec, and his hand lifted, as if he was going to pat Alec on the shoulder. Then his hand dropped. He looked into Alec's face, and his eyes were so sad.

"You're a good man, Alec," he said at last. "You're a better man than I am."

Alec loved his father and would never be cruel to him. So he didn't say: *I had to be.* Instead he reached out and pulled his father into an awkward hug, patting him on the shoulder before he stepped back.

"We'll talk later."

"Whenever you like," said Robert. "I've got all the time in the world."

Alec waved to his dad, then ran up the steps of his building. He opened the door and bounded up his stairs to find Lily alone. The door of his loft was open a crack, light filtering through, but Lily was standing in the shadows and appeared to be filing her nails.

"Lily," Alec said dangerously, "where is Rafael?"

"Oh, him." Lily shrugged. "He heard Magnus singing some Indonesian lullaby, and he bolted inside. Nothing I could do. Shadowhunters. They're speedy."

Neither of them mentioned Magnus's wards, which couldn't be forced by any magic or any strength Alec knew of. Magnus didn't have wards up for anyone defenseless, anyone who might need his help. Of course a child could go through.

Alec fixed her with a reproachful glare but was distracted

by the deep, lovely murmur of Magnus's voice through the open door. His tone was warm and, as it often was, amused. Alec thought of Jem telling Tessa, *Your voice is the music I love best in all the world.*

"Ah, there's that smile," said Lily. "It's been two days, and I missed it."

Alec stopped smiling and made a face at her, but when he looked at her properly, she was fiddling with the zipper of her leather jacket. There was something about the set of her mouth, as if she'd set it determinedly so it wouldn't tremble.

"Thanks for coming with me," Alec said. "Also, you're the worst."

That made her smile. Lily wiggled her fingers in farewell. "Don't you forget it."

She slipped away like a shadow, and Alec opened the door and stepped inside his apartment at last. His coffee machine was on the counter; his cat was sleeping on the sofa.

There was a door standing open to a room he'd never seen before, which happened sometimes at his place. The room inside had golden-brown floorboards and whitewashed walls. Magnus was standing in the room, with Rafe beside him. Magnus was wearing a red-and-gold silk robe, and Rafe's face was tipped up to watch him as he produced a low, soothing stream of Spanish. It was a beautiful room.

Alec realized Magnus knew he was there because Magnus started translating what he was saying into rapid English, switching between languages with fluid ease so everybody knew what was going on.

"Let's put away the cross for now, and talk about organized religion later," said Magnus, snapping his fingers at the crucifix on the wall. "And let's have a window and let the light in. Do you like this one?"

He gestured easily to the wall, and a circular window opened up onto their street, showing a tree catching the moon. Then he gestured again and the window was red-and-gold stained glass.

"Or this one?" Magnus waved a third time and the window was arched and tall as a church window. "Or this one?"

Rafe was nodding and nodding, his face wreathed in eager smiles.

Magnus smiled down at him. "Want me to just keep doing magic?"

Rafe nodded again, even more vehemently. Magnus laughed and set a hand on Rafe's curly head: Alec was about to warn that Rafael was shy at first and would duck away, but Rafe didn't. He let Magnus stroke his hair, the rings on Magnus's hand catching the light through their new window. Magnus's smile went from gleaming to glowing. He met Alec's eyes over Rafe's head.

"I've been getting to know Rafe," said Magnus. "He told me that was what he liked to be called. We've been doing up a bedroom for him. See?"

"I do," said Alec.

"Rafe," said Magnus. "Rafael. Do you have a last name?"

Rafe shook his head.

"That's all right. We have two. How would you feel about a middle name? Would you like one?"

Rafe broke into a stream of Spanish. From all the nodding, Alec was fairly sure he was agreeing.

"Um," Alec said. "We probably need to talk."

Magnus laughed. "Oh, do you think so? Excuse us for a minute, Rafe." He moved toward Alec, then stopped short.

Rafe's hands were clenched hard on the edge of Magnus's robe. Magnus looked startled.

Rafe burst out crying. Magnus cast Alec a wild glance, then ran his hands distractedly through his own hair. Between torrential sobs, Rafael began to eke out words.

Alec couldn't speak Rafael's language, but he understood nonetheless. *Don't let me see you, and then have to go away into the loneliness that is the world without you. Please, please, keep me. I'll be good, if you would just keep me.*

Alec started forward, but before he was even in the room, Magnus dropped to his knees and touched the child's face with tender hands. All trace of tears disappeared with a shimmer of magic.

"Hush," said Magnus. "Don't cry. Yes, of course we will, my darling."

Rafe put his face down onto Magnus's shoulder and sobbed his heart out. Magnus patted his shaking back until he was quiet.

"I'm sorry," Magnus said at last, and rocked Rafe in the curve of one red-silk arm. "I really do need to talk to Alec. I'll be right back. I promise you."

He stood and tried to move forward, then cast a rueful glance downward. Rafe was still holding on to his robe.

"He's very determined," Alec explained.

"So, completely unlike any other Shadowhunters of my acquaintance, then," said Magnus, and swept off his robe.

Underneath he was wearing a tunic shirt shimmering with gold thread, and loose ratty gray sweatpants.

"Are those sweatpants mine?"

"Yes," said Magnus. "I missed you."

"Oh," said Alec.

Magnus settled the robe around Rafe's shoulders, wrapping him up so he was a red silk cocoon with a startled face on top. Then he knelt down by Rafe again and lifted Rafael's hands in his, holding them together. Inside Rafe's cupped palms, a tiny fountain of glitter leaped in a shining loop. Rafe gave a hiccuping laugh, full of surprised delight.

"There, you like magic, don't you? Keep your hands together and it will keep going," Magnus murmured, then made his escape while Rafe was watching the fountain.

Alec took Magnus's hand, pulling him out of the new room into the main loft and through into their bedroom. He shut the door and said, "I can explain."

"I think I might understand already, Alexander," said Magnus. "You were away a day and half and you adopted us another kid. What happens if you go away for a week?"

"I didn't mean to," said Alec. "I wasn't going to do anything without asking you. Only he was there, and he's a Shadowhunter, and nobody was looking after him, so I thought I could take him to the Institute here. Or to Alicante."

Magnus had been smiling, but now he stopped. Alec felt even more alarmed.

"We're not adopting him?" Magnus asked. "But . . . can't we?" Alec blinked.

"I thought we were," Magnus said. "Alec, I promised him. Do you not want to?"

Alec stared at him for another instant. Magnus's face was tense, intent but confused at the same time, as if he was baffled by his own vehemence. Suddenly Alec was laughing. He'd thought he was waiting to be sure, yet this was better, as all the best things in his life were better than any dream that had come before. Not Alec knowing right away, but seeing *Magnus* know right away. It was so sweet, and so obvious that this was exactly the way things should be: seeing Magnus experience the instant instinctive love as Alec had with Max, as Alec learned with Rafael the slow, sweet, and conscious way of love that Magnus had learned with Max. Opening a new door in their familiar beloved home, as if it had always been there.

"Yes," Alec said, breathless with laughter and love. "Yes, I want to."

Magnus's smile returned. Alec pulled him into his arms, then turned so Magnus had his back to the wall. Alec cupped Magnus's face in both hands.

"Give me a minute," Alec said. "Let me look at you. God, I missed home."

Magnus's fascinating eyes were narrowed slightly, watching Alec back, and his smiling mouth was a little startled, as it often was, though what surprised him Alec didn't know. Alec couldn't just look at him. He kissed him, and that mouth was against his own, the kiss making every tired muscle in Alec's body turn to liquid sweetness. To Alec, love always meant this: his shining city of eternal light. The land of lost dreams reclaimed, his first kiss and his last.

Magnus's arms went around him.

"My Alec," Magnus murmured. "Welcome home."

Now when Alec asked himself *Is this how you want to live your whole life?* he could answer yes, and yes, and yes. Every kiss was the answer yes, and the question he would get to ask Magnus someday. They kissed up against the bedroom wall for long bright moments, then both stepped away from the other with a wrench.

"The—" Alec began.

"—kids," Magnus finished. "Later."

"Wait, the kids plural?" asked Alec, and became aware of what Magnus had heard: the stealthy sound of tiny feet exiting Max's room.

"That hellborn brat," Magnus muttered. "I read him eight stories."

"Magnus!"

"What, I can call him that. It's you who can't call him that, because it's infernally insensitive." Magnus grinned, then squinted at his own stained hand. "Alec, I know you don't really care about your clothes, but you don't usually come home covered in soot."

"Better see to the kids," said Alec, ducking out of the bedroom and the conversation.

In the main room was Max, in his triceratops footie pajamas and dragging his fuzzy blankie, regarding Rafe with wide eyes. Rafe stood on the woven rug before the fireplace, wrapped in Magnus's red silk robe. His eyes narrowed into the death stare that had frightened the other kids at the Shadow Market.

Max, who had never felt threatened by anything in his life, smiled guilelessly up at him. Rafe's scowl faltered.

Max turned at the opening of the door. He padded swiftly over to Alec, and Alec knelt down to embrace him.

"Daddy, Daddy!" Max caroled. "This the brother orra sister?"

Rafael's eyebrows went up. He said something quickly in Spanish.

"Not a sister," Magnus translated from the door. "Max, this is Rafe. Say hi."

Max clearly took this as confirmation. He patted Alec's

shoulder as if to say: *great job, Dad, finally you deliver the goods.* Then he turned back to Rafe.

"What are you? Werewolf?" Max guessed.

Rafe glanced at Magnus, who translated. "He says he's a Shadowhunter."

Max beamed. "Daddy's a Shadowhunter. I'm a Shadowhunter too!"

Rafe regarded Max's horns with an air suggesting: *Can you believe this guy?* He shook his head firmly and attempted to explain the situation.

"He says you're a warlock," Magnus translated faithfully. "And that this is a very good thing to be, because it means you can do magic, and magic is cool and pretty." Magnus paused. "Which is so true."

Max's face screwed up in rage. "I'm a Shadowhunter!"

Rafe waved a hand, his attitude one of deep impatience.

"All right, my blue-ringed octopus," Magnus interposed hastily. "Let's continue this debate tomorrow, shall we? Everybody needs sleep. Rafe has had a long day, and it is incredibly past your bedtime."

"I'll read you a story," Alec promised.

Max dropped his fury as swiftly as he'd assumed it. His blue brows knit. He seemed to be thinking deeply. "No bed!" he argued. "Stay up. Be with Rafe." He sidled up to a stunned-looking Rafael and gave him a big hug. "I'm love him."

Rafe hesitated, then hugged Max shyly back. The sight of them made Alec's chest hurt.

He cast a glance back at Magnus, who had an equally smitten expression.

"It's a special occasion," Alec pointed out.

"I was never very good at discipline anyway," said Magnus, and threw himself down beside the kids on the rug. Rafe edged closer, and Magnus looped an arm around him. Rafe cuddled up. "How about you tell us all a bedtime story about what happened in Buenos Aires?"

"It wasn't that exciting," Alec said. "Other than: I found Rafe. I missed you. I came home. That's it. We'll have to go back and forth to Buenos Aires a few times to finalize the adoption, before we can make it official and tell everyone. Maybe we can all go together sometime."

Rafe said several swift sentences in Spanish.

"Is that so?" asked Magnus. "How extremely interesting."

"What are you saying?" Alec asked Rafe anxiously.

"You aren't getting away with this one, Alec Lightwood." Magnus pointed at him. "Not this time. I have a spy!"

Alec went over to the rug, knelt down, and made earnest eye contact with Rafe.

"Rafe," he said. "Please don't be a spy."

Rafe gave Alec a look of firm incomprehension and burst into a torrent of Spanish for Magnus. Alec was certain at least some of it was Rafe promising to be a spy anytime Magnus wanted.

"Sounds like you did some pretty impressive things in Buenos Aires," said Magnus at last. "A lot of people would have given up. What were you thinking?"

Alec picked Max up, tipped him upside down, then sideways, then returned him to the rug, grinning when Max crowed with laughter.

"All I did was think about being worthy of coming home to you," said Alec. "It was nothing much."

There was a silence. Alec turned, a little concerned, to find Magnus staring at him. That surprised look was on his face again, and there was a softness along with it that was rare for Magnus.

"What?" said Alec.

"Nothing, you stealth romance attacker," Magnus said. "How do you always know what to say?"

He leaned forward easily, keeping Rafe held comfortably against him, to give Alec a kiss on the jaw. Alec smiled.

Rafe was studying Max, who seemed gratified Rafe was taking an interest.

"If you want to be a Shadowhunter," said Rafael, in careful English, "you have to train."

"No, Rafe," said Alec. "Max doesn't need to train."

"I train!" said Max.

Alec shook his head. His baby was a warlock. Alec would train Rafe, but Max didn't need to learn any of that. He looked to Magnus for backup, but Magnus was hesitating, his lip caught between his teeth.

"Magnus!"

"Max wants to be just like you," Magnus said. "I can understand that. Are we going to tell him he can't be whatever he wants to be?"

"He's not—" Alec began, and stopped.

"There's nothing to say a warlock couldn't physically fight," said Magnus. "Using magic to substitute for Shadowhunter attributes. It might keep him safe, because people don't expect a warlock to be trained that way. It wouldn't hurt to try. Besides . . . we found Max on the steps of Shadowhunter Academy. Someone might have wanted him to have Shadowhunter training."

Alec hated the idea. But he'd thought, hadn't he, that he

wished he could train a kid? He'd promised himself that he would never be the kind of father who made the walls of home feel like a trap.

If you loved somebody, you trusted them.

"All right," said Alec. "I guess it wouldn't hurt to show them a few ways to stand and fall. Might get them tired enough for bedtime."

Magnus grinned and snapped his fingers. Practice mats suddenly covered the floor. Max scrambled to his feet. Rafe, head pillowed against Magnus's chest, seemed uninterested until Magnus nudged him gently, but then he got up willingly enough.

"Maybe I can teach Rafe a few magic tricks as well," Magnus mused. "He can't be a warlock any more than Max can be a Shadowhunter, but there are magicians around. He might be a very good one."

Alec recalled a story about a magician with Shadowhunter blood, known as Roland the Astonishing, who had lived a long, happy life with his best beloved. He thought of the Market and the Institute mingling in the streets of Buenos Aires, of Jem and Tessa, of love and trust in a changing world, and showing his sons they could be anything they wanted, including happy. He rose and walked to the center of the room.

"Boys? Follow the moves I make," said Alec. "Stand with me, now. All together."

Through Blood, Through Fire

By Cassandra Clare and Robin Wasserman

J

2012

Once upon a time, in a land not so far away, there was a child who should not have been born. A child of disgraced warriors—his blood the blood of the angels, his birthright forfeit while he slept, unknowing, in his mother's womb. A child sentenced to death for the sins of his ancestors, a child spirited away from the Law that condemned and the family that couldn't yet know how much they might someday need him and his progeny.

Once upon a time, a child was lost—or, at least, such is the story as told by those foolish enough to lose him. No one is ever lost to himself.

The child was simply hiding. As his child, and his child's child, learned to hide, and on through the generations, evading those who hunted them—some seeking forgiveness, some seeking annihilation—until, inevitably, that which had been hidden was revealed. The lost child was found.

And that was the end.

Later, when Jem Carstairs tried to remember how the end began, he would remember the tickle of Tessa's hair on his face as he bent close, breathed deep the scent of her, which that day carried a hint of lavender. They were in Provence—so, of course, everything smelled like lavender. But Tessa was alive with it; breathing her in was like breathing in a sunlit meadow, a sea of purpling blossoms, springtime itself. That was what Jem would remember, later. The desire that time stop, freeze the two of them inside this perfect moment; he would remember thinking, with wonder, that this was how it felt to be perfectly satisfied.

When Tessa Gray returned to that moment, the moment before, she remembered the taste of honey, which Jem had drizzled onto a sliver of baguette, then popped into her mouth. The honey, fresh from the hive behind the estate, was almost painfully sweet. Her fingers were sticky with it, and when she pressed them to Jem's soft cheek, they didn't want to let go. She couldn't blame them.

Memory has a tendency to fog the mundane. What Jem and Tessa were actually doing: bickering about whether the cheese they'd acquired that morning was goat or cow, and which of them was responsible for eating so much of it that a second trip to the fromagerie was required. It was a lazy, loving bickering, as befitted their sun-dappled afternoon. They'd come to this retreat in the French countryside to strategize about the lost Herondale—who, they had recently discovered, was also heir to the Seelie and Unseelie Courts, and so in more danger than anyone had ever imagined. This estate, the use of which had been offered by Magnus Bane, was a safe, quiet place to plan where to go from here. The lost Herondale had made it very clear to Jem that she didn't want to be found, but Jem worried this was because she didn't know the depths of danger she was in. They needed to find her. Warn her. Now more than ever.

The urgency was real, but so was their inability to *do* anything about it, which left many hours to fill, gazing out at the sunlit hillside—and at each other.

Tessa had nearly decided to give in and admit that Jem was right about the provenance (goat), if wrong about who'd eaten the most (Tessa), when a light sparked between them, like a tiny falling star. Except it didn't fall; it froze in midair, getting brighter and brighter, blindingly bright, and forming itself into a familiar shape. Tessa sucked in a sharp breath. "Is that . . . ?"

"A heron," Jem confirmed.

Years before, Jem had enchanted a silver pendant in the shape of a heron and pressed it into the palm of a young woman with Herondale blood. A young woman in danger, who steadfastly refused his help.

With this pendant, you can always find me, he had promised, in the silent voice with which he had once spoken. Jem had been Brother Zachariah then, still bearing the robes and duties of the Silent Brotherhood, but this mission—and this promise—had nothing to do with the Brotherhood. Jem was still bound by it, would always be bound by it. *I trust you will summon me for help, if and when you need. Please trust that I will always answer.*

The woman he'd given that pendant to was a Herondale, the last heir of the lost Herondale, and the silver heron meant that after all these years, she needed him. As Jem and Tessa watched, the bird traced letters of fire on the air.

I turned away from you once, but please help me now. I thought I could do this on my own, but the Riders are closing in. If you will not come for me, come for my boy. I thought I could buy his life with my suffering. I thought if I left him, he would be safe. He is not. Please come. I beg you. Save me. Save my child.

—Rosemary Herondale

The light winked out. Jem and Tessa were already in motion. In the century and a half they'd known each other, much had changed, but this truth endured: when a Herondale called, they would answer.

L.A. traffic wasn't as bad as everyone said. It was exponentially worse. Six lanes, all of them nearly at a standstill. As Tessa inched forward, shifting lanes every time a space opened up, Jem felt like he was going to crawl out of his skin. They'd Portaled from France to Los Angeles, but the closest location that was familiar enough to them for the Portal to work was halfway across the city from the source of the distress call. Magnus had reached out to his network of West Coast acolytes and secured them transport to get the rest of the way. The turquoise convertible didn't exactly scream "incognito," but it was enough to carry them the handful of miles from Echo Park to Rosemary Herondale's house in the Hollywood Hills. The ride should only have taken a few minutes. It felt like it had been a year.

I turned away from you once, but please help me now.

The words echoed in Jem's mind. He'd spent decades searching for the lost Herondale—finding her, finally, only to lose her again. But after she'd refused his offer of protection, he'd made her a promise. He would come when she called. He would save her when she needed saving.

I thought I could do this on my own.

James Carstairs would always come to the aid of a Herondale. He would never stop repaying the debts of love.

She had summoned him, using the necklace, and he would do everything in his power to honor his promise, but—

Please come, I beg you. Save me.

There was more than just one life at stake now.

Save my child.

What if they were too late?

Tessa put her hand on Jem's. "This isn't your fault," she said.

Of course she knew what he was thinking. She always did.

"I had her, and I let her walk away." Jem couldn't stop picturing it, that morning on the bridge in Paris, when he'd begged Rosemary Herondale to accept his protection. He had asked a Herondale to trust him and been judged unworthy.

"You didn't *let* her do anything," Tessa pointed out. "She made her own choice."

"The Herondale way," Jem said wryly.

"You let her know you would always be there if she needed you, and now that she does—"

"I'm twiddling my thumbs five miles away, useless."

"Enough." Tessa abruptly swerved onto the shoulder of the road and sped past the clogged lanes, then careened onto the first exit ramp they came to. Instead of slowing down, she picked up speed as they hit the surface streets, weaving wildly from lane to lane to sidewalk. Soon, finally, they found their way into the hills, the road narrowing to a single lane of hairpin turns bounded by a vertiginous drop. Tessa didn't slow down.

"I know you have superhuman reflexes, but—"

"Trust me," she said.

"Infinitely."

He couldn't tell Tessa the other reason he felt guilty—it wasn't simply that he'd let Rosemary slip through his fingers all those years ago. It was what he'd done for her since, which suddenly seemed like next to nothing. Ever since he'd sloughed off his life as Brother Zachariah and fought his way back to James Carstairs—and back to Tessa Gray, the other half of his soul, his heart, his self—he'd given himself permission to be happy. They'd visited Shadow Markets all over the world, keeping watch for Rosemary, always searching for ways they might be able to assist her from a distance. They'd even visited the Market here in L.A. several times, but they had found no trace of her there. What if, despite his best intentions, Jem had missed something, some opportunity to find and help Rosemary before it was too late? What if, lost in his own happiness with Tessa, he'd enabled her suffering?

The car screeched to a stop in front of a small Spanish-style bungalow. The yard was a riot of color: monkeyflowers, hummingbird sage, desert mallow, jacaranda blossoms. A gauntlet of sunflowers watched over the path to the door, nodding in the breeze, as if to welcome them.

"It's like a house from a storybook," Tessa marveled, and Jem agreed. The sky was an impossible blue, dotted with cotton-candy clouds, and the mountains on the horizon made it feel like they were in an Alpine village, rather than the middle of a sprawling metropolis. "It's so peaceful," she added. "Like nothing bad could ever happen here—"

She was interrupted by a piercing scream.

They erupted into motion. Jem shouldered the front door open, readying his sword to face whatever lay beyond. Tessa followed close behind, her hands sparking with angry light. Inside, they found a nightmare: Rosemary lying still in a pool of blood. Looming over her, a massive faerie, his body covered in thick bronze armor, a longsword raised overhead. Its point aimed straight at Rosemary's heart.

In many ways, Jem Carstairs was no longer a Shadowhunter. But in the most important ways, he would always be a Shadowhunter.

He launched himself forward, a whirl of deadly motion, sword stick a silver blur as he hacked at the faerie with the full, righteous force of Shadowhunter rage. His blows glanced off the creature's body without leaving a single mark. Tessa raised her hands and dispatched a blinding white wave of energy at the faerie—he absorbed it without flinching, then, almost carelessly, grabbed Tessa in one massive hand and flung her across the room. She slammed into the wall with a thud that caused Jem physical pain. Jem threw himself in the faerie's path, kicked, spun, swung the sword down sharp and sure in what should have been a mortal blow. Any ordinary faerie— any ordinary Downworlder—would have been felled. This one only laughed, shoved Jem to the floor, and pinned him there beneath a massive foot. Leaving Jem helpless to do anything but watch as the longsword found its mark and stabbed Rosemary through the chest.

The faerie stepped back, freeing Jem to rush to her side—too late. He tore off his shirt, pressed it desperately to Rosemary's gushing wound, determined to keep her life from draining away. Too late.

"I have no quarrel with you, Shadowhunter," the faerie said, then gave a sharp whistle. An enormous bronze steed crashed through the bungalow's front windows in a hail of glass. The faerie hoisted himself onto the horse. "I suggest you refrain from quarreling with me." The horse reared and leaped into the air.

And just like that, horse and Rider were gone.

Rosemary's face was deathly pale, her eyes closed. She was still breathing, if barely. Jem put pressure on the wound, willing her to hold on. Tessa knelt beside him.

He let out a sharp breath, his heart clenching. "Are you hurt?"

"I'm fine. But Rosemary . . ." Tessa gripped Rosemary's hands and closed her eyes in concentration. Seconds passed as she summoned the will to heal. He could see the effort written on her face, the torment. Finally, Tessa turned to Jem, a hollow look in her eyes. He knew what she would say before she said it.

"It's a mortal wound," she murmured. "There's nothing to be done."

Tessa had volunteered as a nurse during one of the mundane world wars—she knew a mortal wound when she saw one. And Jem, during his decades in the Silent Brotherhood, had seen too many Shadowhunters beyond help. Far too many in the Dark War. He too could recognize death in all its guises.

Rosemary's eyes flickered open. Her lips parted, as if she was trying to speak, but she managed only a rasping breath.

There was still one Herondale they could save. "Your child," Jem said. "Where is he?"

Rosemary shook her head, the effort of motion causing her obvious pain.

"Please," she whispered. There was so much blood. Everywhere, blood, her life streaming away. "Please, protect my son."

"Just tell us where to find him," Jem said. "And on my life, I will protect him, I swear—" He stopped, realizing there was no one to receive his promise. The shuddering breath had given way to stillness.

She was gone.

"We'll find him," Tessa promised Jem. "We'll find him before anyone can hurt him. *We will.*"

Jem hadn't moved from Rosemary's body. He held her cool hand in his own, as if he couldn't bring himself to let go. She knew what he was feeling, and it hurt. This was the joy and punishment of loving someone the way she loved Jem—she felt with him. His guilt, his regret, his powerlessness and fury: as they consumed him, they consumed her, too.

Of course, it wasn't just Jem's guilt, Jem's fury. She had plenty of her own. Every Herondale was a part of Will, and so a part of her. That was what it meant to be family. And she had knelt by the cold body of too many Herondales. She could not stomach another meaningless death.

They would find Rosemary's son. They *would* protect him. They would ensure this death was not in vain. Whatever it took.

"It's not just that she's dead," Jem said quietly. His head was lowered, his hair a curtain over his face. But she'd memorized his face, his every expression. She'd spent so many hours, since his return, gazing at him, unable to believe he was really here, restored to life—restored to her. "It's that she died alone."

"She wasn't alone. She's not alone." This was not the first time she and Jem had helped a Herondale into eternity. Once, she had sat on one side of Will, Jem on the other, both of them longing to hold on to him, both summoning the strength to let him go. Jem had been Brother Zachariah then, or that was what the world had seen: runed face, sealed eyes, cold skin, closed heart. She had only ever seen her Jem. It still seemed a miracle that he could open his eyes and see her back.

"Wasn't she?" Very gently, Jem unclasped Rosemary's necklace. He dangled the long silver chain, letting the heron charm spin slowly, gleaming in the afternoon light. "I thought this would be enough—a way to reach out if she needed me. But I *knew* she was in danger from the fey. I shouldn't have underestimated that!"

"I recognized that faerie, Jem," Tessa said. "The bronze braid, the designs on his armor—all those etchings of the sea—that was Fal of Mannan." She'd studied the Riders of Mannan during her time in the Spiral Labyrinth, part of her efforts to better understand the Faerie world. They were very old—ancient, even, from an age of monsters and gods—and they served at the pleasure of the Unseelie King. These were no ordinary faeries. They were more powerful; they were made of wild magic. Perhaps most terrifyingly, they could lie. "Seraph blades are useless against the Riders of Mannan, Jem. They're born assassins—a walking death sentence. Once he found her, no power on earth could have stopped him."

"So then what hope is there for the boy?"

"There's always hope." She risked putting her arms around him then, and very softly extricated Rosemary's hand from his grip. "We find the boy first. Then we make sure the fey never do."

"Not until we're ready for them, at least," Jem said, a note of steel entering his voice.

There were those who believed that because Jem was so kind, so capable of gentleness and generosity, because Jem loved so selflessly, that Jem was weak. There were those who suspected he was not capable of violence or vengeance, who assumed they could hurt Jem and the ones he loved with impunity, because he did not have it in him to strike back.

Those who believed this were wrong.

Those who acted on it would be sorry.

Tessa squeezed the heron charm tightly, its beak pricking sharply against the soft meat of her palm. She could feel Rosemary's essence simmering in the silver, and reached for it with her mind, opening herself to the traces of the woman left behind. It was second nature to her now, Changing into someone else. Usually she needed only to close her eyes and let it wash over her.

This was different. Something felt—not wrong, exactly, but *sticky*. Like she had to yank herself out of her own form and forcibly shove it into another. The transformation felt difficult, almost painful, as it had in her earliest days in London, her bones and muscles and flesh tearing and distorting themselves into alien form, body rebelling against mind, while mind fought its own battle, defending its territory against the colonizing force of an *other*. Tessa forced herself to stay calm, focused. Reminded herself that it was always more difficult to embody the dead. She felt herself shrinking, fading, firm limbs narrowing to Rosemary's delicate, bony frame, and as she did so, the horror flooded in, those final moments. The flash of the longsword. The hot breath of the faerie Rider. The unthinkable pain and pain and pain of the blade thrust once, twice, and finally, fatally. The terror, the despair, and beneath it, the fierce, loving rage on behalf of the boy who must, somewhere out there, survive, he must, he must, he—

"Tessa!"

Then Jem was there, steady, his arms on her shoulders, his gaze firm and kind, his love a tether to keep her from floating away. Jem, always, bringing her home to herself.

"Tessa, you were screaming."

She breathed. She focused. She was Rosemary and she was Tessa, she was the Change itself, the possibility of transformation, the inevitability of flux, and then, mercifully, she was clear.

"I'm okay. It's okay." Even now, after more than a century of Changing, it was strange to hear herself speak with another woman's voice, to look down and see another woman's body as her own.

"Do you know where he is? The boy?"

My boy. Tessa could hear the wonder in Rosemary's voice, could feel the other woman's ongoing surprise that it was possible to love like this. *They won't have him. I won't allow it.*

There was fear, but mostly rage, and Tessa realized that "they" were not the fey. "They" were the Shadowhunters. This was one secret she would keep for herself. Jem didn't need to know that Rosemary had died as she'd lived: convinced they were the enemy.

"Let me go deeper," Tessa said. "She's spent years burying what she knows about him, but it's there. I can feel it."

Rosemary's being was in battle with itself. She'd been entirely consumed with her son, with the fierce need to protect him, but had also spent these years trying with all her might to forget him, to force all thought of him from her consciousness, for his own safety. "She knew the greatest danger in his life was *her*," Tessa said, horrified by the sacrifice this woman had made. "She knew the only way to keep him alive was to let him go."

Tessa let herself sink into the memory—she let go of *Tessa* and gave herself wholly over to *Rosemary*. Focused on the boy, on the strongest memories of him and what had become of him, and let them possess her.

She remembered.

"I don't understand," her husband is saying, but the desperation in his eyes, the grip of his hands on hers as if he knows what will happen when he lets go? That says different. That says he does understand, that this has to be the end, that their son's safety is more important than anything. More important, even, than the two of them, which Rosemary used to think was everything.

Things were different, before she was a mother.

Christopher is three. He looks like and unlike his mother, like and unlike his father. He is their love come to life, their two hearts intertwined and given shape and breath and cherubic cheeks and golden hair and a nose to kiss and a forehead to stroke and a perfect, perfect body that has never known pain or horror and never should. Must never.

"It's about him now. That's all that matters."

"But we're already so careful. . . ."

For one year, they have forced themselves to live apart. In one small apartment, seedy blocks from the Vegas strip: her son and her husband—who now calls himself Elvis, but who has been Barton and Gilbert and Preston and Jack and Jonathan, who has changed not just his name but his face, over and over again, all for her. In an even smaller, much lonelier apartment in a sad stretch of desert behind the airport: Rosemary, feeling their absence with every breath. She haunts their shadows, watches Christopher on the playground, at the zoo, in the pool, never letting him see her. Her son will grow up unable to recognize his mother's face.

She allows herself monthly encounters with her husband—an

hour of stolen kisses and all the details of a childhood passing without her—but that was selfish. She sees that now. Bad enough that the Shadowhunters were able to get as close as they did. Now the fey have sniffed her out. She's set up charms around the apartment, a warning system—she knows their emissaries have been there; her position has been compromised. And she knows what will happen if they find her. If they find him.

"You have to go deeper underground," she tells her husband. "You have to change your identities again, but this time, I can't know what they are. If they find me . . . you can't let me lead them to you."

And he is shaking his head, he is saying no, he can't do this, he can't raise Christopher alone, he can't let her go knowing he can never have her back, he can't risk her facing danger without him, he can't, he won't.

"I have the heron," she reminds him. "I have a way to summon help if I need it."

"But not my help," he says. He hates the necklace, he always has, even before it was tainted with the Shadowhunter's enchantment. He tried to sell it once, without telling her, because he knows her heritage only brings her pain; she forgave him. She always forgives him. "What if you need me?"

She knows he hates it, the idea that she would call on a stranger over him. He doesn't understand: this is because a stranger's life means nothing to her. She would let the world burn if it meant keeping Jack and Christopher safe.

"What I need is for you to keep him alive."

The world believes Jack—for that is how she first loved him and how she always thinks of him—is a crook. Untrustworthy, venal, without capacity for trust or love. Rosemary knows better. Most people are spendthrift with their care, spreading it around without discretion.

Jack loves only two things in this world: his wife and his son.

She wishes, sometimes, that he would include himself on that list. She would worry less for him if she thought he allowed any worry for himself.

"Okay, but what if we win?" he says.

"What do you mean?"

"Let's say you defeat the evil faeries and you convince the Shadowhunters you're of no use to them. What if everyone just stops looking for you, and for Christopher, and it's finally safe to be together. How will you find us?"

She laughs, even in her despair. He has always been able to make her laugh. This time, though, he doesn't see the joke. "That's never going to happen," she says gently. "You can't even risk hoping for that to happen."

"Then let's go to the Clave, all of us. Let's throw ourselves on their mercy, ask for their protection. You know they'd give it to you."

This cuts her laughter off abruptly. The Shadowhunters are without mercy. Who knows that better than she? She squeezes his hands, tight enough to hurt. She is very strong. "Never," she says. "Never forget that the Shadowhunters are as grave a threat to Christopher as anyone else. Never forget what they were willing to do to my ancestor—to one of their own. They will not get their hands on him. Promise me."

"I swear. But only if you promise too."

There is no other way. He won't do what she asks, won't disappear forever, unless she leaves one thin thread between them. One hope.

"The place you first told me who you really are," he says. "The first place you trusted me with yourself. If you need help, you go there. Help will find you. I will find you."

"It's too dangerous—"

"You don't need to know where we are. You don't need to find us. I'll never go looking for you, I promise. And Christopher will be safe. But you, Rosemary—" His voice catches on her name, as if he knows how rarely he will allow himself to voice it again. "If you need me, I will find you."

They don't say good-bye. Between them, there can be no such thing as good-bye. Only a kiss that should last forever. Only a closed door, a silence, a void. Rosemary sinks to the ground, hugs her knees, prays to a god she does not believe in that she will have enough strength never to let herself be found.

"I know how to find him," Tessa said, already pulling herself out of the Change. It was, again, harder than it should have been. An unfamiliar friction holding the Rosemary shape in place.

Except it wasn't entirely unfamiliar, was it? Something tickled the back of her mind, a memory just out of grasp. Tessa reached, almost had it—but it skittered away, gone.

It felt wrong to be in Los Angeles without checking in on Emma Carstairs. But Jem reminded himself that involving her in this could bring danger to her door, and the girl had faced enough. She reminded him of himself sometimes—both of them orphans, both of them taken in by an Institute, adopted into someone else's family but harboring, always, the secret pain of losing their own. They had both found salvation in a *parabatai*, and Jem could only hope that Emma had found in Julian what he'd always found in Will: not just a partner but a refuge. A home. No one, not even a *parabatai*, could replace what had been lost. Even now, there was a hole in Jem's heart, a raw wound where his parents had been ripped away. This was a limb that could not be replaced, only compensated for. As it had been when he lost Will. As it would be if he ever lost Tessa.

Loss was an inevitability of love, pain the inescapable price of joy. Everyone had to learn this someday—maybe this was what it meant to grow up. He wished, for Emma, that her childhood could have lasted just a little longer. And he wished that he could have been there for her when it ended. But this was always the cold calculus when it came to Emma Carstairs: balancing his desire to be part of her life with the consequences. When he was a Silent Brother, he would have been taunting her with something she couldn't have—her only remaining family, who could, nevertheless, not be her family. Now, as Jem Carstairs, he would have happily taken her into his care, but he was no longer a Shadowhunter—and choosing him would mean Emma would have to give up her entire world. The Law was hard—it was also, so often, lonely.

He kept telling himself: soon. Soon, when he and Tessa had gotten their bearings again. Soon, when he had helped Tessa find the lost Herondale, that piece of Will lost to Will's world. Soon, when the danger had passed.

He worried, sometimes, that these were all flimsy excuses. He'd been alive, one way or another, for over a hundred and fifty years. He should know by now that danger never passed. It only paused, and then only if you were lucky.

"You sure this is the place?" Jem asked Tessa. She'd Changed into Rosemary again, and he could barely look at her. Sometimes Jem missed the cool distance the Silent Brotherhood had forced on him, the way no emotion, however powerful, could penetrate his stony heart. Life was easier without feeling. It wasn't life, he knew. But it was easier.

"Unfortunately, this is definitely the place."

Every city had a Shadow Market, and in a way, they were all the same Market, branches of a single tree—but that didn't stop each Market from taking on the character of its environs. From what Jem could tell, Los Angeles's environs were: tanned, health conscious, and obsessed with automobiles. The Shadow Market was located on a tony corner of Pasadena, and everything there was shiny, including its occupants: vampires with bleach-white fangs, bodybuilding faeries whose bulging muscles sheened with gold-spangled sweat, witches with neon hair and self-writing screenplays for sale, ifrits hawking glittering "star maps" that, on closer examination, had nothing to do with astronomy but were in fact self-updating maps of Los Angeles with a tiny photograph of Magnus Bane marking each location the infamous warlock had caused some infamous chaos. (Tessa bought three of them.)

They threaded through the crowds as quickly as they could. Jem was relieved to no longer bear the robes of the Silent Brotherhood, the ineradicable mark of his creed. There was a taste of the frontier to the Shadow Market, a sense that the rules applied here only as far as anyone was willing to enforce them. Faeries cavorted openly with their fellow Downworlders; warlocks did business with mundanes that should never be done; Shadowhunters were, for obvious reasons, unwelcome.

Their destination lay just beyond the buoyant chaos. In the liminal space between the Shadow Market and the shadows, there stood a ramshackle structure with no sign and no windows. There was nothing to suggest it was anything but a ruin, certainly nothing to mark it as a seedy Downworlder bar, home away from home for down-on-their-luck Downworlders for whom even the Shadow Market wasn't quite shadowy enough. The last thing Jem wanted to do was let Tessa set foot inside, especially wearing the face of someone the Unseelie Court intended to assassinate—but since he'd met her, no one had *let* Tessa do anything.

According to Tessa, Rosemary and her husband had a deal. If Rosemary ever needed him, she would come to this place and somehow make it known that she needed him, and he would appear. It was that middle part of the plan that seemed a little too vague for comfort, but there was no way out but through, Tessa had said cheerfully, then kissed him. Even in someone else's body, even with someone else's lips, her kiss was all Tessa.

They went inside. Tessa went first, Jem following a few minutes later. It seemed prudent to appear they were not together. The bar wasn't much of one. It was just as ramshackle inside as it was out. The large werewolf bouncer at the door sniffed him once, warily, grunted something that sounded very much like "behave," then waved him inside. The crumbling walls were blackened by scorch marks, the floor spattered with beer and, by the smell of it, ichor. Jem surreptitiously clocked the other denizens for potential threat: One bikinied faerie slow dancing with herself, despite the silence, teetering drunkenly on her sky-high heels. One werewolf wrapped in a tattered silk cape, slumped facedown on a table, his scent suggesting he'd been there for days. Jem watched just long enough to make sure he was still breathing, then took a seat at the bar. The bartender, a wizened, balding vampire who looked like he'd been hiding from the sun since long before he Turned, looked Jem up and down, then slid him a drink. The glass was spotted, its contents a filmy pale green. Whatever floated in the center looked like it might once have been alive. Jem decided it was probably safer to stay thirsty.

Three stools away, Tessa hunched over a glass of her own. Jem pretended not to notice.

The faerie sidled between them, her forked tail caressing the rim of Jem's glass. "What's a guy like you, et cetera?"

"Excuse me?"

"You know, all tall, dark, and handsome and"—she shot a glance at the guy in the corner, now snoring with such force that his table rattled beneath him with each exhale—"upright. You don't look like the kind of guy who would hang out around here."

"You know what they say about books and covers," Jem said.

"So you're not as lonely as you look, then?"

Jem realized Tessa, pretending not to listen, was suppressing a smile—and only then understood that the faerie was flirting with him.

"I could help you with that, you know," she said.

"I came here to be alone, actually," Jem said, as politely as he could. The faerie's tail slipped from his glass to his hand, tracing up and down his fingers. Jem pulled away. "And, uh, I'm married."

"Pity." She leaned in, too close, her lips brushing his ear. "See you around, Nephilim." She strutted out of the bar, freeing Jem to concentrate fully on the conversation Tessa was having with the bartender.

"Do I know you?" the bartender asked. Jem stiffened.

"I don't know," Tessa said, "do you?"

"You look familiar around the edges. A little like a girl who used to come in here all the time, with her boyfriend. Bad news, that guy, but she wouldn't hear it. Head over heels, like only a kid can be."

Out of the corner of his eye, Jem caught Tessa's slight smile. "Oh, I don't know that I'd put an age limit on 'head over heels.'"

The bartender gave her an appraising look. "If you say so. Not this girl, though. She grew up to be the flaky kind. Ran off on him and their kid, I heard."

"Terrible," Tessa said dryly. "And Mr. Bad News?"

"Maybe not such bad news. Loyal enough that he's still coming back here after all these years. The kind of guy a certain type can lean on when they need help, if you get me."

"And how would a certain type go about finding him?" Tessa asked. Jem could tell she was trying very hard to keep the eagerness out of her voice.

The bartender cleared his throat, began halfheartedly wiping down the bar. "The right kind of woman, I'm told, would know exactly how to find him," he said, without looking at her. "Because he's exactly the same bird he used to be, just a little less of a crook." He put special emphasis on the words, and Jem could tell by Tessa's expression that they meant something to her. His heart leaped.

Tessa jumped to her feet and tossed a few dollars on the bar. "Thank you."

"Anything for the girl as pretty as a rose. Good luck to—" The dagger seemed to materialize in the center of his forehead. He was dead before he hit the ground. Jem and Tessa whirled around to find Fal of Mannan and his bronze horse thundering through the doorway, bearing down on them with inhuman speed, Fal's longsword falling, Jem's body reacting before his mind had time to process, every second of a lifetime of Shadowhunter training poured into a storm of slashing kicking leaping fighting—all this in under a second, all this ineffectual, because the blade was already falling, was dropping Tessa to the floor in a limp pile of blood and flesh, and Fal of Mannan, impervious, had already taken flight by the time Jem dropped to his knees beside her pale form.

"I suggest you stay dead this time," the faerie advised, and was gone.

She was so pale.

Her features were melting back into her own. The Change always released when she lost consciousness, but something was wrong this time, almost as unsettling as the wound. Her features had nearly returned to Tessa's when, like a taut rubber band suddenly released, they snapped back to Rosemary's. And back again, and again, as if her body couldn't decide whom it wanted to be. Jem pressed the wound, tried to hold in the blood, didn't care whom she looked like, just wanted her body to choose life over death. *The faerie in the bikini.* The thought cut through his haze of panic. Maybe she'd been planted there to spy for the Riders, knowing this place had special meaning for Rosemary and her family; maybe she'd simply recognized "Rosemary" as a woman with a target on her back, a woman who was supposed to be dead, and done her faerie duty. It didn't matter how it had happened. What mattered was that Jem had overlooked her as a threat, which made this his fault, and if Tessa didn't—

But he stopped the thought before it could continue. The wound would have killed a mundane. Maybe even a Shadowhunter. But Tessa's body had shaped itself to Rosemary's form at the time of the attack, the form of a woman who was not just Shadowhunter but heir to the faerie throne—who knew what magic the body might be working on itself in its struggle to survive? Maybe that was why the Change wouldn't let her go—maybe that was her body's way of staving off death until she could heal. Tessa moaned. Jem scooped her into his arms, begging her to hold on.

He had learned much about healing in the Silent Brotherhood, and he did what he could. He thought about how she'd sat by what they all thought was his deathbed, his supply of *yin fen* finally exhausted, the demonic poison overtaking his system, and remembered telling her that she had to let him go. He remembered, too, sitting with the dying Will, giving him permission to leave. He didn't know whether it was strength or selfishness now, but he refused to do the same for Tessa. Not yet: they had waited so long for a life together. They had only just begun.

"Stay," he begged her. "Fight." She was so cold. So light in his arms. Like something essential had already fled. "Whatever it takes, you stay here. I need you, Tessa. I have always needed you."

She wasn't dead. A full day had passed, and she wasn't dead. But she wasn't awake, either, and she hadn't stopped Changing, from Tessa to Rosemary and back again. Sometimes she lasted minutes, once even an hour, in a single form. Sometimes the Change whipped back and forth so quickly that she seemed to have no form at all. Her skin was slick with sweat. At first it was cold to the touch. Then, as fever tore through her, it burned. She had been given medicines—to staunch the blood loss, to give her strength, endurance—remedies that Jem, no longer a

Silent Brother, couldn't treat her with himself. The moment he had gotten her to safety, he'd summoned help.

Or rather, because he and Tessa weren't part of the Clave and had no claim over the Silent Brotherhood, no power with which to summon, he'd *asked* for help. Begged for it. Now Brother Enoch was here, mixing tonics, enacting the complicated, secret rituals that Jem had once been able to do himself. Never before had he regretted leaving the Silent Brotherhood, returning to the land of mortals and mortal peril, but to save Tessa he would have happily pledged the rest of his eternity to those parchment robes, that heart of stone. Instead he could only stand beside Enoch, helpless. Useless. Sometimes, Brother Enoch even made him leave the room.

He understood; he had done the same himself, many a time, secreting himself with the patient, never giving much thought to the torture their loved one might feel on the other side of the wall. In his first life, Jem himself had been the patient, Tessa and Charlotte and Will hovering anxiously around his bed, reading to him, murmuring in comforting voices as he swam between darkness and waking, waiting for him to get stronger, and for the day he would not.

Exiled to the hallway of the small apartment that Magnus— via his ever-expanding and ever-ambiguous network of "friends"—had secured for them, Jem sagged against the wall. *I'm sorry, Will*, he thought. *I never knew.*

To watch the person you loved most fight for every breath. To watch them slipping away, powerless to hold on. To see the face you loved contort with pain, the body you would die to protect trembling, shuddering, broken. It wasn't that Jem had never endured this before. But always before, there had been an intercessor between him and the raw horror of absence. When he was growing up as a Shadowhunter, Jem had always, in the back of his mind, been conscious of the fact that he would die young. He had known he would die long before Will or Tessa, most likely, and even when Tessa or Will flung themselves at danger—as they did so often—there was a part of Jem that had understood he would not be forced to stay very long in a world without them. There had been moments too, in the Silent Brotherhood, when he had stood by Will or Tessa's side, uncertain if they would live or die—but the pain of that had always been mitigated by the same icy distance that mitigated everything else. Now, though, there was nothing in his way, nothing to distract his gaze from the terrifying truth of it. Tessa could die, and he would live on without her, and there was nothing to be done but wait and see. To endure this took all the strength Jem had.

Will had never flinched from Jem's suffering—over and over again, he had endured. He had sat by Jem's bed, held Jem's hand, seen Jem through the darkest of hours. *You were the strongest man I knew*, Jem said silently to his lost friend, *and I never even knew the half of it.*

The door creaked open, and Brother Enoch emerged. Jem still marveled at how alien the Silent Brothers seemed to him now that he was no longer among them. It had taken him some time to get used to the silence in his mind, the chorus of voices that had accompanied his every moment for decades suddenly gone. But now he couldn't imagine it. It felt like trying to remember a dream.

"How is she?"

The wound is no longer a mortal threat. Her shape-shifting abilities seem to have prevented it from having the expected effect.

Jem nearly collapsed with relief. "Can I see her? Is she awake?"

The Silent Brother's runed face was immobile, his eyes and mouth sewn shut, and yet Jem could still sense his concern.

"What is it?" he said. "What aren't you telling me?"

The wound is healing. Her Changing has saved her, but I fear now it is the Changing that poses the greatest threat. Her body, her mind are trapped within it. She seems unable to find her way back to herself—the Change will not let her go. It is as if she has lost her hold on what makes her, essentially, Tessa Gray.

"How do we help her?"

There was true silence then.

"No." Jem refused to accept this. "There's always something. You have a *millennium* of knowledge to draw on. There must be *something*."

In all those years, there has never been a being like Tessa. She is a strong woman, and a powerful one. You must have faith she will find her own way home.

"And what if she doesn't? She just stays like this, in limbo, forever?"

The Changing takes its toll, James. Every transformation requires energy, and no body can sustain this level of energy indefinitely. Not even hers.

The voice in Jem's head was so cool, so measured, it was easy to imagine he didn't care at all. Jem knew better. It was simply that caring, for a Silent Brother, took a different, alien form. This much, Jem could remember: the icy distance from life. The inhuman calm with which events were processed. Words like "care," "need," "fear," "love": they had meaning; it was just a meaning unrecognizable to anyone who could sleep and eat and speak, who lived a life of animal passions. He remembered how grateful he was for the rare moment—almost always, a moment with Tessa—in which he felt a spark of true emotion. How he'd longed for the fires of human passion, for the privilege of *feeling* again, even fear, even sorrow.

Now he almost envied Brother Enoch the ice. This fear, this sorrow; it was too great to bear. "How long, then?"

You should go to her now. Stay with her, until . . .

Until it was over, one way or another.

Tessa knows and does not know that this is a dream.

She knows that Jem is alive and so this must be a dream, this corpse in her lap wearing Jem's face, this body decaying in her arms, skin sloughing from muscle, muscle flaying from bone, bone dissolving to dust. He belonged to her, so briefly, and now he is dust, and she is alone.

He is cold, he is lifeless, he is meat, her Jem, meat for maggots, and they swarm his flesh, and somehow she can hear them, chittering and gobbling, millions of mouths nibbling to nothing, and she screams his name but there is no one to hear but the wriggling death worms, and she knows it to be impossible, but still, she can hear them laugh.

Jem is alive, his eyes bright with laughter, his violin raised to his chin, his music the music he wrote for her, the song of her soul, and the arrow that sails toward him is swift and sure and coated with poison, and when it pierces his heart, the music stops. The violin breaks. All is silence forever.

He flings himself between her and the Mantid demon and she is saved but he is speared in half, and by the time she can catch her breath enough to scream, he is gone.

The Dragonidae demon breathes a cloud of fire and the flames consume him, a blinding blue-and-white fire that burns him from the inside out, and she watches the flames shoot from his mouth, watches his eyes melt with the heat and run down his smoldering cheeks, and his skin crackles like bacon, until, almost mercifully, the light is too bright, all-consuming, and she turns away, only for a single moment of weakness, but when she turns back, there is only a pile of ash; everything that was Jem is gone.

A flash of sword, and he is gone.

A wailing beast swooping out of the sky, a talon raked across pale skin, and he is gone.

And he is gone.

She is alive, and she is alone, and he is gone.

When she can no longer bear it, when she has watched love die ten times, a hundred times, felt her own heart die with him, when there is nothing left but an ocean of blood and a fire that's burned away all but the excruciating pain of loss after loss after loss, she flees to the only place she can, the only safe harbor from horror.

She flees into Rosemary.

The night air is thick and sweet with jacaranda. The hot rush of the Santa Ana winds feels like a hair dryer aimed at her face. Her hands are scratched and bloody from the trellis thorns, but Rosemary barely notices. She drops from the trellis, excitement surging through her the moment her feet touch cement. She made it. The mansion glows pearly in the moonlight, a hulking monument to privilege and privacy. Inside, protected by their alarms and their security patrols, her parents sleep soundly, or at least as soundly as two paranoiacs ever can. But Rosemary is, for the night, free.

Around the block, a jet-black Corvette idles by the curb, its driver in shadow. Rosemary leaps in and favors him with a deep, long kiss.

Since when do you have a Corvette?

Since I found this little guy idling behind the In-N-Out, just begging for a new owner. Like a lost puppy, *Jack says.* I couldn't exactly say no, could I?

He hits the gas. They speed away, screech of the wheels tearing through the hushed silence of Beverly Hills.

He's lying about how he got the car, probably. He lies about everything, her Jack Crow. He's probably even lying about his name. She doesn't care. She's sixteen, she doesn't need to care, she just needs to see the world, the real *world, the Downworld, the world her parents are so obnoxiously determined to keep her away from, and he's happy to show her. He's only one year older than she, so he says, but he's already lived enough for twenty lives.*

They met at the beach. She was cutting school—she was, always, cutting school—looking for trouble, not realizing she was looking for him. He aimed her at a strolling couple, all golden hair and glowing tans like they'd stepped out of a catalog for L.A. living, had her ask them for directions, distract them while he lifted the purse. Not that he told her this was his plan. He told her nothing ahead of time, other than trust me, *and so she waited until they were alone, sharing a burrito bought with stolen coin, to ask why he wasn't more worried about stealing from the fey. It had not occurred to him that she had the Sight, that she could see truth beneath their glamour. She said,* What did you think, I was just some bored little rich girl? *He did. She informed him she* was *a bored little rich girl: bored because she could see how much more interesting the world could be. He said,* What do you think of me, that I'm just some cute bad boy you can use to piss off Mommy and Daddy? *She said,* If Mommy and Daddy knew you existed, they'd have you murdered. And no one said you were cute. *One truth and one lie: he is very, very cute,* swoop of dark hair over hooded brown eyes, knowing smile saved only for her, face like a stone, sharp in all the right places. It's true, if her parents knew about him, they would want him dead. Which was usually all it took. That first day, he took her to a Downworlder café in Venice. She has always had the Sight, and her father has it too, of course. But her parents have fought so hard to keep her away from Downworld, to stop her from knowing its delights and terrors. This is her first taste—literally, a sundae that, whatever the faeries had infused it with, tasted like summer sunlight. When she kissed him, he tasted like chocolate fudge.

Tonight he will finally, after weeks of pleading, bring her to the Shadow Market. She lives for these nights with him—not just because of him but because of the world he's opened to her.

He's right, though—also because she knows how much it would piss off her parents.

He makes her wait with the mergirls selling seaweed bracelets while he conducts his business, so she waits and watches and wonders at the magical chaos swirling around her. She's not so awestruck that she doesn't notice the hooded figure shadowing Jack, the werewolf with the handlebar mustache perking up as he passes by, the djinn who tenses at his approach and throws a glance to someone behind her, and she may not know Downworld but she has been taught since childhood to recognize danger, to sense the signs of enemies lying in wait. She has been schooled only in the hypotheticals of battle, learned to gauge, fight, strategize, flee, all in the cosseted comfort of her own home, and has always wondered whether practice could ever prepare her for reality, whether her training would evaporate in the face of terror. Now she has her answer: she knows an ambush when she sees one, and there is no hesitation about what to do next.

She screams. Drops to the ground. Clutches her ankle. Screams,

Jack, Jack, Jack, something bit me, I need you, *and like lightning he is at her side, a tenderness on his face she never knew was possible. He scoops her into his arms, murmurs assurances, until she whispers her warning in his ear,* ambush, *and they run.*

The Corvette is flanked by three werewolves. Jack shouts at her to run, save herself, as he launches himself into the fight, but she hasn't put in all those hours and years of training simply to run. It's different, fighting a real enemy—but not that different. She whirls and leaps, slips the dagger from her ankle holster, slashes and stabs, and she can feel the burn in her cheeks, the fire in her heart as the werewolves flee in defeat and she and Jack fling themselves into the Corvette, screech away, speed wildly into the hills and around the hairpin turns of Mulholland Drive, without speaking, without looking at each other, until he swerves hard onto a lookout point and the car squeals to a stop. Then he's staring at her. Let me guess, *she says,* I've never looked more beautiful. *She knows her cheeks are flushed, her face shining, her eyes sparkling. He says who cares how she looks.* It's the way you fought! The way you think! *He asks where she learned how to do what she did. She can't tell him why her parents have made certain that she knows how to defend herself, that she hasn't left the house without a weapon since she was five years old. She simply says there's a lot he doesn't know about her. He says he knows enough. He says,* I think I'm in love. *She whacks him, hard, tells him it's rude to say that as a joke, even to a girl like her, hard as* adamas. *He says,* What makes you think I'm joking?

Her parents want to move again.

She refuses. Not this time, not again.

They want to know if it's because of him, that guy, the one you sneak out with, *and she can't believe they know. They're having her* followed. *They are not sorry. They tell her she doesn't understand how dangerous the world is,* that world, the Downworld, *and she says that's because they won't let her. Sixteen years old and she's never lived anywhere longer than a year, because they never stop moving. When she was a child, she accepted their explanations, believed the nightmarish fairy tale of the monster lurking in the dark, longing to destroy them. But the monster has never shown itself, the danger has never manifested, and she has begun to wonder whether her parents are simply paranoid, whether running and hiding has become easier for them than staying still.*

It's not easy for her. She's never had a real friend, because she's forbidden from telling anyone who she actually is.

She is alone.

She has one thing: him. She will not let them take that away.

Her mother says, You're sixteen, you have plenty of time to fill your life with love, but only if we keep you alive long enough to do so. *She says she's already filled her life with love, she loves him, she's staying. Her father says,* You're too young to know what love is, *and she thinks about Jack, about the touch of his hand, the silent laughter in his crooked smile. She thinks about him holding an umbrella over her head to protect her from the rain, about him asking her to teach him to fight, so he can protect himself. She thinks about training him, how he loves that she's stronger, faster, better, and thinks about sitting with him, still and silent, watching the waves.*

She is young, but she knows. She loves him.

Her father says they are leaving in the morning, all of them, a family. He says no more sneaking out.

So she runs out the door in plain sight, openly defies her parents for the first time, and they are too slow, their warnings too familiar, to stop her. She leaves, with nowhere to go—Jack is taking care of some typically vague business somewhere vaguely downtown, and so she walks the deserted streets, skirting freeways, melting into the shadows of underpasses, murders the minutes until she can be sure her parents have gone to sleep. She knows exactly how to slip into the house without waking them, but there's no need.

The doors are flung wide open.

Her mother's body is in the grass, in pieces.

Her father's blood is pooling across the marble entryway. He is holding on for her. He says, They found us. He says, Promise me you'll disappear, and she promises and promises and promises but there's only his corpse to hear.

She flees without ID or credit card, nothing that could be used to trace her, not that the enemy uses technology to trace, but these things can never be counted on, and her parents are dead.

Her parents are dead.

Her parents are dead because she slowed them down, because they knew it was time to go and she insisted they stay, she fought, she complained, she sulked, they loved her and she held it against them and now they are dead.

She waits at Jack's favorite bar, the one by the Shadow Market that tries its best to look like it doesn't exist. She waits for him there, because he always comes back eventually, and when he does, alarmed to see her, and to see her covered with blood, she collapses in his arms.

Then she tells him the truth.

She tells him she is a Shadowhunter, by line if not by choice. She is fey, by spirit and blood if not by choice. She tells him she is hunted, she is dangerous to all those who love her, she is leaving forever. She tells him this is good-bye.

He doesn't understand. He wants to come with her. She tries again.

Tells him the Unseelie Court wants her dead, has sent an ancient group of faerie assassins with godlike powers to murder her. To let him stay with her would mean signing his death warrant. She tells him staying with her would mean giving up his identity, his city, his whole life. He says, You're supposed to be smart, but you don't get it. You are my life. You are my identity. I will not give you up. As for everything else? *He shrugs.* Who needs it?

*She laughs. She shakes with laughter. Cannot believe she's laughing. Then feels the wet on her cheek, feels him press her face to his chest, wrap his arms around her, realizes: she's not laughing, she's weeping. He promises he will always protect her. She says—out loud, for the first time in her life—*I am a Herondale. I'll protect you. *He says it's a deal.*

It doesn't feel like living on the run. It feels like stones skipping across a lake. They dip into a life, wherever they feel like it— Berlin, Tokyo, Rio, Reykjavik—they establish identities, connections to Downworld, and when Jack burns one too many bridges or Rosemary sniffs out a faerie or, that one time in Paris, they discover a Shadowhunter on their trail, they slough off their identities, change their names and faces, resurface elsewhere. They consider, sometimes, going underground, living as mundanes, but this was her parents' choice, and it proved a fatal one. They will be smarter, safer, and when they build new identities for themselves, they build a network of contacts to call on if the need comes. Contacts, but never allies, never friends, never anyone who would ask too many questions when they appear or disappear. No obligations, no ties, no roots. They need only each other—and then they have Christopher, and everything changes.

She insists on having the baby in secret. No one can know there's another link in this cursed chain. Even when she was pregnant, she realizes later, she understood at some level what she would have to do.

Once she has Christopher, she finally understands her parents, their lives consumed by fear. Not for themselves but for her. She refuses to impose that on her son. She wants a better life for him, something more than barbed wire and security alarms. She wants him to have a home. She wants him to know trust, to know love. She wants to save him from hiding.

Jack hates it. So you want to protect him from having to keep his secret by keeping it for him? You want to keep him from knowing he has a secret? And she says yes, exactly, and then he will grow up unafraid of the world.

Jack says growing up unafraid of the world is a good way to get destroyed by it.

She waits until the baby is old enough to eat solid food, old enough to survive without her, or—more to the point—that she can persuade herself he can survive without her. She doesn't know if she can survive without him, without either of them, but it's time.

She sends them away.

She is lying on the floor. She is dying. There are strangers here, but she is alone. She is hiding in the secret place in her mind where she keeps her memories of Jack and Christopher. She thinks, maybe she knew this was inevitable, why else return to L.A., where it would be so easy to find her?

She is so tired of being alone. She is tired of missing her son and her husband, tired of forcing herself not to look for them. At least in L.A., she can feel close to the past, to the family she's lost. This is the only city that's ever felt like home, because this was where she found her home in Jack's arms, and in her weakest moments, this is where she imagined a home for them, Rosemary and Jack and

Christopher, a family again, a fairy-tale life in the bungalow. She planted a garden she thought Christopher might like. She filled her days imagining them with her, and now, dying, she imagines them with her still.

Maybe she has won. Maybe Fal will believe the line has died with her, and Christopher can be safe. This is the relief in dying. This, and knowing that if she's wrong, if she's failed, she will be saved having to watch him suffer. She will never watch him die because of who his mother is. This is her last thought, as the pain carries her into darkness. She will never have to know a world without Christopher—

And then she is Tessa again, and she is at Will's side, and Jem is there, and Will is slipping away, and she is trying to fathom how she will face a world without him.

And then Tessa is on a bridge, the Thames beneath her, a miracle beside her. Love reawakened, love returned. Jem, her own true, real, flesh-and-blood James Carstairs, returned to her from silence and stone, and Tessa, whose heart has remained so full through the years and years of empty days, is finally no longer alone.

And then she is standing by a great sea, mountains looming against a crystalline sky. The waves crash loud and sure against the beach, and Jem is beside her, his face as beautiful as the sea. She knows this moment has never been, yet here they are, together. I can't believe this is real, *she says*, that you're here with me.

Come back to me, *Jem says.*

But she is right here, with him.

Stay with me, *Jem says. Please.*

But where would she go?

He's aging, right in front of her, skin sagging, hair graying, flesh withering from the bones, and she knows, she's losing him, she will watch him die as she watches everyone die, she will have to learn all over again to survive in a world without love.

He says, Please, Tessa, I love you.

He is crumbling before her eyes, and she thinks of Rosemary, enduring so many years without the ones she loved most—knowing that her family lived, but could not be with her—and she is grateful, because Jem is here. Now. That's enough, she says to Jem. We have right now. We have each other.

Jem says, Please, Tessa, stay with me, I love you, *and she holds on to him, will keep holding, for as long as she can, unafraid of—*

—Tessa woke to find Jem by her side, his hand warm in hers, his eyes closed, his voice low, urgent, chanting, "Stay with me, I love you, stay with me—"

"Where would I go?" she said weakly, and, as his gaze met hers, his face broke into the most beautiful smile she'd ever seen.

Everything hurt, but the pain was a welcome reminder of life. Jem's lips were impossibly soft against hers, as if he was afraid she would break. Tessa didn't recognize the room she was lying in, but she recognized the hooded figure who glided into the room upon Jem's frantic call. "Brother Enoch," she said warmly. "It's been some time."

He has been very worried about you, the Silent Brother said in her mind.

Tessa's fever dreams were already fading, but she felt like she was vibrating with love—and despair. She understood the panicked relief in Jem's eyes, because she had lived inside her own terror, watched him die again and again, and even now, awake, the dreams felt too solid, too much like memory.

She felt the traces of Rosemary in her mind, those last desperate seconds of life giving way to death, almost willingly, and understood: it was easier to die protecting the people you loved than to watch them die in your stead. What horrific choices mortality had to offer.

That was the devil's bargain of Jem's return, the truth she had tried to escape. He could live for centuries, but never truly live—never love—or she could have him back, fully alive and fully *mortal*, inevitably to lose him for good. It hadn't been her choice to make, of course. But Jem had chosen her. She could never regret this.

The Silent Brother asked Jem to step outside and leave them in privacy for a moment, and Jem, laying a final kiss on her forehead, took his leave. Tessa propped herself up in bed, her strength already returning.

Do you remember what happened? Brother Enoch asked.

"I remember that Fal attacked, and then . . . there were so many dreams, and they were so vivid. And . . ." Tessa closed her eyes, trying to retrieve the details of the strange lives she'd lived in her head. "They weren't all mine."

You were trapped for several days inside the Change, Brother Enoch said.

"How could that happen?" Tessa asked in alarm. When she'd first experimented with her powers, there was always fear attached to the transformation. To let herself sink so fully into another person's body and mind was to risk losing herself. It had taken much time and will to make herself trust the Change, trust that no matter how many forms she forced herself into, she remained, indelibly, Tessa Gray. If that faith was misplaced, then how could she ever risk Changing again? "Was it something about the weapon?"

It was not the weapon that caused this.

The cause is in you.

"You sure you're up to this?" Jem asked as he and Tessa approached the L.A. Shadow Market.

"For the hundredth time, yes." She spun around in a very un-Tessa-like pirouette, and Jem smiled, doing his best to disguise his worry. Brother Enoch had given her a clean bill of health, but she was trying too hard to seem like everything was well. And the harder she tried, the more Jem suspected that it was not.

He trusted Tessa, to the ends of the earth. If there was something wrong, she would tell him when she was ready. In the meantime, though, he would worry.

"We've wasted enough time," Tessa said. "Rosemary's counting on us to find her son."

It turned out Jem had been right that something the bartender said tipped off Tessa about how to find Christopher Herondale's father, the man once known as Jack Crow. *He's exactly the same bird he used to be, just a little less of a crook.*

"It's a riddle," Tessa had explained, once she shook off the haze of her fever dreams. "And not even a particularly good one. What's another word for 'crow' . . . that's just a *little less* than a crook?"

"A *rook*," Jem had realized quickly. It gave them, at least, a question to ask—and, given Jack Crow's proclivity for shady Downworlders and small-time crime, the L.A. Shadow Market seemed the obvious place to ask it. Even in the middle of the night and miles in from the coast, the Market smelled like sunshine and ocean. It was crowded, that night, with sun-tanned witches selling enchanted hemp bracelets, werewolves peddling elaborate wrought-iron mounting equipment that attached weapons to luxury cars, and booth after booth of artisanal, organic juices, all of which seemed to feature some combination of ancient mystical potion and banana.

"Guaranteed to boost muscles, manhood, and personal magnetism by two hundred percent?" Tessa read skeptically as they walked past a warlock juicer.

"Also an excellent source of vitamin C," Jem noted, laughing.

They were both trying so hard to seem normal.

It didn't take very long to find someone who'd heard of a petty criminal by the name of Rook.

"You looking for *Johnny* Rook?" a grizzled werewolf asked, then spit on the ground. Rook apparently had his own booth in the Market but hadn't been seen that night. "You tell him Cassius says hello, and that if he ever tries to scam me again, I'll happily rip his face off with my teeth."

"We'll do that," Tessa said.

They got a similar answer from everyone they spoke to— "Johnny Rook," it seemed, had torn a swath of bad will through the entire L.A. Downworlder community. "It's amazing he still *has* a face to rip off," Tessa observed, after a pretty, young witch explained in great detail the way she would go about disfiguring him if she ever got her long-awaited chance.

"He's not very good at this hiding-out thing, is he?" Jem said.

"I don't think he wants to be very good," Tessa said, with the faraway look she sometimes got when she was hearing some-one else's inner voice. "After all this time, all these identities, he comes back home, makes a name for himself at the Shadow

Market—a name painfully close to the one Rosemary knew him by? He wanted her to come find him."

"She came back to L.A. too. Maybe she wanted the same thing."

Tessa sighed, and neither of them said the obvious, that if they'd only loved each other a little less, Rosemary might still be alive, and her son might have a better chance of staying that way.

They roamed the Market—no one knew where to find Johnny Rook that night, and most seemed delighted by the prospect that he might have disappeared forever. Tessa and Jem heard about Johnny's bad attitude, bad business practices, badly fitting trench coat, bad habit of feeding information to whoever asked for it, including—the vampire complaining about this had paused here to aim a murderous look at Jem— filthy Shadowhunters. Until finally, as the sun was rising and the last vendors were departing, they heard something they could use: an address.

Once again, the traffic was terrible. Tessa and Jem finally arrived at the right neighborhood, only to find themselves circling the shady streets for an alarmingly long period of time, unable to locate Rook's house. Tessa eventually realized this was due to unraveling misdirection spells that surrounded their destination, the magic flickering through a few last bursts of power as it faded. *Why unraveling?* Tessa wondered with a sense of dread. At least the deterioration of the spell meant they'd be able to find Rosemary's husband and son.

But they were not the only ones looking. They arrived, again, too late. The house was a ruin of blood and ichor, Mantid demons wreaking bloody destruction in desperate battle with—Tessa's eyes widened—*Emma Carstairs?* There was no time to ask questions, not with the insectoid demons swarming angrily in search of warm-blooded prey. The Riders of Mannan would never have sent demons to do this job, but after what Tessa had learned about Rook, she supposed it was no surprise he had more than one enemy to worry about. Though perhaps his worries were at an end: the ruined body lying in a pool of blood was surely Johnny Rook's. As she launched into action, slicing a razored foreleg, spearing a bulging eyestalk—she spared a moment of sorrow for Rosemary, who had died so desperately hoping that her husband would live.

But all was not lost. Because there, miraculously alive despite the swarm of ravening Mantids, was the treasure Rosemary had sacrificed everything to protect: her son. He was crouched against the wall. As Emma and Jem waged fierce battle against the remaining demons, Tessa approached the boy. She thought she would have recognized him anywhere—not just from Rosemary's memories of her child as a toddler, but from Tessa's own memories of her children and grandchildren, her memories of Will. The determination in his blue eyes, the fierce, graceful way he held himself in the face of danger—there was no doubt, this was a Herondale.

She introduced herself. He said nothing. He was so young, and trying so hard to look brave. She honored this effort, speaking to him as a man, rather than a child needing her care. "Get up, Christopher."

He didn't move, his gaze straying toward—then quickly away from—the body. The boy's jeans were coated in blood, and Tessa wondered if it belonged to his father.

"My father. He . . ." His voice trembled.

"You must grieve later," Tessa told him. He was, by blood if not by training, a warrior. She knew his strength better than he knew it himself. "Right now you are in great danger. More of those things may come, and worse things as well."

"Are you a Shadowhunter?"

She flinched at the disgust in his voice.

"I am not," she said. "But—" Rosemary had tried so hard to keep this from him. Had sacrificed everything so he could live in ignorance of the darkness surrounding him. That life was over now, that lie was dead, and Tessa would be the one to deal it the final, fatal blow. "But you are."

The boy's eyes widened. She extended a hand. "Come now. On your feet, Christopher Herondale. We've been looking for you a long time."

Jem gazed out at a picture-perfect landscape—white crests on a sun-dappled sea, the peaks of the palisades poking at a storybook blue sky, and beside him, Tessa Gray, the love of his many lifetimes—and tried to ascertain why he felt so uneasy. Christopher Herondale, or Kit, as he preferred to be called, was safely under the protection of the L.A. Institute. Jem and Tessa hadn't failed Rosemary, not entirely—they'd lost her but saved her son. Returned a lost Herondale to the Shadowhunter world, where, hopefully, he would find a new home. He and Tessa would soon part—she'd been summoned to the Spiral Labyrinth to look into some troubling reports of illness in the warlock community, while Jem went in search of Malcolm Fade's body and the Black Volume of the Dead. He had a feeling that what Fade had begun here in Los Angeles was only the beginning of a graver danger. All of these were ample reasons to feel uneasy, but that wasn't it.

It was Tessa, who was still holding herself at some remove from him, as if there was something she couldn't bear for him to know.

"This place," Tessa said, sounding troubled. Jem put an arm around her shoulders, held her close. These felt like stolen moments together, before they turned to their respective missions. He breathed her in, trying to memorize the feel of her, already preparing for her absence. "There's something so familiar about it," Tessa said.

"But you've never been here before?" he asked.

She shook her head. "No, it's . . . it's more like something I saw in a dream."

"Was I there with you?"

Tess's smile had an unmistakable trace of sorrow. "You're always in my dreams."

"What's wrong?" Jem said. "Is it Rosemary? I can't help but feel her death is on my shoulders."

"No!" Tessa insisted. "We did everything we could for her. We're still doing everything we can—Kit is safe, for the moment, and hopefully the Riders of Mannan still have no idea he exists. Maybe the Unseelie Court will consider their job done."

"Maybe," Jem said dubiously. They both knew it was unlikely to end here, but at least they'd bought Kit some time. "I wish we could do more for him. No child should have to see his father murdered."

Tessa took his hand. She knew exactly what Jem was thinking about—not just all the orphans scattered through the Shadowhunter world who'd watched their parents cut down in the Dark War, but his own parents, tortured and killed before his eyes. Jem had told no one but Tessa and Will the full horror he'd endured at the hands of that demon, and telling the story even once was almost more than he could stand.

"He's in good hands," Tessa assured him. "He's got a Carstairs by his side. Emma will help him find a new family, as we did with Charlotte, Henry, and Will."

"And each other," Jem said.

"And each other."

"It won't be a replacement for what he's lost, though."

"No. But you can never replace what you've lost, can you?" Tessa said. "You can only find new love to fill the void left behind."

As always, the memory of Will sat between them, his absence a presence.

"We both learned that lesson too young," Jem said, "but I suppose everyone learns it eventually. Loss is what it means to be human."

Tessa started to say something—then burst into tears. Jem wrapped his arms around her, holding her tight against the racking sobs. Smoothed her hair, rubbed her back, waited for the storm to pass. Her pain was his pain, even when he didn't understand its source. "I'm here," he whispered. "I'm with you."

Tessa took a deep, shuddering breath, then met his gaze.

"What is it?" he asked. "You can tell me anything."

"It's . . . it's you." She touched his face gently. "You're with me now, but you won't always be. That's what it means to be human, like you said. Eventually I'll lose you. Because you're mortal, and I'm . . . me."

"Tessa . . ." There were no words to say what he needed to

say, that his love for her stretched beyond time, beyond death, that he had spent too much time these last few days imagining his own world without her, that even unfathomable loss could be survived, that they would love each other for as long as they could—so instead, he held her tight, let her feel his arms sturdy and sure around her, physical evidence: *I am here.*

"Why now?" he asked gently. "Is it something Brother Enoch said?"

"Maybe I didn't realize how much I'd shut myself away from humanity all those years in the Spiral Labyrinth," she admitted. "You fought in the War, you saw so much violence, so much death, but I was hiding—"

"You were fighting," Jem corrected her. "In your way, which was as essential as mine."

"I was fighting. But I was also hiding. I didn't want to be fully in the world until you could be there too. And now, I suppose, I'm waking up to being fully human again. Which is terrifying, especially now."

"Tessa, why *now*?" he said again, alarm growing. What could Brother Enoch have told her to send her into this kind of spiraling panic?

Tessa took his palm and pressed it flat against her stomach. "The reason I had so much trouble Changing back to myself is that I'm not *only* myself right now."

"You mean . . . ?" He was almost afraid to hope.

"I'm pregnant."

"Really?" He felt like a live wire, the idea of it, a *baby*, lighting his synapses on fire. He had never let himself hope for this, because he knew better than anyone how difficult it had been for Tessa, watching her children age as she did not. She had been a wonderful mother, she had loved being a mother, but he knew what it had cost her. He'd always assumed she would never want to endure that again.

"Really. Diapers, strollers, playdates with Magnus and Alec, assuming we can persuade Magnus to wait a few years before he starts training our child to blow things up, the whole nine yards. So . . . what do you think?"

Jem felt like his heart would burst. "I'm happy. I'm—'happy' doesn't even begin to cover it. But you . . ." He examined her expression carefully. He knew her face better than his own, could read it like one of Tessa's beloved books, and he read now: terror, longing, sorrow, and most of all, joy. "You're happy too?"

"I didn't think I could ever feel this way again," Tessa said. "There was a time when I thought there was no more joy left to me. And now . . ." Her smile blazed like the sun. "Why do you look so surprised?"

He didn't know how to say it without hurting her, making the pain fresh again by reminding her of her loss—but of course, she could read his face just as well as he could read hers. "Yes," said Tessa. "I might lose them someday. As I'll lose you. I can't bear the thought of it."

"Tessa—"

"But we bear so much that seems unthinkable. The only truly unbearable burden is living without love. You taught me that." She laced her fingers through his, squeezed tight. She was so unimaginably strong. "You and Will."

Jem cupped her face in his hands, felt her skin warm against his palms, and felt grateful all over again for the life that had been returned to him. "We're having a child?"

Tessa's eyes shone. The tears had stopped, and in their wake was a look of fierce determination. Jem knew what it had cost her to lose Will, then to lose the family she'd built with him. Jem had lost a piece of himself when his *parabatai* died; Will's absence had left behind a void that nothing could fill. There was, all these years later, still pain. But the pain was evidence of love, was a reminder of Will.

It was easier not to feel. It was safer not to love. It was possible to make oneself silent and still as stone, to wall oneself off from the world and its losses, to empty one's heart. It was possible, but it was not human.

It was not worth losing the chance to love. He had learned this from the Silent Brotherhood and, before that, from Tessa. And before that, of course, from Will. They had both tried so hard to hide from the pain of future loss, to stay solitary, safe from the dangers of connection. They had failed so beautifully.

"We're having a child," Tessa echoed him. "I hope you're ready to give up sleep for a few years."

"Fortunately, I've got plenty of practice at that," he reminded her. "Less so when it comes to diapers."

"I hear they're much improved since the last time I needed them," Tessa said. "We'll have to figure it out together. All of it."

"You're sure?" Jem said. "You want to take all this on yourself again?"

She smiled like Raphael's Madonna. "The nappies, the sleepless nights, the endless crying, the love like you've never imagined was possible, like your heart is living on the outside of your body? The chaos and the fear and the pride and the chance to tuck someone in and read them to sleep? To do all of that with you? I couldn't be more sure."

He took her in his arms then, imagining the life growing

inside of her and the future they would have together, a family, more love to fill the absences left by those they'd lost, more love than either of them had ever imagined still possible. The future was so precarious, shadowed by a looming danger neither of them fully understood, and Jem wondered what kind of world his child would be born into. He thought of all the blood that had been shed these last few years, the growing sense among the Shadowhunters he knew that something dark was rising, that this Cold Peace after the war might be only the eerie calm at the eye of the hurricane, those still, silent moments in which it was possible to deceive yourself into imagining the worst was over.

He and Tessa had been alive too long to deceive themselves, and he thought about what might happen to a child born at the eye of such a storm. He thought about Tessa, her will and her strength, her refusal to let loss after loss harden her against love, her refusal to hide any longer from the brutality of the mortal world, her determination to fight, to hold on.

She too had been a child born of storms, he thought, as had he, as had Will. All three had risen in love through their struggles to find happiness—and without the struggle, would the happiness have been so great?

He closed his eyes and pressed a kiss to Tessa's hair. Behind his lids, he did not see darkness but the light of a London morning and Will there, smiling at him. *A new soul made of you and Tessa*, Will said. *I can hardly wait to meet such a paragon.*

"Do you see him too?" Tessa whispered.

"I see him," Jem said, and he held her even more tightly against him, the new life they had created together between them.

The Lost World

By Cassandra Clare and Kelly Link

The world and everything in it had changed . . . people passed me as I sat—people who laughed and joked and gossiped. It seemed to me that I watched them almost as a dead man might watch the living.
—Arthur Conan Doyle, *The Fate of the Evangelion*

2013

"So you didn't sense any kind of demonic energy or other kind of supernatural emanation from the tarn?" Ty asked.

It was March, and outside the Scholomance the world was wintry white, as if all the Carpathian Mountains were in mourning. Ty was writing at his desk, in the black notebook where for six months he had been keeping a record of the side effects, benefits, and discoverable qualities of Livvy's resurrected state.

Early entries ran along the lines of *Incorporeal. Invisible to all with some exceptions. Some animals appear to sense her. Most cats, for example, though cannot entirely be sure since cats do not talk. Can, with some effort, make herself invisible to me. Have asked her not to do this. Find it worrying. Does not sleep. Does not need food. Says she believes it is possible she can taste things that I (Ty) eat. Will test this—Livvy wait in other room while I taste various foods—but not the most pressing of experiments, and there is the question of whether or not this is entirely related to Livvy's current state or whether it is due to being twins or the undeniable fact that I have made all of this happen. Magnus says there is very little reliable information. Sense of smell unimpaired. Tested her on clean and dirty socks as well as various herbs. Insensible to extremes of heat or cold. Says that she is happy to be here with me. Says that she loves me and wishes to stay with me. Proof, can we assume, that some things (some emotions or relationships) survive the grave?*

"No?" Livvy said. Often, while Ty wrote, she hovered at his shoulder, to see what he wrote down and to qualify his notes with her own observations. But at the moment, she was more interested in something she had discovered carved into the wall just below the headboard of Ty's bed. If she made an effort, she could push herself through the wooden headboard, just like a ghost in one of Dru's movies, who could walk through walls. How she would have liked to show off this ability to her sister—but she and Ty had agreed that she should not manifest in front of the rest of their family.

Behind the headboard of Ty's dorm-issue bed, the tops of letters just faintly visible, someone had gouged a rough sentence into the wall, and a date. "'I did not choose this life,'" Livvy said out loud.

"What?" Ty said, sounding startled.

"Oh," Livvy said hastily. "That's not an observation, Ty. It's something that someone carved here on the wall. There's a year, too. '1904.' But no name.'"

Ty had been at the Scholomance for four months now. And where Ty went, Livvy went too. Four months at the Scholomance, and six months since Livvy had come back as a ghost when the catalyst Ty was using in his attempt to resurrect her had failed him, and the spell from the Black Volume of the Dead had gone awry. At first Livvy had not been entirely herself. There were pages in Ty's notebook about the gaps in her memory, the ways in which she did not seem to be the same person. But, gradually, she had come back to herself. Ty had written in his notebook: *Jet lag, when one travels between coasts or countries and experiences a change in time zones, is part of the human condition. It is possible that Livvy is experiencing some version of this. A writer once called Death "that unknown country." Presumably Livvy had to travel, at least psychically, quite far to come back to me.*

All in all, the last few months had been a time of great and alarming changes—Livvy's ghostly return from the dead had been neither the greatest nor the most alarming. The Cohort and their supporters were now shut off in Idris, while supporters of the Clave had been exiled to all the corners of the globe. No one could get into Idris and none could get out. "What do you think they're eating?" Ty had asked Livvy. "Each other, hopefully," Livvy replied. "Or zucchini. Lots of zucchini." She felt sure that no one honestly enjoyed zucchini.

The Scholomance, too, had changed. Historically it was the institution where Centurions were trained, and Livvy had heard the Centurions who descended on the L.A. Institute speak of the place. It had become a recruiting ground for the Cohort, and it had sounded thoroughly horrible. Those Cohort sympathizers were now in Idris, and that was no great loss as far as Livvy could see. Every member of the Cohort she had ever met had been a bully, a bigot, or a petty-minded bootlicker. The zucchini of the Shadowhunter world. Who missed them? The real problem now was not that they were gone but that they were not gone enough. There they were, lurking inside the wards of Idris, planning and plotting only the Angel knew what.

Some of the Scholomance's instructors had gone to Idris with the Centurions, and now Jia Penhallow, the former Consul, was in charge here. She'd decided to step down as Consul so that she could have time to rest, but once her health improved, she wanted something useful to do. Her husband, Patrick, was with her, and Ragnor Fell had stepped in too, to teach and offer guidance. Catarina Loss was a frequent presence as well. She spent more time at the new Academy on Luke Garroway's farm in upstate New York, but she would stop by the Scholomance now and then to restock the infirmary or heal unusual magical maladies.

There were other changes. Kit had gone off to live with Jem and Tessa, while Helen and Aline were now ensconced at the Los Angeles Institute. Livvy wished with all of her ghostly heart that she and Ty could have stayed in Los Angeles, but Ty had been adamant. Going off to the Scholomance was the penance he must endure for his great crime—the great crime of attempting to bring Livvy back. Not very flattering, Livvy thought, to now be the ghostly albatross that Ty wore around his neck, but better a ghostly albatross than simply a dead sister.

Ty said, "No one chooses this life." He had put down his pen.

He sounded as if he were somewhere far away. Livvy didn't think he was talking about the Scholomance.

She said hastily, "I saw animal tracks around Dimmet Tarn. It isn't fully iced over—I heard some of the other students say that this year is warmer than any on record. Can you imagine more snow than we've had? It looks as if animals come down to drink from Dimmet Tarn. I wonder what they are."

"A Carpathian lynx, perhaps," Ty said. "They are supposed to haunt the area."

"Same," Livvy said. But Ty didn't laugh at her joke.

He said, "You were away for nearly three hours. I noted it

in the book. I felt as if some part of me was falling asleep. Pins and needles."

Livvy said, "I felt it too. Like a rubber band being stretched."

The past week, when Ty was not in classes, they had been experimenting with timed intervals in which Livvy moved progressively farther and farther away from Ty. Dimmet Tarn was only just past the Scholomance, less than a quarter of a mile away from Ty's room, but it was the farthest Livvy had ventured. She'd hovered over the surface of the water for so long she had almost begun to feel hypnotized by the unmoving black stillness beneath her. She had been able to see the reflection of leafless trees on the tarn, but no matter how close she pressed her face to the flat inky surface of the water, she had not been able to see herself. She could see her hand if she held it out, but not the reflection of her hand, and that had made her feel very strange. So instead she looked only at the water and tried to let go of all her unhappinesses and worries. The only thing to hold on to was Ty.

So eventually she had withdrawn her attention from Dimmet Tarn and she had come back to him. She said, "I would have liked to see a Carpathian lynx."

"They're endangered," Ty said. "And very shy."

"And I am very invisible," Livvy said. "So I feel my chances are quite good. But please mark down that Dimmet Tarn is quite an ordinary tarn. Those old stories, I think, must be only that. Stories."

"Further investigation required, let us say," Ty said. "I will continue to do research in the library."

They had picked Dimmet Tarn as a destination for Livvy not only because the distance was a useful measure but because there were lots of interesting stories about Dimmet Tarn among the other students at the Scholomance. It had once been a place of great uncanniness, supposedly, but none of the stories were in agreement as to the nature of its uncanniness. Some stories said that it was once a place beloved of the faeries. Others said that there was a great clutch of demonic eggs far down at the bottom of the tarn, so deep down that no sounding rope could give a true measure. Another story said that an unhappy warlock had enchanted the water so that to swim in it would curse the swimmer with a toe fungus that eventually hatched miniature blue and green toadstools, which sounded improbable, but then warlocks were often improbably petty. It was one of the potential side effects of immortality. You got very bad at letting go of things.

"Did you try to submerge yourself?" Ty asked.

"Yes," Livvy said. Much like pushing through a headboard, she had been able to push herself down into the water. It had been nothing like swimming had been back in Los Angeles, where the water was green or blue or gray, depending on the time of day and whether the sun was shining, and all the waves wore a cap of white froth and came rushing up noisily on the wet sand. Dimmet Tarn was black, utterly black, as black as night but without stars or moon or the promise that dawn would ever come. Black as tar, black as—nothingness.

Livvy had not felt the water of Dimmet Tarn, but she had sunk into it all the same, slowly, until her head was beneath the surface, darkness below her, the suggestion of the winter sky above shrinking until it was gone altogether and she saw and felt nothing. She had sunk down and down into that void, that blackness, that nothingness, until it was not clear to her whether she was still sinking at all. Nothingness was all around her. Only that strand that connected her to Ty remained, as thin as it could be and yet stronger than the strongest metal.

She and Ty had theorized that perhaps since she was now, as a ghost, uncanny herself, she might be able to discover the secret of Dimmet Tarn. Livvy had liked the idea she might have a superpower of some kind, be useful in some way, and Ty liked the idea that there might be a local mystery that they could solve. But if Dimmet Tarn was keeping an occult secret, Livvy had not discovered it.

"They're going to ring the bell for dinner soon," Livvy said.

"I hope it's not olive loaf," Ty said.

"It is," Livvy said. "Can't you smell it?"

"Ugh," Ty said. He put down the black notebook and picked up the red one in which he kept his timetables. He flipped back a page and said, "That's three times in four weeks."

Livvy had worried about what it would be like for her brother, to be so far away from home, but Ty had adapted surprisingly well. He'd drawn up a schedule for himself on the first night, and he followed it faithfully. He laid out his clothes each night for the following morning, and before he fell asleep he checked his alarm clock against the watch he wore around his wrist. Ty kept one of Julian's old empty lighters in the pocket of his jeans, for when he needed to keep his fingers busy, and he wore his headphones around his neck during classes like a kind of talisman.

After he'd failed to resurrect Livvy from the dead, Ty had thrown his phone into the Pacific Ocean so he wouldn't be tempted to try other spells from the Black Volume. He had a new phone now, but he hadn't uploaded his photos. More penance, Livvy thought, although Ty hadn't said so. Instead, he had a triptych of paintings by Julian on the wall above his desk: one of their parents, one of all the Blackthorn siblings and Diana and Emma, with the ocean behind them. The third painting was of Livvy, and Livvy often found herself staring at it so that she wouldn't forget her own face. Not being able to see yourself in a mirror was not a big deal, compared to other parts of being dead, but all the same it was not very pleasant.

Ty wrote a letter to Julian every week, and he wrote Dru and Mark and Diana and Tavvy and Helen postcards, but Livvy couldn't help but notice that he never wrote Kit at all. She knew Kit had been angry at Ty for trying the resurrection spell, but surely Kit had gotten over that by now? If she brought up Kit, though, Ty shrugged and put his headphones on.

In general, though, Ty seemed to be fitting in just fine at the Scholomance. Better than Livvy would have imagined, before her death, had she imagined such a thing. Ty hadn't made any friends, but he managed everything that the instructors asked of him, and if he was mostly quiet or withdrawn otherwise, no one seemed to think that was strange. There were a lot of Shadowhunter kids at the Scholomance now who were worried or afraid or occasionally went off to cry in a corner. Ty was keeping his head down. No one except for Livvy, and maybe Julian, would have known there was something wrong.

But there was something wrong. And Livvy had no idea how to fix it, especially since she had no idea what was wrong. All she could do was be there. She had promised him that she would always be there. He had saved her from death, and she loved him.

Anyway, she didn't have anywhere else to be.

Sometimes, while Ty was studying or sleeping, she went exploring. To the library, where the great silvery tree grew through the broken ceiling like a promise that no wall or hardship (or promise) endured forever.

Sometimes she lingered by a student reading by themselves in the library, or perched on a window ledge, looking out at Dimmet Tarn. She would press all her attention upon them, testing them, to see if she could make herself known. "Can you see me? Can you see me?"

But no one saw her. Once, late at night, Livvy came across two girls kissing in an alcove, one with curly black hair and the other fair. They were only a year or two older than she, and Livvy wondered if this was their first kiss. The fair-headed one drew back at last and said, "It's late. I should get back to my room. Books aren't going to read themselves."

The curly-haired girl sighed but said, "Okay, but that's true of kisses, too. I'm not going to make out with myself."

The other said, "Good point."

But this time the curly-haired girl was the one who broke away from the embrace, laughing. She said, "Okay, okay. It's late and you've got the kissing thing down. Top marks. And there'll be time for more kissing later. So much time for so much kissing. Go read your books. See you at practice tomorrow?"

"Sure," the fair-haired girl said, and ducked her head, blushing. Livvy trailed her all the way back to her room. "Can you see me? Can't you see?" she demanded. "Life is short! Oh, can't you see? There's less time than you think, and then it's gone."

Sometimes Livvy wondered if she was going crazy. But it was easier in the day, when Ty was awake. Then she wasn't so alone.

After dinner, which was indeed olive loaf, while he was getting ready for bed, Ty said, "Everyone keeps talking about Idris. About what might be going on in there."

"Jerks being jerks is what's going on there," Livvy said.

"No one can get in because of the wards," Ty said. "But I was listening to them and I had an idea. No one can get in, but what if *you* could get in?"

"Me?" Livvy said.

"You," Ty said. "Why not? You can pass through all sorts of things. Walls. Doors. We could at least test it."

"Well," Livvy began, and then was silent. A feeling came over her, and she realized that the feeling was excitement.

She grinned back at her twin. "You're right," she said. "We should at least test it."

"Tomorrow, after Volcanoes and the Demons that Dwell in Them," Ty said. He made a note in his schedule.

But that night, while Ty was sleeping, Livvy found herself pulled toward Dimmet Tarn again, toward the nothingness of its depths. Every time she thought of Idris, and the experiment that she and Ty would try tomorrow, she thought of her own death, of the blow that Annabel had struck. That moment of pain and dislocation. The stricken look on Julian's face as she fled her body.

Of course Annabel wasn't in Idris now. Annabel was dead. And of course, even if Annabel had still been alive, Livvy shouldn't be afraid of her murderer. A Shadowhunter shouldn't be afraid. But the thought of her own body on the cold stone of the Accords Hall, the thought of her body burnt upon a pyre, the thought of Lake Lyn, where she had returned, all of these pursued her as she sank into the blackness of Dimmet Tarn and let its nothingness hide her.

It was almost morning when at last she rose up, pearly light already sliding over the crust of snow around the tarn. And there, too, on the lip of the tarn was a small crumpled heap as if someone had dropped their hat or scarf.

Livvy drew near and saw that it was a kitten, starved and motionless. Its paws were torn by the ice, and there were marks of bright blood in the snow. Its ears were long, tipped in black, and its coat was spotted with black as well. "You poor thing," Livvy said, and the kitten opened its eyes. It looked right at Livvy and snarled noiselessly. Then its eyes closed again.

Livvy fled back to the Scholomance, to Ty.

"Wake up, Ty!" she said. "Hurry, wake up, wake up!"

Ty sat bolt upright. "What is it? What's wrong?"

"There's a Carpathian lynx down by Dimmet Tarn," Livvy said. "A kitten. I think it's dying. Hurry, Ty."

He threw a coat over his pajamas and pulled on his boots. He bundled up a blanket in his arms. "Show me," he said.

The kitten was still alive when they got back to Dimmet Tarn, Ty's boots breaking through the snow with each step. He sank, sometimes, to his knees. But Livvy, of course, floated above the snow. There were advantages, sometimes, to being dead. Livvy could admit that.

You could see the small rise and fall of the lynx's chest. Small wisps of breath rose from its black nose.

"Is it going to be okay?" Livvy asked. "Will it live?"

Ty knelt down in the bank of snow beside the lynx. He began to wrap it in the blanket. "I don't know," he said. "But if it lives, it will be because you saved it, Livvy."

"No," Livvy said. "I found it. But I can't save it. You'll have to be the one who saves it."

"Then we'll both have saved it," Ty said, and smiled at her. If Livvy had had a notebook, she would have written it down. It had been a long time since she'd seen her brother smile.

Ty found a box and put an old sweater in it. From the kitchen he got a plate of chicken casserole and a bowl to fill with water. When the lynx wouldn't eat or drink, he went to the infirmary and asked Catarina Loss what to do.

"She says to moisten a piece of cloth—a T-shirt, maybe? Or a hand towel?—and then drip water into its mouth."

"Then do it," Livvy said anxiously. How useless she felt!

"Catarina gave me a hot water bottle too," Ty said. He reached into the box and unwrapped the bundle of blanket enough to put the hot water bottle in as well. Then he began to drip water onto the lynx's mouth until the fur was wet all around its face.

Ty was more patient than Livvy thought she could have been. He dipped the smallest section of T-shirt sleeve into a bowl of water and then wrung it out gently, until the animal's mouth opened and a pink tongue poked out. Ty dripped water onto the tongue, and when the lynx swallowed it, he picked up the bowl and tipped it slowly so that the lynx could drink without moving its head. After that, he tore the chicken into small pieces and fed the pieces to it. The lynx ate ravenously, making small, angry noises.

At last the chicken was gone. "Go get more," Livvy said.

Ty said, "No. Catarina said not to let it eat too much at first." He tucked a towel in around the lynx, and then covered over the box with a jacket. "We'll let it sleep now. I'll give it more later."

"What about a name? Are you going to give it a name?"

Ty scratched his head. Livvy saw, with a pang, that he had the faintest beginnings of a beard on his face. But he, of course, would continue to grow older. One day he would be a man, but she would always be a child. Ty said, gaze fixed on one black-tipped ear, all that was visible of the lynx, "But we don't know if it's a boy or a girl."

"Then we can give it a gender-neutral name," Livvy said. "Like Stripes or Hero or Commander Kitty."

"Let's see if it lives first," Ty said. By mutual agreement, they put off the plan to test Livvy's capabilities to bypass the boundaries of Idris until the next day. Ty attended his classes, and Livvy watched over the lynx, and in between Ty's classes he supplied their ever more lively captive with scraps of food and bowls of milk. By the time the dinner bells were ringing, they had ascertained the lynx's gender and Ty's arms were bloody with scratches. But the lynx was asleep and purring in his lap.

There was a makeshift litter box in the closet, and as it turned out, Ty's fidget toys also made excellent cat toys.

"Irene," Ty said. Once again, Livvy saw, he was smiling. "Let's call her Irene."

In the end, he skipped dinner altogether. And that night, Livvy did not go back to Dimmet Tarn. Instead she watched over her brother, Irene curled around his head on the pillow, her glowing eyes closing and opening, always fixed on Livvy.

There was a new note in Ty's book. It said, *Lynx sees her. Is this because the Lynx (have given her a name, Irene) was close to death? Or because she is a cat, though larger than house cats? Inconclusive. More research needed, though large cats may be hard to come by.*

✻ ✻ ✻

If it hadn't been for the matter of Idris, Livvy could have spent the whole next day playing with Irene. She and Ty had discovered that if Livvy drew her foot along the ground, back and forth, Irene would try to pounce, over and over. She could not understand why she couldn't catch Livvy. "Like a laser pointer," Ty said. "You're the red dot that always escapes."

"That's me," Livvy said. "The elusive red dot. So, Idris. How do we do this?"

Shadowhunters used Portals to go to Idris. Only now, Idris was warded and Portals wouldn't work. Livvy, being dead, didn't need Portals. When Ty had come to the Scholomance, he had stepped through a Portal and Livvy had willed herself to go with Ty. To be in the place where Ty was.

Ty said, "It should be the same as Dimmet Tarn. Or when I'm in class and suddenly you just show up. Hold Idris in your mind, like a picture. Let yourself go there."

"You make it sound easy," Livvy said.

"Something ought to be easy," Ty said. "Everything can't be hard all the time."

"Fine," Livvy said. "Here we go."

She thought of Idris, of Lake Lyn. Of the moment she was no longer dead. Saw it in her mind and held it there. And then she was no longer in the room with Ty and Irene. Instead she was floating above the great stillness of Dimmet Tarn.

"Great job, Livvy," she told herself. But she didn't go back to Ty. Instead she thought of Idris once more, and imagined, this time, that she was alive again. She thought of how once, when she'd been very young, she had Portaled with her family from the beach outside the L.A. Institute into Idris. Had that been the first time she'd gone to Idris?

She closed her eyes, opened them, and found herself beside the ocean in L.A. The sun was just coming up, turning the foam atop the waves to fiery lace. And there was the Institute where her family would be waking up soon. Making breakfast. Did they think of her? Dream of her and then wake and think of her again?

"This isn't where I want to be," she said, and knew it wasn't true. She tried again. "This isn't where I'm *supposed* to be."

The sun was rising, and she tried to feel its warmth—something other than its brightness. To warm herself. What she would have given to feel that wet velvet crust of the top layer of sand under her feet, to feel the cold grittiness of the sand underneath change in temperature as the warmth of her human feet soaked away. To scream herself hoarse, knowing that no one would hear over the roar of the surf. She squatted and tried with every particle of herself to pick up a piece of beach glass. But it was a useless endeavor. She had no more effect on the world than a fragment of dream. It seemed to her, in fact, that she was shrinking, growing smaller and smaller until she no longer stood on the sand, but was instead slipping between the icy grains, now large as boulders around her.

"No!" she said. And was no longer on the beach in Los Angeles. Instead she was back at Dimmet Tarn, her bare feet skimming the deep black.

"Get a grip on yourself," she told herself sternly. "And try again. What's the worst that could happen?"

This time, instead of thinking of Idris, Livvy thought of the way in which it was bounded. She thought of the wards that kept out everyone who was not welcome. She imagined Idris, picturing the terrible dessert they served at least once a month at the Scholomance, in which unidentifiable pieces of fruit were embedded in a vast Jell-O dome. There were certain advantages to being dead: you were not expected to be enthusiastic about terrible desserts simply because they were desserts. But nevertheless, even dead, she remembered the consistency of Jell-O, and she imagined Idris as if it had been encased in gelatin instead of magic. She imagined traveling to Idris, to the shore of Lake Lyn, as if she were pressing up against a Jell-O mold. Doing this, she could almost feel the wards of Idris resisting her: tingling, slippery, and only the slightest bit yielding. Still she persisted, imagining pressing all of her incorporeal self against their magic.

Livvy closed her eyes, and when she opened them, she was in a green meadow where she had never been before. There were sugar-white mountains against the horizon, and insects, buzzing languorously like secrets, in among the blades of grass. She was not in Idris. What was even the point of being a ghost if you didn't get to infiltrate the bad guys' lair in order to haunt jerks like the Cohort?

"This would prove that you fail at life, Livvy, except, you know," she said to herself. And then was surprised, because it seemed that someone had heard and was answering her.

"If they failed, would it really matter?" the voice said. A male voice with a strong Spanish accent. Livvy could see no one, but she could hear the voice as if the speaker stood beside her. "Then we could fight. I'm tired of this. We've been sitting around on our asses for months now, eating basic rations and arguing about the pettiest of goals."

"Shut up, Manuel," said a voice that Livvy knew. Zara. And now she recognized Manuel's voice as well. "We have been told to check the wards, and so we will check the wards. Obedience is a virtue in a Shadowhunter. So is patience."

"Patience!" Manuel said. "Like you've ever practiced patience in your life, Zara."

Livvy could see nothing but the meadow around her, the far white peaks of the mountain range. But she found that she could feel Idris, warded against her, pressing against her consciousness. Though she couldn't penetrate the wards, apparently she could eavesdrop through them. They must be standing right there, Livvy on one side of the wards and Zara and Manuel on the other.

"I am practicing enormous patience right now in not killing you," Zara retorted.

"I wish you would," Manuel said. "Then I wouldn't have to suffer through another dinner of dandelion greens and half a parsnip garnished with unseasoned pigeon while your father's cronies bicker about whether we mark the start of this new age by naming ourselves Raziel's Chosen Angels or the Birthright or the Glorious Front. Why not just call ourselves Super Amazing People Who Did the Right Thing but Now Have Run Out of Coffee and Staples?"

"You think with your stomach," Zara said.

Manuel ignored this. "Meanwhile, out there, there are Downworlders having baguettes slathered with Brie, and chocolate chip cookies, and vats and vats of coffee. Do you know how awful it is to spy on people who are eating delicious things like chocolate croissants when you don't even have a cube of sugar? By the Angel, I never thought I would say this, but I miss the food at the Scholomance. What I would give for olive loaf. Olive loaf!"

Livvy thought, *I'm dead and I wouldn't eat olive loaf. But then, I wouldn't hang out with Zara, either.* She could still see nothing of Idris inside the wards, but as she tried to push through again, glittering symbols she did not recognize appeared, hanging in the air.

"This will be a brief chapter in the history of the Imperishable Order," Zara said. "Or whatever historians end up calling us. Anyway, the point is, when we see that the time is right to leave Idris and we have the whole world to set to rights, no one is going to bother recording that you missed olive loaf. They're going to write about all the battles that we won, and how good we looked winning them, and how all our enemies like Emma Carstairs died pitifully choking on their own pleas for mercy."

"Last time I looked, she was partying on a beach," Manuel said. "As if she wasn't thinking about us at all."

"Good," Zara said. "Let them not think about us. And then let us be the last thing they ever see. Come on. The wards are holding. Let's get back before there's nothing left for lunch."

And like that, the voices were gone. Livvy was alone in the green meadow, Idris as inaccessible as ever. But she had succeeded, sort of, hadn't she? She hadn't gotten past the wards, but she had gathered information. She'd learned, what? That the Cohort was low on food, and just as unpleasant as ever. They had some sort of plan to emerge at some unknown date from Idris, in some kind of surprise attack. Most important, they seemed to be able to spy, somehow, on the outside world. She should go back to Ty and report what she had learned. All she had to do was tug on that strand of necromantical magic that connected her to Ty, and she would go flying back. This was the farthest she had ever gone from her twin, and it was not entirely a comfortable sensation. And yet it *was* a sensation and Livvy found herself savoring it. There was so little left to feel. For months now she had been less than a shadow at Ty's heels. Now, stretched so far away from him, she felt both more and less solid than she had been.

She sank into the grassy meadow, feeling herself growing smaller and smaller until the blades of grass towered around her. The noise of the insects changed—where before it had been shrill, now it slowed and grew thunderous. Why could she hear and see but not touch anything? She stretched out her hand toward a towering stalk of grass and then drew it back with a gasp. There was a bead of blood on her palm as if she had cut herself on the green edge. And when she raised her hand to her mouth, her blood was the most delicious thing she had ever tasted. She closed her eyes, savoring the taste, and when she opened them again, she was floating above the placid black nothing of Dimmet Tarn.

There was something she was supposed to do. There was someone who knew her, who knew what she should be doing. She could feel them tugging at her, as if she were a balloon on a tenuous string. They were pulling her away from the black reflective surface in which she could see no face, hard as she looked, and she let herself be reeled in.

Then she was in a room with a tall, rather thin boy with messy hair who was pacing up and down, fiddling with an empty lighter, a small creature stalking after him, pouncing at his heels. "Livvy!" the boy said.

As he said this, she recognized both herself and him. He was quite tall now. Hardly a boy now at all. It wasn't that she was growing smaller. It was just that he was growing, would continue to grow, and she was dead. That was all.

"Ty," she said.

"You've been gone all day," he said. "It's three in the morning. I stayed up because I got worried. It felt like you were . . . well, far away. It felt like something was . . . wrong."

"Nothing was wrong," Livvy said. "I just couldn't get into Idris. But I think I was just outside of it, somehow. Just outside the wards. I overheard people talking. Zara and Manuel. They were checking the wards and talking."

"Talking about what?" Ty said. He sat down at his desk and flipped open his notebook.

"Mostly about how hungry they were. But I think they have a way to spy on us. Well, not us, but you know. They can spy on everyone out here outside Idris. And they're planning some kind of surprise attack."

"When?" Ty said, busily writing.

"They didn't say. And 'surprise attack' is overstating it. They mentioned in a vague kind of way that when they did attack us, we were going to be really surprised and then really dead. Because they think they're super awesome and all we do is sit around and eat delicious croissants. And then they finished testing the wards and went away, and I couldn't hear anything else."

"Still," Ty said. "Those are two pieces of information. We should go tell someone. I could tell Ragnor. Or Catarina."

"No," Livvy said. "I'm the one who figured it out. I want to be the one who gets to tell. I'll go find Magnus and tell him. Didn't Helen say in her last letter that Magnus was spending time at the Los Angeles Institute?"

Ty didn't look at her. "Yes," he said at last. "That seems fair. You should go. Only, Livvy?"

"What," she said.

"While you were gone," he said, "did you feel different? Did you feel anything strange?"

Livvy considered his question. "No," she said. "Write that down in the book. That I didn't feel anything strange at all. You don't need to worry about me, Ty. I'm dead. Nothing bad can happen to me now."

Irene was curled up on Ty's bed now, leg extended as she fastidiously groomed one haunch. Her unblinking golden eyes stayed fixed on Livvy. They said, *I belong here. Do you?*

"You and Irene take care of each other while I'm gone, okay?" Livvy said.

"You're going now?" Ty said. He grimaced as if the thought was causing him physical discomfort.

"Don't wait up," Livvy said, and then the room around her was gone, and she was once again standing on the beach beside the Los Angeles Institute, the sun slipping down below the darkening waves of the Pacific Ocean. The rush of the water down the sand was wrong somehow.

She could see lights blazing in the windows of the Institute. She wasn't sure, but most likely they had already had dinner. Someone, probably Helen or Aline, would be doing the dishes. Tavvy would be getting ready for bed. Someone would read a book to him. Mark and Cristina would be in New York, most likely. Was Mark more settled in the human world now? It had always seemed so strange to her, how he had been taken from them and then restored. How alien he had seemed when he came back. And yet now she had become something even stranger.

She wished to be inside the Institute suddenly, away from the blackness of the water so like the blackness of Dimmet Tarn. And so she was inside. She found herself in the kitchen. Helen was sitting at the table, the dishes still waiting to be washed. Aline's head rested against her shoulder. Her arm was around Helen's shoulders. They looked utterly at home, as if they had always lived there. As if they had never been exiled to a small frozen island far away from their family.

"It's nice to have Mark home for a few days," Helen said.

Aline turned her face into Helen's neck. "Mmm," she said. "Do you think we could trust him to hold down the Institute for a few hours? I was thinking I could book a spa day for the two of us."

"No," Helen said. "Probably not. But let's do it anyway."

It was wonderful to see how settled in Helen and Aline were, but it was also all extremely unfair, Livvy felt. Everyone else got to come home. Mark. Helen. Even Ty would come home someday. But she would never truly be home again. A shudder of envy and despair and longing went through her, and as if she had any material effect on the world at all, the pile of dishes beside the sink suddenly toppled over, sending shards and bits of food all over the counter and floor.

"What was that?" Aline said, standing up.

Helen groaned. "A tremor, I think. You know, welcome to California."

Livvy fled the kitchen, up to Dru's room, where her sister sat on her bed, watching one of her horror movies on the Institute's battered television.

"Hey!" Livvy said. "You like scary movies so much? Well, here I am! The real deal. Boo!"

She got right into Dru's face, being as loud as she could. "Here I am! Can you see me? Dru? Why can't you see me! I'm right here!"

But Dru went on watching her stupid movie, and Livvy felt herself shrinking, growing smaller and smaller until she could have slipped right into the still, black calm of her sister's pupil as if it were a pool of water and lodged herself there. She could be safe there. A secret from everyone, even Dru. And then Ty wouldn't have to worry about her anymore. He would be safe too.

"Safe from what, Livvy?" she asked herself.

The screen of the television went dark then, and the witchlight sconces over Dru's bed flickered and went out. "What the hell," Dru said, and got up. She went over to the wall and touched the sconce. The room filled with light again.

There was a knock on the door, and when Dru opened it, Helen and Aline were there. Helen said, "Did you feel anything just now?"

"We were in the kitchen and then a bunch of dishes fell," Aline said eagerly. "Helen says it might have been an earthquake! My first one!"

"No," Dru said. "I don't think so? But the TV went off a second ago. So, maybe?"

In the doorway behind Helen and Aline, Mark appeared. Helen said, "Did you feel it too?"

"Feel what?" Mark said.

"A tiny earthquake!" Aline said, grinning.

"No," Mark said. "No, but Magnus just got a message from Jem. He says Tessa's in labor. So he's gone to them."

"Of course," Helen said dryly. "Because Magnus is exactly the person I want to keep me company when I'm about to give birth."

"I bet he gives amazing baby presents, though," Aline said. "And to be fair, I think that he feels he should have been there when Tessa and Will had their children, considering. Where are Julian and Emma right now? We should let them know."

"Paris," Helen said. "They like it so much there they keep extending their stay. Or do you think Magnus has let them know too?"

Magnus! Livvy realized that she had entirely forgotten why she had come. She had information for him. Well. In one moment she was in Dru's room, ignored and forgotten by a good number of the people she had loved most in the whole world. In the next, all the doors of the Los Angeles Institute flung themselves open and all the windows of the Institute shattered outward and Livvy did not even notice because she was suddenly beneath a full moon above a black pond carpeted in lily pads, fat velvet pads of the softest gray in the moonlight. Frogs, invisible in the shadows, were singing.

She knew, without knowing how she knew this, that she was now in the countryside, somewhere outside London. This was Cirenworth Hall, the estate where Jem and Tessa lived with Kit Herondale. Julian had visited there, and described it in a letter to Ty. There were horses and cows and apple trees. Tessa had an herb garden, and there was a glass conservatory that Jem had converted into a kind of music studio. How nice life was for the living! Jem, too, had gone away from the world for whole lifetimes and been allowed to return. Oh, why couldn't Livvy do the same? Why was she the only one who could not return and take up her life again?

It must be very late at night here, or else very early in the morning, but as with the Institute, lights were blazing in all the windows of the house. She drifted toward it, and then was inside. She was in another kitchen, this one very different from the cheery contemporary kitchen of the Institute. The walls were white plaster, hung with bundles of herbs and copper pots. Enormous beams dark with age ran across the whitewashed ceiling. Sitting at a long, scarred oaken table was Kit, playing solitaire and sipping from a mug. It might have been tea, but Livvy suspected from the face that he made as he sipped that it was something alcoholic instead.

"Boo!" she said, and Kit fumbled the mug, spilling liquid all down his pants.

"Livvy?" he said.

"That's right," she said, pleased. "You can see me. It gets really, really boring being invisible to everyone."

"What are you doing here?" Kit said. Then, "Is he okay? Ty?"

"What?" Livvy said. "No, he's fine. I'm looking for Magnus, actually. There's something that I need to ask him. Or tell him. I think I'm supposed to tell him something."

"Are *you* okay?" Kit said.

"What, aside from being dead?" Livvy said.

"Just, um, you seem a little off," Kit said. "Or something."

"Yeah, well, dead," Livvy said. "But other than that."

"Magnus is in the old conservatory with Jem and Tessa. Tessa's in labor, but, like, they seem like it's not a big deal or anything. They're just sitting around and talking about stuff. But, you know, it was kind of freaking me out. Like, she's going to have a baby, you know? Which is cool! But I thought I should give them some space."

"Okay, thanks," Livvy said. "Great to see you, Kit. Sorry I scared you. Sort of."

And then she was in the conservatory, which had been completely outfitted for a musician. There was a grand piano in one corner, and various instruments hanging on a beautiful wooden cabinet. Jem was playing a cello, his long hands drawing the bow across the strings as if he were coaxing out those low, beautiful, belling notes. Tessa was pacing, slowly, along a glass wall, one hand on her great belly and the other on her back. Magnus was nowhere to be seen.

Livvy wasn't really thinking about Magnus, though. Not anymore. All of her attention was focused on Tessa. On the hand that rested on the pregnant belly. She could not take her eyes away.

There was a voice in Livvy's head, way below the song that Jem was playing, below the sounds of the living hearts that beat in the conservatory: Jem, Tessa, and the unborn baby. She almost recognized the voice. It belonged to someone who had once been very dear to her. "Livvy," it was saying. "Something's wrong. I think that something's wrong."

Livvy did her best to ignore the voice. She thought, *If I make myself very small, I bet that I could do the thing I am thinking of. I could make myself so very small that I could slip into that baby. I wouldn't take up much room at all. A baby is hardly a person at all, really. If I took the place of whoever the baby is going to be, if I wanted a do-over, it wouldn't hurt Tessa and Jem at all. They would be good parents to me. And I would be a good daughter. I was good when I was alive! I could be good again. And it isn't fair. I shouldn't have died. I ought to get another chance. Why shouldn't I have another chance?*

She drew closer to Tessa. Tessa groaned.

"What is it?" Jem said, putting down his bow. "Is it my rank, terrible playing? Magnus may have magically transformed this space to be hospitable to instruments, but I am still an amateur when it comes to the cello." His face changed. "Or is it time? Shall we go back to the house?"

Tessa shook her head. "Not yet," she said. "But drawing nearer. Keep playing. It helps me."

"Magnus will be back soon with the herbs you wanted," Jem said.

"There's still time," Tessa said. "There's still time too if you don't want to be the one to deliver this baby. Magnus could fetch someone."

"What, and miss my chance at the big time?" Jem said. "I'd like to think that all my years as a Silent Brother weren't totally pointless."

Livvy was shrinking, shrinking, shrinking down almost to nothingness. All the darkness outside the glass walls of the conservatory was pressing in as if they were all submerged beneath Dimmet Tarn, but she could still escape. She could be a living girl again.

Jem got up and went over to Tessa. He knelt down in front of her and laid his head against her belly. "Hello there, Wilhelmina Yiqiang Ke Carstairs. Little Mina. You are welcome, little Mina, my heart. We are waiting for you in joy and hope and love."

Tessa rested her hand on Jem's head. "I think she heard you," she said. "I think she's hurrying now."

"Livvy!" said the other voice. The one that Livvy didn't want to hear right now, the one that tugged at her as if it were a leash. "Livvy, what are you doing? Something's wrong, Livvy."

And oh, the voice was right. Livvy came back to herself. What had she been thinking of doing? She had been going to—and as she realized what she had been about to do, all the walls of the conservatory exploded outward into the night in a great cloud of glass shards.

Jem and Tessa both cried out, crouching down. And then Magnus was there in green silk pajamas beautifully embroidered with Pokémon. "What in the world?" he said, bending over to help Jem and Tessa up.

"I don't know," Jem said wildly. "Demons? A sonic boom?"

Magnus looked around the conservatory. A strange expression came over his face when he saw Livvy.

"I'm sorry!" she said. "I didn't mean to, Magnus!"

Looking hard at her, Magnus said to Jem and Tessa, "Not a demon, I think. There's nothing dangerous here now. Come on. Let's get you back to the house. I have your herbs, Tessa. Kit's brewing you a nice cup of tea."

"Oh good," Tessa said faintly. "The intervals between contractions are getting shorter. I thought there would be more time. Are you sure we shouldn't be more concerned about whatever broke all the windows?"

"Everyone always thinks they'll have more time," Magnus said. He was still looking right at Livvy as he said it. "And no. I don't think you have to be concerned at all. I would never let anything happen to you. Think of it as part of the christening! You know that when they christen a ship, they break a bottle of champagne against the forward bow. Your baby just gets the deluxe version. Imagine her voyage! Her life, I predict, will be full of wonders."

"Come on," Jem said. "Let's get inside the house. Magnus, will you bring my cello?" He took down his violin from the cabinet, and with his other hand, he took Tessa's arm and began to walk her toward the house, over the dark ground strewn with broken glass.

Magnus said, "Oh, Livvy."

"I almost—" she said.

"I know," he said. "But you didn't. Go find Kit and stay with him. I'll come to you in a little while to fetch Tessa's tonic."

Kit seemed relieved, actually, to have company, even if company was only a ghost. "What happened out there?" he said. "What happened to the conservatory?"

"I think that was me," Livvy said. "I didn't mean to, though."

"Is this the kind of thing that you've been getting up to at the Scholomance?" Kit said. "Is that why you came to find Magnus?"

"No!" Livvy said. "I haven't done anything like this. Well, not until today. I think I smashed some plates at the Los Angeles Institute. And I made the lights go out in Dru's room while she was watching a scary movie."

"Nice," Kit said. "So, like, basic poltergeist stuff."

"I didn't mean to do any of it!" Livvy said. "It just sort of happened. I'm sorry I wrecked the conservatory."

"Maybe you could try not to do anything like that again," Kit said.

"Sure," Livvy said. "Of course. I don't *want* to do anything like that again."

There was a glint off something Kit wore on a chain around his neck. "Oh," Livvy said, looking closer. It was a heron made of silver.

"It belonged to my mother," Kit said. "Jem and Tessa gave it to me a while ago. I found it again this morning. I'd forgotten about it."

"It's so pretty," Livvy said.

Kit said, "I'd give it to you if I could. She used it to summon Jem and Tessa to her side when she was attacked. In the end, it didn't save her. So I guess I have a grudge against it."

Livvy said, "I'm sorry."

"Why?" Kit said. "You didn't kill them. Anyway, everything's okay?" He was looking at his hands very intently, as if he thought there might be something wrong with them.

"What?" Livvy said. "Yes. Everything's fine. Oh. You mean Ty."

Kit didn't say anything, but he nodded. He looked as if he wished he hadn't asked at all, and also as if he were listening with all of his being.

It was ridiculous, Livvy thought. You could tell how much he missed Ty. As much as Ty missed him. She didn't understand boys at all. Why couldn't they just say what they felt? Why did they have to be so stupid?

"He's okay," Livvy said. "He's doing well at the Scholomance. He has a Carpathian lynx in his room! He doesn't really have any friends, though. He misses you, but he won't talk about it. But other than that, he's fine."

As she said it, though, she realized that she wasn't sure at all that Ty was fine. The strand that bound her to Ty—that filament of magic—felt wrong, somehow, as if it were slackening. She could feel Ty reaching for her, but weakly.

"Livvy?" Kit said.

"Oh no," she said. "No, I think I have to go back. I think I shouldn't be here."

Now Kit looked truly alarmed. "What's wrong?" he said.

"Ty," she said. "It's hurting him that I'm here. Tell Magnus

I'm sorry, but I have to go. Tell him to come find me. I have information for him about Idris."

"About Idris?" Kit said. "Never mind. I'll tell him. Go!"

And Livvy went.

She must have been back at the Scholomance in the space of a breath, although to be fair, since she didn't breathe anymore, she was only guessing that was how long it took. She was in Ty's room, but Ty wasn't there. Only Irene, looking accusingly at her from the door, which she appeared to be attempting to chew open.

"Sorry," Livvy said, and then felt ridiculous. This time she let her awareness of Ty, where he was, pull her toward him, and yet that was not where she found herself. She found herself, instead, hovering once more over Dimmet Tarn.

"No!" she said. And, feeling as if she were fighting her way to him through some impenetrable and gloomy dark chasm, she came at last to her brother.

He was lying in a bed in the infirmary, looking very pale. Catarina Loss was by his side, and a boy that Livvy recognized from Ty's classes. Anush.

"He just collapsed," Anush was saying. "Is it food poisoning?"

"I don't think so," Catarina Loss said. "I don't know."

Ty opened his eyes. "Livvy," he said, so softly that her name was barely a sound at all.

"What did he say?" Anush asked.

"Livvy," Catarina said, laying her hand on Ty's head. "His sister. The one who was slain by Annabel Blackthorn."

"Oh," Anush said. "Oh, how sad."

Catarina Loss said, "His color is improving a little, I think.

Are you good friends?"

"Uh, not really?" Anush said. "I don't know who his friends are. If he has friends. I mean, he seems like a good guy. Smart. Super focused. But he kind of keeps to himself."

"I'm going to keep him in the infirmary overnight," Catarina Loss said. "But if it occurs to you to come back to visit him, it wouldn't be the worst thing in the world. Everyone needs friends."

"Yeah, sure," Anush said. "I'll come back later. See if he needs anything."

Catarina Loss poured a glass of water for Ty and helped him sit up to take a drink. "You fainted," she said in a neutral voice. "Sometimes new students take their course of study too seriously and forget about things like getting enough sleep or eating."

"I don't forget things like that," Ty said. "I have a schedule so that I don't forget."

"You came to me the other day about the lynx," Catarina Loss said. "How is she doing? I see there are scratches on your arm."

"She's great!" Ty said. "She eats everything I bring her and she's drinking fine too. How long have I been here? I should go make sure that she's okay."

"You've only been here a little while," Catarina Loss said. "When Anush comes back, you can tell him to look after her for tonight. I think he'd be happy to do that. Do you think you could eat something?"

Ty nodded, and Catarina Loss said, "I'll see what delights the kitchen can supply. Stay in bed. I'll be right back."

When she was gone, Livvy said, "Ty!"

Ty frowned at her. He said, "I could feel you getting farther and farther away. It hurt, Livvy. And you were getting stranger and stranger, the farther away you got. I could *feel* you. But you didn't feel like you anymore. You felt—"

Livvy said, "I know. I felt it too. It was scary, Ty. *I* was scary. You're going to have to write that down in your notebook. I don't think it's good when I'm away too long. I think the farther away from you that I get, the more dangerous it is for both of us. The longer I stayed away, the more I forgot things. Like who I was. Like you. Why I should come back."

Ty said, "But you did come back."

"I came back," Livvy said. "Almost too late. But I'm here now. And just in time. Irene is gnawing her way through your door."

She grinned at Ty reassuringly, and Ty smiled back. Then his eyes closed again.

"Ty?" she said.

"I'm fine," he said. "Just really tired. Going to sleep for a little while, Livvy. Will you stay with me while I fall asleep?"

"Sure," she said. "Of course I will."

He was asleep when Catarina Loss returned with a tray of food, and still asleep when Magnus Bane came through the door several hours later in a puffy scarlet down parka trimmed in black fake fur that came all the way down to his ankles. He looked as if he had been mostly swallowed by a very fat eiderdown dragon.

Catarina Loss was with him. "A girl!" she said. "I've been knitting a blanket for her, but it isn't done yet. Wilhelmina Yiqiang Ke Carstairs. That's quite a big name for a very small baby."

"Mina for short," Magnus said. "Oh, she's lovely, Catarina. She has Jem's fingers. A musician's fingers. And Tessa's chin. So how's our patient?"

"He'll be fine," Catarina Loss said. Then, "Though what was wrong with him in the first place isn't quite apparent to me. He seems perfectly healthy. I'm due to teach a class. Will you still be here in an hour or so?"

"I'll be here or somewhere close at hand," Magnus said. "Come and find me when you're done."

When Catarina Loss was gone, Magnus said to Livvy, "Well. There is apparently something that you must say to me. And then there is something that I must say to you."

Livvy said, "I know. I think I know what you must say to me. But first let me tell you about Idris." And she told him everything she had heard Zara and Manuel say.

"We knew that sooner or later they plan to attack us," Magnus said at last. "But now that we know they are spying on us, we will have to find out how. And perhaps if it is possible for them, then it is also possible for us to spy on Idris. But I don't think we can risk you doing it again."

"No," Livvy said. "Because every time I get too far away from Ty, things start to go wrong. I start to change. I get stronger, I think. I can do things! Like I did with the conservatory. I broke dishes, too, and I think I almost hurt Tessa's baby somehow. And Ty, it's bad for him, too, when we're apart. That's why he ended up in the infirmary. Because I was gone too long."

"Yes," Magnus said. "Smart girl."

"If I had stayed away longer," Livvy said, "would he have died?"

"I don't know," Magnus said. "But the magic he tried to use to bring you back from the dead was dark magic, Livvy. Necromancy. A spell from the Black Volume of the Dead! And a failed spell, at that. When the spell failed, the thing that kept you here, that bound you, was Ty. Your twin. That's not normal for ghosts. Most of them are bound to an object. Things like a ring or a key or a house. But you're bound to a person. It makes sense that you need to stay close to Ty now. And that he has to stay close to you. I think that when you are away from him for too long, you become less yourself. More powerful. Less human. More a hungry ghost. Something dangerous to the living."

"When I was in the conservatory," Livvy said, forcing the words out, "I felt as if I could swap places with Tessa's baby. That I could be alive again, if I were willing to take her baby's life. Her baby's place."

Magnus said, "Necromancy is a very dark art. Yes. Perhaps you could have. Or perhaps you might have killed the baby or Tessa, and ended up with nothing at all. Magic can have a high price, Livvy."

"I don't want to hurt anybody," Livvy said. "That's what Annabel did. I don't want to be like Annabel, Magnus. I don't! But I don't want to be dead, either! It isn't fair!"

"No," Magnus said. "It isn't fair. But life isn't fair. And you died bravely, Livvy."

"Stupidly," Livvy said. "I died stupidly."

"Bravely," Magnus said. "Though I admit that sometimes I wish Shadowhunters were a little less brave and used their heads a little more."

Livvy sniffed. "Well," she said. "Ty is good at that. Using his head."

"Ty is exceptional," Magnus said. "I expect great things from him. And from you, too, Livvy. Because if you do not do great things, then I fear you may do terrible things. The two of you have remarkable potential."

"Me?" she said. "But I'm dead."

"Nevertheless," Magnus said. He reached into his pocket and said, "And I have a present for you. Well, it's from Kit, too. It's for you and Ty." He held out a silver chain from which hung the figure of a bird. A heron, Livvy realized.

"You're bound to Ty," Magnus said, "but it's a necromantical bond. I was poking around for something to use that might work to bear a little of the weight that bond must be on you and Ty, and Kit asked what I was doing. He gave me this, and I have altered it a little. Given it some potency. If Ty wears it, it should shield him a little from any side effects of being bound to the dead. And it should sustain you a little. It should ease some of the strangeness of being in the living world. You can touch it. And, too, should you or he feel in need of help, you can use it to call on me. Or Ty can. Once it belonged to Kit's mother. It was given to her by Jem, so that when she was in danger she could summon him. Now it will serve you and your brother."

Livvy stretched out a finger. Stroked the silver heron. "Oh," she said. "I can! I can feel it!"

Magnus said, "Yes. Well. Good."

"Like one of Ty's fidget toys," Livvy said. "Like Julian's lighter." She was running her fingers along the chain now. "Is the baby okay? Mina?"

"Yes," Magnus said. "She's fine. Everyone is fine. The conservatory, on the other hand . . ."

Livvy thought, suddenly, of Dimmet Tarn. She said, "You've been here before, to the Scholomance?"

"Yes," Magnus said. "Many times, over the years."

"Have you ever been to Dimmet Tarn?" Livvy said.

"Yes," Magnus said. "A most unimpressive body of water. You must find it a sad change from the Pacific Ocean."

"Yeah, well, there are stories that it's supernatural in some way," Livvy said. "But nobody knows how. Ty and I were trying to see if we could find out anything about it."

Magnus said, "Let me see. There were stories about it, but I never paid much attention to them. What was it?"

He sat in silence for a minute, and Livvy sat companionably with him. Ty stirred as if he were dreaming in a way that made Livvy think that he would wake up soon.

"Yes!" Magnus said. "Of course. The story was this. That if you went to Dimmet Tarn and looked into the water for long enough, you would see something of your future. That was the enchantment placed on it by some warlock or other. Funnily enough, I believe he was from Devon, actually. Dimmet is a Welsh word. Why? Did you go there? Livvy? Did you see something there?"

"No," Livvy said at last. She tried to think of what it had been like, sinking into that vast dark nothingness. "I didn't see anything. It was nothing at all."

"I see," Magnus said in a tone that suggested he saw everything she wasn't saying. "But let us say that there was someone who happened to look into dismal Dimmet Tarn and let's say they saw something they didn't like. Something that suggested a future they didn't want. And let's say that this someone came and talked to me. Do you know what I would tell them?"

"What?" Livvy said.

Magnus said, "I would tell them this. That the future isn't fixed. If we see a path in front of us that we would not choose, then we can choose another path. Another future. Dimmet

Tarn be damned. Would you agree with that, Livvy?"

He stared hard at Livvy and Livvy stared right back. She couldn't think of anything to say at all, but finally she set her mouth and nodded.

From the bed, Ty said, "Livvy!" His eyes opened and found her, and he said, "Livvy," again. This time he didn't sound despairing. He hadn't noticed yet that Magnus was there at all.

A terrible wailing came from the doorway as Ty spoke. It was Irene, her whiskery jaws stretched open and all of her fur standing on end. Livvy would not have thought that such a tiny animal could have produced such a large noise. Still wailing, Irene leaped onto the bed and butted Ty in the chin. The noise she was making changed to smaller, angry inquiring trills like a hot teakettle who had a lot of questions but suspected she wasn't going to like any of the answers.

"What on earth is that?" Magnus said.

"This is Irene," Ty said. "She's a Carpathian lynx."

"Of course!" said Magnus. "A Carpathian lynx. How silly of me." His eyes met Livvy's. "A boy, a Carpathian lynx, and a ghost. Truly I expect great things from you and your brother, Livvy. Here, Ty. This is for you." He dropped the Herondale necklace into Ty's palm. "Livvy will explain its purpose. Suffice it to say that if you need me for any reason at all, you can use it to summon me. Livvy's been telling me about Idris, about what she overheard. But I have been up all night long, and I need some strong tea. I'm going to go find Ragnor Fell and make him find me some strong tea."

He made as grand an exit as anyone can make when they are wearing an oversize down coat, and as he exited, Anush entered, his arms bloody with scratches.

Anush gazed after Magnus in astonishment. "That was Magnus Bane," he said to Ty. "Was he here to see you?"

"Yes. He's our friend," Ty said.

Anush said, "I knew that you know him, but I didn't realize you had a just-dropping-by-the-Scholomance-to-see-you type of relationship! Sorry about that animal. I went to your room to see if I could bring you back a book or some clothes or something, and she got away from me. She's so pretty. But she's so mean."

"Her name is Irene," Ty said, looking fondly at the lynx curled up beside him.

Anush said, "Again, rhymes with 'mean.' Do you want me to go get some scraps from the kitchen for her?"

When Anush was gone, Livvy told Ty everything that had happened while she had been in Los Angeles and in the conservatory in England. Ty said, "I'm so sorry, Livvy."

"For what?" she said.

"For doing this to you," he said.

"Oh, Ty," she said. "I would have done it for you. It isn't a thing that should be done, but I would have done it anyway. And so we would be in just the same mess we're in now. Besides, I think I'm getting the hang of this ghost thing."

Ty nodded. He turned the necklace over and over in his hand, then held it out, dangling the heron over the bed so that the sunlight caught the silver, and Irene batted it with her paw. Livvy thought of Kit sitting at the table in the kitchen, so carefully not asking her anything about Ty.

She reached over and caught the chain in her hand. Gently untangled it from Irene's sharp claws. Holding the necklace still, Livvy said, "This belonged to Kit. You'll have to write him.

To say thank you. You'll write him and give the letter to Magnus to take back when he goes."

"Okay," Ty said at last. "But he won't write back."

"Then you'll keep on writing until he does," Livvy said. "Necromancy is bad. We're all agreed on that. But postcards are pretty harmless. You know. Something scenic on the front." Dimmet Tarn flashed in front of her. That black nothingness. "Wish you were here. That kind of thing."

She held the chain tighter. Rubbed the small links between her fingers. Maybe that was her future. Black nothingness. But right now she had Ty. She could choose the path that led away from Dimmet Tarn for as long as she could. She had an anchor. She would hold on as tightly as she could.

Forever Fallen

By Cassandra Clare and Sarah Rees Brennan

Awake, arise! Or be forever fallen.
—Milton

New York, 2013

Jem Carstairs and Kit Herondale came through the Portal together, from the black midnight velvet of the English woods into the orange-starred deep blue of a New York street in the evening. Kit eyed the silver stream of honking cars with the same expression he'd worn since Jem suggested going: a mixture of excitement and nerves.

"They didn't, uh, exactly welcome me at the L.A. Shadow Market the last few times I went," Kit said. "You're sure this will be okay?"

"I am," Jem assured him.

The yellow and red lights of cars played over the intricate scrollwork and arched windows of the abandoned theater. The Shadow Market on Canal Street was much like he remembered it from a decade ago and more, though Jem himself was so different. To a mundane, steel shutters and boards covered the entrance. To Jem and Kit, they were silver and wood beads, a curtain that chimed a song as they passed through.

A warlock woman paused when she saw them.

"Hello, Hypatia," said Jem. "I think you know Kit?"

"I know that two Shadowhunters make even more trouble than one," said Hypatia.

She rolled her starry eyes and passed on, but a werewolf Jem knew from the Paris Shadow Market stopped and chatted with them for a moment. He said it was a pleasure to meet Kit, and always a pleasure to see Jem.

"Congratulations, by the way," he added.

Jem glowed. "Thank you."

Jem had been surprised to find that he was welcome in most Shadow Markets now. He had been to many, over the years, and quite a few of the vendors and attendants were immortal. People remembered him, and after a time, they had stopped fearing him. He hadn't even realized it, but he had become a familiar sight, his visits marking a Market night as lucky: he was the only Silent Brother most of them had ever seen. The first time he'd gone to a Shadow Market once he was no longer a Silent Brother, hand in hand with a warlock woman, seemed to confirm the Shadow Market people's opinion that he was close to being one of their own. Showing up with Kit, who had basically grown up in the Shadow Market in Los Angeles, pretty much cemented that.

"You see?" Jem murmured. "No problem."

Kit's shoulders were relaxing and his blue eyes beginning to shine with a familiar wicked gleam. He pointed out several interesting features of the Market that Jem was already aware of, a Market boy showing off, and Jem smiled and encouraged him to keep talking.

"They do it with magic mirrors," Kit whispered in Jem's ear when they stopped to see two mermaids doing tricks in a tank.

The mermaid glared at Kit, and Kit laughed. They stopped at a stall to buy candied moonflowers, since Kit had a fiendish sweet tooth.

"I know you," said the faerie vendor. "Aren't you Johnny Rook's boy?"

Kit's smile died a swift death. "Not anymore."

"Whose are you now?"

"Nobody's," Kit answered quietly.

The faerie vendor blinked, a second eyelid sliding in sideways and making the blink rather impressive. Jem reached out to touch Kit's shoulder, but Kit was already moving on, browsing the sweets as if he found them deeply fascinating.

Jem cleared his throat. "I hear there is a special stall run by warlocks and faeries, offering potions and illusions? My friend Shade told me of it."

She nodded understanding and leaned down to whisper in his ear.

The stall devoted to the faerie-and-warlock joint venture was a carved wooden caravan parked in an antechamber of the Canal Street building. The caravan was painted bright blue and adorned with paintings that moved: as Jem and Kit approached, birds took flight from several gilded cages and soared free over the bright-blue painted sky.

The faerie woman had mushrooms growing in her hair, and ribbons looped around them. She seemed very young, and enthusiastic about selling Jem the medicine he asked for. Jem lifted the porcelain lid to examine its contents carefully and apologized for doing so.

She waved this off. "Perfectly understandable, considering what it's for. Lovely to meet you properly at last. Any friend of

Shade's. Such a distinguished gentleman. Perhaps it's the Irish in me, but I do love a fellow in green."

Kit became overwhelmed by a fit of coughing. Jem smiled discreetly and patted him on the back.

"Also . . . ," the faerie said in a rush. "I saw you once, about eight years ago, when you were still . . . I only got one glimpse, but you seemed so hauntingly sad. And so hauntingly attractive."

"Thank you," said Jem. "I'm very happy now. Your cough seems to be getting worse, Kit. Do you need medicine as well?"

Kit straightened up. "Nope, I'm good. Come on, Brother Hauntingly Attractive."

"There's no need to mention this to Tessa."

"And yet," said Kit, "I'm gonna."

"Congratulations!" the faerie woman yelled after Jem.

All of his knowledge as a Silent Brother told him the potion was harmless and would do its work. Jem offered another smile over his shoulder to the woman and let Kit pull him toward the row of stalls in the next room across the way. The Market was growing more crowded, so crowded that all the faeries who could take wing were flying overhead. One was being pursued by a werewolf, who was yelling that the faerie had unfairly snatched the last hat in her size. The fleeing faerie's winged shadow darkened a golden head and broad shoulders that struck Jem as familiar.

"Isn't that Jace? I think that's—" Jem began, turning to Kit. Then he saw Kit's face was white.

Kit was staring over at a tall boy with dark hair and headphones, browsing through a stall and running his fingers through the dried herbs. Jem laid his hand on Kit's shoulder. Kit seemed oblivious, rooted to the spot, until the boy turned around and had blue eyes and a crooked nose, and was not Ty Blackthorn.

"I have what we came for," Jem said. He spoke with his usual, and carefully cultivated, calm. "Shall we go, or do you want to look around? We can do whatever you want."

Kit's jaw was still set. Jem knew that look. Herondales were always flames, he thought. They loved and suffered as if they would burn away with the sheer force of their own fire.

"Let's go home," Kit mumbled.

In spite of his slight disappointment, Jem found himself smiling. It was the first time Kit had called their house that.

The man, who had never had the chance to be Jace Herondale and who was no longer Jace at all, was starting to think that coming here had been a bad idea.

The Seelie Queen had been the one to insist he should have a new name, when he made his way to Faerie wanting protection for Ash and help with his plans. The Queen had answered all his questions about Clary, but her help hadn't come free. Royalty tended to make demands.

"I'm accustomed to the other Jace," she said with a regal sneer. "Though I admit, not overly fond. What else can we call you?"

Jonathan, he'd thought first, and flinched at even the thought of that name, which had surprised him. He hadn't done much flinching in Thule.

"Janus," he'd told the Queen. "The god with two faces. The god of endings and beginnings, and passages between strange doorways."

"The god?" the Queen repeated.

"My father gave me a classical education," Janus told her. "To go with my classical good looks."

That had made the Queen laugh. "I see some things do not change, no matter the world."

She saw nothing. Nobody in this world could know what he had been forced to become.

It was in Faerie that Janus had heard of the faerie-and-warlock stall and the magic it could do, and he hadn't been able to resist. He knew Shadowhunters were not welcome at Shadow Markets. He'd thought that if he wore a hood and cloak, the risk would be minimal.

Unfortunately, several people were looking at him as if they recognized him. Well, let them think that the Jace of this world made a regular practice of haunting the Shadow Market. He had nothing invested in protecting that Jace's reputation.

Janus turned. A werewolf slammed into him and cursed.

"Hey, Shadowhunter, watch where you're going!"

Janus had his hand on his dagger when another werewolf came by and slapped the first werewolf upside the head.

"Do you know who you're talking to?" he demanded. "That's Jace Herondale, the head of the Institute."

The werewolf paled. "Oh my God. I'm so sorry. I didn't know."

"Please forgive him. He's from a horrible desert wasteland and he doesn't know what's going on," said the other werewolf.

"I'm from Ohio!"

"That's what I said."

The two werewolves gazed at Janus in apologetic misery. Janus was very confused, but he slowly let go of the hilt of his dagger. This pair might be more useful alive.

"*So* sorry," the second werewolf stressed.

"It's . . ." Janus cleared his throat. "It's fine."

"He's also the Consul's *parabatai*," said the werewolf. "You know, Alec Lightwood."

Janus felt something twist deep in his gut. The sensation surprised him. He was used to feeling nothing at all.

He held the thought of Alec being Consul in front of his mental eye, like a peculiar stone he was studying. He'd heard from the Queen that in this new strange world everything was different and everyone was alive, but when he had imagined those he'd known once alive again, he'd imagined them unchanged. Alec as Consul. He couldn't imagine it.

"I'm actually here on . . . a secret mission," he said. "I'd appreciate it if you kept quiet about seeing me."

"I thought so," said the second werewolf. "Cloak. Hood. 'Secret mission,' I said to myself."

Janus's smile became less real and far more easy. "I can tell you're perceptive. Perhaps in the future, if I needed your help—"

"Anything we can do!" the werewolves rushed to assure him. "Absolutely anything."

Janus kept smiling. "Oh good."

It *was* good to make allies—especially those who were stupid and eager to please.

Janus headed to what he had come for, the bright blue caravan where he had been assured that faeries and warlocks together could produce impenetrable glamours.

In Thule, there was no more warlock magic. There were no more warlocks at all. But there were demons crawling everywhere across the surface of that world, thick as flies on spoiled meat, and Sebastian could make the demons create illusions. Very occasionally, when Janus had pleased Sebastian, he would give him such a gift. Only sometimes, and it was never enough.

A faerie with mushrooms in her hair let him into the caravan. She seemed young, and she quailed when his eyes fell on her, but he paid the price she and the warlock demanded. It was exorbitant. He would have paid more.

The inside of the caravan was a wooden shell that had a jewel hidden within. The faeries had not been wrong when they said the combined magic could produce an extraordinary result. She was the most convincing illusion he had ever seen.

She was small, always so small. Her hair fell in red loops and swirls around her face and her shoulders. He had wanted to follow every loop with his finger, work out the precise shape of each curl, as he'd wanted to trace connections between every golden freckle. He'd wanted to know her completely.

"Clary," he said.

Her name sounded foreign in his mouth. He hadn't said it often, even in Thule, where whatever he felt had been buried under layers and layers of a weight like cement.

"Come here," he said. He was surprised by the roughness in his own voice. His hands were shaking. It felt like a distant, even despicable weakness.

She moved toward him. He caught her by the wrists and pulled her roughly against his chest.

Holding her was a mistake. That was where the illusion began to collapse. He could feel her trembling, and Clary would not have done that. Clary was the bravest person he knew.

The illusions were never convincing enough. No illusion could love you back. No illusion would ever look at him the way Clary had once looked at him. And though he didn't know why he needed that, he did. He had needed it before, and the severing of his bond with Sebastian had made it a thousand times worse.

Clary. Clary. Clary.

He fooled himself for another moment, pressing his lips against her forehead, then her cheek, then burying his face in the cloud of her bright hair.

"Oh, my darling," he murmured, reaching for his knife as her eyes widened in realization and fear. "My darling. Why did you have to die?"

Kit ran up the stone steps to his room, slamming the door behind him, as soon as they retured to Cirenworth Hall. Jem thought it might be best to give him privacy, for a little while.

He was still slightly worried as he climbed the steps himself, following the sound of a song echoing off the slate walls.

"Black for hunting through the night
For death and mourning the color's white
Gold for a bride in her wedding gown
And red to call enchantment down.

Saffron lights the victory march,
Green will mend our broken hearts.
Silver for the demon towers,
And bronze to summon wicked powers."

It was a variation on an ancient Shadowhunter song; Jem could not have guessed how old. His father had sung it to him when he was a child.

When he pushed open the door, the world narrowed down for a moment to a single room, and that room was full of soft light. There was a cluster of shining witchlights arranged in the old-fashioned iron grate, and pearlescent rays caught in Tessa's brown curls as she bent over the cradle, rocking it gently. The cradle had been carved more than a hundred years ago from an oak felled in these woods. Jem had seen it made, with careful hands and patient love. The cradle rocked just as smoothly now as it had then.

Plaintive grizzling drifted from the cradle, and Jem leaned over to see its occupant. She lay on soft white bedding, piles on piles of fleeciness so it seemed she slept on a cloud. Her shock of hair was very black against the sheets and her small face was screwed up in outraged distress.

Wilhelmina Yiqiang Ke Carstairs. For their lost Will, the first and only possible name, and *wild rose*, because all those who Jem loved best grew in beautiful rebellion. He'd wanted a Chinese name for his darling, and wanted to commemorate lost Rosemary, who had trusted Jem and Tessa with what was infinitely precious to her and was now infinitely precious to him: Rosemary had trusted him with Kit. Rosemary was the herb meant for remembrance, and Zachariah meant *remember*. The longer Jem lived, the more surely he believed that life was a wheel, coming full circle, and bringing you to those you were meant to love. She had an imposing name, their little one, and it might have been longer had they included Gray, but Tessa said that warlocks chose their own name, if she chose to be a warlock. Mina might choose to be a Shadowhunter. She might be anything she pleased. She was everything already.

Jem was often lost in admiring her, but he did not let himself do so for long tonight. Instead he lifted her in his arms. Her hands flew out like startled starfish and came to rest, the smallest tenderest weights, against his collarbone. Mina's dark eyes popped open all the way, and she went quiet.

"Oh, I see how it is," Jem's wife whispered, laughing softly. "Daddy's girl."

"She knows I brought her something from the Market," said Jem, and gently rubbed the faerie salve on Mina's soft pink gums.

Mina wriggled and fussed as he did so, kicking her legs as if she were swimming in a race, but when Jem was finished the salve seemed to do its work quickly. Then she settled, her small face bewildered but happy, as if Jem had performed some peculiar and marvelous feat.

Tessa said it was early for a baby to start teething. Mina was remarkable and advanced in all sorts of ways, Jem considered proudly.

"*Qiān jīn*," Jem murmured to her. "You are more like your mother every day."

She was very like Tessa. Whenever he pointed this out, Tessa and Kit seemed skeptical.

"I mean, she's a baby, so she mostly looks like a kind of screwed-up turnip," said Kit. "In . . . uh, a good way. But if she looks like anyone . . ."

Kit had shrugged. Tessa had the same expression on her face now as Kit had worn then.

"Still no," Tessa informed him. "She looks just like you."

Jem lifted Mina up and toward the witchlights, one hand cupped protectively around the fragile curve of her head. Happiness came easily to Mina. She crowed with delight, witchlight radiant around her ruffled cap of black hair and her round waving arms, and he was dazzled and overwhelmed by the sheer immensity of his good fortune.

"But—she's so beautiful," Jem said helplessly.

"And where might she get that from? I love you forever, James Carstairs," said Tessa, leaning her dear head against his shoulder. "But you are a fool."

Jem drew Mina back in and held her close, and she nuzzled her dimpled cheek against his, burbling to him joyfully. From the day she was born, Mina had gurgled at ceilings and walls and into the tiny caves of her cupped hands. Her gurgling grew higher pitched and more excited when she was in Tessa's or Jem's arms, trying to attract their attention. She talked in her sleep as her mother did. She was always talking, and Jem was always listening, and soon he would understand every word.

Their daughter was so like Tessa. Jem knew what he knew.

Janus zipped his jacket up to hide the blood as he passed a faerie stall. He'd decided he'd risked his luck long enough and he should make his way home.

"Yo, Jason," called a black-haired vampire girl in a blue minidress. She was looking at him expectantly, but from what she'd called him, she couldn't know him that well.

"Actually, it's Jace," said Janus casually, still moving for the exits.

He didn't understand what he'd said wrong, but he understood it had been something. Instant alarm flashed across her face, and she darted away through the crowd, making it out of the Market, but even a vampire wasn't faster than Janus. Nobody was.

He cornered her in an alleyway, backhanding her when she fought, pinning her thrashing limbs. He got his dagger to her throat, but she didn't stop struggling.

"You're *not* Jace," said the vampire girl. "What are you? Eidolon? Shape-shifter? Herondale cosplayer?" She squinted at him.

He was going to have to break her neck, he realized. Tedious. Vampires were hard to kill, but he was still stronger than they were. "I am Jace Herondale," he told her. It was a relief to say it to someone, even someone who was going to die. "A stronger, better Jace Herondale than you have in this world. Not that you'll understand a word I say."

He reached for her throat, but she was staring at him with a look of realization. "You're from Thule," she said. "Alec told me about this freaky other world where Clary died and everything was screwed literally to hell. And Jace was bound to Sebastian Morgenstern. You're *that* Jace."

She glared up at him defiantly, and something about her face rang a dull, funereal bell.

"I know who you are too," Janus said slowly. "You're Lily Chen. In my world, Sebastian killed you."

"He did?" Lily looked outraged. "To hell with that guy. Irony intended."

"You're the girl Raphael Santiago started a war for."

Lily abruptly and entirely ceased fighting. It was startling enough that Janus almost let go, but his father had trained him to be remorseless.

"What?" Her voice trembled. "Raphael?"

"When Sebastian was taking over," Janus said slowly, lost to memory, to the time when Clary fell and the world broke, "the warlocks were gone. The faeries were with us. Sebastian asked the vampires and the werewolves to join him. Most of the vampires left were rounded up by Raphael Santiago, the head of the New York vampire clan, and Sebastian was in talks with him. Raphael was not pleased by what had happened to the warlocks, but he said he was the practical type. He wanted protection for his vampires. We thought we might be able to come to an arrangement. Only Sebastian found out you were sending secret information to a werewolf girl. He asked if you wanted to have fun with him, and you said you did."

Janus was surprised he even remembered that time. He'd been blind with pain back then, before Sebastian made him stop thinking of Clary so often. Sebastian had said he was pathetic and useless and *feeling*. So he'd made it stop.

"I wish I could resist killer parties," said Lily, "but I can't. This is a fully plausible scenario."

Her voice was almost absentminded. Her eyes were searching Janus's face.

"Sebastian killed you and showed Raphael what was left. Raphael said you were stupid, and it served you right. Six hours later he led every vampire he could, and some of the werewolves, out of the talks. He set the building on fire as he went. I had to pull Sebastian out from the burning rubble. Next we heard, Raphael was with Livia Blackthorn and the resistance."

"He's alive?" Lily's voice was sharp. "In your stupid, messed-up world. Raphael's alive?"

The words burst out of her mouth. "Take me to him."

Even though Janus had been expecting it, the words were shocking, so shocking that the truth fell from his own mouth without him meaning to say it. "There isn't any hope for that world. Even the sun has been blotted out."

His head ached as soon as he spoke. The pain felt like Sebastian being displeased with him, even now.

"Then bring him here," said Lily. "Please. Go back and bring him here."

Her hands were no longer shoving at him, but clinging to him, almost pleading.

"If I did," Janus ground out, "what would you do for me?"

He saw her mind working, behind her watchful black eyes. She wasn't stupid, this vampire girl.

"Depends," she snapped. "What are you going to ask me for?"

"Let's be clear," Janus said. "You'd do anything for this."

The vampire girl's sharp face softened. She liked Jace, Janus realized. She trusted him. Some part of her still thought Janus was her friend. She was underestimating him, not on guard as she should be. She didn't really think he would hurt her.

"I guess so," she said. "I guess I would." She leaned back against the alley wall. "Would it help if I told you that you were still hot?"

"Probably not," Janus said.

"Don't repeat that to the other Jace," said Lily. "He shouldn't be encouraged. You know, I think some people might find you *more* hot. Little less of a pretty boy, little more rugged thing going on. It's a trade-off."

"Most things are," Janus agreed.

"I'm not hitting on you, by the way, I'm just making observations here."

Janus shrugged. "Wouldn't do any good if you were."

"Still a one-woman man, huh?"

"Still," Janus said very quietly.

Lily was gazing at him as if she was sorry for him. As if she could know how he felt. He wanted to put out her eyes, to stop her looking at him like that, but she might be useful.

"Let's make a bargain," Janus suggested. "You do me one favor, when the time comes, without asking questions, and I will do what I can to bring Raphael to your world. It isn't going to be easy, and it will take time. You don't tell anyone you've seen me. If you do, I can always send a message back to Thule telling them to kill Raphael."

She winced.

"Do we have a deal?" Janus said.

There was a long silence. Janus could still hear the songs and bells of the Shadow Market flowing on, past this dark alley with the undead.

Then Lily said, "We have a deal."

He let Lily leave, and followed her quietly. He saw her take out her phone, as if she might call somebody and warn them. But she didn't. She put her phone back in her pocket.

It was almost funny. Janus knew no way back into that other world, but it didn't matter if this girl was smart or if she wanted to be good, because she was wild and clawing and frantic to believe him. Hope made everybody a fool.

To make people obey, all you had to do was first make sure they were desperate. Janus should know that well enough. He'd been desperate for years. *Don't repeat that to the other Jace*, Lily had said. As if Janus was planning to have any conversations with the other Jace, the one from this world, the one who'd gotten lucky. Janus didn't need to talk to him. Janus would learn everything he had to know about this world, so he could pass himself off as the other Jace.

Then he would kill this world's version of himself and take his place. Beside Clary.

It was near dawn when Mina woke crying. Tessa stirred, but Jem dropped a kiss on her bare shoulder and murmured, "I'll go, love."

Tessa had suffered pains that Jem could not, bringing Mina into the world. His wife would never lose sleep with the baby while Jem was in the house. That was Jem's privilege.

Jem crept up to Mina's room, quiet so as not to wake Kit and to let Tessa go back to sleep.

When he reached her room, though, he saw Kit was awake. Kit was already in the baby's room, with Mina in his arms.

"Hey," Kit said to the baby, speaking seriously as if to a teammate. "C'mon, do me a solid, will you, Min? You've been waking them up all week. I bet they're tired."

Mina's small face was tearstained, but she had clearly forgotten her tears before they were dry. She was smiling a gummy smile, apparently enchanted by this new experience.

"Jem always talks about how advanced you are, so how about advancing to the part where you sleep through the night?" Kit said. "I wonder if having a mom who is an immortal warlock means that you've been maturing faster than other babies."

Mina had no response for this. Kit didn't hold Mina often, though he would bend over the cradle or someone else's arms and awkwardly offer her attention when he came into a room where she was. He did give her his forefinger to hold frequently, and now that Mina could focus better, she would hold her hands out imperiously when Kit came near. Jem was sure she knew Min-Min was Kit's name for her, and Kit was the boy who held her hand.

Now she was bundled inelegantly in Kit's arms, the long white woolen blanket Catarina Loss had knitted for her trailing. Kit tripped over it as he walked the floor and stumbled. Jem tensed to lunge across the room and catch them. But Kit caught himself against the wall, though he let out a curse as he did so and promptly looked horrified and belatedly tried to cover one of Mina's ears.

"Please don't tell Jem and Tessa I said that word in front of you!" Kit exclaimed.

Mina, who clearly thought Kit was playing a game with her, gave him another sleepy smile that split her small face, then yawned like a kitten. Kit bit his lip and hummed a broken line of a song to her, several times over. Soon she was drooling against Kit's T-shirt, which had a design on it that Kit had informed Jem meant superheroes. Kit patted her on the back.

"There we go," Kit murmured, sounding proud of himself. "It's our secret."

Jem watched Kit and Mina for a little while longer, then crept back to his room, letting Kit return to his own bed believing he'd helped Jem and Tessa to rest.

Janus kept thinking of that word, "Consul," and Alec, and he decided he should survey the situation for himself. He couldn't pass himself off as Alec's *parabatai* if he didn't know about Alec's life. His father had always said that knowledge was power to be used in battle.

It was too dangerous to go to the Institute and risk someone seeing him, but Janus remembered where Magnus's loft had been. He concealed himself and watched the door until Alec emerged. It was one of the sunny spring days in New York that was better than summer, the sky full of clear light and soft breezes.

Alec was where Alec had always wanted to be: walking easily by Magnus's side. There were two children with them. One had very dark, short, crisply curling hair, and even though he was too young to bear Marks, there was still a suggestion of grace about him that said *Shadowhunter*. His small fingers were curled securely within one of Magnus's ringed hands. Magnus's other hand was tucked, with Alec's, in the pocket of Alec's ratty, unzipped hoodie. The other kid was glamoured to look like a mundane, but Janus saw beneath it to blue skin and horns. The warlock boy was up on Alec's shoulders, laughing and kicking his feet against Alec's chest.

It took Janus a moment to realize the strangest thing. Alec's chest and shoulders were broader than they had been in his world. Alec had died when he was still a boy always a little afraid to be in love.

Consul, thought Janus. *You must be so proud.*

Janus followed as they made their way to the Brooklyn Botanic Garden, where the cherry trees were blooming. Alec and Magnus seemed to be taking these kids to the cherry blossom festival.

The kids were excited. The pink clusters of flowers formed a soft avenue around them, a pink marble arch come alive, petals falling like bright confetti into their hair. The little boy on Alec's shoulders caught the petals in his hands. The trees provided plenty of cover so that Janus would not be seen.

There were *taiko* drummers under a bandstand, and people

dancing in the grass. Alec set the warlock child down, and he immediately ran into the crowd of dancers and began to strike dramatic poses. Magnus went and danced with the little kid, though Magnus's dancing did not involve any falling on his butt.

The Shadowhunter boy copied Alec, leaning against a tree with his arms folded in the same way Alec's were, until Magnus beckoned and said, "Rafe," and the boy's small surly face lit up and he ran to him. Then he held Magnus's hands and let Magnus pirouette him about, his shoes lighting up as he twirled in the dust.

Alec watched them for a while, fondly, then wandered away to buy ice creams. A couple of Downworlder teens, a young werewolf girl and a faerie boy, were waiting in the line and watched him come with nervous delight.

"It's our Consul!" said the werewolf girl.

"He's not technically ours," said the faerie boy. "He belongs to the Shadowhunters who aren't assholes. Maia is your leader and King Kieran is mine."

"I can have a Consul as well as a pack leader if I want," muttered the werewolf. "He's coming right over! What do we say?"

"I cannot lie, Michelle!" said the faerie. "You know this! You have to pretend to be cool for both of us."

Alec nodded to them, a little strained with strangers still, but trying to be friendly in a way the Alec Janus had known might not have.

Alec smiled crookedly into their silence and offered, "Hey, here for the festival?"

The faerie boy gasped out, "Yes!"

"Me too," said Alec. "Family outing. Those are my kids over there, with my husband. Over there. That's my husband."

Alec said "my husband" so proudly, as if the word was a new

and dearly prized acquisition with the shine still on it, something he wanted to show everybody.

My boyfriend, Clary had called Janus, a few times, and it had made him so happy to finally be hers, to think she might be proud he was hers. He'd been embarrassed to show how happy he was. He remembered the emotions now and they prickled like pins and needles, like dead limbs starved of blood finally beginning to wake up. And like pins and needles, they hurt.

"Oh, congratulations," Michelle the werewolf said to Alec, looking as if she might cry. "Your husband. That's so nice."

The boy nodded vigorously.

"Um, thanks," said Alec. "Nice to meet you. Enjoy the festival."

He went back to his family, where the kids hailed the ice creams with great joy. Alec slid his arms around Magnus, and they danced a little together, Alec slightly clumsy in a dance as he never was in battle, but smiling, with his eyes shut and his cheek laid against Magnus's.

The young couple wandered off with their ice creams, which were decorated with rose petals and which the faerie seemed to enjoy more than his girlfriend, chattering excitedly about the amazing experience they had just had.

Janus watched them, and when they wandered off among the trees for privacy, he let them see him.

"You're Jace Herondale," breathed the werewolf girl, obviously thrilled. "Jace Herondale *and* Alec Lightwood. This is literally the best day of my life. I can't wait to tell Mom."

"Actually," said Janus, "I'd appreciate it if you didn't tell anybody. You two are about the same age my friends and I were when we saved the world. I think I can trust you two. I think you could do great things. I'd love your help."

They looked at each other with awkward, surprised enthusiasm. "Help with what?" said the werewolf.

Janus told them. It seemed to go well at first. Their eyes were shining. They wanted so badly to be heroes. He'd wanted to be one himself, once.

The werewolf girl, who seemed to know more of Alec and Jace in this world, was nodding eagerly. The faerie boy nodded less and said very little. Janus wasn't certain of him. After he was done talking and pretended to leave, Janus swung around and quietly followed them. He could feel his Soundless rune sparking against his skin: a novel sensation after so long.

"I don't care who he is," said the faerie boy. "I don't trust him. I'm going to tell the King."

Well, win some, lose some. The important thing was knowing when to cut your losses.

Janus cut their throats and buried the two young lovers side by side under the green leaves of the springtime trees. He made sure to close their eyes and clasp the girl's hand safe in the boy's before he smoothed the soil over them, so they were sleeping peacefully together. He gave them the death he would have wanted for himself.

Mina woke early in the morning. This time Jem got to her first, before Kit or Tessa had a chance to stir. Mina smiled with surprised delight when she saw Jem's face over the side of the crib, as if she'd worried that this time he wouldn't come.

"There is never any need to worry, Mina mine," said Jem. "Silly melon."

He dressed her in the red romper with a blue rabbit on the front that Magnus had sent them, then put her in his front pack. Mina cooed excitedly as he did so. She loved an outing.

They walked together through the woods to the village. The village was very small, and there was a great bakery they often patronized. The two ladies who ran the bakery were very welcoming.

"Aw, look," he heard one of the ladies whisper to the other, quietly enough so he wouldn't have heard them if he did not still have Shadowhunter hearing. "He brought the baby again!"

Jem bought *pain au chocolat* for Kit, because he liked it, and apple-and-raisin pastries for Tessa.

"My wife doesn't like chocolate," he explained. "But my—but Kit does."

"Right, your wife's . . . nephew?" The woman's tone was friendly as well as curious.

"Nephew, cousin." Jem shrugged. "Same family. We were very glad when he agreed to come live with us."

The woman winked. "My little sister says he's a total beast."

Jem didn't think that was a very nice thing to say about Kit.

"You guys seem like such a happy couple," the woman continued, which *was* nice. "Have you been together long?"

"We've only been married a few years," said Jem. "But we had a very long engagement." He accepted the paper bag of pastries with a smile and waved Mina's dimpled hand at them. "Say bye to the kind ladies, Mina."

"So cute!" he heard the woman whisper as the door of the bakery closed behind them. "I'm dying."

"Hear that, Mina mine?" Jem murmured. "They think you're cute. They're right, of course."

Mina waved at the trees in loose uncoordinated movements, like a tiny queen accepting tribute. He took the long way through the woods, past the thatched pub where they had afternoon tea sometimes, and across the bridge so Mina could babble to the brook.

Through the shifting green leaves and radiant splashes of sunlight, Jem saw the slate roof and uneven white plaster of the small manor house that was their home.

This house, nestled on the edge of Dartmoor, had been in the Carstairs family for a long time. Jem's uncle Elias Carstairs had owned it once and lived there with his family. Out of concern for Kit, Jem and Tessa had enlisted Magnus to put up wards around the house that prevented those with ill intentions from crossing onto the property.

At the side of the house, blue-shuttered French doors hung open, showing a white-painted kitchen splashed with sunlight. Jem's family was having breakfast at a massive farmer's table. Tessa was in a white robe, and Kit was still in his superhero pajamas, and they hailed the coming of pastries with acclaim.

"Mina and I journeyed far, and have returned bearing love and baked goods."

"My adventurous Mina," said Tessa, kissing Mina's silky hair, then tipping up her face for Jem's kiss. "Are you ready to defeat evil vampires using your knowledge of technology and the train timetables, like in *Dracula*?"

"Saw that movie," said Kit.

"Read that book," Tessa shot back.

"I have no idea what you two are talking about," Jem said, on cue. "But Mina was much admired in town."

Tessa raised an eyebrow. "I'm sure she was."

"But one of the lady's sisters was unkind about Kit. Don't

make friends with her, Kit. She called you a beast."

Kit beamed. "Really? Did someone really say that? Who said that?"

"Oh, is that good?" asked Jem.

"I *have* been working out," said Kit happily to himself.

"I didn't know that was good either," Tessa confided to Jem. "Language changes so often through the years, it's hard to keep track of. Especially slang. It's fascinating, but sometimes I liked the earlier meanings of the words best."

"Yeah, well, Min has to know how people speak in this day and age," Kit said sternly.

Mina cooed and reached out her hands to him, and Kit surrendered his forefinger to her grasp. He continued to eat *pain au chocolat* with his free hand.

"You want the other kids to think you're cool, right, Min?" he asked her as she burbled agreement. "You're lucky I'm here."

Tessa swooped on Kit from behind, ruffling his golden hair with the hand not holding her pastry, on her way to get Jem coffee from the stove.

"We're all lucky you're here," she told him.

Kit bowed his head, but not before Jem saw his face flush, pleased and shy.

Once he buried the kids, Janus went back and found that Magnus and Alec had wandered in the opposite direction, farther afield from the music. Alec and the kids were playing soccer with a fluorescent pink ball. Alec, being Alec, was half playing, half patiently teaching them. Janus remembered when they were kids, how whenever he or Isabelle wasn't as good as Alec was, Alec would practice with them endlessly until they were better than Alec was himself. Every time, he would do that. Janus had forgotten, until now.

The Shadowhunter boy was good at soccer when he was concentrating, but he was constantly abandoning the game and zigzagging back to Magnus, hovering by his side like an adoring bumblebee.

Janus envisioned what Magnus had become in his world, the pitiful thing his body had been. It was odd to see Magnus whole and well, sitting under a cherry blossom tree. He was wearing buckled purple boots, skinny jeans, and a tank top that had BABE WITH THE POWER scrawled on it in pixie dust. He was leaning against the tree, cat's eyes slitted lazily, but he smiled whenever the Shadowhunter boy returned to him, and after the fifth time he made a small gesture, and the falling cherry blossoms began to circle around the boy's head, winding intricate patterns like bracelets around his arms, brushing against his plump cheeks and making him giggle.

The warlock boy was very intense about soccer, short legs pumping furiously over the grass. Eventually he seemed to become concerned Alec might win, and he picked up the ball and ran away with it, back to Magnus and the other kid.

"I won!" announced the warlock boy. "I always win."

Magnus kissed the boy on the cheek and laughed, and the sound of his laugh made a smile light on Alec's face as he jogged up to them. Janus had forgotten how much more Alec had begun to smile, once Magnus was in his life.

"I heard you lost your soccer game?" teased Magnus. "I heard the Consul is a big loser?"

Alec shrugged. "No kiss for me, I guess."

He was flirting, Janus realized. Alec hadn't lived long enough to learn how to do that, not in the confident way he was now.

"Oh, there just might be," said Magnus.

The Shadowhunter kid was still playing with the floating blossoms. The warlock kid put his ball on the ground and trotted after it as it glided gently away.

Alec leaned down, taking Magnus's pixie dust shirt in both hands to pull Magnus up toward him. Magnus's spiky head tipped back, and one of Alec's arms went around Magnus's waist.

Janus remembered another world. Alec had still been clinging to what Magnus had become, at the very last. Those strong scarred archer's hands, always swift to protect and defend, held him fast. Even in death, there seemed no way to break Alec's grip.

Janus hadn't had the chance to take Clary in his arms one last time, as Alec had with Magnus. Janus understood the choice his *parabatai* had made, the only choice he could've made with evil on his threshold and all he loved in ruins.

When Janus and Sebastian found them lying together in the rubble, Sebastian had been furious. He had wanted to capture Alec alive. Alec knew secrets about the resistance, about small pockets of hidden free humans: information Sebastian craved and that Alec had died to hide.

With a howl, Sebastian had kicked at Alec's body. The desolate lack where the *parabatai* bond had been screamed. It was one of the few times Janus was able to think, *Kill him.*

Now, in the sunlight of the park, the undergrowth crackled. Janus spun around to face the enemy, cursing himself for being distracted, for being sentimental, as Sebastian and Valentine always said he was.

"What're you doing, Uncle Jace?" asked the warlock boy, clutching his ball and clearly pleased at making a much greater discovery. His round face was smiling and curious.

Janus went still.

"Are you playing hide-and-seek?" the boy continued.

Slowly, Janus's hand moved toward his dagger.

He whispered, "Yes."

The boy darted into the bushes and put his arms around Janus's leg. Janus's hand tightened on his knife.

"I love you, Uncle Jace," the boy whispered, with a conspiratorial grin, and Janus shuddered. "Don't be sad. I won't tell where you're hiding."

Janus drew his knife. Warlocks were not safe to be around. It would be a quick, clean kill, and better for Alec, in the end.

"Max!" Alec shouted. He didn't sound concerned now, but if there was no response, he would be.

Max, thought Janus. Long ago, the youngest Lightwood. In this world Magnus was alive, so Alec was alive. Alec was the Consul, and they had children. Alec had named his son for that lost Max.

Janus let go of his knife. He let go of the boy. His hands were shaking too much to hold on to either.

Little Max darted out of the bushes with his arms outstretched, making a zooming sound as if he were an airplane, and ran back to his family. When they went home from the park, Max was still holding on to his ball, trotting at Magnus's side as Magnus sang a soft Spanish lullaby, while the Shadowhunter boy slept, drooling on Alec's shoulder.

Janus did not follow them out of the park. He stayed by the gates and watched them go.

The words of Janus's *parabatai* oath echoed in his head, worse than a death sentence. *Where thou diest, will I die, and there will I be buried.* He had not kept his oath, but he'd wanted to. Death would have been welcome. Death would have meant being with Clary.

Long ago in the other world, when Sebastian was sleeping, Janus had gone back for Alec, but the bodies had vanished. Janus hoped now that they had not been eaten by the roving, starving demons. He hoped Maryse had burned Alec and Magnus both. He wished that a kind wind had carried their ashes away, and let them stay together.

When they first moved into Cirenworth Hall, the house in England that they intended to be their family's home, Jem and Tessa had noticed how often Kit's eyes fell on the valuables they had decorated the house with.

One evening they collected up everything they could think of and placed all their most prized possessions in Kit's room, lining them up on tables and windowsills.

When Kit went into his room next, he stayed in there for some time and was absolutely quiet. Eventually Jem and Tessa tapped on his door. At his assenting mumble, they pushed open the door and looked inside. They found Kit standing in the middle of the room. He hadn't touched anything.

"What does all this mean?" Kit asked. "Do you think I'd take them and—do you want me to—?"

He sounded lost. His blue eyes fell on Tessa's first editions, on Jem's Stradivarius violin, as though they were signposts and he was trying to find his way in a terribly strange land.

Jem said, "We want you to stay, and to know that the choice

is entirely yours, and we wanted to show you something. We want you to know there is nothing in this house more precious to us than you."

Kit had stayed.

The home the Seelie Queen had given them stood on a hollow hill near bone-white sea cliffs, a hundred leagues from either Seelie or Unseelie Court, and far from any prying eye that might spy the Queen's long-lost and long-sought-for son.

Within the house, the walls flickered with shadows. As Janus came through the doorway into the dark, the shadows trembled in the wind that crept in with him.

Ash was draped over a sofa, long legs stretched out, dressed in the faerie clothes the Queen had provided. Black silk, green velvet. Nothing but the finest for her boy. Ash hadn't aged much since they had come from Thule. He still looked sixteen, which was the age Janus believed him to be. He was holding up a piece of paper to the light, studying it intently.

When he heard the door close, Ash turned his head, the white-gold gossamer-fine hair he had inherited from his father falling around his curved faerie ears, and hastily tucked the bloodstained piece of paper away into his pocket.

"What's that?" Janus asked.

"Nothing important," said Ash with a slow blink of his grass-green eyes. "You're back."

"Do you think I would have had eyes that color," Sebastian had said once, late at night when he was in one of his most melancholy moods, "if our father had not . . . done what he did, and made me what I am?"

Janus had not been able to reply. He couldn't imagine

Sebastian or his flat shark's eyes, dead as the sun and black as the eternal night in their world, as anything other than they were. When he looked in Ash's eyes, green as springtime, green as new beginning, he thought of someone else entirely.

It was hard to keep secrets from Sebastian. He always took them away. But Janus had kept that one.

"It's good to be back," Janus told Ash slowly.

He didn't like it much in Faerie, but Ash was here. He'd needed a secure place for Ash. Ash was going to change everything. Ash was the key. Nothing bad could happen to him.

Janus knew Ash wanted him to like it here more than he did. When they came here, Ash had asked the Queen, his mother, for a piano. Now the piano stood near the doors, sleek and shining darkly, reflected by all the mirrors. Janus tried not to look at it.

"You said you used to play once," Ash offered when the piano came.

Ash seemed disappointed when Janus said he no longer remembered how.

Janus had imagined Ash would be happy and safe, back with his mother, but the Queen said Ash couldn't stay at Court.

"I lost a daughter who will never return," she'd told them, thorns in her voice. "I lost a son who returned past hope. I will never risk him again. He must be kept secret and secure."

So Ash lived in this isolated house, this cliff-top palace, and Janus lived here with him. For now.

Janus didn't like the idea of abandoning Ash to live in the New York Institute. But that was where Clary was.

Wherever you are is where I want to be.

Janus needed water to wash away the bitter taste in his mouth. He went to get it, and Ash followed him. Ash's step was faerie soft and Shadowhunter trained, entirely noiseless, like having a pale shadow.

When Ash first came to Thule, Sebastian had been pleased. Sebastian had always liked the idea of blood binding someone to him. He'd seen it as a sign that he was doing everything right, that another world had delivered an heir to him, since in Thule, the Seelie Queen had died before she had ever given birth.

It pleased Sebastian's vanity that Ash resembled him. Sebastian had thought that finally here was what he had always wanted: someone like him. Sebastian embraced Ash and allowed Janus to do the same. For a while Sebastian played with Ash, tried to teach him, but Sebastian grew tired of his toys quickly and broke them.

Sebastian had not been patient with Ash for some time before the end.

Once Sebastian had been training Ash, and Ash had made a mistake. Sebastian had gone for Ash with a whip.

Sebastian's face was startled and offended when Janus moved between them and caught the lash between his hands. The whip split Janus's palms open, and blood dappled the ground.

"Why not whip him? Father did it to *me*." Sebastian's voice was the whip now. "And I'm strong. He didn't do it to you, and you were weak until I got my hands on you. I should do the best thing for my boy, shouldn't I?"

Janus was already convinced. He should drop the whip and let Sebastian hurt Ash.

But his words were racing ahead of his thoughts, as if he couldn't control them. "Of course. It's just that there are so many things for you to do. Training a boy should be the general's work, not the ruler's. You are higher than this. You know I want only to serve you and never to fail you. Let me train him, and if he isn't satisfactory, then the lash can be his guide."

He could feel Sebastian was bored with training anyway. After a moment Sebastian cast whip and boy aside and strode off. Ash watched Sebastian walk away.

"Hell of a father," Ash murmured.

"Don't talk like that," Janus ordered.

Ash's face changed when he transferred his gaze from Sebastian to Janus, lingering on Janus's bloody hands. When Ash's eyes were not so hard and guarded, he reminded Janus of Clary. It made him think of how Clary had once looked at Simon or at Luke, before Clary and Luke died and Simon disappeared. When Sebastian came for Clary's mother, Luke had tried to stand in Sebastian's way.

"I will do as you tell me," Ash offered suddenly. "Since you're going to be my teacher. You'll see. I'll make you proud."

After that, Janus trained Ash, but Janus should never have stepped in. Sebastian noted how many hours Janus spent with Ash and decided he wanted to see results from all this training.

Sebastian kept a pit of demons under the floor of Psychopomp, his favorite nightclub. It made for a nice show-piece and a convenient method of disposing of those disloyal to the Star. Sebastian ordered that Ash be given a sword and dropped into it.

Ash did not protest or struggle. He let Janus lead him forward, to the very edge of the pit. Then he stepped out into the empty air and fell.

A dark wave of demons closed over him.

Sebastian and Janus both leaned forward, Janus sick with a pain he did not understand and Sebastian smiling like a guardian angel. They watched as Ash's head broke through the wave of demons, a swimmer fighting his way to the surface in a dark sea. He rose—and rose, and rose again. He soared into the air, black wings spreading from his back.

"Ah." Sebastian sounded delighted. "So it has come to pass."

"What is it?" Janus had demanded. "What's happening to him?"

"He is becoming more," said Sebastian. "The Unseelie King worked magic upon him, and he has the blood of Lilith in him. Those are the wings of an angel—one of the fallen sort. They were always in his blood, but Thule has drawn them out of him."

Sebastian was applauding, laughing as Ash spun and flew low, slashing with his silver sword, slicing through the necks of a dozen demons at once. Ichor splashed the walls of the pit.

Janus's hands itched.

He had beaten Sebastian once, long ago, when he was someone else.

We were both trained by Valentine. But I tried harder, because I loved my father and I wanted to please him so badly. Then there was Robert and Maryse and Isabelle and Alec, always Alec, every one of them teaching me whatever they knew, so I could protect myself. Because they loved me. I was better than Sebastian. I was better.

He'd trained with Clary, too, a few times. He'd meant to teach her everything he knew, so she could always protect herself. So they could fight together. Ash was as fearless and determined as she was. Janus could teach him everything, so Ash would always be safe. He did not know why, but it was important that Ash always be safe.

When Janus watched Ash fight, he thought that when Ash was grown, he might beat Sebastian too. He crushed the treacherous idea down, but he couldn't help smiling a small smile down at Ash.

Ash's lip curled back from his teeth. It was his father's sneer, his father's scorn, aimed at Sebastian himself. Then his green eyes passed with total withering indifference over Sebastian, and caught on Janus. Ash smiled up at him.

Janus went cold.

So did Sebastian's voice. "My father," he mused. "My sister."

"Please," Janus begged. He couldn't talk about Clary. "No. Please."

Sebastian never did have any mercy. "My father, my sister, my son. They were all mine. And yet they all wanted *you* more. Valentine's sweet boy. Clary's golden prince. Ash's guardian angel."

Nobody else ever dared speak Clary's name aloud.

"You might as well know," Sebastian said. "Nothing you feel for Ash is real. The Unseelie King gifted him with many gifts. The wings are but an outward expression of that. He also has the power to command perfect love and perfect loyalty. You have no choice but to want to protect him."

Janus froze. His heart beat slowly, thickly in his chest. It never occurred to him to doubt Sebastian. He had seen the way Annabel was with Ash. How she would have laid down on broken glass so he could walk on her.

This was why. *This* was why. Nothing Janus felt for Ash was real.

Sebastian ordered that the pit be closed. Ash flew up, straight and dark as an arrow, and knelt at the pit's edge, his sword gleaming. His wings beat softly in the still air of Thule.

"Are you angry, Jace?" Sebastian said. "That I told you the truth?"

Janus had shaken his head. "No. I exist to serve you."

It was true. Sebastian was stronger. Whatever Janus had done once, Sebastian had beaten him in the end.

"Yes." Sebastian sounded thoughtful. "You're mine. And so is the world. But the world's hollow these days, isn't it?"

The world had been hollow since Clary died. Janus had never expected to find meaning again. He thought of that later, when he bound Ash's wounds, and when they trained. If Ash had power over him, Janus thought, he didn't use it. He never ordered Janus to do anything he didn't want to do.

Ash listened to him. He was careful. He didn't defy Sebastian. He kept training. Ash was very good, but it didn't please Sebastian any longer.

Sometimes Janus caught Sebastian looking at Ash in a way Janus recognized. There was an edge and steel to that look, as if it were a dissecting knife.

One day, when Sebastian was sleeping—it was a little easier to do certain things when Sebastian was sleeping—Janus took Ash outside and talked about traveling, about going somewhere, about not upsetting his father.

Janus tried to explain, tried to work out how he could possibly explain. He couldn't say: *He wants to hurt you, and I don't.* That would be impossible. Janus and Sebastian only wanted the same things.

Janus ended up on his knees in the ashes, trying to choke

out the words. Ash did what his father had never done, and went on his knees too. He'd put his arms around Janus.

"Come with me," he said.

"I can't," Janus gasped through waves of agony. "You know I can't."

He screamed then. It felt right, doing what Sebastian wanted, it was right. He didn't know how to do anything else, and when he tried, it went wrong. It hurt too much. He kept screaming.

"Don't," Ash said. "Don't."

"Do you understand what I am trying to tell you?" Janus asked, his voice blurred. His head rang with pain and his mouth was full of blood from biting his tongue, but he was used to blood.

"Yes," Ash had whispered. "I understand. You can stop."

The next time Ash and Sebastian were together, Ash pretended indifference as usual. But Janus caught a covert look in those green eyes, as cold as any in Sebastian's. *Ash hates Sebastian now*, Janus realized, and he knew that he'd made everything worse.

He'd known Ash was doomed. But Sebastian had died instead, and now Janus and Ash were in another world. It had not been easy to get here. But it was worth it. Everything could be different here.

Janus finished his glass of water, and tried to breathe, and glanced over to where Ash stood. Ash was watching him, and Janus swept the pale hair off Ash's brow. He tried to be gentle. It always made him feel steadier, in this world and the other, to look at Ash. Sebastian's son, with Clary's green eyes. The only thing besides Sebastian Janus was allowed to love. Ash, who was beloved and still not safe, Ash, who was all Janus had.

For now.

"There's blood on your hands," Ash murmured.

Janus shrugged. "That's nothing new."

He sat at the carven oak table, where the last acorn that had ever fallen from the dead tree was set in the table's center. He laid his weary head in his arms. Once Sebastian had told Janus that Sebastian was always burning, but it was better when he had Janus, when they were burning together. Now Sebastian was dead, and Janus was still burning. Ash laid a cool hand on Janus's shoulder.

"I thought you would get better here," Ash said, his voice low. "But you're not. Are you?"

Janus lifted his head, for Ash's sake. "I will be," he promised. "Soon."

"Oh yes. I'd almost forgotten," Ash remarked, withdrawing. "When you go away and leave me."

Janus looked at him in surprise. "Why would I leave you?"

"Because you only love me because you have to," said Ash. "It's the spell. Perfect loyalty. Did you think I didn't know?"

Ash's eyes were green ice. They didn't look anything like Clary's then.

Janus went back to Magnus's, hardly knowing why he did so. He was aware it would be madness to go near the Institute, but surely this was safe. He wore all black, like the Shadowhunter he used to be. He stood concealed by the shadow of a wall near Magnus's loft, waiting for someone he knew to come out, but instead he saw light and movement behind the windows. Perhaps they were staying in this evening. It was a foggy, misty night, after all.

Then a voice coming from the other direction said, "I'll kill you, Jace Herondale."

The last time Janus had seen Simon in his world, Simon had said something similar.

Simon's face had been moon pale and sixteen years old, always sixteen years old. He'd looked like a lost child, but in that world so many were lost children.

Now Simon was walking down a street in New York. He was taller and older, his skin tanned and runed, and he was carrying groceries.

Simon wasn't a vampire, Janus realized. He was—he was a *Shadowhunter*. What had *happened* in this world?

"Yeah?" Simon said, his voice amused. "Yeah, yeah, yeah. Keep bragging, it's what you're best at. Prepare to be decimated. You are not as good at video games as you think."

He shifted his brown paper shopping bag to the crook of his elbow, his phone pressed between shoulder and ear.

"Yes, I got the cupcakes," he added. "And you're doing your job, right? Keep all the Lightwoods out of the kitchen! You can't let them touch anything."

There was a pause.

"Isabelle is the love of my life, but her seven-layer dip is like the nine circles of Hell," said Simon. "Don't tell her I said that! Are you telling her I said that literally while you are on the phone with me? You are so dead."

Simon hung up and dropped his phone in the pocket of his jeans, shaking his head. Then he let himself in through the door. He seemed to have a key. Janus sidled around to the fire escape and clambered up to the second floor. Kneeling, he peered in through the window.

Through the rain-wet glass he saw someone dancing, laughing, long black hair swirling around her shoulders. After a dazed moment, Janus realized who it was. Isabelle, alive. Isabelle, striking poses and laughing. Alec went to the window and gave her a hug, one-armed, as she showered the squirming child tucked under Alec's other arm with kisses.

Janus had been with Valentine, and then with Sebastian, longer than he had been with these, his family. Sometimes it had seemed like a sentimental dream—*more of your weakness, Jace*—that he'd ever had the Lightwoods at all. Alec, Isabelle, Max, Maryse, Robert. His family.

But what had he done to Maryse?

What he'd had to do, Janus reminded himself, clenching his hand around his sword hilt. The best thing, the right thing. He couldn't be weak.

There was brightness at the edge of Janus's vision, as there often was, taunting and tormenting, never coalescing into anything real. Except this time, it did. So many times since Clary died, Janus had swung around thinking he would see her, hoping desperately for a ghost, for a whisper, for anything but this endless darkness without her. He had to stop wishing for her, stop hoping for her, stop searching for her. He had to burn his heart out until there was nothing left but ash. No matter where he looked, she was never there.

Until now.

Now he understood why Isabelle had been striking poses.

Clary was drawing her.

She had wedged herself into a window seat opposite Isabelle, her sketchbook balanced between them, her profile outlined against the glass. This time, she did not fade away or go wrong. This time, she was real.

She'd died in his world when she was a girl, but here she was a woman. She had scars from runes on her arms, her skin was a little darker and her freckles a little lighter, and her eyes were the color of the grass that no longer grew in Thule. Her hair was twisted up into a bun at the back of her head, a few fiery tendrils escaping. She glowed like a light. She was everything.

Wherever you are is where I want to be.

He was dizzy with the yearning to hold her, overwhelmed by the urge. *Why not*, he thought for a reckless moment, though he knew he was not allowed to be reckless. He had been once. He could see himself doing it: going to her, going to them. Telling Clary everything, and resting at last, with his head on her knee.

Then *he* came into the room, and the world went black and red with furious despair.

He was all in black, as Janus was, but he was smiling: looking around easily, casually, with an absolute air of belonging. Alec smiled at him. Isabelle leaned over and poked him in the side with a painted fingernail. And Clary, Clary, his Clary—she lifted her beautiful face up to his and gave him a kiss.

He was there, the Jace from this world, and Janus hated him. Janus wanted to kill him, and he could do it. Why should he have everything, when Janus had nothing? He should have been the one to remain in this dimension. Not Jace.

The rain hit the windows and blurred those within from his sight. He strained to see a glimpse of Clary's bright hair, and could not. She was lost to him again. He was bitterly tired of her being lost. He couldn't breathe with the pain of it. He clambered down the fire escape and stumbled to the nearest alley, where it was dark, where he would be hidden, where he could scream out all the agony in his soul. He tried, but as in a nightmare, no sound came out.

Janus wanted to remember Clary's face at the window. But he could not see hers without seeing Jace's. That smooth young face, the bright head held arrogantly high, the clear golden eyes that had never seen his *parabatai* dead, the hands that had never killed Maryse and countless others. That face had never known a world blackened and ruined after the loss of Clary. That was the boy who fought on the side of the angels, all grown up. *Valentine's sweet boy. Clary's golden prince.* Janus understood the wretched, murderous jealousy in Sebastian's voice now, the jealousy of all you could never be.

Janus could never be that boy again or the man he had become.

His shuddering breaths sounded almost like sobs, but he stopped breathing when he heard her voice. Clary's. As if she was standing only a few feet away.

"How can *all* the vampires be drunk?" said Clary. "No, I mean, I understand how, Maia, I just don't know why anybody thought that would be a good idea."

There was a pause. Janus crept to the mouth of the alleyway. It still seemed impossible to believe, but she was there. Clary was standing outside, a phone pressed between her shoulder and her ear as she paced back and forth, a slim vivid shape against the darkness. She was fighting her way into a coat and trying to keep hold of an umbrella. In doing so, her stele fell to the sidewalk, unnoticed, rolling until it came to a stop against a trash can.

". . . Well, I assumed we both blamed Elliott," Clary said.

"Say no more! Simon the former Downworlder and his trusty *parabatai* are on their way to keep the peace." Clary half turned toward him. Streetlights made the raindrops caught in her hair glimmer like a radiant veil.

This was another world. There were still angels here. Janus crept from the alleyway, picking up her stele.

". . . *Who* invited a stripper called Faerie Buns?" Clary demanded into the phone.

She stepped closer to him. His hand tightened on the stele. He knew that to approach her in his current state was madness, but she was so close. . . .

"I don't even know what to say about the stripper. Bye, Maia," said Clary, shaking her head as she ended the call.

Janus took a few steps and was beside her, just outside the pool of the streetlights.

"Hey," Clary said, still distracted by her phone. "I thought you were staying behind."

She wasn't looking up at him. He swallowed and held out the stele. "I chased after you," he said, his voice sounding strange to his own ears. "You left this inside. You should have it with you."

"Oh," Clary said, taking it from him and slipping it into her coat. "Thanks. I thought it was in my pocket."

She lifted the umbrella so it sheltered him, too, and leaned slightly against him. No more fantasies, no more dreams. He knew then that none of the illusions he'd tried to fool himself with had ever even come close. Every detail had been wrong, everything in the world had been wrong, and everything about himself.

He'd been crawling across the scorching sand of the desert

where her dead body lay for years, but now there was a shimmering oasis before him. She was here. She was alive again. She was with him, and he would have suffered through every long day of every hopeless year again to touch her for a moment more.

Clary was warm, and breathing. She was staying that way, no matter what he had to do or who he had to kill to keep her safe, to keep her with him. She leaned against him with perfect trust.

A rain-bright curl brushed against Janus's shoulder, and he felt blessed, saved, though he'd failed to save her. It could all be different here.

"The vampire-and-werewolf meet 'n' greet has descended into total chaos," Clary reported, her voice indescribably sweet in his ears. "But Simon and I will get things under control. You go have a good time."

He wanted her to go on talking, to let him hold her and drink up every word, but she was waiting for him to say something. He had to say something. He knew he was being stiff and strange, and he knew from the tension in her body that she could tell something was not right, but he had no idea how to fix it, how to relax, how to be the person he once was.

His voice cracked. "I—I missed you."

She had to believe him. He had never meant any words so much.

"Aw," said Clary, her cheek against his shoulder. "Nobody but me would ever believe you're as sweet as you are."

His whisper was hoarse. "Nobody but you would ever believe I'm sweet at all."

She laughed. He'd made her laugh. It had been so many silent years since he last heard that sound. "This shouldn't take long. I told Maia that Simon and I would drop in and maybe escort a couple of the worst offenders back to the Hotel Dumort. Normally Lily would keep a handle on things, but Maia says Lily's really drunk too."

"I'll come with you." Janus breathed in the scent of her hair. "I'll keep you safe."

"No need," Clary told him. She began to draw away.

Janus held on, crushing her against him. He would not let her leave him. Not again.

She lifted her head. He glimpsed her beautiful face in a flash of moonlight followed by shadow, saw her eyes narrow. "What's wrong with you, Jace? You're acting really weird—"

No. No. You believe it's me, you know it's me, you know I'm the one who really belongs with you.

The words stuttered through Janus's mind. He wanted to quiet the unease in her voice. He wanted her to lean against him again. Her touch made the world right.

There was the sound of a van's wheels, squealing to a stop on the street outside. "That's Simon," Clary said. "Don't worry. I'll come back soon."

You will come back. But not to me.

He let her go. It took all his strength. She smiled when he did, clearly puzzled by the way he was acting. *She knows,* he thought in terror, but then he had his reward.

She stood on tiptoe and kissed him on his starving mouth. The memory of a thousand years ago came to him, kissing Clary in an alley full of rain, the feel of her wet skin, the scent of her sweat and perfume and the taste of her mouth. Her arms were around him; her body was curvier now, fuller, and the roundness of her hips under his hands and the feel of her breasts through her jacket overwhelmed his reeling senses, making him dizzy. He could scarcely breathe, but he would rather have her than air. The kiss painted every shadow gold.

She drew away, and now the expression on her face was more confused than ever. She pressed her fingers to her lips. Her eyes searched his face, even as his heart beat unevenly in his chest. He stepped back, into the deeper shadows. She was starting to guess, he thought.

"I love you," he told her. "So much. Someday you'll know how much."

"*Jace*," she said, and then Simon honked the horn of the van.

Clary exhaled, her breath condensing to mist. "Go have fun. You've been working too hard," she said, smiled a swift uncertain smile, and dashed away to Simon's van.

Janus crumpled as the van peeled away, falling to his knees on the drenched and dirty cement. He kissed the ground where Clary had stood. He huddled there, face pressed against the stone, shuddering on his knees.

He wouldn't be able to kill Jace easily and take his place by Clary's side. They would all know. He knew none of their jokes, the way they interacted. He had barely been able to fool Clary for a few stolen moments in the dark. Even now, she suspected him, and later on, she might ask Jace why he'd been acting so strange. . . . Janus couldn't bear to think of it. He could never fool them all in the light. Not yet.

He did not realize for some time that he was soaked to the skin, shaking with cold and rage. He hated them all. He hated Alec and Isabelle and Magnus and Simon. He hated and loved

Clary in equal measure and it was like poison in his throat. For all these years he had been tortured and they had not noticed or cared or missed him.

He would show them what that darkness could be like, one day.

The woods and the gardens were full of memories, but so was their home. Jem and Tessa had put up pictures on the stone walls, black-and-white photographs carefully preserved: of Will, of James and Lucie, who were Mina's half brother and half sister separated by a more than a century. Someday they could point out each face to Mina and tell her their names and that they would have loved her.

Memories were like love: wound and cure, both at once.

That night, they were all together in the nursery, reading Mina her bedtime story. Mina was in Tessa's lap, gumming avidly at the edge of her rubber book. Tessa finished the story and looked down at Kit, who was lying on the carpet, propped up on his elbows.

"I transformed into your mother once," Tessa told him in a low voice. "I know you never knew her."

Kit stiffened but tried to pass it off casually, as he did most things.

"Yeah, I'm still absorbing the fact that I'm literally Rosemary's baby," he remarked.

"Read that book," Tessa said with a faint smile.

"Saw that movie," returned Kit.

"I have no idea what you two are talking about," said Jem, as he usually did when they played Read that book/Saw that movie.

Later Tessa would give him the book, or Kit would cue up the movie on his laptop.

"I don't want to hurt you," Tessa said. "I know I can't replace her or make up for the loss of her. But I wanted to tell you that your mother, the lost Herondale, the descendant of the First Heir—she loved you. She never wanted to leave you. She spent her life running because she thought that was the best way to protect you. She'd always been running: it was the only way she knew. But the happiest time for her was the time when she returned to your father, and they lived together in hiding for a few years, and she had you. I don't get memories as clearly as I once did, but I can remember being her, remember holding you when you were as small as my Mina is now. I know the song she used to sing to you."

Kit scrambled up now. He sat at Tessa's feet with his head bowed as she began to sing. Jem reached for his violin. He played a tune of love and loss, of searching and finding, a melody that ran like a river beneath the bridge of his wife's voice, the melody he loved best in all the world.

"I gave my love a story that had no end. I gave my love a baby with no crying."

She sang the song of Rosemary Herondale, and Jem thought of how impossibly lucky he had been. It could all have been darkness for him, and silence, forever, until he lost hope even for what came after death. If there had been no Tessa, if he had lost her, too, if she had not been immortal—but then she would not have been who she was. That might have been part of what drew him to her first, when he was a dying boy a century and more ago, and she was the loveliest girl he'd ever seen: a girl who had traveled to him across the sea, impossible and magical and beautiful beyond stories or music, a girl who would live forever.

At last, he was no longer doomed, and she was still so lovely.

Jem played a song for Will, for all those he loved on the farthest shore, and for his wife and his baby and the boy who was safe in his keeping, here together in this warm small room at home. One day they might be parted, but they could remember this moment and this melody.

"The story that I love you," Tessa sang. *"It has no end."*

Jem believed her.

Janus visited the Seelie Queen before he went back to Ash.

"You knew my plans had no chance of succeeding," he said to her, his voice flat. "You knew that I could not pretend to be that—that arrogant fool."

"He has the arrogance of luck and being loved," said the Queen. "But would you really want all of them to love you and believe you were him? Or would you rather be loved as your own self?"

"You know what I would want," he said.

Her smile was the curve of a cat's tail. "And you can have it. Let us make new plans."

The Queen had always wanted him to stay in the house of mirrors by the sea, he realized that now. She wanted him to be Ash's guardian, Ash's guard who nobody could pass.

Janus could do that. He wanted to do that. He would help her to her heart's desire, if she would give him his. They talked for a long time. The Queen seemed pleased by the idea that they had someone in New York who would do Janus a favor. She said she could slip Lily a forgetting potion, until the time came for

Janus to collect his favor. The Queen suggested several more ideas, and then said that Ash was waiting.

The Queen was right.

This time Janus did not catch Ash by surprise. Ash met him as Janus made his way up the winding road to home.

Ash had been out flying. Janus watched as Ash landed, alighting in the long grass of the cliff by the sea. His black wings folded down against his narrow back and his broadening shoulders, and there was a bright expectancy on Ash's face that was almost like hope.

Ash had looked at his father, Sebastian, that way long ago, but it hadn't lasted. He looked at his mother, the Queen, that way, but the brightness was beginning to fade now, as Ash learned how different his mother was from his childish memories and yearnings.

Ash only had Janus, but Janus would not fail him as his parents had.

"You're back. I was watching out for you," said Ash.

"How did you know I was coming?" Janus asked.

"I didn't. I just sometimes look out to see if you might come. That's all."

Ash shrugged, but Janus didn't think his shrug was as indifferent as Ash made it seem.

"I saw Clary," Janus said quietly. "She'll be with us, one day."

"I thought . . ." Ash looked puzzled. "I thought you were going to live with her in the New York Institute."

"Plans change," said Janus.

"What's the new plan?" Ash said. "Will you stay?"

My last hope, Janus wanted to say. *I will always love you and never leave you. I knew this world must be better than ours, because you come from this one.*

"What if I did?" Janus asked Ash. "What would you say if I said I would stay with you and train you?"

Ash kicked at a pebble. "I would say that I didn't understand why," he said. "I know you know you don't have real feelings for me. You want to stay and protect me because the Dark Artifices make it so. You *have* to love me and be loyal to me. But distance makes that feeling fade. I know my mother actually loves me, in her way, because she still missed me when I was gone. But I thought that you—once you started traveling to the human world so often—"

"I didn't know that," said Janus, thinking back to Sebastian's long-ago words about Ash's power to inspire love. "That distance makes it fade."

"It does," Ash said. "So if you want to go now—"

"I don't," said Janus, a swell of warmth, like a small tide, lifting his heart. "I never felt any differently about you in the mundane world than I do when you're right next to me. You're mine."

Ash smiled. "Who else's?"

The Queen's son and Sebastian's. Lilith's blood and Valentine's and Clary's. *He was well named,* Sebastian had said once. *He was born to rule over a land turned to ash.*

Janus had seen what Sebastian had done to a world. Time to see what Ash did to this one. When Janus's plans were complete—when the world became chaos and death—Janus and Ash could both belong.

This was a second chance. When the darkness came, Janus could protect Clary. He could keep his family safe. Everybody he loved, starting with Ash.

"If I teach you to be a Shadowhunter, if I teach you to bear runes, it will hurt."

"That's okay," Ash replied. "The old Unseelie King hurt me. My father hurt me. I'm used to it."

"I don't want to hurt you," murmured Janus.

"I know," said Ash. "That's why it's okay."

Valentine had taught Janus through discipline that sometimes seemed harsh, and it had been right to teach Janus that way, but Ash was different. He was strong and smart and quick, and he would learn fast. Janus would never have to kill Ash or stand by and watch him be killed. Sebastian was dead, and Janus still breathed. Sebastian was dead, and Janus and Ash were free.

Ash hesitated. "What did you see out there? In the mundane world?"

His voice was fascinated and almost yearning. Ash had been a captive most of his life, a winged thing in a golden cage. Even now he could not go far from their home. There were too many dangers for the son of the Queen, and Ash had such a bright future ahead of him: so bright it was like the sun, impossible to contemplate. Janus shouldn't have left Ash alone, but he'd make it up to him.

Janus would do better than tell Ash hollow words. Ash must be defended. If he had to, Janus would deal with anyone who posed a threat to Ash or his plans for Ash. This new Unseelie King might be a problem. Far worse, there were rumors about a danger the Queen would not speak of, but that Janus had heard about nonetheless: the descendant of someone called the First Heir. Whoever it was, if they dared threaten Ash, if anyone ever dared threaten Ash again, Janus would hunt them down and present Ash with their heads.

The blue waves crashed against the stones, miles down from the cliff at their feet. It made Janus recall a poem about the ocean in Faerieland.

> *For whatsoever from one place doth fall,*
> *Is with the tide unto an other brought:*
> *For there is nothing lost, that may be found, if sought.*

"It's a beautiful world out there," Janus answered. "I was thinking I'd wrap a bow around it and give it to you."

Soon Janus would have Clary, and Ash would have the world. They only had to wait.

Ash smiled. Behind his green eyes, a predator lurked, like a tiger half-obscured by leaves. "I'd like that," he said.

Tessa was putting Mina down for her nap. Jem lay in the long grass beneath the oak tree, with his cat curled against his chest, almost napping himself. Church pressed his flat, fuzzy face on the place where he could feel Jem's heartbeat. Jem could feel the cat's purr reverberating through his chest, as if his heart and the cat's contentment were combining to form the same song.

"It took us a long, long time to be happy," said Jem. "But here we are. I think it was worth it, don't you?"

Church purred agreement.

They were waiting, as the sun dipped lower in the sky, for Kit to stop feinting and parrying, fighting intently with nothing but air, and notice they were there.

"Oh, hey, Jem," said Kit at last, lowering his broadsword and wiping the sweat from his brow with one suntanned forearm. "Hey, bad cat."

"He's a sweet cat, really," said Jem. "You have to learn how he likes to be petted."

"I know how he likes to be petted," said Kit. "By you and no one else. That cat is waiting for the chance to literally pee in my Cheerios." He pointed the sword accusingly at Church. "I'm watching you."

Church seemed unimpressed.

They'd cleared a training ground for Kit at the bottom of the garden. It had been the first request he made, hesitantly and with many assurances that it was fine if it wasn't convenient, and Tessa had used magic and Jem a scythe to clear a space at once. Kit trained there every day.

"I saw you running laps at dawn," Jem observed.

"Wow, that's a horrible thing to say about anybody." Kit shrugged uncomfortably, as if trying to shift the weight of a burden. "I'm not . . . very naturally gifted at this Shadowhunter thing. The Blackth—other people, they were born in Institutes, raised to it, but mostly my dad taught me card tricks. I don't think demons will be impressed by my card tricks. Though they are pretty excellent."

"You don't have to be a Shadowhunter," said Jem. "I'm not one. But I was. It was what I wanted, once. I know what it looks like, when you want something so much it almost breaks you."

To fight. To be *parabatai* with Will. To kill demons and protect the innocent, to live the kind of life his parents would be proud of, when he saw them again. And the thought that carried Jem through the worst nights as he grew to manhood, to find love like his parents' love, transforming and sanctifying. He had to last, until love came.

Love had been worth the wait.

"If you're asking whether I'm working out my emotional pain through a punishing physical regimen," said Kit, "my answer is obviously a manly yes. But I was hoping time would speed up when I did, and a rock soundtrack would start up, and I would get buff via a montage like in the movies. All the superhero movies and that one boxing movie have lied to me."

"You're getting better," said Jem.

Kit grimaced. "I still get winded easily."

"When I learned to fight, I was dying from slow poison," said Jem. ". . . And I was, yes, still faster than you."

Kit laughed. His eyes were Herondale eyes, but his laugh was all his own, mischievous and cynical and a little innocent, despite that.

"Train with me," said Kit.

Jem smiled.

"What?" Kit asked anxiously. "Do you . . . not want to?"

"I said that to somebody once," said Jem. "A long time ago. He did train with me. And now I'll train you."

Kit hesitated, then said, "Will?" and Jem nodded. "Do you . . ." Kit bit his lip. "Do you still think about him a lot?"

"I loved him better than I love myself," said Jem. "I still do. I think about him every day."

Kit blinked quickly. There was pain behind his eyes, the hidden kind, the sort Will had carried along with his secrets for so many years. Jem did not know its exact meaning or shape, but he could guess.

"Whoever you have loved, and however you loved them," said Jem, "anyone you loved would be lucky."

Kit was staring at the ground again, at the dust of the training ground. *We are dust and shadows*, Will used to say.

"Yeah, well, that's a minority opinion," Kit mumbled. Then he lifted his chin, blue eyes defiant, throwing a challenge at pain. "Tessa says my mom loved me, but I never knew her. She didn't know me. My dad knew me, and he didn't care. Don't say he did. I know he didn't. But he loved my mom, apparently, so it wasn't that he couldn't love anyone. It was that he couldn't love me. And—and the—and—nobody else has, either. I wasn't enough, to stop—I wasn't enough. I've never been enough, not for anyone, and I'm trying, but I don't know if I ever will be."

Jem didn't know exactly what had happened at the Los Angeles Institute, where he and Tessa had left Kit believing he would be safe. It was clear Kit had been badly hurt, there with Emma and the Blackthorns. Jem believed the Blackthorns all had good and open hearts, but they had suffered great losses while Kit was with them, and sometimes when people were wounded they hurt others. They were all very young, and Kit had not been with them long.

Jem did know enough to see Johnny Rook must have done something truly wrong, if he'd had all Kit's life to show him that he was loved and never convinced him.

"I loved my parents," said Jem. "And they loved me."

Kit blinked. "Um, good for you."

"I had a happy childhood with them in Shanghai, the kind of childhood you should have had, the kind of childhood everyone should have. Then they were tortured and murdered in front of me, and I was tortured too, and the Shadowhunters told me I would die. I knew I would die. I could feel the poison coursing in my veins. And I remember lying curled in a cabin at the bottom of a boat, on my way to England, feeling utterly small, hollow and hopeless and miserable. I thought I might die that way, that I couldn't bear the torture of loving and losing someone, not ever again. But then . . . there was Will, and I loved him, and he loved me. If your father's heart was too little and wretched to love someone else after losing your mother, then I pity him, but I know it was his fault. None of yours."

The wind went sighing through the leaves, but it was only a soft sigh. Summer was coming, and winter would not be for a while yet.

Kit laid his sword down and walked over to the tree where Jem was sitting. He came and sat in the grass in front of Jem, as he'd sat at Tessa's feet while she told him about his mother.

"All this 'being the descendant of the First Heir' stuff," said Kit. "I don't know what to do about it, but I know I have to be ready. I think about evil faeries, and Herondales, and my dad, and I don't know how to be anything but a big mess."

Jem did not know what would come either, but he was sure of one thing. Kit would not run when danger called. Kit would stand and fight. The search for the lost Herondale, Jem refusing the Greater Demon Belial's temptations, Jem being turned away and then called back by Rosemary Herondale, had all led to this. Rosemary's child was Jem's now. It was Jem's job to teach Kit how to fight as well as he could.

"Think of the people you love," said Jem, and Kit startled. "It doesn't matter if they didn't love you back, or if they did. You keep them here."

Jem reached out and laid his hand against Kit's chest, felt it beating too swiftly beneath his palm.

"Do you want to keep them somewhere small and mean, with the walls closing in?"

Kit shook his head silently, lips pressed tight together.

"No," Jem said softly. "You won't. You choose to be yourself, your best self. You can be descended from gods and monsters. You can take the light they left you and be a lamp shining out all their light made new. You can battle the darkness. You can choose always to fight and hope. That is what it means to have a great heart. Don't be afraid of being yourself."

"But . . ." Kit fumbled for words. "I know that you and Tessa took me in because of Will. And I'm—I'm grateful, I want to—I can be like—"

His shoulders shook and Jem reached out, putting his arms around Kit. He felt Kit's muscles lock, almost straining away, then felt the moment when Kit chose to lean in and lay his head down on Jem's shoulder.

"No," Jem told him fiercely. "Don't be grateful. Where there is love, Kit," he murmured into the wild gold of his hair, "there is no need for gratitude. And I love you."

Kit shook, and nodded, once.

"Okay," Kit whispered.

Jem felt tears drop hot into the curve of his neck. He held Kit safe in his arms, until his tears were dry and they could both pretend he had not wept. He held Kit until Church growled jealously and tried to squirm in between them.

"Dumb cat," Kit muttered.

Church hissed and swiped at him. Jem gave Church a disappointed look, then stood and offered Kit a hand.

"Come inside where it's warm," Jem said. "Tomorrow, we'll start you on weights so you can learn the right balance to strike with that sword. For now I can hear Tessa and Mina. Let's go be with our family."

The doors were already standing invitingly open. As they came closer Jem could see Tessa, in a gown the same gray as her eyes, gray as the river under the bridge where she had met him year after year after year. She was laughing.

"I couldn't get Mina to sleep," she called. "She thinks you might go on an adventure without her."

Kit said, "Not today."

He went in ahead of Jem, and Mina wriggled in her mother's arms, eagerly reaching out toward them.

Jem smiled at the sight of his daughter, and paused long enough to think, *Will, my Will. You would be so proud.*

Jem went inside to his wife and his baby and his boy, to his long-awaited home. Above the low slate roof, sunset had dyed the clouds a color darker than gold. This evening the whole sky was bronze, as though to summon wicked powers.

Acknowledgments

Thank you to Cathrin Langner for fact checking, Gavin J. Grant and Emily Houk for keeping us organized, and Holly Black and Steve Berman for their cheerleading and support. Thank you also to Melissa Scott for her assistance with "Every Exquisite Thing," and to Cindy and Margaret Pon for their translation help. Our everlasting love and thanks to our friends and families.

About the Authors

CASSANDRA CLARE was born to American parents in Tehran, Iran, and spent much of her childhood traveling the world with her family. She lived in France, England, and Switzerland before she was ten years old. Since her family moved around so much, she found familiarity in books and went everywhere with a book under her arm. She spent her high school years in Los Angeles, where she used to write stories to amuse her classmates, including an epic novel called *The Beautiful Cassandra* based on the eponymous Jane Austen short story (and from which she later took her current pen name).

After college, Cassie lived in Los Angeles and New York, where she worked at various entertainment magazines and even some rather suspect tabloids. She started working on her YA novel *City of Bones* in 2004, inspired by the urban landscape of Manhattan, her favorite city.

In 2007, the first book in the Mortal Instruments series, *City of Bones*, introduced the world to Shadowhunters. The Mortal Instruments concluded in 2014 and includes *City of Ashes*, *City of Glass*, *City of Fallen Angels*, *City of Lost Souls*, and *City of Heavenly Fire*. She also created a prequel series, inspired by *A Tale of Two Cities* and set in Victorian London. This series, the Infernal Devices, follows bookworm Tessa Gray as she discovers the London Institute in *Clockwork Angel*, *Clockwork Prince*, and *Clockwork Princess*.

The sequel series to the Mortal Instruments, the Dark Artifices, where the Shadowhunters take on Los Angeles, began with *Lady Midnight*, continues with *Lord of Shadows*, and concludes with *Queen of Air and Darkness*.

Other books in the Shadowhunters series include *The Bane Chronicles*, *Tales from the Shadowhunter Academy*, *The Red Scrolls of Magic*, and *The Shadowhunter's Codex*.

Her books have more than fifty million copies in print worldwide and have been translated into more than thirty-five languages. Visit her at CassandraClare.com.

SARAH REES BRENNAN was born and raised in Ireland by the sea, where her teachers valiantly tried to make her fluent in Irish (she wants you to know it's not called Gaelic) but she chose to read books under her desk in class instead. The books most often found under her desk were Jane Austen, Margaret Mahy, Anthony Trollope, Robin McKinley, and Diana Wynne Jones, and she still loves them all today. After college she lived briefly in New York and somehow survived in spite of her habit of hitching lifts in fire engines. She began working on *The Demon's Lexicon* while doing a creative writing MA and library work in Surrey, England. Since then she has returned to Ireland to write and use as a home base for future adventures. Her Irish is still woeful, but she feels the books under the desk were worth it. Sarah is also the author of the Lynburn Legacy series and the novels *Tell the Wind and Fire* and *In Other Lands*. Follow her on Twitter at @sarahreesbrenna or visit her at sarahreesbrennan.com.

MAUREEN JOHNSON is the *New York Times* and *USA Today* bestselling author of several YA novels, including *13 Little Blue Envelopes*, *Suite Scarlett*, and *The Name of the Star*. She has also done collaborative works, such as *Let It Snow* (with

John Green and Lauren Myracle), and *The Bane Chronicles* (with Cassandra Clare and Sarah Rees Brennan). Maureen has an MFA in writing from Columbia University. She has been nominated for an Edgar Award and the Andre Norton Award, and her books appear frequently on YALSA and state awards lists. *Time* magazine has named her one of the top 140 people to follow on Twitter (@maureenjohnson). Maureen lives in New York, and online on Twitter (or at maureenjohnsonbooks.com).

KELLY LINK is the author of the collections *Stranger Things Happen*, *Magic for Beginners*, *Pretty Monsters*, and Pulitzer Prize finalist *Get in Trouble*. Her short stories have been published in *The Magazine of Fantasy & Science Fiction*, *The Best American Short Stories*, and *The O. Henry Prize Stories*. She has received a grant from the National Endowment for the Arts. She and Gavin J. Grant have coedited a number of anthologies, including multiple volumes of *The Year's Best Fantasy and Horror* and, for young adults, *Steampunk!* and *Monstrous Affections*. She is the cofounder of Small Beer Press and coedits the occasional zine *Lady Churchill's Rosebud Wristlet*.

Link (kellylink.net/@haszombiesinit) was born in Miami, Florida. She currently lives with her husband and daughter in Northampton, Massachusetts.

ROBIN WASSERMAN is a graduate of Harvard University and the author of several successful novels for young adults including the Seven Deadly Sins series, *Hacking Harvard*, the Skinned trilogy, and *The Book of Blood and Shadow*, as well as *Girls on Fire*, her first novel for adults. A recent recipient of a MacDowell fellowship, she lives in Los Angeles.